palgrave advances in james joyce studies

Palgrave Advances

Titles include:

Phillip Mallett (*editor*)
THOMAS HARDY STUDIES

Lois Oppenheim (*editor*)
SAMUEL BECKETT STUDIES

Jean-Michel Rabaté (*editor*)
JAMES JOYCE STUDIES

Forthcoming:

Patrick Finney (*editor*)
INTERNATIONAL HISTORY

Robert Patten and John Bowen (*editors*)
CHARLES DICKENS STUDIES

Frederick S. Roden (*editor*)
OSCAR WILDE STUDIES

Anna Snaith (*editor*)
VIRGINIA WOOLF STUDIES

Nicholas Williams (*editor*)
WILLIAM BLAKE STUDIES

Jonathan Woolfson (*editor*)
RENAISSANCE HISTORIOGRAPHY

Palgrave Advances
Series Standing Order ISBN 1–4039–3512–2 (Hardback) 1–4039–3513–0 (Paperback)
(*outside North America only*)

You can receive future titles in this series as they are published by placing a standing order.
Please contact your bookseller or, in the case of difficulty, write to us at the address below
with your name and address, the title of the series and the ISBN quoted above.

Customer Services Department, Macmillan Distribution Ltd, Houndmills, Basingstoke,
Hampshire RG21 6XS, England

palgrave advances in james joyce studies

edited by
jean-michel rabaté
university of pennsylvania

First published 2004 by
PALGRAVE MACMILLAN
Houndmills, Basingstoke, Hampshire RG21 6XS and
175 Fifth Avenue, New York, N.Y. 10010
Companies and representatives throughout the world

PALGRAVE MACMILLAN is the global academic imprint of the
Palgrave Macmillan division of St Martin's Press LLC and of
Palgrave Macmillan Ltd.
Macmillan® is a registered trademark in the United States,
United Kingdom and other countries. Palgrave is a registered
trademark in the European Union and other countries.

ISBN 1–4039–1210–6 hardback
ISBN 1–4039–1211–4 paperback

This book is printed on paper suitable for recycling and
made from fully managed and sustained forest sources.

A catalogue record for this book is available
from the British Library.

Library of Congress Cataloging-in-Publication Data
Palgrave advances in James Joyce studies / edited by Jean-Michel Rabaté.
     p. cm.
   Includes bibliographical references and index.
   ISBN 1–4039–1210–6
     1. Joyce, James, 1882–1941—Criticism and interpretation—History—20th century.
2. Joyce, James, 1882–1941—Criticism and interpretation. 3. Ireland—In literature.
I. Rabaté, Jean-Michel, 1949–

PR6019.O9Z7775 2004
823'.912—dc22

                                                                    2004041503

10 9 8 7 6 5 4 3 2 1
13 12 11 10 09 08 07 06 05 04

Printed and bound in Great Britain by
Antony Rowe Ltd, Chippenham, Wiltshire

contents

notes on the contributors

Eric Bulson has a Ph.D. from Columbia University and is the author of several articles on Joyce and Trieste (two are published in the *Journal of Modern Literature*), as well as *James Joyce, An Introduction* (Cambridge University Press, forthcoming).

Ronald Bush is Professor of English at Saint John's College, Oxford University, and the author of *The Genesis of Ezra Pound's Cantos* (Princeton University Press, 1976), *T.S. Eliot: A Study in Character and Style* (Oxford University Press, 1983) and two co-edited volumes, *Prehistories of the Future* (Stanford University Press, 1995) and *Claiming the Stones/Naming the Bones* (Getty Institute, 2002). He is currently completing a biography of Joyce.

Marian Eide is Professor of English at the University of Texas and author of numerous articles on Joyce and Modernism as well as *Ethical Joyce* (Cambridge University Press, 2002).

Michael Groden is Professor of English at the University of London, Ontario, and has co-edited the James Joyce Archive. He is the author of *Ulysses in Progress* (Princeton University Press, 1977) and co-editor of the *Johns Hopkins Guide to Literary Theory and Criticism* (Johns Hopkins University Press, 1994).

R. Brandon Kershner is Professor of English at the University of Florida, Gainesville. His books include *Joyce, Bakhtin and Popular Literature* (University of North Carolina Press, 1989), *James Joyce and Popular Culture* (ed.) (University of Florida Press, 1996) and *The Twentieth Century Novel* (Macmillan, 1997). He recently edited *The Cultural Studies of James Joyce* (Rodopi, 2003).

Garry Leonard is Professor of English at the University of Toronto. He is the author of *Reading Dubliners Again: A Lacanian Perspective* (Syracuse University Press, 1993) and *Advertising and Commodity Culture in Joyce* (University of Florida Press, 1998).

Vicki Mahaffey is Professor of English at the University of Pennsylvania and author of *Reauthorizing Joyce* (1998, second revised edition; University of Florida Press, 1995) and of *States of Desire: Wilde, Yeats, Joyce and the Irish Experiment* (Oxford University Press, 1998).

Laurent Milesi is Professor of English at the University of Cardiff and the author of 50 articles on various modernist authors and literary theory as well as the editor of *James Joyce and the Difference of Language* (Cambridge University Press, 2003).

Margot Norris is Professor of English at the University of California at Irvine. Her books include *The Decentered Universe of Finnegans Wake* (Johns Hopkins University Press, 1976), *Joyce's Web* (University of Texas Press, 1992), *Writing War in the Twentieth Century* (University of Virginia Press, 2000) and *Suspicious Readings of Joyce's Dubliners* (University of Pennsylvania Press, 2003).

Jean-Michel Rabaté is Professor of English at the University of Pennsylvania. His books include *Joyce upon the Void* (Macmillan, 1991), *Lacan and the Subject of Literature* (Palgrave, 2001), *James Joyce and the Politics of Egoism* (Cambridge University Press, 2001) and *The Future of Theory* (Blackwell, 2002).

Sam Slote is a researcher at the University of New York at Buffalo and is currently working for the James Joyce Foundation in Dublin. He is the author of *Silence in Progress of Dante, Mallarmé and Joyce* (Lang, 1999) and co-editor of *Genetic Studies in Joyce* (Rodopi, 1995) and *Genitricksling Joyce* (Rodopi, 1999). He is co-editor of the forthcoming *Genetic Guide to Finnegans Wake*.

Joseph Valente is Professor of English at the University of Illinois at Urbana. His books include *James Joyce and the Problem of Justice* (Cambridge University Press, 1995), the edited volume *Quare Joyce* (University of Michigan Press, 1998) and *Dracula's Crypt: Bram Stoker, Irishness and the Question of Blood* (University of Illinois Press, 2002).

james joyce: a chronology

1882 *February 2.* Birth of James Augustine Joyce at Rathgar, in the south suburbs of Dublin. He is the son of John Joyce and Mary Jane Murray, the eldest child of 15 children, of whom ten survived.

1887 The Joyce family moves to Martello Terrace, Bray, by the seaside.

1888 *September.* James Joyce is accepted by the very distinguished Clongowes Wood College, where he is taught until June 1991.

1889 *December.* Captain O'Shea files a petition for divorce and accuses Charles Stewart Parnell of adultery.

1890 *October 6.* Death of Parnell. James Joyce writes a poem about the leader's betrayal, "Et Tu, Healy."

1892 John Joyce loses his job and the impoverished Joyce family moves to Blackrock.

1893 The Joyces move to Fitzgibbon Street, in the north of Dublin. While the other children are taught at the Christian Brothers School, James is accepted at Belvedere College, a prestigious Jesuit institution.

1894 James Joyce accompanies his father to Cork when the latter is forced to sell what remains of the family's properties.

1895 Joyce is elected a member, then prefect of the Sodality of the Virgin Mary. He is sexually initiated by a prostitute.

1898 Joyce renounces priesthood and becomes very popular among his peers, notably acclaimed for his part in a

	satirical play, *Vice-Versa.* In September, he is enrolled at University College Dublin. He specializes in English, French, and Italian.
1900	Joyce reads a paper on "Drama and Life" at University College. Ibsen thanks him for his enthusiastic review of *When We Dead Awaken.* Joyce writes an Ibsenian first play, *A Brilliant Career,* now lost.
1901	Joyce translates from the German Hauptmann's play *Michael Kramer* and publishes *The Day of the Rabblement,* a pamphlet addressed to the Irish Literary Theatre that he accuses of provincialism. He defends Yeats, Ibsen, Strinberg, and Hauptmann.
1902	Joyce gives a lecture on the Irish poet James Mangan at University College. His brother George dies at the age of 15. After graduating with a B.A., Joyce decides to go to Paris to study medicine. He arrives to Paris in December after a short stay in London.
1903	In Paris, a very destitute Joyce spends most of his time at the Sainte Geneviève library, where he reads Aristotle and Aquinas. He meets Synge and discovers the stream of consciousness technique in Edouard Dujardin's *Les Lauriers sont coupés.* On April 12, a telegram from his father informs him that his mother is dying of cancer. James rushes home where his mother dies on August 13 at the age of 44. Stuck and aimless in Dublin, he writes "epiphanies" and reviews.
1904 *January.*	Joyce writes the first version of the "Portrait of an Artist" for a new review, *Dana.* The text is refused as too obscure. He decides to turn it into an autobiographical novel, *Stephen Hero.*
March.	Joyce teaches for a while in a school at Dalkey. He gets only a bronze medal at a singing competition, the Feis Ceoil, because he cannot sight-read a score.
June.	He meets Nora Barnacle, a young woman from Galway, in the street.
August.	He writes the satirical poem "The Holy Office." "The Sisters," to be the first story in *Dubliners,* is published in the *Irish Homestead.*

September.	He spends a few days at the Martello Tower with Oliver Gogarty and Samuel Chenevix Trench. "Eveline" is published in the *Irish Homestead*.
October.	Joyce and Nora Barnacle, unmarried, leave Dublin together with the idea of living abroad; James will teach English in Berlitz schools. As a first post in Zurich is not available, they go to Trieste, then Pola (now Pula in Croatia), where they settle. They stay in Pola until March 1905.
1905	James and Nora move to Trieste, then the main harbor of the Austrian empire.
July.	Birth of Giorgio Joyce.
October.	Stanislaus Joyce, the brother who had been closest to him, joins them from Dublin and helps them financially. James starts drinking heavily.
1906	First censorship difficulties to publishing *Dubliners* with Grant Richards. James and Nora go to Rome in July, James works in a bank. He is interested in socialism and anarchism.
1907	Disgusted by the city and their poverty, James and Nora go back to Trieste. In May, *Chamber Music* is published in London by Elkin Mathews. Joyce writes several political articles on Ireland for the *Piccolo della Sera*. He also gives lectures in Italian at the Università del Popolo in Trieste. The Triestine dialect will remain the language of the Joyce family, even after they move to Paris.
July.	Birth of Lucia Anna.
September.	Joyce finishes "The Dead." He condenses and rearranges the chapters of *Stephen Hero*, which are transformed into *A Portrait of the Artist as a Young Man*.
1908	Nora has a miscarriage and James suffers eye trouble. He meets Ettore Schmitz, or "Italo Svevo," who will become one of his first admirers.
1909	Joyce publishes an essay on Oscar Wilde in the *Piccolo della Sera*.
July.	Joyce returns to Dublin with his son and meets old friends.
August.	He meets Cosgrave who pretends that he was enjoying Nora's favor while James was courting her. James sends

	indignant letters to Nora and then repents when told by another friend that this was a fabrication, and done out of spite. The subsequent correspondence between James and Nora is tumultuous, obscene and superb.
September.	Joyce returns to Trieste with Giorgio and his sister Eva.
October.	Joyce returns to Dublin: he has convinced a group of Triestine businessmen that there are profits to be made in Dublin as the city has no cinema. Dublin's first cinema, the Volta, opens in December thanks to Joyce's efforts.
1910	Joyce returns to Trieste with another of his sisters, Eileen. He negotiates with George Roberts about the publication of *Dubliners*, in which certain passages or expressions are deemed objectionable.
1911	The publication of *Dubliners* is halted. Joyce writes to the King of England in the hope of clearing the difficulties with censorship.
1912	Joyce gives lectures on Defoe and Blake at the Università del Popolo and tries to get an Italian diploma to teach at a higher level but this fails for administrative reasons. In the summer, Nora leaves for Ireland with Lucia. Soon after, unable to leave her alone, James follows her with Giorgio: this will be his last trip to Ireland.
September.	The publisher Roberts, frightened by British censors, decides to destroy the printed proofs of *Dubliners*. Disgruntled, Joyce returns to Trieste where he publishes the pamphlet "Gas from a Burner," a broadside in which he attacks censorship and derides Dublin's publishers and critics.
November.	Joyce gives a series of twelve lectures on Shakespeare's *Hamlet* at the Università del Popolo.
1913	Joyce teaches English at the Scuola Superiore di Commercio Revoltella in Trieste while giving private lessons and is slightly better off. He completes *A Portrait of the Artist as a Young Man* and starts to draft the first half of *Exiles*. He also composes the private diary he entitles *Giacomo Joyce*, a poetic and ironical account of his infatuation with one of his Jewish pupils.
1914	At Ezra Pound's instigation, the London-based review the *Egoist* starts the serial publication of *A Portrait of the*

Artist as a Young Man. Dubliners is finally published in June. Joyce begins drafting *Ulysses*.

1915   In the midst of World War I, with the help of influential Triestine friends, Joyce and his family are allowed to leave Trieste and go to neutral Switzerland, while Stanislaus is interned in an Austrian prison camp. Settling in Zurich, Joyce meets many new artists and writers, and continues writing *Ulysses*.

1916   Joyce follows the news from Dublin, where the Easter Rising and the following troubles bring about the execution of his friend Sheehy-Skeffington. In December, the American edition of *Dubliners* is published.

1917 *February.*   Joyce finds out that an anonymous admirer has given him £200. He finds out only later that it is Miss Weaver, whose generosity in later years will allow him to keep writing without having to work.

August.   A surgical intervention on his right eye is necessary.

December.   Joyce sends the first chapters of *Ulysses* to Ezra Pound who is enthusiastic.

1918   In February Joyce sends the first three episodes of *Ulysses* to the *Little Review* in New York. In Zurich, Joyce associates himself with a British theatrical company, the English Players, and has a fight with one of its members, Carr. A series of absurd litigations follows. He becomes friend with Frank Budgen and the brothers August and Paul Suter.

May.   *Exiles* is published.

1919   The Joyces return to Trieste in October, but cannot renew the pre-war intimacy with their local friends.

1920 *June.*   Joyce finally meets Ezra Pound in Sirmione, and Pound persuades him to come to Paris.

July.   The Joyces arrive in Paris. Joyce wants to finish the "Circe" episode in Paris and then move to London – but he stays in Paris until the start of World War II. Thanks to Pound's contacts, Joyce is introduced in the literary milieu. Friendships are established with Sylvia Beach, Adrienne Monnier, T.S. Eliot, and Valery Larbaud.

September.   The *Little Review* is suspended for the publication of the "Nausicaa" episode, and condemned in February 1921.

December.	Joyce finishes writing "Circe."
1921	Valery Larbaud declares his enthusiasm for *Ulysses*. Sylvia Beach is ready to publish it in France in order to avoid censorship. Joyce meets Marcel Proust very briefly during a dinner party.
June.	The first proofs of *Ulysses* are sent from Dijon by the printer Darantiere. While energetically adding to the proofs, Joyce finishes the last episode, "Penelope."
November.	Joyce gives Larbaud the "scheme" of the correspondences in preparation for a December talk presenting *Ulysses* to a French audience.
December 7.	More than 250 people attend the presentation and many readers subscribe in spite of Anglo-American censorship.
1922 *February 2.*	On Joyce's birthday, three copies of *Ulysses* arrive from Dijon. His fame is immediate, accompanied by a whiff of scandal.
April.	Nora leaves for Ireland with the children, but the civil war forces them to come back.
1923	Joyce visits England and begins drafting fragments of *Finnegans Wake*, known only as *Work in Progress* until 1938.
1924	The first fragment of *Work in Progress* is published in the *Transatlantic Review*.
1925	The Joyces move to 2 Square Robiac, where they stay until April 1931. Joyce is almost blind for several months, and will continue to suffer from very weak eyesight requiring numerous surgical interventions over the years.
1926	*Exiles* is performed in London. Joyce meets Eugène and Maria Jolas, who are then launching *transition*, an international avant-garde review. The journal's manifestos on avant-garde writing and the "language of the night" always take Joyce as a model. In December, Lucia Joyce appears in a ballet at the Comédie des Champs-Elysées.
1927	At Joyce's request, an international manifesto is published against Samuel Roth's piracy of *Ulysses* in the U.S. In July, the collection of poems called *Pomes Penyeach* is published by Shakespeare and Co. In

	November, Nora undergoes an operation due to cancer and has a hysterectomy.
1929 *February*.	Publication of the French translation of *Ulysses*.
May.	Publication of the twelve essays on *Work in Progress* by Samuel Beckett, William Carlos Williams and others, under the title of *Our Exagmination Round His Factification for Incamination of Work in Progress*. Lucia's performance in an international dance competition is acclaimed but, disappointed because she is not awarded a prize, she decides to abandon dancing. Her subsequent depression and instability are unmistakable signs of growing mental illness. Joyce is quite distressed and for a while tries to find a cure for his daughter by himself. *Tales Told of Shem and Shaun* is published.
1930	Publication of *Haveth Childers Everywhere*. Joyce meets Paul Léon, a Russian-born lawyer, who will become his closest friend and self-appointed private secretary.
December.	Giorgio marries Helen Castor Fleischman.
1931 *March 26*.	*Anna Livia Plurabelle* is read in Adrienne Monnier's bookstore. Its French translation is published in the *Nouvelle Revue Française* soon after. Joyce and Nora are officially married in London, where they plan to move.
December.	John Joyce dies in Dublin.
1932 *February*.	Lucia, who has grown increasingly violent and self-destructive, is hospitalized in a clinic. Joyce can no longer deny the reality of his daughter's schizophrenia. Stephen James Joyce, the son of Giorgio and Helen, is born.
1933	Judge Woolsey reverses the banning of *Ulysses* in the U.S. He declares that the book is "emetic" but not "aphrodisiac." An American publication becomes possible.
1934	Lucia is admitted to the Burghölzi clinic near Zurich where she is examined by Jung who concludes that she embodies the schizoid element of her father's personality: she drowns when he can still swim.
1935	Lucia is interned in Doctor Delmas's psychiatric clinic at Ivry. Until the 1939 departure from Paris, Joyce visits her every week.

1936	Publication of *Chaucer's ABC* with Lucia's illustrated letters.
1937	Joyce works with Nino Frank on the translation of *Anna Livia Plurabelle* into Italian.
1938	On August 2, Eugène Jolas guesses the title of *Finnegans Wake* (Joyce had kept the book's title a secret and guessing the title had become a society game – Jolas's correct guess won him a sum of money). The book, dated 1922–39, is completed on November 13.
1939 *May 4.*	Publication of *Finnegans Wake*.
September.	Lucia is evacuated to another clinic in Pornichet for fear of German bombardments.
December.	Joyce and Nora leave Paris and go to Saint Gérand-le-Puy where the Jolases are already staying.
1940	In December, the Joyces depart for Geneva, Lausanne and then Zurich.
1941	On January 13, Joyce dies in Zurich of a perforated duodenal ulcer.

list of abbreviations

References to the publications listed below appear throughout this volume as abbreviation followed by page number, unless otherwise specified. Editions other than those cited below are indicated in the chapters' endnotes.

works by james joyce

CW	*The Critical Writings of James Joyce*. Eds. Ellsworth Mason and Richard Ellmann. New York: Viking, 1959.
D	*Dubliners*. Eds. Robert Scholes and A. Walton Litz. New York: Viking Penguin, 1969.
E	*Exiles*. New York: Penguin, 1973.
FW	*Finnegans Wake*. New York: Viking Penguin, 1939. References appear as page number plus line number.
JJA	*The James Joyce Archive*. Ed. Michael Groden et al. New York and London: Garland Publishing, 1977–79.
Letters I	*Letters of James Joyce. Vol. I.* Ed. Stuart Gilbert. New York: Viking, 1957; reissued with corrections, 1966.
Letters II	*Letters of James Joyce. Vol. II.* Richard Ellmann. New York: Viking, 1966.
Letters III	*Letters of James Joyce. Vol. III.* Richard Ellmann. New York: Viking, 1966.
P	*A Portrait of the Artist as a Young Man*. Ed. Chester G. Anderson. New York: Viking Penguin, 1968.
SH	*Stephen Hero*. Eds. John J. Slocum, Herbert Cahoon, and Theodore Spencer. New York: New Directions, 1963.

SL   *Selected Letters of James Joyce*. Ed. Richard Ellmann. New York: Viking, 1975.

U   *Ulysses*. Ed. Hans Walter Gabler. New York: Vintage, 1984. References appear as episode number plus line number.

other works

JJ I   Ellmann, Richard. *James Joyce*. New York: Oxford University Press, 1959.

JJ II   Ellmann, Richard. *James Joyce: New and Revised Edition*. New York: Oxford University Press, 1982.

introduction: the whole of joyce

jean-michel rabaté

The main ambition of this collection of new and specially commissioned essays is to address Joyce's *oeuvre* as a whole. One important editorial decision has been to avoid essays devoted to individual works and to highlight main issues and themes while stressing the organic and quasi-systematic nature of a work grasped as globally as possible. We assume that Joyce's books form a true "corpus," from early unpublished notebooks and drafts to the serial publication of stray chapters from a *Work in Progress* that slowly accrued to produce *Finnegans Wake*. One consequence of this principle is that ideally it should be possible to apply insights garnered from later texts to earlier pieces. A presupposition shared by all the authors in this collection is that Joyce's works and life obey an organic logic, and that this logic opens up a general problematic hinged around the discovery of a new type of writing. There all the recurrent echoes, thematic links and ideological questions find a key to their interrelations and cumulative evolution. The same should be true of this collection as well: even if the approaches follow a progression, one may begin at any point one chooses and move either forward or backward. In Joyce's case, of course, one will have to take into account the learning curve in the aesthetic and political issues he dealt with, along with his increased mastery of style and technique. Nevertheless, the fact remains that there is a fundamental unity in Joyce's entire *oeuvre* and that we need to make sense of it.

However, Joyce may be deemed "organic" in certain senses but not in all. For instance, the progressive canonization of Joyce as last century's major writer has implied a careful bracketing off of *Finnegans Wake*, left to either specialists or devotees. Against this view, and without implying any hierarchy in either importance or difficulty (for indeed some of the earlier and allegedly transparent texts often turn out to be more difficult to interpret than the verbal intricacies of the *Wake*), all the contributions to this collection take *Finnegans Wake* as part and parcel of the Joycean corpus. Besides, if most critics faced with the thorny problem of having to learn as many facts as possible end up knowing quite a lot about Joyce's life and often use these biographical insights to tackle his texts, there has recently been a growing awareness that Joyce's position facing Irish culture and history was not that organic. Joyce has often been described as caught up between an Irish past that he partly embraced and partly repudiated and an internationalist ethos often equated with high modernism. In other words, one may safely assert that Joyce was never an "organic intellectual" in Gramsci's sense.

A recent study of several waves of Marxist approaches shows critics who rejected Joyce as the prototypical alienated petit-bourgeois who bought into a deluded view of history as cyclical and reactionary.[1] Joyce was often classified along with Kafka as a negative source of inspiration, a nihilist who misses out on opportunities of struggle or liberation. On this politicized view, most protagonists portrayed by Joyce do not seem very "organic" in any sense, from Stephen's rather visceral fear of an old Irish peasant at the end of *A Portrait of the Artist as a Young Man* to Gabriel Conroy's refusal to go the West of Ireland, as his wife suggests, in "The Dead." And in *Ulysses*, Bloom's Jewishness, real or imaginary, suffices to set him apart from a group of Dublin citizens who seem reluctant to accept him fully.

Joyce's works may also look frozen in time, stuck in June 1904, a low moment in Irish history, even if it has been memorialized and rendered eternal by *Ulysses*. For the year 1904 was marked by political disappointment among Irish nationalists at a time when Parnell's figure loomed large but more like a lasting hangover, an unredeemable compound of failure, intrigue and division, the paradigm of betrayal and political impotence that Joyce kept in his memory when he went abroad. Thus when *Ulysses* was published in 1922 in France, nothing in the novel seemed to even remotely echo the stirrings of the recent nationalist rebellion. Nevertheless, the Easter Rising of 1916 became a main motive in the *Wake*. There again, one might say that it was published a little too late: in 1939, the new burning issues were the impending World War II, fascism, communism and the apparently bleak fate awaiting Western democracies. The transformation of the Easter Rising into a resurrection myth hardly helped in the context, nor Joyce's selfish lament that the coming war was a disaster because it would prevent his book from being read.

On the other hand, Joyce's organic development may owe little to actual history precisely because it preserves its own temporality. After all, bodies develop in such a way that they keep some biological autonomy, even when the subjectivities that inhabit them are shot through with social discourses and collective passions. Joyce's starting point was found, as is well known, in the then dominant philosophy of neo-Thomism, and in that sense, Joyce's intellectual roots are not very original. Because of this deliberate lack of an original starting point, he managed to find his own strategy in the teachings of Aristotle. Not hesitating to warp and pervert the canonical discourse he was using as a point of departure, he first produced a critical discourse helping him to find a voice and perhaps a way out of the Irish maze. In his commentary on Aristotle's famous statement *"e tekhne mimeitai ten physin"* in the 1903 Paris Notebook ("Aristotle does not here define art; he says only, 'Art imitates Nature' and means that the artistic process is like the natural process," *CW* 145) Joyce lays down the basis of a genetic theory of artistic development that will constitute the backbone of *A Portrait of the Artist as a Young Man*. In Stephen's initiation into a living poetics, he learns that the making of a work of art implies a complex process of "artistic conception, artistic gestation, and artistic reproduction" (*P* 209). What culminates into personal experience is a production of art and artifacts that follows the logic of living beings' evolution. Thus it is not absurd or counter-intuitive to say that the male artist will take on a feminine role in gestation and reproduction; an artist learns how to "give birth" to art and the stages of its progression become identical with an ideal genesis that transcends sexual division.

Aristotle's *Poetics* defines tragic drama as the "imitation of an action" producing pity and terror, but a playwright's aim is not just the creation of a good story or resembling people; a play should create emotions similar to those inspired by suffering characters like Oedipus. When Aristotle's *Poetics* insists that mimesis is the imitation of real "men in action,"[2] it entails that music and dancing can be said to "imitate" passions even better than a play. In his commentary on the *Poetics* (a commentary that Joyce had used), Butcher wrote that "imitation" was synonymous with "producing" or "creating according to a true idea,"[3] which implies a dynamic theory of imitation linked with living processes, hence completely divorced from considerations of formal beauty. Organic truth and consistency in the logical development of plot and character have replaced concerns for beautiful forms. This theory underpins all of Joyce's youthful declarations on "Art" and "Life," including his proud assertion to his mother (as echoed in *Stephen Hero*) that Art should affirm Life. One finds this living and hence almost biological process parodied in the "Oxen of the Sun" episode of *Ulysses*, with a sustained metaphor identifying the stylistic evolution of the English language in its literary uses with the growth of a fetus in the mother's belly. Mrs. Purefoy thus gives birth less to a baby than to a medley of pidgins, all the idioms that attest that English is indeed a world language well adapted to globalization and hybridization. Moving away from the "King's English," Joyce also moved away from the neo-Thomism that dominated Catholic teaching institutions in Ireland at the turn of the century, joining a cosmopolitan modernism that saw itself as part of a more and more unified Europe in which English would function as a universal vehicular language, while heralding an international future marked by globalization and hybridity.

Joyce's subsequent intellectual itinerary made him graft onto neo-Thomist theories of beauty, genres and psychology a Vichian notion of ideal history. Giambattista Vico shares with Aristotle the belief that imitation is a fundamentally human process and is not based upon traditional categories of aesthetics. In Joyce's early aesthetic writings, the concept of "imitation" crucial to Aristotelian poetics paved the way to a new psychological realism. As Stephen explains to his bemused friend Lynch, "Aristotle's entire system of philosophy rests upon his book of psychology" (*P* 208), thus justifying his efforts at paralleling formal structures of the work of art with the stages of the mind's apprehension of it. Psychology and aesthetics are both underwritten by what could be called a genetic reason. Aesthetics cannot become a "science of the concrete" or a "science of the particular" without accounting for the genesis of the perception of beauty and therefore its own genesis. If it fails to do so, it remains a dead letter, pure abstraction devoid of real content. This structural homology generates one of the cruxes of *The Portrait of the Artist as a Young Man*: if we follow literally the reconstruction of esthetic experience the novel contains, we have to explain how any subject is bound to follow in Stephen's steps and apprehend the three stages of the individuation of beauty in objects; all the time we cannot help noticing that this is a quasi-autobiographical narrative.

This entails another type of organicity, which was evident in Joyce's ability to re-read himself and to progress from earlier equivocations and failures, something that he learned from Flaubert. Flaubert discovered that he could progress as a novelist only when he was able to revise and edit his earlier drafts, thus becoming his own critic, editor and rewriter.

He was able to leave enough echoes and traces of an early romanticism in *The Sentimental Education* while mercilessly criticizing its sentimentality and embarrassing stylistic shortcomings. This is a pattern followed by Joyce quite early.

In the first chapter of this volume, Ronald Bush reopens the issue of Joyce's almost symbiotic link to Flaubert, a writer whose every word he had read and memorized (or so he boasted). Flaubert's rare dedication of his life to his craft impacted on the subsequent debate opposing either modernism and modernity or modernism and the avant-garde. If Joyce is often taken for the archetypal "high modernist" (high modernism being supposed to peak in 1922 with *The Waste Land* and *Ulysses*) we cannot take for granted Joyce's paradigmatic status in the now exploding field of modernism. A few dissenting voices have emerged, such as Weldon Thornton who argues for an "Anti-modernism" of Joyce's *Portrait of the Artist as a Young Man*. In fact, Joyce's work taken as a whole forces us to re-examine the category of modernism. Is Joyce to be listed as a canonical high modernist, an "anti-modernist" who turned "post-modernist," or should he be more simply inscribed within a general history of modernity? While there are some features that make Joyce an exception in the modernist field (for example, his love for Aristotle and Vico), experimental texts like *Finnegans Wake* clearly belong to a history of the "modern," if not of the historical "avant-garde." Bush goes back to the exemplary role *Madame Bovary* played in the middle of the nineteenth century in order to show how the entire Joycean canon should be situated within a concept of modernism that goes back to literary ancestors like Flaubert and Nietzsche.

However, modernism cannot be limited to a restricted elite art that would be opposed to or cut off from a debased or trivial Victorian culture. A number of recent books, starting with Cheryl Herr's (1986) *Joyce's Anatomy of Culture*, have focused on Joyce's use of popular magazines, contemporary advertising, Victorian clichés and all the trivia of mass culture. Joyce knew how to exploit the dormant resources of late Victorian culture while pushing it to another level. In consequence, *Ulysses* has been derided by Wyndham Lewis as an "incredible bric-à-brac in which a dense mass of dead stuff is collected"; note that in this mass he includes "1901 toothpaste" as well as "several encyclopedias."[4] In Chaper 2, Garry Leonard introduces us to the exhilarating mixture of the high and the low that is specific to Joyce's art of recuperation.

Moving toward a firm geographical basis for the whole creative effort of Joyce, Chapter 3 by Eric Bulson provides a rationale for the strong sense of location underpinning Joyce's entire creation. Joyce is famous for having recreated Dublin on paper while living first in Italy then in Paris. This chapter addresses his sense of place which often generates a "composition of place" linked with systems of mnemotechnics (he needs to produce a "composition of place" as Saint Ignatius had requested it) in the early works as well as his construction of an increasingly layered culture that nevertheless rest on a few localizable places: Dublin, Gibraltar, without forgetting Trieste or Zurich. From the formative influence of Dublin to the crucial role of the Triestine background, Bulson addresses Joyce's references to real and fictional places. Dublin maps out a whole "geography of the soul" which will reach universal proportions.

It was because of the stability of this imaginary focus that Joyce could broaden the scope of his attacks on British imperialism and colonialism while developing his own artistic program. If the young Joyce showed sympathy for socialism, anarchism and left-wing Irish groups, how far does he go in the critique of nationalism that *Ulysses* deploys? Are Bloom's Jewishness and his friendship with Arthur Griffith related issues? Irish critics like Emer Nolan have questioned the general agreement about Joyce's antinationalistic stance. In Chapter 4, Joseph Valente analyzes the tangle of concepts connected with issues of internationalism and colonialism with their attendant critique of concepts of racism and nationalism.

In Chapter 5, Marian Eide takes her point of departure in Joyce's aesthetic theory to lead to a discussion of genres in the mature works. If in all of these one observes a specific type of organic growth that seems to be generated by the text, can we still classify or organize them in terms of Joyce's aesthetic genres, or should we invent new categories? Eide follows the evolution of the concept of form from Aristotle's *Poetics* to the more experimental attempts with verbal chaos in *Ulysses* and the later texts.

Moving from the concept of genre to that of gender, Vicki Mahaffey, Chapter 6, reopens the vexed issue of Joyce's feminism or anti-feminism in an original manner by focusing on the issue of fantasy. Comparing the status of fantasies about gender in *Dubliners* and *Ulysses*, she shows how Joyce's characters learn to play with fantasy from unfulfilled yearnings to full-fledged hallucinations, from unacted desires to visions of androgyny, and hesitate between perverse cruelty and comforting imaginary solace. Here Mahaffey takes a middle position between French feminists like Cixous and Kristeva who see Joyce close to a paradigm of *écriture feminine* and American feminists who have denounced Joyce's appropriation of the feminine psyche. By tackling the question from the point of view of bisexual fantasies, Mahaffey gives imagination an edge over strict definitions of gender and shows how its very excesses allow for the transgression of ancient dichotomies, finally triggering the rebirth of desire.

That Joyce imagined and desired via the medium of language is a universally acknowledged feature of his work. In Chapter 7, Laurent Milesi explores the link between Joyce's stylistic mastery and his linguistic experiments. Starting from Joyce's early claim that one should "study languages" (to quote an early paper), Milesi analyzes the radical linguistic turn taken by *Finnegans Wake*. Why such a profusion of rare and exotic languages to write the *Wake*? Can one say that the linguistic turn observable in Joyce is a regressive attitude, leading him from high modernism to Vico's anti-modern attitude, or is it to be paralleled with contemporary drifts in philosophy, from Wittgenstein to Heidegger? Joyce blended into an international modernism looking toward the future of a unified Europe in which English would function as a universal vehicular language, a future marked like our own by globalization and hybridity.

Obviously, Joyce's keystone science was the "science of language," or his adaptation of comparative linguistics based on pseudo-etymologies, a humanistic project launched by Vico. Among forthcoming essays that would be devoted to the *Wake*, Joyce wanted four new contributions written by friends, among which there would be one devoted to chemistry and biology in *Finnegans Wake*. In the progression of his writing, Joyce increasingly stressed the role of sciences in an ideal education marked by the medieval trivium and quadrivium. He kept abreast of his times in his last work by introducing references to television and the atomic bomb before they were actually in use. Does *Finnegans Wake* owe its verbal dynamism to theories of historical archetypes, or should one look closer at sciences like biology, nuclear physics, optics or information theory to make sense of the book's totalizing claims? In Chapter 8, Sam Slote uses astronomy and physics examples to illustrate the links between Bloom's "scientific" temperament in *Ulysses* and the relativistic universe created by *Finnegans Wake*.

The use of scientific knowledge is typical of Joyce's creative method: he would pepper his writings with quotes from and paraphrases of other people or other books. In Chapter 9, Brandon Kershner takes up the issue of Joyce's formative readings which include Homer, Dante and Shakespeare in order to problematize these not just in terms of influences but also as contributing to a new sense of internal dialogism in the texts. This leads logically to a discussion of Joyce's impact on culture as whole at a time when the very concept of "culture" was being re-examined. Joyce has forced us to widen the meaning and scope of "culture," especially in his later texts when the term ends up including myths, religions and all "sacred" texts. Here the creative role played by quotations and an increasingly intertextual universal culture is examined.

From universal culture to universal history, there is a leap that Joyce was ready to make. In Chapter 10, Margot Norris analyzes Joyce's debt to a philosophy of history that he absorbed from Vico, but also from Hegel absorbed indirectly through Quinet and Michelet. Joyce's recreation of history, first Irish but then "universal," has attracted more and more critical attention. If Joyce's aesthetic theories imply an immersion in the neo-Hegelian theory of a Bernard Bosanquet, Joyce's link with his own Irish past through his name and family remains elusive. Is it only Irish history that can be called a nightmare? How serious was Joyce in his belief in a cyclical history? We have now realized that the idea that high modernism ignored history is based on a misunderstanding both of history and of modernism, and it is therefore crucial to reopen the problematic of the theory of universal history that underpins Joyce's later writings.

Our recent cultural history has been marked by the emergence of the literary manuscript as an object for collectors (including national libraries) and as an object of study. In Chapter 11, Michael Groden, who has been instrumental in publishing Joyce's manuscripts in facsimile, throws new light on the issue of a "genetic" textuality. The debate triggered by the 1984 revised edition of *Ulysses* edited by Hans Walter Gabler has forced Joyce scholars not only to become textual specialists but also to take a position on genetic and editorial issues. The publicity given to the manuscripts acquired by the National Library of Ireland in 2002 gave even more urgency to a debate that emerges at a time when new possibilities are offered by hypertexts. Crucial theoretical issues remain pending. Should one read all of Joyce's *Wake* notebooks before attempting to make sense of *Finnegans Wake*? What is the minimum amount of textual erudition and historical knowledge one needs in order to read *Ulysses*? Arguing that a new literary competence, a new literacy, has been launched, Groden brings his expertise to bear on a tangled but necessary debate.

Finally, it was necessary to examine the generations of critics who have approached Joyce's *oeuvre* and cumulatively created something that has often been dubbed "the Joyce industry." Any reader will find new bearings for a study of Joyce by having access to a rapid overview of the many trends and schools that have followed one another. Besides, it was Joyce himself who initiated the process when he entrusted his friends Gilbert and Budgen with the task of explaining *Ulysses* in markedly different ways. Just a few years later, Joyce similarly masterminded the writing and publication of essays on his latest work even before the publication of *Finnegans Wake* – hence it is clear that the "Joyce industry" was engineered by Joyce himself. Moreover, some key critics have had a great impact on the reception of the works; in the 1950s, Hugh Kenner created a small revolution when he showed that Stephen Dedalus was often treated ironically; in the 1980s, Hans Walter Gabler opened a raging debate about the text of *Ulysses*. Here we will meet some of the interpretive communities that have decided to "play" along with Joyce.

Last but not least, a thematic bibliography will give a sense of the scholarship currently available. This is a selected and selective bibliography that will help a reader find relevant titles among innumerable items in an overwhelmingly capacious Joycean library.

notes

1. See Trevor Williams, *Reading Joyce Politically* (Gainesville: University of Florida Press, 1997).
2. S.H. Butcher, *Aristotle's Theory of Poetry and the Fine Arts* (London: Macmillan, 1895), p. 123.
3. Ibid., p. 153.
4. Wyndham Lewis, "An Analysis of the Mind of James Joyce", in *Time and Western Man* (1927), ed. Paul Edwards (Santa Rosa: Black Sparrow Press, 1993), p. 89.

1
joyce's modernisms

ronald bush

We tend to take for granted Joyce's inclusion in the field of modernism, but recently dissenting voices have emerged. Readers like Margot Norris, for example, prefer to associate Joyce with the avant-garde or with post-modernism rather than with the aesthetic of figures like Pound or Eliot. On the other hand, critics like Leo Bersani have suggested that certain nineteenth-century survivals demonstrate that *Ulysses* is pre-modernist, and Weldon Thornton has contended that, if modernism is to be linked to the psychology of Locke and Hume, then Joyce, who calls eighteenth-century individualism into question, must be "anti-modernist."[1] Joyce's work in fact forces us to re-examine the broad categories of modernity and modernism, starting with a longer perspective than most of us are used to taking.

Historians and philosophers commonly use "modernity" as a synonym for the Enlightenment – eighteenth-century Europe's turn away from the traditional authority of the past (especially of religion) and toward the autonomy of reason and of the individual. But as Robert Pippin has argued in a book called *Modernism as a Philosophical Problem*, the Enlightenment, which vested authority in the discourses of science, philosophy, and history and produced two centuries of mechanistic explanations of man and nature, also provoked, as early as the Romantic philosophy of the late eighteenth and early nineteenth centuries, a revisionary version of itself, no less rooted in skepticism toward authority. "As envisioned by a line of thinkers from Baudelaire to Nietzsche," he writes, the Enlightenment's great restlessness was driven by a sense that it had not yet been "'modern' enough" – that the optimistic official self-understanding of modernity – "Enlightened, liberal, progressive, humanistic – had been ... a far too smug and unwarranted self-satisfaction."[2]

10

This second tradition of modern thought has long since become as prominent as the first. But confusingly historians and philosophers sometimes describe it not simply as "modern" but as "post-modern" (because it builds on and follows the historical Enlightenment – this, needless to say, is a very different sense of the "postmodern" from what we mean when we call Pynchon's fiction "post-modern"); or "anti-modern" (because it explores the contradictions of early Enlightenment arguments); or "modernist" (because it constitutes a reaction to modernity). In philosophy as well as literature, Pippin reminds us, "modernism" suggests

> a complex and ambiguous designation, since it often denotes both heightened and affirmative modern self-consciousness … as well as an intense dissatisfaction with the sterile, exploitative, commercialized, or simply ugly forms of life apparently characteristic of social modernization (or "bourgeois" forms of modernization).[3]

A similar ambivalence adheres to the social theorist's account of modernity, which, building on the philosopher's, both affirms rationality and progress in societies that reject traditional, hierarchical structures like feudalism and take on secular, individualistic, urbanized, 'differentiated' (i.e., specialized or compartmentalized) and industrialized forms, and decries a fundamental loss in these societies, in the form of Marx's "alienation" or Durkheim's "anomie".

The great figures in this revisionary Enlightenment tradition often sound like reactionaries because of their dissatisfaction with an incomplete modernity, and this is if anything more true for literary figures like Baudelaire or Flaubert, whose modernity involves not only the revolutionary gesture of resisting the authority of classical and neoclassical literary convention, but also horror of the intellectual and social hypocrisies of "bourgeois" society. Though propelled by the great wave of Enlightenment skepticism, such figures focused their energies primarily not on the old regime but on modernity's optimistic and insufficiently grounded belief in the progress of science and the forms of modern capitalism. These attitudes and systems, they concluded, blind to their own contradictions and irrationalities, continue (no less than more traditional institutions like the Church) to obstruct true human self-understanding. So Flaubert, for example, accounts himself both artist and critical thinker, as in a famous letter of 1853:

At the present moment I believe that a thinker (and what is an artist if not a triple thinker?) should have neither religion, country, nor even any social conviction. Absolute doubt now seems to me so completely substantiated that it would be almost silly to seek to formulate it.[4]

And it was just such thinkers as this that Ralph Waldo Emerson had in mind when he wrote in "Historic Notes of Life and Letters in New England" that

There are always two parties, the party of the Past and the party of the Future; the Establishment and the Movement. ... the schism runs under the world and appears in Literature, Philosophy, Church, State, and social customs. ... [The Party of the Future values above all things] "the faculty of life, which spawns and scorns system and system-makers; which eludes all conditions"; which makes or supplants a thousand phalanxes and New Harmonies with each pulsation.[5]

Before James Joyce's "modernism" interacted with the formalist procedures of his mostly younger contemporaries, then, it was formed by Emerson's and Flaubert's vision of art as an advanced guard of "modernity," with which Joyce was exquisitely aware. He prominently alludes to it in his first published literary essay, on Ibsen. ("It may be questioned whether any man has held so firm an empire over the thinking world in modern times [as Ibsen]. Not Rousseau; not Emerson; not Carlyle; not any of those giants of whom almost all have passed out of human ken" CW 48).

Moreover, living in a country where the effect of industrial modernization had not yet taken full hold, Joyce felt the strong need of both the discourses of scientific and post-scientific modernity. As an Irishman, in fact, one had to have great courage radically to insist on either, and Joyce seems to have grasped that necessity early. According to his brother Stanislaus, as a very young man Joyce more than anything else prized "extraordinary moral courage – courage so great that I have hopes that he will one day become the Rousseau of Ireland" (DD 30).[6]

In the terms of these prefatory remarks, Stanislaus's hopes, which James instigated and shared, imply two related but distinct aims, corresponding to the two main strands of Joyce's modernism. On the one hand, having the moral courage to "become the Rousseau of Ireland" implied a will as political progressive to lead Ireland toward enlightened social change into the modern world, and the young James Joyce was ferociously intent on "uprooting" all the "feudal principles" of Irish society (DD 54). Joyce, however, also desired to fashion out of his own life an Irish version of the *Confessions* and to expose rather than advance the pretense of Western rational conviction. In *Stephen Hero*, the early version of *A Portrait of the Artist as a Young Man*, he calls attention to the way the *Confessions*, confounding the puzzlement of Rousseau's English biographer,[7] dares to acknowledge "the young [Rousseau's] stealing his mistress's spoons and allowing a servant-girl to be accused of the theft at the very moment when he was beginning his struggle for Truth and Liberty" (*SH* 40).[8]

Joyce became not just "modern" but "modernist" when he began to value the second of these kinds of "moral courage" as highly as the first. At that point he did not end his commitment to "being modern" (*DD* 54) – enlightened, modernizing, and progressive – but he did increasingly devote himself to examining the buried and conflicted motives behind modernity's two-centuries-old search for "Truth and Liberty." Inclined by temper to social critique, his modernizing impulses came to fix themselves irrevocably on an idea of art that had as much to do with politics and philosophy as with form, an activity that not long before his adolescence Nietzsche had pronounced more "enlightened" than philosophy, because art could not help but treat all notions of tradition, nature, biology, history, and logic as hypotheses to be entertained, rather than systematic truths to be applied.

Then as now, not everyone approved. By the time of Joyce's youth Nietzsche's insights had been echoed in the aesthetic movement, but the respectable middle classes in Britain had attacked Wilde's claims to seriousness like hounds after prey. Their fury was repeated in Joyce's maturity by Marxists and then after Joyce's death by Marxicizing pundits of various stripes. To such intellectuals, the self-conscious skepticism of "modernist" art is an interesting game or a distraction – from this point of view, a distinction without a difference. "Enlightenment" philosophers, sociologists of "modernity," and political economists studying "modernization" tend to read the snowballing difficulties of the nineteenth and twentieth centuries as preludes to a better time. Yet one distressing feature of Western experience has been that those intent on advancing modernity have all too frequently been undone by complexities that lie waiting, like the hidden folds of Leviathan, within the rational curatives that bid so fair in their studies and their drawing rooms.

The most interesting and the most significant thing about Joyce's career may be that while he remained fixated on art he managed to avoid both modernism's tendency to degenerate into mere formalism and the pressure of its enemies to caricature and destroy art's oppositional values.

Instead, he studied his predecessors and fashioned in his work a critical self-consciousness built on their projects (and in part on their failures). In what follows, I propose to situate Joyce's modernist project in relation to two of the most important of these predecessors – Flaubert and Ibsen. This will involve looking (as Joyce did) not just at their work, but also at the different ways their work was read and at their own response to the way they were popularly received. All three of these elements combine to produce what is sometimes called the "social practice" of art.[9]

joyce and *madame bovary*

I begin with *Madame Bovary*. As has also been the case with Joyce, critics from Flaubert's time to our own have argued over whether Flaubert is to be considered primarily a social critic – a realist historian of modernity, or a literary innovator – a modernist. In our own generation, the case for *Madame Bovary* as a novel of social critique has been forcefully stated by Stephen Heath, who points out how carefully it chronicles the course of modernization in early nineteenth-century France.[10] Heath observes that Flaubert makes the social setting of *Madame Bovary* "money on the move." A relentless hunger for money drives the "economic and social transformation" of a story that takes place at the moment a new road joins the sleepy market town of Yonville to the Amiens highway. The most fundamental and sweeping aspect of Flaubert's transformation can be found in the buried narrative of five financial failures on which he constructed his plot: the decline of Charles Bovary's father, the financial disappointment of Charles's first wife, the worsening fortunes of Emma's father, "who loses money every year on his farm and finishes up paralysed"; the collapse of the Café Francais, "engineered by L'heureux and beyond which lies the foreseeable collapse" of the Lion d'or; and the ruin of the Bovary household by L'heureux and Homais. Indeed the entire plot can be framed by the fate of Charles's family line: "Charles's father had speculated in the manufacture of cotton goods, his daughter ends as a worker in a cotton-mill."[11]

In *Madame Bovary* then, no less than in *The Communist Manifesto*, which was written at approximately the same time, we are shown how the forces of modernization – the efficiencies of industrialism, the reduction of value to cash exchange and the breakdown of traditional social relations – transfigure every facet of social life. As Flaubert himself summed it up in a letter to Louise Colet (January 29, 1854) while composing *Madame Bovary*, a "mediocrity" synonymous with modernity is creeping in everywhere; the very stones under our feet are becoming dull, and our highways are boring beyond words. Perish though we may (and perish we shall in any case), we must employ every means to stem the flood of trash [*merde*] invading us. We must take flight in the ideal ... . And so we must raise our voices against gloves made of shoddy, against office chairs, the mackintosh, cheap stoves, against imitation cloth, imitation luxury, imitation pride. Thanks to Industrialism, ugliness has assumed gigantic proportions. How many good people who a century ago could have lived perfectly well without Beaux Arts now cannot do without mini-statues, mini-music, and mini-literature! ... We are all fakes and charlatans. Pretense, affectation, humbug everywhere – the crinoline has falsified the buttocks. Our century is a century of whores, and so far what is least prostituted is the prostitute.[12]

"Mediocrity" signifies an imitation, made cheaply to sell, and Flaubert wonders, here as in *Madame Bovary*, whether anything in French society can withstand the ineluctable forces of money, materialism, and charlatanry that contribute to the psychology of the marketplace, where things are valued not because they are real but because people conditioned by their surroundings live and dream about marketplace simulations of reality. Those who hated *Madame Bovary* when it was published recognized Flaubert's social animus immediately, and held it most abhorrent that the book shows every one of the institutional pillars of French moral judgment to be thus undermined and on the point of collapse. In the words of the state prosecutor who tried to censor the novel, the argument that *Madame Bovary* condemns Emma's adultery is difficult to accept because

in the book there is not one person who could condemn her ... . Could it be in the name of conjugal honour ... . Why, conjugal honour is represented by an idiotic husband ... . Could it be in the name of religious sentiment? But this sentiment is personified in the Curé Bournisien, a priest ... believing only in physical sufferings.[13]

Most shocking of all in the prosecutor's eyes was the personification of "public opinion" in the "grotesque" chemist Homais.[14] In fact (the reason for the prosecutor's shock), what Flaubert questions is not simply public opinion but the rational, scientific, liberal world of nineteenth-century French thought. For, as a more recent commentator has pointed out,

Flaubert satirizes not just superstitious traditional culture nor a caricatured version of rational modernity, but the Enlightenment itself. Flaubert's portrait of Homais is not "the contempt of Aristophanes, or Molière, or Shakespeare, directed at the usual human foibles. Homais is not the standard, sly, self-serving buffoon. He is made to mouth the rhetoric of the Revolution as if he represents the Revolution and not its perversion; he identifies himself as a 'modern,'" and should be understood as a figure of "social modernization."[15]

Flaubert's skewering of modernizing cant finds its epitome in *Madame Bovary* in connection with the Doctor Larivière, who attends Emma's deathbed and who

> belonged to that great school of surgeons [and] that generation, now extinct, of philosophical practitioners, who, cherishing their art with a fanatical love, exercised it with enthusiasm and wisdom … . Disdainful of honors, of titles, and of academies, hospitable, generous, fatherly to the poor, and practicing virtue without believing in it, he would almost have passed for a saint if the keenness of his intellect had not caused him to be feared as a demon. His glance, more penetrating than his scalpels, looked straight into your soul, and would detect any lie, regardless how well hidden.[16]

Against this reading of the "realist" *Madame Bovary*, however, it must be pointed out that the art that Flaubert himself "cherished" goes well beyond either rational critique or his disdain for "fig-leaf morality," as *Madame Bovary* acknowledges by permitting Dr. Larivière an entrance so belated that his intervention can only be futile.[17] Though acutely sensitive to social and economic life, the primary focus of the novel was not, as this reading emphasizes, social and economic, nor were its sympathies principally with an emerging class of workers. Though Flaubert shared Marx's dislike of the bourgeoisie, he puts no faith in a political triumph of the oppressed (in contemporary French terms, the people) or in the inevitable progress of applied reason. His reading of nineteenth-century France was in this respect especially bleak:

> '89 demolished royalty and the nobility, '48 the bourgeoisie and '51 *the people*. Now there is *nothing*, only a rascally and imbecile rabble. We are all sunk at the same level in a common mediocrity … . Social equality has entered the sphere of the Mind."[18]

It is not primarily through scientific precision that *Madame Bovary* interrogates modernization, but via a radical skepticism whose target is not cant but reason itself. Flaubert's only "scalpel" is Art. Not the artistic or Romantic temperament, which can be contaminated by marketplace clichés, but a discipline which Flaubert wrote in a letter "in the precision of its assemblages, the rarity of its elements, the polish of its surface, the harmony of the whole" exhibits "an intrinsic virtue";[19] – what Flaubert in another, more famous letter calls "a second nature":

An author in his book should be like God in the universe, present everywhere and visible nowhere. Art being a second nature, the creator of that nature must behave similarly. In all its atoms, in all its aspects, let there be sensed a hidden, infinite impassivity. The effect on the spectator must be a kind of amazement. "How is all that done?"[20]

This is the basis for the famous Flaubertian "style," less a thing in itself than a thousand coordinated ways to hold the forces of modernization at a distance:

What seems beautiful to me, what I should like to write, is a book about nothing, a book dependent on nothing external, which would be held together by the internal strength of its style, just as the earth, suspended in the void, depends on nothing external for its support; a book which would have almost no subject, or at least in which the subject would be almost invisible ... . I believe that the future of Art lies in this direction. I see it, as it has developed from its beginnings, growing progressively more ethereal.[21]

In other words, since the tools to change the world are within the world and contaminated by its "mediocrity," the sole remaining social resistance to "modernity" becomes a stubborn belief in art valued for its own sake. Only this kind of disinterested and indeed absurd authenticity, Flaubert implies, can withstand the general dishonesty. In modern life, the writer is

either commercial agent, meeting the demands of the mass culture, or self-conscious artist, split between the necessity of writing and its impossibility ... what can it mean to write in this world with this language? ... writing in opposition to industrial literature and its world, outside its parameters of production and consumption.[22]

To get ahead of my story, the ultimate futility of even artistic discipline would be inevitably impressed even on Flaubert. But it is important to understand that Flaubert's "stubbornness" was no mere unthinking formalism. More than simply an escape into art for art's sake, *Madame Bovary* enacts through a rigorous philosophical skepticism the successive moves of the Enlightenment's analysis of its own contradictions, concerning which the critique of liberal hypocrisy was only the first step.

As a writer of fiction Flaubert's fundamental decision was to reject an omniscient narrator, so that no speech acquires authority outside his fictional dialectic. Flaubert's fashioning of *le style indirect libre*, which more than anything else enabled Joyce's technique in *Dubliners, A Portrait of the Artist as a Young Man*, and to a signficant extent *Ulysses*, serves to root the characters of *Madame Bovary* in the particularities of individual experience and to suspend each of them in an open dialectic of fictional discourse. The prime beneficiary of the first function is Emma herself, whose concrete realization surpasses anything heretofore accomplished in psychological fiction. But the negative thrust of *le style indirect libre* is to strip the speech of all Flaubert's characters of an implied moral authority and place every utterance within implied double quotes, making us conscious of each instance as something distanced, ironized, framed. This is the effect of philosophical "aestheticization": every speech, and at a deeper level every social, political or moral statement, is entertained rather than asserted, with special animus against the more "intellectual" or "advanced" instances of rational discourse. As the state prosecutor lamented, there is no prime or ur-discourse in the novel. All are equally suspect.

Flaubert's practice also anticipates the main line of modern philosophy. As Robert Pippin reminds us, the development of "modern" thought from Descartes to Kant, Hegel, Nietzsche and Heidegger has been precisely toward a self-conscious or "aestheticized" acknowledgment of contingency. In Pippin's words, in every attempt to assess modernity from Kant to Nietzsche and Heidegger, philosophy has arrived at the conclusion that

[modern reality] had to be affirmed much more honestly and consistently, and not qualified by ... [a] typically modern [trust in] the public authority of philosophy and science in culture as a whole. For many of these writers, [only] an "aestheticization" of the modern spirit ... would fulfill its premise.[23]

Ultimately, the philosophical imperative to aestheticize, to hold as Nietzsche would have it, all notions of tradition, nature, biology, history, and logic at the distance of "as-if," would displace philosophy itself from its position as the Queen of the intellectual disciplines and replace it with literature, or what Richard Rorty has called "ironism."[24]

Flaubert's modernism, plumbing the problematic depths of Enlightenment individualism, inevitably calls his own illusion of psychological depth into question. The last generation of Flaubert's critics has also discovered that Flaubert's *style indirect libre* is surprisingly unreliable and necessarily involves (to quote the title of a book by Jonathan Culler) *The Uses of Uncertainty*.[25] That is, Flaubert creates enough ambiguity about his narrative point of view to make it impossible to trust his realistic conventions. He establishes "an indeterminacy of narrative voice that unsettles the moral security of the reader and renders decisive judgment about characters or story difficult to attain."[26] Flaubert undermines his own representation, and subjects his own surgical rigor to the same critique he applies to Emma's second-hand romantic dreams. Both are aesthetic conventions, and relying on them endorses that which art cannot give – a rock of stability or value which might serve in the world as substitute for Homais's degraded science or Bournisien's degraded religion.

Implicitly claiming a more advanced "modernity" than positivist science, liberal politics, practical philosophy or rational religion, in the mid-nineteenth century self-conscious modernism focused on its own futility, on the conviction that aesthetic discourse can be trusted only as a negative or oppositional force and never as replacement science or philosophy or religion. In Stephen Heath's qualification to his "realist" interpretation of *Madame Bovary*, Flaubert's conception of impersonality

has nothing to do with ... some voice of knowledge *à la Balzac*, a sort of witness to things who guides our reading and decrees meanings ... . It is not a question of an "objective" position *in* the work but of a play of visions, perspectives, perceptions across the characters and their doings and their world, of a tissue of discourses, ideas, orderings of meaning; leaving the reader deprived of any given grounds as to "what to think," not taken in hand by some privileged voice. Impersonality is accompanied by uncertainty, nothing is sure, nothing definitive. Flaubert's truth is that there is no concluding truth other than the conclusion that there is no such truth, and art is true as the recognition of that; with impersonality as its mode of recognition, against *bêtise*, the stupidity of conclusions. *Tout mentait*, "it was all lies": this is Emma's fundamental discovery one day after leaving Léon.[27]

"All lies." Even art. For Flaubert's "aestheticism" necessarily concludes in self-critique. Nothing is more painful in *Madame Bovary* than the paradox that the heroine of the most perfect work of nineteenth-century literature is destroyed for subjecting the world to the energies of the aesthetic imagination. Henry James's criticism of Flaubert (that Emma's sensibility is far too limited) is in this sense beside the point; even a much more intelligent center of consciousness would in the terms of Flaubert's modernism have come to the same end, since it would remain vulnerable to that implied self-critique of an unironized vision of art that runs through every nerve of the novel. One of the intuitions inscribed in Emma's fall is how quickly art turns into idolatry, anticipating the way that, in Pippin's words, after disillusionment with political and social forms of autonomy, independence and self-determination, "everywhere pursued ... by modern men and women, but nowhere truly realized,"

> modernist suspicions about social and intellectual pretensions to autonomy (or bourgeois optimism in general) helped generate at the same time (and somewhat paradoxically) the hope that art itself (for its own sake, as non-representational, *sui generis*, self-defining) would both be, and in dress, taste, personal style, be a model for, a renewed modern view of self-definition.[28]

Ultimately and inevitably, though, even modernist art, approached in any way but sustained irony, becomes in late bourgeois society a fad of modern life, a symptom of the disease it would diagnose. It is to Flaubert's credit that he saw this far (which is to say, very far indeed) into the philosophical and social foundation of his writing. But having said that, one must also say that he came fully to understand as much only after he had finished his book, in response to a near-tragedy of his own.

The prosecution of *Madame Bovary* has become legend. In April 1856 Flaubert sold the manuscript of the novel to his friend Maxime du Camp, co-editor of the liberal *Revue de Paris*, for 2,000 francs. But Du Camp demanded that Flaubert cut it, both because he feared prosecution over the passages which dealt with sex and religion, and because he did not understand the purpose of its literary indirection.[29] Flaubert was enraged, but was eventually worn down. He cut out offending passages, but insisted that the review publish a disclaimer that the author no longer considered the work his own. In the end the cuts and the disclaimer made no difference. The book and the review provoked prosecution for corrupting public morals, with a potential sentence for Flaubert of a year in prison. The trial, in January 1857, centered around whether the novel celebrated or censured Emma's adultery and, as observed above, the imperial prosecutor, Pinard, perceptively argued that Flaubert had so hollowed out the institutions of French life that not one was left strong enough to condemn her. But the judges were less subtle, and with most of Flaubert's subsequent critics, agreed with the defense counsel, Sénard, that Emma's fate would incline young readers to turn away from adultery and that "if anything, Flaubert had been too harsh in his punishment of Emma."[30] Flaubert and the journal were acquitted, but, inevitably, the *Revue* was shut down slightly afterwards in a similar action. Still, with a perverse poetic justice, more than 20 years later, the prosecuting lawyer was publicly unmasked as the author of pornographic verses.[31]

What came next, if by now predictable, caught Flaubert utterly off guard and constituted the most painful irony of all. Forced by his good friend's revisions and the resistance of the state to realize that no nineteenth-century fiction could be "dependent on nothing external," publishing forced him to realize how difficult it was to avoid the social forces he loathed. His name assured by the trial, he suffered something worse than censorship. He acquired immense popularity as the author of a dirty book. The sales were immediate and very large. Flaubert was appalled at his success, won for all the wrong reasons amid praise of the kind Homais himself might have coined. Swept into stunning celebrity by the forces of the marketplace, he never really recovered. More misanthropic than ever, for the remainder of his life he published and he fumed.

Nor, if we listen to Jean-Paul Sartre, did the irony stop there. In the thesis of Sartre's unfinished but monumental three-volume biography, *L'Idiot de la famille*, this rage, which had driven the writing of *Madame Bovary* from the beginning, reinforced instead of weakened the bourgeois system that Flaubert despised. Intended to undermine the reality of French life, Flaubert's fiction in Sartre's view helped late nineteenth-century France to resign itself to the way things were: it strengthened both the futile self-hatred of the French middle class and a generalized resignation to the political status quo. In Dominick La Capra's paraphrase of Sartre, it performs "the predominantly symptomatic function of reinforcing capitalism and justifying alienation. But it is not simply symptomatic. It actually aggravated conditions that informed it and to which it responded."[32]

And so, having been convinced that he had worked through the problems of modernity and that his masterpiece would be protected by its calculated sophistication from the literal-minded stupidities of the practical world and from the weak misreading of the dandy, Flaubert discovered that he was still part of the problem. He had insisted that the work of art lies beyond social utility with "its own intrinsic value." But he could not prevent society from assigning the work a value of its own. Nor could he prevent meretricious value being assigned to his own rejection of social utility: in the upper echelons of the market his art would become "by virtue of its uselessness, a luxury of decoration, a fetishism of style."[33]

A hundred years later the issues are not very different.

> The idea that modern art can maintain an independent, critical, "negative" perspective on modern social existence (the kind of thing [Theodor] Adorno tried to promote as a defense of modern art) [has] turned] out to be a grotesquely self-serving illusion. Modernist art [now seems] simply the deepest expression of the modern crisis, understood either as paradigmatically "bourgeois art," or ultimately as nihilistic, self-consuming and as much a historical dead-end as bourgeois civilization itself ... . [It is only] the last game played by Western bourgeois high culture, an elitist code designed only to preserve and celebrate the "subjectivist" point of view of an exhausted but still immensely powerful upper middle class.[34]

At best it has created an "exhausted, co-opted, everywhere displayed and commercialized 'culture of rupture.'"[35]

But what are the alternatives?

joyce, *a doll's house,* and *when we dead awaken*

Joyce's adolescent hero, Henrik Ibsen, shared much of Flaubert's understanding of modern life, but in his drama created a more "ethical" construction of modernism, both in the sense that it insisted on the therapeutic relations between art and life and in the sense that its form involved an openness that corresponded to Ibsen's Kierkegaardian belief in individual choice and growth. Especially in *A Doll's House,* moreover,

Ibsen's writing and its transmission engaged with both the progressive and the skeptical traditions of modern thought.

The obvious alternative to the tragedy of Emma Bovary for an entire generation of British progressives was represented by the refusal of Ibsen's Nora Helmer to continue to live in a doll's house. In the same year that *Madame Bovary* was translated by Karl Marx's daughter, Eleanor Marx, she and her unmarried partner Edward Aveling published a feminist pamphlet entitled *The Woman Question* with a vision of the future couched in Ibsen's terms. In "a society in which all the means of production are the property of the community, a society which recognises the full equality of all without distinction of sex," they predicted, "there will no longer be one law for the woman and one for the man … . nor will there be the hideous disguise, the constant lying, that makes the domestic life of almost all our English homes an organized hypocrisy."[36]

To readers familiar with *A Doll's House*, it was clear that the last of these predictions is but a precis of Ibsen's plot, the penultimate an explicit reference to one of Nora's speeches in its last act. It was logical, then, for Marx and Aveling to supplement their feminist manifesto by making sure that "people understand our Ibsen a little more than they do."[37] In January 1886 they arranged to stage Ibsen's play in their drawing room in Great Russell Street. Ibsen had published *Et Dukkehjem* in 1879, but, although it had created a furor on the continent, by 1886 it had yet to make a real British impact. Translated in 1882 by Francis Lord as *Nora*, it attracted little attention outside a small circle, and when adapted by Henry Arthur Jones and Henry Herman in 1884 as *Breaking a Butterfly*, it was reconstructed as an inoffensive domestic comedy.[38] With increasing frustration, Eleanor persuaded her friend George Bernard Shaw to take part in a drawing room production of Mrs. Lord's translation. For Shaw it was "his first exposure to Ibsen in performance" and may well have sparked some of the enthusiasm that would turn him into the foremost proponent of Ibsen in English.[39] But he was only one player in an intellectually stellar cast. Eleanor played Nora, Aveling played Helmer, Shaw played the blackmailer Krogstad, and William Morris's daughter May played Kristina Linde.[40] The presentation was the most important predecessor of the blockbuster June 1889 production of the play newly translated as *A Doll's House* that was produced by Charles Charrington and starred his wife Janet Achurch (both prominent socialists). This production revolutionized British drama and established Ibsen's reputation as (so William Archer claimed in the July 1889 *Fortnightly Review*) the most famous man in the English literary world.[41]

Yet the Aveling production, crucial to Ibsen's transmission as a "socialist" writer, carried a frame of reference very much of its own making and apparent from the way Marx and Aveling wrote about *A Doll's House* in *The Woman Question*. Not only do they there make no allusion to the fact that Nora leaves her family in the play, they end the essay with an image of socialized domestic bliss: "Husband and wife," they prophesy,

> will be able to do that which but few can do know – look clear through one another's eyes into one another's hearts. For ourselves, we believe that the cleaving of one man to one woman will be best for all, and that these will find each in the heart of the other, that which is in the eyes, their own image.[42]

The Avelings' domestic utopia is completely consistent with the sequel (*A Doll's House Repaired*) that Eleanor penned with Israel Zangwill in 1891, in which Nora is portrayed as a "repentant woman listening obediently to her husband's exhortations on ideal womanliness, and Helmer as a considerate husband."[43] It is also consistent with Eleanor's Marx's conception of her relationship – she and Edward, she believed, were two of the "but few" who had already achieved a rational substitute for marriage. (Or, in a less optimistic reading, that they were a couple held together by the courage and will of a liberated woman: Aveling was a man with a reputation for being "irresponsible and unscrupulous" about money and promises. Eleanor Marx often felt estranged but "felt she was bound to Aveling by her own free will.")[44]

When *A Doll's House* finally gained its English sensation three years later, ordinary reviewers understood neither the Avelings' interpretation nor their enthusiasm. They dismissed the play as immoral, morbid, and dreary, which only made the Avelings' circle more eager to take up Ibsen's claim. Overnight he became "the dramatist of the avant-garde [and] the spokesman of liberal values in Europe ... a reputation he retained for decades."[45] Thus, although he was admired for his writing by George Moore, Henry James, Thomas Hardy, and Yeats, "the strongest and most conspicuous signs of interest in Ibsen's work" were to be found in radical circles.[46] And although Shaw, in "The Quintessence of Ibsenism" (1891), played down Ibsen's socialist affiliations, more enthusiastic admirers were not so fastidious. They adopted Ibsen for his skepticism toward bourgeois conventions and his support of feminism – what Ibsen himself called "the transformation of social conditions ... in Europe [that] is very largely concerned with the future status of the workers and of women."[47]

Yet serious socialists and feminists had reservations, nor was there always a unity of purpose between them. The socialist Beatrice Webb considered Ibsen's endorsement of "Truth and Freedom and the Emancipation of Women" "old fashioned stuff" that distracted energy from economic issues.[48] And feminists like Havelock Ellis's wife Edith Lees considered Ibsen an equivocal ally and wrote that Ibsen's importance was largely that it "drove thinking women *further together* towards their emancipation."[49] Both were suspicious of Ibsen's flashes of anarchism and individualism, which were as difficult to reconcile with socialism as with feminism, although they could appear more radical than either. As Ibsen told his Danish disciple Georg Brandes in 1871,

> undermine the concept of the state, set up free choice and spiritual kinship as the one decisive factor for union, and that is the beginning of a liberty that is worth something. Changing the form of government is nothing more than tinkering with degrees ... rotten, all of it.[50]

Eleanor Marx especially seems to have harbored doubts about Ibsen's individualism, and in *The Woman Question* slighted such attitudes as they appeared in *An Enemy of the People*.[51] But she continued her fervent support, going so far as to learn Norwegian to translate *The Lady from the Sea*, because for her *A Doll's House* demonstrated once and for all that, as she had argued in her introduction to *Madame Bovary*, once women are liberated from restricting custom, they will see the world as it is. On that day, she wrote, citing Nora Helmer's words, "there will no longer be one law for the woman and one for the man."

Swayed by Enlightenment optimism, however, Eleanor Marx had gotten her Ibsen wrong. In his first jottings toward the play that became *A Doll's House*, entitled "Notes for a Modern Tragedy," Ibsen had asserted that there are indeed

> two kinds of moral laws, two kinds of conscience, one for men and one, quite different, for women. They don't understand each other; but in practical life, woman is judged by masculine law, as though she weren't a woman but a man ... . A woman cannot be herself in modern society. It is an exclusively male society, with laws made by men and with prosecutors and judges who assess feminine conduct from a masculine standpoint.
>
>   [My heroine] has committed forgery, and is proud of it; for she has done it out of love for her husband, to save his life. But this husband

of hers takes his standpoint, conventionally honourable, on the side of the law, and sees the situation with male eyes.[52]

Far from advancing a universalist feminism and a common law for men and women, then, Ibsen began *A Doll's House* to explore the reality of opposing moral conventions. Nor does *A Doll's House* suggest that it is likely they will be harmonized. In fact, the action turns on just the opposite. Nora, having argued, when Krogstad proposes to blackmail her for forgery in Act I, that she does not believe in a law not concerned with love ("Hasn't a daughter the right to protect her dying father from worry and anxiety? Hasn't a wife the right to save her husband's life? I don't know much about the law, but I'm quite certain that it must say somewhere that things like that are allowed"[53]) reasserts these beliefs more vociferously to her husband Torvald (who holds her accountable by the same logic) in Act III (*DH* 228). Then, as part of the illumination that drives her departure, she insists on the authority of her own values. (When Torvald admonishes her that "no man would sacrifice his *honour* for the one he loves," Nora replies that "Thousands of women have" [*DH* 230].)

The strongest current readings of *A Doll's House* also acknowledge the subversive force of its feminist critique, but also affirm the play's stress on what Ibsen's biographer Michael Meyer has called "the need of every individual to find out the kind of person he or she really is."[54] It is a work, in other words, that portrays opposing spheres of value and portrays them with full understanding that they are incompatible. No less than *Madame Bovary*, *A Doll's House* subtly suggests that the choice between perspectives turns on interests rather than truths, and that any choice between them is ultimately arbitrary. No less "aestheticizing" than Flaubert's practice, this technique is offered not in the key of Flaubert's horror of the bourgeois world, but with a sense of Kierkegaardian existential choice. About to slam the door, Nora tells Torvald "we must both be perfectly free" (*DH* 231); her departure does not solve her problems so much as begin a step into the unknown, since she "can't be satisfied any longer with what most people say, and with what's in books" (*DH* 228). As a rejection of accepted truths, *A Doll's House* presents yet another variation of skeptical aestheticism, an ironic reduction of all truth to the status of as-if and an unequivocal rejection of assumptions like Eleanor Marx's about universalist progress.

This philosophical aestheticism lies at the heart of Ibsen's dialectical procedure, not only in individual plays but in the logic of succeeding compositions. Indeed an open dialectic like Ibsen's is only possible within an aesthetic structure, both in the limited sense of a work of art and in the larger philosophical sense of a discourse fashioned to distance the truth-value of propositions. As Errol Durbach has pointed out, Ibsen's dying word was "*Tvertimod*" – "on the contrary"; it was the last expression of a willingness "to entertain an idea and its opposite in a single visionary moment" and a fundamentally "dialectical frame of mind."[55]

A Doll's House especially needs to be read as a struggle between opposites, a dialectic rather than a manifesto. Throughout, Nora, reacting against a life of hypocrisy, is opposed to her friend Kristina Linde, who has been living without a family in the darkness of separation and purposelessness. In the progress of the play, Nora is impelled out into the cold while Kristina seeks to re-enter a domestic world. At the end they cross, but although Nora commands our attention, *A Doll's House* is deliberately constructed so that each woman's choice questions the other's, and so there is no easy way for us to decide between their opposing claims. In Durbach's words, "Nora's slamming the door on the doll's house must be seen in the dramatic context of Mrs Linde's motives for reentering that secure domestic world, and to see the play as recommending domestic revolution is to miss its surprising *tvertimod*."[56] The value of either choice is relative, dialectical. There is no question of improving things simply by changing "surroundings." And although it was vital, as Ibsen said later in his life, to solve the "problem of women," that was not the "whole object" of *A Doll's House* or his other work.[57]

It was almost inevitable that the open ending of *A Doll's House* would prove unacceptable. Its shock generated a number of sequels of the kind Eleanor Marx Aveling produced, nor was Ibsen displeased. Every rewriting underlined the distinction between a kind of philosophical aestheticism that forces us to encounter the painful contradictions of life and a safer kind of composition that insulates us from such contradictions.

Nevertheless, the distinction was in constant danger of blurring. The contradictory choices of a Nora Helmer and a Kristina Linde were, despite Ibsen's dramatic revolution, only elements of a play, and, as everyone knows, plays are meant to satisfy our need for order and pleasure.

For Ibsen, the inevitability of this kind of reduction was a constant worry. Aestheticizing his own experience, in the end he might succeed only in derealizing everything he loved. Such broodings, we have seen, had led Flaubert into more and more advanced forms of unhappiness a generation before, and the same was to prove true of Ibsen. Exile from his native Norway, recurring estrangements from his wife, and an inevitable alienation from the women and workers whose rights he had so vehemently defended[58] were the equivalent in Ibsen's life to Flaubert's misanthropy. And yet, like Flaubert, Ibsen came to incorporate his frustration into his work, most importantly into the increasing self-consciousness of aesthetic self-critique.

Michael Meyer comments on the extent of Ibsen's self-consciousness in an account of Ibsen's career focused on his last play, *When We Dead Awaken* (1899):

> Ibsen had been planning to write an autobiographical book which would relate his life to his work. Did he perhaps, before starting *When We Dead Awaken*, decide to write that book in dramatic form? For the play certainly covers that ground; it is Ibsen's final account of a struggle with himself. He had portrayed different facets of himself in most of his plays: the unsatisfactory husband preoccupied with his work (Tesman in *Hedda Gabler*, Allmers in *Little Eyolf*), the uncompromising idealist who brings unhappiness to those he loves most (Brand, Gregers Were, Dr Stockmann), the egotistic artist (Ejnar in *Brand*, Hjalmar Ekdal, Lyngstrand in *The Lady from the Sea*), the ruthless old man who despises the world and neglects his wife (Solness, Borkman). But nowhere do we find so complete and merciless a self-portrait as the character of Arnold Rubek. The aging artist [is] restless in his married life, restless in the homeland to which he has returned after a long sojourn abroad, restless in his art.[59]

Meyer omits to say that in *When We Dead Awaken*, Ibsen, while criticizing the consequences of mere aestheticism, makes a heroic attempt to reaffirm the kind of aestheticization that involves a philosophical cycle of existential unmooring and recommitment. In the play, Ibsen's alter ego Rubek is forced to encounter a living emblem of his alienation in the person of his former sculptor's model, who left him in horror when she realized he had taken their spiritual collaboration and turned it into something trivial. The play turns not upon the issue of art versus love but upon a realization that art in a real sense is not just composition but a terrifying leap into a future enabled by the opening of aesthetic detachment. The artist in this sense possesses an existential obligation to follow where the work leads. Irene, the returned model, forces Rubek to realize that in his caution he had betrayed not only her and their sculpture (called "Resurrection Day" because in a generic sense this kind of art necessarily requires the resurrection of the artist), but his own life as well. He has ceased to be an artist or a human being and has turned himself into what she derisively calls a "poet," a "weak" artist whose cowardice is excused by "self-forgiveness for your lifetime of sins both of thought and deed" (*WWDA* 271). For her, his cowardice resulted in a "self-murder" – a "mortal sin against myself" (*WWDA* 271). But had he instead accepted the freedom to grow, her "death" would have been a rebirth into a new life initiated by a living work of art, the existential equivalent of a child. She and the work were "hidden away in tombs" (*WWDA* 271), but she returns to bring him back to a moment of renewed crisis and genuine freedom. (A moment that James Joyce, reviewing the play the year it was first produced, called a "soul crisis" – a recognition at the heart of the play that "life is not to be criticised, but to be faced and lived.")[60]

In *When We Dead Awaken*, Ibsen is careful to distinguish this kind of proto-existential openness both from the formalism with which it struggles and from a certain kind of nihilism which it closely resembles. The counterparts to Rubek and Irena in the play are a hunter named Ulfheim and Rubek's wife, Maia. They too are released into a dizzying freedom, but with no future purpose in sight must choose between the destruction of the void and a safe and simulated freedom. The final counterpoint to Rubek's and Irena's plunge into the future is Maia's nursery-rhyme insistence that

> I am free, I am free, I am free!
> No longer the prison I'll see!
> I am free as a bird, I am free! (*WWDA* 290)

Compared with Flaubert's, Ibsen's can seem a less socially engaged and more optimistic response to modernity. And yet it proceeds by the same dialectic of suspicion, self-conscious of its own peculiar variety of bad faith. For Ibsen's Nora Helmer, modern love guarantees no prosperity or continuity, and involves high and inevitable costs. And for Arnold Rubek, modern art can be nothing more and nothing less than recurrently betting one's existence on a step into the void.

joyce, irony, flaubert, ibsen

In 1898, a year before *When We Dead Awaken* was translated into English, James Joyce began his career as a critical thinker. It was the year (at the age of 16) that he entered University College Dublin, itself a testimony to the modernizing hopes of Irish nationalism, and began to profess strong socialist beliefs that would guide his life and work for a decade and more. About socialism, about marriage, he was a "modern" in the progressive tradition. He remained a socialist until 1907 and probably longer, he refused to marry, he wrote the first two versions ("A Portrait of the Artist" and *Stephen Hero*) of his autobiographical novel, *A Portrait of the Artist as a Young Man*, as documents of socialist defiance.[61]

But Joyce had, by 1898, begun to form himself on the modernist *as well as* the socialist readings of the progressives' favorite texts. He would tell anyone who asked that he had "read every line" of Flaubert, the best of "the great nineteenth century masters of fiction,"[62] but without need: the lineaments of Flaubert's style in *Madame Bovary* are inscribed in everything he wrote through *Ulysses*.[63] As for *A Doll's House*, he informed his friend Arthur Power that the only way to understand Ibsen (who "had been the greatest influence on the present generation; in fact you can say that he formed it to a great extent") was to start from

> the purpose of *The Doll's House* ... the emancipation of women, which has caused the greatest revolution in our time in the most important relationship there is – that between men and women; the revolt of women against the idea that they are the mere instruments of men.[64]

The difference, however, between Joyce and so many other turn-of-the-century progressive "moderns" had less to do with the divergence of their interests (they in fact diverged very little) than with his understanding of the social dynamics of modern art. Attending not only to the "message" of Flaubert and Ibsen, but to the lessons to be learned from their social practice – the way the form of their work engaged with nineteenth-century society – he understood how easily even sophisticated art could be turned by society into a consumerist fashion or on its own terms degrade into something much tamer than it was – formal aestheticism, social engineering, or nihilism. Moreover, Joyce also heeded the lessons of Flaubert's and Ibsen's lives. It was the example of Joyce's struggle to publish *Dubliners* and then *Ulysses* that taught us to read the paradoxes of Flaubert and modern art in the marketplace. And it was Joyce's awareness of the way Ibsen registered the "cross-purposes and contradictions of life," placed at the center of an essay entitled "Ibsen's New Drama" in the 1900 *Fortnightly Review* (p. 16) on *When We Dead Awaken*, that launched his career at the age of 18 and kept Ibsen's focus on the relations between men and women at the center of the avant-garde agenda. Seven years later, in "The Dead," Joyce went back to *A Doll's House* and used it as the basis of the first masterpiece of twentieth-century literature. For, as Margot Norris has perceptively observed, "The Dead" is first and foremost a "husband's version of Ibsen's plot of a [Christmas] party that ends in a ruinous marital exchange."[65]

By the time "The Dead" was written, however, there were modern tragedies to heed beyond those of Flaubert and Ibsen. That of Oscar Wilde, for example, whose philosophical assault on gender roles and on gender itself had pushed the dialectic of modernity well beyond the different laws of *A Doll's House* and had alerted society to the subversive charge of aesthetic skepticism. Joyce's response to his predecessors was cumulative and consistent: he attempted not to find a core problem and then derive the rational principle on which it could be solved, but, as Ibsen had done in *When We Dead Awaken*, to illuminate the contradictions of modernity by exploring his own implication in them, as individual and (as representative modern artist) as opponent. Neither "The Dead" nor *A Portrait of the Artist as a Young Man* nor *Ulysses* nor *Finnegans Wake* can be said to resolve any of the problems of modernity, but they encounter them in a progressively more self-conscious fashion, in part by incorporating the histories of his predecessors into accounts of his own life, more tellingly by enlarging upon the way their ironies reflected on their own involvement in the problems they explored.

Starting in the early drafts of *A Portrait of the Artist as a Young Man*, he put a version of his own life at the center of his fiction, and allowed the ironic procedures of the fiction to suggest: first, the power of "showing" to surpass the rhetoric of "telling" both in presenting and in qualifying rationalist criticisms of modern life; second (as with Flaubert), the futility of its own formal aestheticism too simply conceived; and third (as with Ibsen), an openness and a possibility for growth that a critical understanding of the relations between art and life maintained in the face of deterministic notions of either.

Tokens of these positions may be seen in the evolution of Stephen Dedalus's feminist inclinations from the first draft of *A Portrait of the Artist as a Young Man* (*Stephen Hero*) into the final version and then *Ulysses*. As Homer Obed Brown long ago pointed out, *Stephen Hero* is full of Joyce's own rebellious opinions placed in Stephen's mouth and reinforced by a narrator whose primary function seems to be to reaffirm his perspicacity.[66] One can see this quite clearly in the episode of Stephen's dying sister Isabel (*SH* 165), where his heartfelt sympathy for the "futility of his sister's life" in the conditions of patriarachal Ireland is dramatically contrasted with the insensitivity of his father and endorsed by the narrator, who tells us how "acutely" Stephen sympathized and how "sorry" he was to see her lying dead. Scenes like this substantiate Stephen's positive response a few pages earlier to Emma Cleary's question "are you a believer in the emancipation of women" and confirm Margot Norris's observation that *Stephen Hero* is an explicitly feminist text.[67] No less feminist, Joyce's more mature writings, "The Dead," for example, or more pertinently the revised *A Portrait of the Artist as a Young Man*, prefer, however, as Richard Brown has put it, to "articulat[e their] feminist critique by examination of anti-feminism," whether it be in the patronizing sophistication of Gabriel Conroy or the apparently less forward-looking Stephen of *A Portrait*.[68] That is, they proceed by a probing Flaubertian irony which multiplies the contextual relations framing intellectual attitudes and remain suspicious of positive assertions of a political kind.

In *A Portrait*, moreover, Joyce also applies Flaubertian irony to the formalist variant of his own aestheticism, in order to self-consciously distinguish himself from it. So, for example, in the key section of the novel in which Stephen discusses his theory of art, Joyce substitutes for what had been in *Stephen Hero* an unironized discussion of Ibsenite practice a long disquisition on art based on a formalist and simplified version of Aquinas. The point, as Margot Norris argues in *Joyce's Web*, is by a series of pointed and ultimately comic juxtapositions to distance the aesthetics from Joyce's own and make it clear that Stephen's theory is a way of evading rather than engaging reality.[69]

Yet *A Portrait* also employs, in a way that will be dramatically intensified by *Ulysses*, a more open irony, of the kind Joyce drew attention to in his essay on Ibsen, which supersedes both the "realistic" or "scientific" irony, verging on satire, of the progressives' reading of Flaubert, and the "indeterminist" irony proposed by Flaubert's avant-garde readers. Just as the multiple potentialities of a figure like Nora are held open by the alternative dramatic frames of *A Doll's House*, with a final emphasis on her need as a free agent to arbitrarily choose from among them, so the selves open to Stephen in *A Portrait* and *Ulysses* are suggested by an ironic multiplicity of narrative frames (to start, the mythical frames of Icarus, Dedalus, Telemachus, and Hamlet), which imply different interpretive visions of Stephen's future and assert his need to consciously choose between them.

Joyce invokes Ibsen's less Christian version of Kierkegaard's assertion (in his doctoral thesis on *The Concept of Irony*[70]) that such irony is a mode of freedom in his 1900 essay on *As We Dead Awaken*, which identifies the play's "all-embracing philosophy, a deep sympathy with the cross-purposes and contradictions of life."[71] And by his mid-teens he had located it at the center of his work, and had constructed *Ulysses* (as Arnold Goldman long ago pointed out) as a novel balanced (over the void) between opposing ethical interpretations of its characters' lives.[72] Given the facts of the novel, we (and they) read their futures in different ways, and our (their reading) of what happens to them on the mysterious morning after the novel concludes depends completely on which perspective and which values we (they) choose. *Ulysses'* structural and thematic preoccupation with the "paradoxes and tensions" at the heart of the mystery of human change is an essential component of his mature modernism.[73]

In *Finnegans Wake*, these issues of irony and self-consciousness, art and life, stasis and growth, are transposed from the concerns of narration to a drama of language and interpretation that takes part in the response of the reader. In a book about the unconscious, where things mean not either/or but both/and, the reader is both forced to impose his or her own interpretation of Joyce's language, and, as Jean-Michel Rabaté puts it in *James Joyce and the Politics of Egoism*, required to become self-conscious of his or her responsibility for constructing the text (and the world).[74]

conclusion

There were those at the beginning of the century, of course, as there are those now, who would argue that the ethical neutrality of even Joycean irony is an evasion of the first responsibility of the philosopher. (As Karl Marx famously wrote, it is the duty of the philosopher not to understand history but to change it.) For them, modernism is perhaps a moment of cultural transition and more likely an unfortunate detour. Social criticism of modernism in the 1890s reaction against aestheticism, in the Marxist criticism of the 1920s and 1930s, and in neo-Marxist social criticism of the 1980s and 1990s, would have it that modernism has no future, having already been superseded by the progress of modernity. To take only one very recent example, Edward Said, in an essay entitled "Representing the Colonized: Anthropology's Interlocutors," argues from the perspective of post-colonialism that modernism represents a kind of half-way house – a stage of cultural understanding rooted in a situation in which "Europe and the West" were for the first time forced "to take the Other seriously," but which proceeded no farther than the "formal irony of a culture unable either to say yes, we should give up control, or no, we shall hold on regardless" – that is, with "paralyzed gestures of aestheticized powerlessness." For Said, that stage of understanding is dead, and he foresees an era of post-colonial resolution of modernity's problems based on a post-modern hybridity that goes beyond modernism's ironies and establishes a better world "on the idea of a collective as well as a plural destiny for mankind, Western and non-Western alike."[75] His assurance is currently echoed by many others – by Marianna Torgovnick, for example, the author of an enthusiastically received study of modernist primitivism, who laments the colonialism, racism and sexism implied in the ambiguities of modernism's encounters with the Other, and who aspires to an affirmation beyond irony – to what she calls "a neutral, politically acceptable vocabulary" of non-Western culture which would acknowledge the collective destiny of post-colonial hybridity in a post-modern world.[76]

Yet, as Marjorie Perloff inquires in a response to Torgovnick, what idiom have we developed to transcend the sophistication of that irony? What "neutral" vocabulary might we now employ to supersede the dialogism which is the self-reflexive heart both of the ethnographic encounter and of modernist irony – the kind of formalized self-questioning which, if it opens itself to the charge of ethical fence-sitting, at least acknowledges the phenomenological structure of the dilemma? Don't we, she continues, when we fantasize we are enlightened beings "who live at the end of the twentieth century [and] can see the hidden and not-so-hidden colonialism, racism, and sexism of the early twentieth century as in themselves they really were," expose exactly the same kind of hubris that undermined the righteous efforts of the imperialists that modernist writers fixed in their ambiguous gaze?[77] And do we not, I would add, increase the likelihood of repeating the tragic irony of Enlightenment optimism? As with nineteenth-century Orientalists, might we not, as idealistic reformers, look forward once more to finding ourselves not part of the solution but part of the problem?

The most recent, or "post-colonial" school of Joyce critics has returned once more to the progressive elements in Joyce's modernity, and of course they are right. But we would lose a great deal if we forget that Joyce's modernism was not only progressive but critical, and that much of his achievement consisted in updating the combination of idealism and skepticism embodied in the histories of *Madame Bovary* and *A Doll's House* for the twentieth century. Despite the heated misgivings of his more "progressive" critics, after all, starting in 1900 James Joyce extended the future of "modernism" for 40 glittering years.

notes

1. See Margot Norris, *Joyce's Web: The Social Unraveling of Modernism* (Austin: University of Texas Press, 1992). Leo Bersani's account of Joyce's "conservative ideology of the self" can be found in his essay "Against *Ulysses*" in *The Culture of Redemption* (Cambridge: Harvard University Press, 1990). See especially p. 176. See also Weldon Thornton, *The Anti-Modernism of Joyce's Portrait of the Artist as a Young Man* (Syracuse: Syracuse University Press, 1994).
2. Robert B. Pippin, *Modernism as a Philosophical Problem* (Oxford: Blackwell, 1991), pp. 6–7, 32.
3. Ibid., p. 29.
4. Letter to Louise Colet of April 26, 1853, translated in *The Letters of Gustave Flaubert*, ed. Francis Steegmuller, 2 vols (Cambridge: Harvard University Press, 1980), Vol. 1, p. 185.
5. Ralph Waldo Emerson, in *Lectures and Biographical Sketches* (Boston: Houghton, Mifflin and Company, 1884), pp. 307, 332.
6. Stanislaus Joyce, *The Complete Dublin Diary*, ed. George H. Healey (Ithaca: Cornell University Press, 1971). Here and in subsequent citations references will be indicated parenthetically in the text using the abbreviation *DD*, followed by page numbers.
7. Most probably John Viscount Morley, *Rousseau and His Era* (1873). For the embarrassment Joyce refers to, see for example Morley, Vol. II (reprinted, London: Macmillan, 1923), p. 142: "But Rousseau's egotism manifested itself perversely. This is true to a certain small extent, and one or two of the disclosures in the Confessions are in nauseous matter, and are made, moreover, in a nauseous manner."
8. Joyce here confuses spoons with ribbon, and misremembers the incident near the beginning of the *Confessions* in which Rousseau blames the cook, Marion, for stealing a little pink and silver ribbon that he had himself taken. See the *Confessions* as translated by J.M. Cohen (London: Penguin, 1958), p. 86.
9. For a more theorized account of Joyce's critical aesthetics, see Norris, *Joyce's Web*, especially chapters 1 and 2. Norris, however, probably oversimplifies Eliot's modernism in her effort to distinguish it from Joyce's, and gives too little credit to Wilde's self-consciousness.
10. Stephen Heath, *"Madame Bovary"* (Cambridge: Cambridge University Press, 1992). See also Dominick La Capra, *"Madame Bovary" on Trial* (Ithaca: Cornell University Press, 1982), especially chapter 4.
11. Heath, *"Madame Bovary,"* pp. 56–7.
12. Flaubert, *Letters of Gustave Flaubert*, Vol. I, p. 212. The letter is cited in La Capra, *"Madame Bovary" on Trial*, p. 67.
13. Translated into English from the French Edition Definitive by Eleanor Marx-Aveling: *Madame Bovary: Provincial Manners* (London: Vizetelly and Co., 1886). See Marx's Introduction, p. xiii. Subsequent citations of the novel are from this edition.

14. Ibid., p. xiii.
15. Pippin, *Modernism as a Philosophical Problem*, p. 40.
16. Flaubert, *Madame Bovary*, pp. 233–4.
17. See La Capra, *"Madame Bovary" on Trial*, p. 186. La Capra, however, goes too far in suggesting that Larivière's futility marks him as a "false model" like one of Emma's "romantic novels" ("or at least a model that is used falsely").
18. Letter of September 22, 1853, to Louise Colet, translated by Heath, *"Madame Bovary,"* p. 14.
19. Letter of April 13, 1876, translated by La Capra, *"Madame Bovary" on Trial*, p. 77.
20. Letter of December 9, 1852, to Louise Colet. See Flaubert, *Letters of Gustave Flaubert*, Vol. 1, p. 173. Cited by Heath, *"Madame Bovary,"* pp. 104–5.
21. Letter to Louise Colet of January 16, 1852, translated in Flaubert, *Letters of Gustave Flaubert*, Vol. 1, p. 154. Cited in Heath, *"Madame Bovary,"* p. 7.
22. Heath, *"Madame Bovary,"* p. 145.
23. Pippin, *Modernism as a Philosophical Problem*, pp. 6–7.
24. Richard Rorty, *Contingency, Irony, and Solidarity* (Cambridge: Cambridge University Press, 1987). See especially chapter 4, "Private Irony and Ritual Hope."
25. Jonathan Culler, *Flaubert: The Uses of Uncertainty* (Ithaca: Cornell University Press, 1974; revised edition, 1985).
26. La Capra, *"Madame Bovary" on Trial*, p. 60.
27. Heath, *"Madame Bovary,"* p. 106.
28. Pippin, *Modernism as a Philosophical Problem*, p. 118.
29. The full transcript of the trial can be found in the Pléiade Flaubert, ed. Albert Thibaudet and René Dumesnil, *Oeuvres*, Vol. I (Paris: Gallimard, 1951). For a good, brief account of the resistance, negotiations, and trial, see Benjamin Bart, *Flaubert* (Syracuse: Syracuse University Press, 1967), pp. 354–66. A more tendentious account of the trial can be found in La Capra, *"Madame Bovary" on Trial*, chapter 2, pp. 30–52.
30. Bart, *Flaubert*, p. 361.
31. See Bart, *Flaubert*, pp. 356, 362.
32. Jean-Paul Sartre, *L'Idiot de la famille*, 3 vols. (Paris: Gallimard, 1971–72). See Vol. III, p. 325. Cited, translated, and explicated in La Capra, *"Madame Bovary" on Trial*, p. 88. On Sartre and Flaubert, see La Capra, *"Madame Bovary" on Trial*, pp. 81–99 and *passim*.
33. Heath, *"Madame Bovary,"* p. 43.
34. Pippin, *Modernism as a Philosophical Problem*, p. 41.
35. Ibid., p. 119.
36. Edward Aveling and Eleanor Marx-Aveling, *The Woman Question* (London: Swannsonnenchein, Le Bas and Lowrey, 1886), pp. 14–16.
37. Eleanor Marx to Havelock Ellis, December 1885, cited in Yvonne Kapp, *Eleanor Marx* (London: Lawrence and Wishart, 1972–76). 2 vols. See Vol. 2, p. 103.
38. Ibid., p. 161.
39. Ian Britain, "A Transplanted Doll's House: Ibsenism, Feminism and Socialism in Late-Victorian and Edwardian England," in Ian Donaldson, ed., *Transformations in Modern European Drama* (London: Methuen, 1983), pp. 14–55. See p. 17.

40. For accounts of the productions, see Chushichi Tsuzuki, *The Life of Eleanor Marx, 1855–1898: A Socialist Tragedy* (Oxford: Oxford University Press, 1967), pp. 164ff., Kapp, *Eleanor Marx*, Vol. 2, pp. 103ff. and Britain, "A Transplanted Doll's House," pp. 16–17.

41. For the reception of the 1889 production, see Errol Durbach, *A Doll's House: Ibsen's Myth of Transformation* (Boston: Twayne, 1991), pp. 19–20. Durbach notes that the production was also reviewed (anonymously) by Shaw and by Harley Granville Barker, who called it "the most dramatic event of the decade."

42. Aveling and Marx-Aveling, *The Woman Question*, p. 16.

43. Tsuzuki, *The Life of Eleanor Marx*, p. 182. See also Kapp, *Eleanor Marx*, Vol. 2, p. 517.

44. Tsuzuki, *The Life of Eleanor Marx*, p. 165.

45. Durbach, *A Doll's House*, p. 20.

46. Britain, "A Transplanted Doll's House," p. 24.

47. Ibid., pp. 25–31.

48. Ibid., pp. 32–3.

49. Ibid., p. 32.

50. Ibid., p. 40.

51. Ibid., p. 56.

52. Michael Meyer, *Ibsen* (1967; reprinted London: Cardinal Books, 1988), p. 466.

53. Henrik Ibsen, *A Doll's House and Other Plays*, trans. Peter Watts (London: Penguin, 1965), pp. 175–6. Subsequent citations are indicated parenthetically in the text by *DH*, followed by page number.

54. See Meyer's reading in *Ibsen*, p. 478: "its theme is the need of every individual to find out the kind of person he or she really is and to strive to become that person. Ibsen knew … that liberation can only come from within; which is why he had expressed to Georg Brandes his lack of interest in 'special revolutions, revolutions in externals.'"

55. Durbach, *A Doll's House*, p. 6.

56. Ibid., p. 92.

57. See Meyer, *Ibsen*, p. 817. These words, from an 1898 speech to the Norwegian Society for Women's Rights in which Ibsen was resisting the kind of narrow reading imposed upon him by those only interested in the cause of feminism, has often been cited (as it is by Meyer and Durbach) as a reason to discount the real feminist sympathies of the play. To do so is itself a simplification, however, as Joan Templeton demonstrates in "The *Doll House* Backlash: Criticism, Feminism, and Ibsen," *PMLA* 104:1 (1989), pp. 28–40.

58. For Ibsen's class alienation, see Britain, "A Transplanted Doll's House," pp. 44ff.

59. Henrik Ibsen, "When We Dead Wake" ["When We Dead Waken" was the title Joyce knew and preferred], in *Ghosts and Other Plays*, trans. Peter Watts (London: Penguin, 1964), p. 271. Subsequent citations of this translation are indicated parenthetically in the text by *WWDA*, followed by page number.

60. James Joyce, "Ibsen's New Drama," first published in the *Fortnightly Review* for April 1, 1900, and reprinted in *The Critical Writings of James Joyce* [*CW*], pp. 47–67. See especially pp. 50, 67.

61. On the seriousness and tenacity of Joyce's socialism, see Dominic Mangiello, *Joyce's Politics* (London: Routledge & Kegan Paul, 1980), especially chapter 3.
62. See Frank Budgen, *James Joyce and the Making of 'Ulysses' and Other Writings* (1934; reprinted Oxford: Oxford University Press, 1972), pp. 186, 184.
63. See Richard K. Cross, *Flaubert and Joyce: The Rite of Fiction* (Princeton: Princeton University Press, 1971).
64. Arthur Power, *Conversations with James Joyce*, ed. Clive Hart (1974; reprinted Chicago: Chicago University Press, 1982), p. 35.
65. Norris, *Joyce's Web*, p. 99.
66. See Homer Obed Brown, *James Joyce's Early Fiction: The Biography of a Form* (Cleveland: Case Western Reserve Press, 1972), pp. 63ff.
67. See Norris, *Joyce's Web*, pp. 15ff.
68. See Richard Brown, *James Joyce and Sexuality* (Cambridge: Cambridge University Pres, 1985), p. 93.
69. Norris, *Joyce's Web*, p. 20: in the "self-reflexivity" of interrogating a practice comparable to but less self-conscious than his own, Joyce "critici[zes], rather than reinforc[es], the autonomy [and] separatism" of insufficiently theorized modern art.
70. See Soren Kierkegaard, *The Concept of Irony*, ed. and trans. Howard V. Hong and Edna H. Hong (Princeton: Princeton University Press, 1992), pp. 286–301.
71. See *CW*, 66.
72. On Kierkegaard's revision of Aristotle on identity and change, see Arnold Goldman, *The Joyce Paradox: Form and Freedom in His Fiction* (London: Routledge & Kegan Paul, 1966), pp. 154ff.
73. Ibid., p. 162.
74. Jean-Michel Rabaté, *James Joyce and the Politics of Egoism* (Cambridge: Cambridge University Press, 2001), p. 22.
75. Edward Said, "Representing the Colonized: Anthropology's Interlocutors," *Critical Inquiry* 15 (Winter 1989), pp. 224, 222–3.
76. Marianna Torgovnick, *Gone Primitive: Savage Intellects, Modern Lives* (Chicago: University of Chicago Press, 1990), p. 21.
77. Marjorie Perloff, "Tolerance and Taboo: Modernist Primitivisms and Postmodernist Pieties," in *Prehistories of the Future: The Primitivist Project and the Culture of Modernism*, ed. Elazar Barkan and Ronald Bush (Stanford: Stanford University Press, 1995), pp. 339–54. See p. 339.

2
james joyce and popular culture

garry leonard

In Joyce's fiction, all is not sweetness and light. Indeed, the presentation of "culture" in his fiction gleefully annihilates Matthew Arnold's (1925) rather suspiciously high-handed definition of it as "to know the best that has been thought and known in the world." With this definition, Arnold does not merely distinguish "high art" from "low art" in his definition. Culture *is* "high art." For Arnold, what others might designate as "low art" or "popular culture" is not culture at all. Its only relationship to culture is as a threat, and, as such, it should first be regretted, and then, as far as possible, ignored.

Matthew Arnold makes a rather odd cameo appearance in *Ulysses* when Stephen is imagining the world of Oxford University: "Shouts from the open window startling evening in the quadrangle. A deaf gardener, aproned, masked with Matthew Arnold's face, pushes his mower on the somber lawn watching narrowly the dancing motes of grasshalms" (*U* 1.172–5). "Watching *narrowly*" may well stand in for the visual equivalent of Joyce's critique of Arnold: a cultural watchdog patrolling the border protecting those who reserve the right to determine and preserve a self-perpetuating cultural meaning system advantageous to their personal and economic self-interest, from those who feel systematically disenfranchised and would challenge this same cultural meaning system in an effort to get their own concerns included within the purview of "legitimate." Arnold presents the gathering and appreciation of "culture" as something as neutral as collecting butterflies. The resulting collection, however, especially after it has been naturalized as no more than "what is the best that has been thought and known," also serves as the basis for granting legitimacy to a dominant hegemonic discourse and thereby, without having to argue the point, permanently excluding competing forms of discourse as illegitimate.

Of course, there is a significant diminution of Arnold in Joyce's image: he is at Oxford, sure enough – a center of education, a virtual factory for the production of a cultural meaning system in Imperial England, and thus very much where we might expect the great educator to be – but the center has not held. He now trims overgrown grass, "watching narrowly" as what he has clipped flies off in a steady stream. What is different is that nobody else is watching; if this curious reincarnation of Arnold still imagines he is preserving British culture, all we can see is an irrelevant caretaker mowing the lawn, ignored by all the young men, and gone deaf himself so he cannot hear even their "moneyed voices" carelessly promoting their own rather strained hilarity over some trivial incident unrelated to education: "Palefaces: they hold their ribs with laughter, one clapping another. O, I shall expire! Break the news to her gently, Aubrey!" (U 6.166–7).

And yet, for everything to which Matthew Arnold has grown deaf, Joyce has the ears of a fox and the eyes of a hawk: overheard trivial conversation ("O ... there's a fib," from the close of "Araby" [D 35]), overheard shouts in a public street ("the curses of labourers, the shrill litanies of shop-boys" [D 31]), advertisements ("I walked away slowly ... reading all the theatrical advertisements in the shop-windows as I went" [D 9]), pulp fiction ("I liked better some American detective stories which were traversed from time to time by unkempt fierce and beautiful girls," from "An Encounter" [D 20]), popular song ("She sang I dreamt that I dwelt" [D 106]), vulgar music hall songs ("Polly Mooney ... would also sing. She sang: I'm a ... naughty girl. You needn't sham: You know I am" [D 62]), pantomime ("She heard old Royce sing at the pantomime of Turko the Terrible and laughed with others" [U 1.257–9]), graffiti scratched into a desk (the word "Foetus" in A Portrait of the Artist as a Young Man), even pornography ("For him! For Raoul!" from Sweets of Sin, purchased by Bloom [U 10.609]).

To the question "How low can you go?" Joyce seems to answer: there is no limit. No low art low is low enough to be excluded or ignored. Of course, examples of "low art" are hardly smuggled into Joyce's texts. He seems to feature and highlight them. His very notion of "Epiphany," usually treated as a crucial aesthetic of "high art" modernism, is nonetheless the unexpected convergence of the ephemeral, the trivial and the vulgar, all combining to knock a character out of a self-prescribed and unexamined orbit, and thus producing an ideological freefall experienced as personal dissolution.

And that is what we must especially note: "low art" does not appear merely for the sake of verisimilitude in Joyce; in most cases, it rocks the character's world. For example, a flirtation overheard by the narrator of "Araby" unravels suddenly his oh-so-carefully embroidered romantic quest fantasy to bring back the Holy Grail to his self-appointed and indifferent Guinevere. Interestingly enough, the self-chastisement that floods into his suddenly vacated sense of impending triumph produces just the sort of result Arnold only allows "high" art to be: "I saw myself as a creature driven and derided by vanity" (*D* 35). After all, Arnold describes culture as "the love of perfection" and insists that it "places human perfection in an internal condition ... as distinguished from our animality," and the narrator of "Araby" does seem suddenly ashamed of his "animality" and determined to be more perfect in the future, someone of whom the priests might be proud.

And there's the rub. Arnold has no doubt "perfection" exists, and to strive for it should be an accepted ideal. But when characters in *Dubliners*, or the young Stephen Dedalus, try to re-commit themselves to this sort of "perfection," it is the clear beginning of "moral paralysis," such as the time Stephen dedicates every day, every waking moment, to a different saint in his desperate desire to drown out the call of his own flesh for gratification. Or the time Bob Doran can think of nothing to do but go downstairs and propose to Polly – a "perfection" that will result in his depiction as a hopeless drunk in the "Cyclops" chapter of *Ulysses*. In Joyce's Ireland "perfection" is wielded as a weapon: people who submit to it are henceforth crippled.

Nowhere is this Arnold's stated intent, but it is clear he reserves the right to nominate what is "culture" and so, if "culture" is to be a cudgel to keep the masses at bay, Arnold is the Father Dolan of "high" art, anxious to give a flogging to anyone who appears in need of it. "*The Apache chief!* Is this what you read instead of studying your Roman History?" thunders the aptly named "Father Butler" (*D* 20). Serving British Empire with an obtuseness only equaled later by Haines in *Ulysses*, Father Butler flogs the students with an idea of perfection: "the man who wrote it, I suppose, was some wretched scribbler that writes these things for a drink. I'm surprised at boys like you, educated, reading such stuff. I could understand it if you were ... National School boys" (*D* 20). This class is to be the elite, the guardians of "culture"; it's expected, even perhaps required, that "others" read this wretched scribbling to distinguish them from "the best" who "know" and can justify their superior social status with reference to their impeccable taste.

In other words, people who define culture, as Arnold does, as "the best that is thought and known" already know what they know, and already think what they think, and what they think and know gives them the authority to pronounce on the relative value of everyone else and, at the same time, grants them an unquestionable legitimacy for doing so. As the sociologist Pierre Bourdieu argues,

> [t]he most intolerable thing for those who regard themselves as the possessors of legitimate culture is the sacrilegious reuniting of tastes which taste dictates shall be separated... . At stake in every struggle over art there is also the imposition of an art of living, that is, the transmutation of an arbitrary way of living into the legitimate way of life which cast every other way of living into arbitrariness. (Bourdieu 1984: 57)

Far from avoiding this "struggle," Joyce puts it into play at every opportunity.

Raymond Williams's correction of Arnold is abrupt, concise and even abrasive:

> Culture is ordinary: that is the first fact. Every human society has its own shape, its own purposes, its own meanings ... . We use the word culture in these two senses: to mean a whole way of life – the common meanings; to mean the arts and learning – the special processes of discovery and creative effort. Some writers reserve the word for one or other of these senses; I insist on both, and on the significance of their conjunction. (Williams 1993: 26)

Joyce's well-known series of letters to Grant Richards, insisting that he could not alter *Dubliners*, consistently tries to draw Richards's attention to how the presentation of the "ordinary," which Richards feels can be deleted at no cost to the stories, is, in fact, the heart and soul of *Dubliners* because the particular shape, purpose and meaning of Irish Catholic culture in Dublin – the essence of the "moral paralysis" he hoped to show – required that he show how culture is ordinary and the sole engine driving our construction of the "everyday."

And it is the everyday, not Arnold's neo-Platonic fantasy of perfection, that shapes what we are able to know and what we are able to think. When Maria in "Clay" sings, "I Dreamt That I Dwelt" she forgets to sing the second verse, instead repeating the first, and, as the narrator reports, "no one tried to show her her mistake" (*D* 106). Of course, the forgotten second verse tells of a marriage proposal – something Maria has never received and never will, thus assuring her that her last days will be spent in the cheerless confines of the Dublin by Lamplight Laundry. But it is the conjunction of her forgetting and the silent, unanimous decision not to correct her that shows how ordinary culture is used, in an ordinary way, by ordinary people, to preserve the illusion that a highly constructed "reality" is nothing more than an ordinary event, on an ordinary day.

"It is a very bold man," Joyce writes to Richards, "who dares to alter in the presentment, much less deform, what he has seen and heard … I cannot alter what I have written." And what Joyce sees and hears is what his fellow citizens in Dublin turn away from and ignore: "I am nauseated by their lying drivel about pure men and pure women and spiritual love forever: blatant lying in the face of truth" (*Letters II* 191–2). Often in Joyce's fiction what is important is what is not said, not seen, not heard, or rather the way things are not said: "No, I wouldn't say he was exactly … but there was something queer … " says Old Cotter in "The Sisters" and later that evening, restless in bed, the narrator tells us how he "puzzled my head to extract meaning from his unfinished sentences" (*D* 11). In other words, though the narrator could never conceptualize this, he is a Cultural Studies practitioner, approaching a cultural moment as a semiotic web of significance, one in which he finds himself suspended.

Or, to cite Clifford Geertz's description of analyzing culture, he is "sorting out the structures of signification … and determining their social ground and import." For Geertz, culture is "public because meaning is" (Geertz 1973: 4–5). No doubt because of his background as an anthropologist, he ignores the possibility of an individual meaning, and interests himself in "systems of meaning," insisting that meaning is always generated and internalized with reference to group dynamics. So "culture" is the system of meaning constituted by webs of significance within group dynamics and "the question as to whether culture is patterned conduct or a frame of mind, or even the two somehow mixed together, loses sense. The thing to ask [of actions] is what their import is" (Geertz 1973: 12–13). And, of course, as my reading of the end of "Clay" suggests, this is the thing to ask of inaction ("no one tried to show her her mistake"), as well.

the everyday

Joyce's sustained interest in "low culture" extends beyond artifacts of culture. For him, the way his characters interact with the trivial and the ephemeral is a way to demonstrate "moral paralysis" and colonial mentality in Dublin and show it to be not simply a system of thought, but a material practice. As Althusser and de Certeau argue, it is the practices of everyday life, and not just ideas about it, that bind us, and blind us, to the dominant social order. To use "Clay" again as an example, Maria, who constantly hears remembered compliments playing through her head with the soothing consistency of elevator music, also values a decidedly trivial object: "She took out her purse with the silver clasps *and read again* the words A Present from Belfast. She was very fond of that purse because Joe had brought it to her five years before when he and Alphy had gone to Belfast on a Whit-Monday trip" (*D* 100, my emphasis). What matters to Maria is not what the object is – a purse – but how it signifies an exchange that once occurred that suggests she is valued and loved, against all the mounting evidence to the contrary.

There are numerous instances in Joyce where what people buy is incidental to what the moment of exchange is configured by them to signify. The narrator of "Araby," not unlike Maria in "Clay," allows the contemplation of purchasing something – he doesn't know what – for someone – though she barely acknowledges him – and yet we're told his constant thought on this intended purchase is able to generate a wish to "annihilate the tedious intervening days" (*D* 32). Maria, for her part, visits two cake shops and elaborately discriminates between them, not unlike the contemporary shopper stunned by the nearly psychotic variety of "stuff" presented by the modern mall. Buying something is everything to Maria; her day – one suspects her life – revolves around anticipated purchases, and when she nearly cries at discovering the loss of her plum cake, it is the loss of her dignity she indirectly laments.

One of the most frightening experiences for Stephen Dedalus occurs when he is walking down the street in Cork with his father, and, suddenly, "he could scarcely interpret the letters of the signboards of the shops." Simultaneous with this partial aphasia, he is overcome with a frightening feeling of hyper-insularity in which "nothing moved him or spoke to him from the real world unless he heard in it an echo of the infuriated cries within him. He could respond to no earthly or human appeal … " (*P* 92). Significantly, the next portion of the novel details the temporary joy Stephen feels as he establishes social relations with the people around him through buying things with the money from his essay prize:

For a swift season of merrymaking the money of his prizes ran through Stephen's fingers. Great parcels of groceries and delicacies and dried fruits arrived from the city ... . In his coat pockets he carried squares of Vienna chocolate for his guests while his trousers' pockets bulged with masses of silver and copper coins ... . then the season of pleasure came to an end. (*P* 97–8)

Stephen's "season of pleasure" suggests the extent to which merchandise is eroticized by twentieth-century advertising and marketing techniques.

In fact, the last of his essay money is spent on an overtly erotic product: a prostitute. Would Stephen have become an artist at all if there were a way to extend the "swift season"? True he declares, "how foolish his aim had been!" after his unabashed orgy of consumerism – but only after he has run out of money (*P* 98). The circulation of advertised objects in Joyce's fiction – including objects that are purchased, objects that are received, and objects that fail to enchant – allows Joyce to make explicit the volatile link between consumerism and consciousness in the twentieth century. Bloom's several purchases of his breakfast kidney, his cheese sandwich, the novel *Sweets of Sin*, and a bar of lemon soap (as well as his complex contemplation about whether or not to buy Molly some lingerie) are all actions that might be said to form the superstructure of his day, built up from the infrastructure of his desires and anxieties. Indeed, the primary manner in which Bloom summarizes June 16 is to list everything he has bought. Conversely, many of the "crises" that occur to Joyce's characters directly result from some type of disruption in the process of commodity consumption.

Michel de Certeau suggests that "from advertising to all sorts of mercantile epiphanies, out society is characterized by a cancerous growth of vision, measuring everything by its ability to show or be shown" (de Certeau 1984: xxiv). The overriding "reality" in "A Little Cloud" that strikes the final blow and makes Little Chandler feel he can never "get on" like Gallaher, turns out to be a purchase he made on credit that is visible all around him, pinning him down: "Could he not escape from his little house? Was it too late for him to try to live bravely like Gallaher? Could he go to London? There was the furniture still to be paid for" (*D* 83).

Anywhere that buying, selling, giving, or wanting something is featured in Joyce's fiction, we can also see the complex tactics and strategies that people employ to constitute the experience of their everyday life. Tactics and strategies are two terms for which de Certeau offers a detailed definition in his attempt to highlight the political dimension that is present in each "trivial" act of consumption:

A tactic insinuates itself into the other's place, fragmentarily, without taking it over in its entirety ... Strategies, in contrast, conceal beneath objective calculations their connection with the power that sustains them from within the stronghold of its own "proper" place or institution. (de Certeau 1984: xx)

Tactics, for example, can be employed by the colonized to resist the strategies of the Imperial ideology that surrounds them. Of course, more often in Joyce, as my examples from "Clay" and "A Little Cloud" demonstrate, the "tactics" collapse and the strategy invades, leaving the Dublin consumer with a shattered sense of self, and a feeling of bewildered inferiority. This is one of the fundamental ways Joyce details the construction of everyday acts of consumption in order to illustrate the various power relations that constitute everyday life.

T.S. Eliot famously wrote in "The Love Song of J. Alfred Prufrock," "I have measured out my life with coffee spoons," but Joyce is far more contextual than this. He asks: where did you buy the coffee? What brand? How was it advertised and how did that affect the choice? What were you thinking while you bought it? What was happening around you as the final exchange took place? In other words, all moments of exchange in Joyce must be submitted to a "double reading" because they have a literal meaning and a symptomatic meaning: first, observe the literal transaction (plumcake, a souvenir for Mangan's sister, furniture) and then look at the lapses, the evasions, the distortions, the silences, even the blushes: when Maria takes too long looking at the plumcake, a young clerk asks impatiently if it's wedding cake she wants. This may be sarcasm, and she's certainly guessing Maria would be the mother looking for wedding cake for a daughter's wedding, but Maria blushes, and by this we know, against all appearances, she is indulging her consciously denied fantasy that she might yet someday be married and rescued from her anonymous existence in the Dublin by Lamplight Laundry.

To offer an example from *Ulysses*, Stephen Dedalus comes upon his sister Dilly employing a "tactic" of consumption that attempts to address her anxiety that she will be trapped in Dublin forever. Stephen has told her tales of Paris, and she buys a French primer off a book cart. In one of the most poignant moments in *Ulysses*, Stephen gives a "double reading" to the purchase:

– I bought it from the other cart for a penny, Dilly said, laughing nervously. Is it any good? ...

He took the coverless book from her hand. Chardenal's French
primer.
– What did you buy that for? he asked. To learn French?
  She nodded, reddening and closing tight her lips.
  Show no surprise. Quite natural.
– Here, Stephen said. It's all right. Mind Maggy doesn't pawn it on
you. I suppose all my books are gone.
– Some, Dilly said. We had to.
  She is drowning. Agenbite. Save her. Agenbite. All against us. She
will drown me with her, eyes and hair. (*U* 10.863–76)

Dilly's instant embarrassment at having been discovered in the act of
exercising this tactic leaves no doubt that her purchase will prove futile
in the long run. In a rather uncharacteristic act of compassion, Stephen
tries to convince her that he views this profoundly pathetic tactic of
consumption as a successful strategy: "Show no surprise. Quite natural."
And yet his next comment, "Mind Maggy doesn't pawn it on you,"
inadvertently highlights the fact that her tactic only, as de Certeau puts
it, "insinuates itself into the other's place, fragmentarily, without being
able to keep it at a distance." In Stephen's metaphor for Dilly's tactic of
consumption, the French primer happened to float by, and, although she
has convulsively grabbed on to it, she is still drowning. Since Stephen, just
like Dilly, has no permanent footing, no "place that can be circumscribed
as proper," any attempt to rescue her would drown him too. What is
compelling about the passage is what is *not* said, what is avoided, and
the only sign of all this "absence," just as with Maria and her plumcake,
is Dilly's "reddening" blush. Joyce's text, in other words, can be read
symptomatically: a problem struggling to become articulate is diverted,
evaded, and suppressed. The "trivial" act of buying a used French primer
tellingly conveys the heartache and alienation that is a simple everyday
occurrence within the systematic colonial poverty of Joyce's Dublin.

Such apparently trivial, ephemeral, and arbitrary moments are often
presented in Joyce's fiction as fundamentally more authentic than
"historical events" not despite their insignificance but *because* they are
insignificant. "Official" versions of "historical" events are actually the
distortion, whereas the never to be historicized events of the everyday
are beneath notice, and therefore, for Joyce, most notable.

As my reading of moments of consumption suggests, the momentary
is momentous because it remains unexplained and unaccounted for by
what the Marxist critic Gramsci called "hegemonic discourse." Discourse

more generally can be understood as the various conceptual frameworks that facilitate some modes of thought and exclude or invalidate others. In this way, various institutions sustain their privileged position as arbiters of "the best that is thought and known" (to bring in Arnold again). They do so by developing definitions that permit and encourage the formulation of some ideas while making others, literally, "unthinkable." But Joyce's fiction interrogates such definitions to expose what they exclude.

When Stephen declares to Haines he is "a servant of two masters" and "a third who wants me for odd jobs," Haines is utterly perplexed. Even as Stephen says this, he has a decidedly unofficial image of Queen Victoria: "A crazy queen, old and jealous. Kneel down before me" (*U* 1.640). Finally Stephen is stirred to bluntness: "The imperial British state, Stephen answered, *his colour rising* ... " (*U* 1.643, emphasis added). Once again, a blush signals the intensity of the suppressed affect behind the statement. But Haines is supremely unrattled by the remark, and he effortlessly recasts it in more official, politically neutral language: "I can quite understand that, *he said calmly*. An Irishman must think like that, I daresay. We feel in England that we have treated you rather unfairly. It seems history is to blame" (*U* 1.647–9, emphasis added). Haines's apparent concession that an Irishman must think like that is really an exclusion: nobody else thinks like that, nor need they do so.

After that, 500 years and more of oppression are summarized by Haines as "history" and then this history is itself blamed, neatly vacuuming out any sense of agency or responsibility for anything that has happened during the colonization of Ireland. "Treated you unfairly" becomes another staggering euphemism which reduces a systematic abuse of power, conducted over the course of centuries, to a mere spat of "unfairness," as if it were a game of cricket and all that need be done is replay the game with a renewed sense of sportsmanlike conduct. No wonder when Stephen gives his history lesson in the next chapter he is as disinterested in dates and events as his apathetic students, and does not blame them for their indifference: "For them, too, history was a tale like any other too often heard, their land a pawnshop" (*U* 1.46–7).

He goes on to think of history as the "possible" become "actual." But what interests him is all the "possibilities" ousted by "actualities." He goes so far as to wonder if there might somewhere be "a warehouse" where these ousted possibilities might yet be stored. The "warehouse," I would suggest, is nothing less than the easily ignored world of "low" art and "popular" culture. In the short story "An Encounter," Father Butler, servicing Empire, confiscates "low" art in order to secure "high" art as the only allowable text: "This page or this page? This page? Now, Dillon, up! Hardly had the day … . Have you studied it? What have you there in your pocket?" (*D* 20). What Dillon has, clearly of more interest to him than "official" history, is a cheaply printed text – *The Apache Chief* – detailing events that Father Butler denounces as the refuse of history: "What is this rubbish? … . Is this what you read instead of studying your Roman History?" So, to play this out, a man who is in the service of England historicizes British imperial ideology (Roman history was widely viewed by the British as an apt analogy for British imperial rule) by valorizing as "history" an earlier and excessively heroic account of imperial conquest.

His dismissal of *The Apache Chief* as "rubbish" is a definitional exclusion of any possible authority the victims of imperialisms might have to tell their own story, denying them alternative sources for drawing on inspiration rather than "official" that reaffirm their inferiority as "the conquered." The young narrator who witnesses the throwing out of the "rubbish" of an alternative discourse is appropriately chastened, but the excitement inspired by the forbidden text can only be excluded, not eradicated: "[W]hen the restraining influence of the school was at a distance I began to hunger again for wild sensations, for the escape which *those chronicles of disorder alone* seemed to offer me" (*D* 20–1, my emphasis). A chronicle is a chronological record of events, a specific sort of history, so a "chronicle of disorder" is, on the face of it, an oxymoron; that is to say, a chronicle that is disordered ceases to be a chronicle. But, in fact, a "chronicle of disorder" is the non-chronological experience of impossible-to-historicize moments, which nonetheless allows for a sense of continuity in one's identify over time. Or, put another way, a chronicle of disorder – popular culture – signifies, in a manner "unfairly" dismissed as "rubbish," a non-narrational history of the everyday as distinct from the narrative history that Haines blames, with self-serving vagueness, for causing any problems Ireland or Stephen might care to name.

The "escape" afforded by chronicles of disorder, in other words, is not an escape from history but rather an escape from the historicized, to the not yet historicized, where the colonial subject may have access to *actual* possibilities ousted by the exclusionary "actualities" imposed by historical narrative. "From its own niche," Senn suggests, "*Ulysses* may have helped to change our views of what history also is; we have now learned to read an age not solely in terms of its great masterpieces and dominant philosophies, but particularly in its newspapers, its advertisements, or its fashions" (Senn 1996: 53). But I would not want to lose sight of what the narrator of "An Encounter" tells us. Such sources as newspapers, advertisements, and fashions are not an overlooked source of history; they are "chronicles of disorder," or records of a different kind of history. We should not use them only to correct or oppose the record of dominant historical narrative, but also to promote awareness of a different record. The "warehouse" of ousted possibilities is the suppressed reality submerged in the artifacts and practices of the everyday; the history of everyday experience operates beneath, beyond, and in between the exhaustive yet still limited monocausality of "official" historical discourse.

The "warehouse" of these locked up possibilities may be glimpsed in the blush of Maria hesitating over her plumcake, the "reddening" of Dilly caught buying a French primer, the "rising colour" of Stephen hazarding a critique of British imperialism to his unflappable British guest. Joyce's refusal to honor the separation of "low" and "high" art is his way of honoring the everyday experience of the oppressed. His demotion of Arnold, formerly the arbiter of "high" culture, to a deaf gardener trimming the lawn at Oxford University is a necessary step if the muted lives of the historically unrepresented are to find a voice. This is not a project Arnold favored, or would even have imagined as possible. His description of the "masses" is a fairly recognizable description of many of the characters in Joyce's fiction: "those vast, miserable, unmanageable masses of sunken people." Arnold is clear that, for such as these, "knowledge and truth in the full sense of the words, are not attainable by the great mass of the human race at all." But, as Jameson has said, "history is what hurts," and those hurt by history have a tale to tell and parts of it will be "sunken" and parts will be "miserable," but there is a raw elegance in the everyday struggle that Joyce honors, and that Arnold, with a dismissive strategy mirrored in the confiscating actions of Father Butler, would seem to denounce as "rubbish." For Joyce, the momentary is momentous; the "everyday" is not where we make history, but where we live despite it, and "low" art chronicles this disorder. If we seek the full splendor of Joyce's accomplishment, examples of "low" art are what we *must* read, and read doubly, instead of our Roman history.

references

Arnold, Matthew. *Culture and Anarchy (1869)*. New York: Macmillan, 1925.

Bourdieu, Pierre. *Distinction: A Social Critique of the Judgment of Taste*. Trans. Richard Nice. Cambridge, MA: Harvard University Press, 1984.

de Certeau, Michel. *The Practice of Everyday Life*. Trans. Steven Rendall. Berkeley: University of California Press, 1984.

Geertz, Clifford. "Thick Description: Toward an Interpretive Theory of Culture," in *The Interpretation of Cultures*. New York: Basic Books, 1973.

Senn, Fritz. "History as Text in Reverse," in Mark Wollaeger, Victor Luftig, and Robert Spoo, eds. *Joyce and the Subject of History*. University of Michigan Press, 1996.

Williams, Raymond. "Culture is Ordinary," in Ann Gray and Jim McGuigan, eds. *Studying Culture: An Introductory Reader*. London: Edward Arnold, 1993.

3
topics and geographies
eric bulson

Joyce made Dublin the capital of literary cities in the twentieth century, a microcosm of the universe, a veritable city of cities, that he brought to life again and again with the utmost care and accuracy. To fully appreciate this achievement, however, it is worth reminding ourselves of the paradox that it was only by leaving Dublin that he could conduct his "topographical symphony" – a phrase he once used in 1912 when writing about a seventeenth-century map of Galway – and bring the city's buildings, houses, monuments, residences, and streets into sharp relief. Claiming Dublin for his fiction was contingent on the audacious act of letting it go so that he could see "the dim fabric of the city," as Stephen Dedalus once does in *A Portrait*, "in the distance along the course of the slowflowing Liffey" (*P* 181).[1]

From this distance, Joyce did not represent a fixed and static Dublin. Rather, he represented a revolutionary montage of "Dublins" through a range of historical juxtapositions and varied naturalist, hyper-realist, and surrealist styles.[2] Though the Dublin of *Dubliners*, *A Portrait of the Artist as a Young Man*, and *Ulysses* is consistently set in the same historical period and transfused with similar social, cultural, and historical energies – a British colonial city in the early years of the twentieth century with a population of roughly 300,000 inhabitants – each image of the city and our experience with it changes. With each new literary form, Joyce created a version of Dublin that was as much an eccentric urban plan as a palimpsest of his own topographies whose full complexity we are still learning to understand and appreciate.[3]

There is a strong critical tradition in place that relishes Joyce's topographical precision. The seed for such an approach was first planted in Frank Budgen's 1934 study, *James Joyce and the Making of Ulysses*. In it

Budgen recounts Joyce's claim that Dublin could be reconstructed from the pages of *Ulysses* and mentions, almost in passing, Joyce's composition of "Wandering Rocks" with a map of Dublin before him and a red pen in hand to trace the paths of Father Conmee and the Earl of Dudley.[4] In his *Fabulous Voyager: James Joyce's Ulysses*, Richard Kain was the first critic to demonstrate to what extent Joyce actually used documentary sources like *Thom's Dublin Directory* when he tracked down more than 30 real Dubliners to correspond with the fictional characters of *Ulysses* and examined the geographical references to chart the novel's "meticulous methods of composition."[5] Robert Adams then followed up Kain's achievement some 20 years later with a rigorous study of the concrete facts and realistic details of the novel in an effort to distinguish between what he called surfaces and symbols: the former being "the things which were put into the novel because they are social history, local color, or literal municipal detail" and the latter "the things which represent abstract concepts of special import to the patterning of the novel."[6]

Critics have not been unanimous in their praise of Joyce's geographical realism and there have been occasional attempts over the years to show that the historical geography of Dublin in his works is biased, incomplete, fictional, and forever lost. In his influential article "James Joyce's Dublin" (1970), the Irish historian F.S.L. Lyons first exposed a subjective urban blind spot.

> Of course, we immediately say, there was not one Dublin, but several different Dublins, and how they looked depended on the eye of the beholder. Viewed from Eccles Street the city might well appear to be the center of paralysis; yet from the new theatre, of Moore's house in Ely Place, or half a dozen other points, life and movement and excitement seemed its most obvious characteristics.[7]

Lyons's recognition that there was in fact a more prosperous side of Dublin completely absent from Joyce's fiction reminds us that he chose a self-interested perspective from which he *wanted* to imagine his native city: it was the seventh city in Christendom, the second city of the British Empire, but it was also the paralytic city, as he saw it, awaiting redemption and renewal through his art. While Lyons forcefully reminds us of the disparity between the real, historical geography of Dublin and Joyce's subjective, incomplete one, Bernard Benstock emphasized that Joyce's geography is above all imaginary, a fictional place that allowed him to record a more universal human experience. Focusing more specifically on

Ulysses, Benstock contended that *"Ulysses* is no more about Dublin than *Moby Dick* is about a whale – although no less," and added further that "Too much familiarity with Joyce's Dublin might indeed be dangerous in attempting a balanced reading of *Ulysses*."[8]

So how does one, to use Benstock's words, attempt a "balanced reading" of Joyce with these competing interpretations in mind? As divergent as these voices might at first seem, they are both invested at some level on the mimetic function of geographical details: the streets and place-names can refer either to real, localized sites pinpointed on a map or imagined, universalizing frameworks capable of containing symbolic worlds. In the end, both of these interpretations point back to an organized place that is no longer "there" in any conventional sense. Whether or not one wants to check Joyce's accuracy against the sources and guidebooks is a matter of personal preference, but first and foremost it is necessary to understand that the geography gave him a ready made design whose details he could include and ignore at will. Instead of entering the fray once again, I will discuss how Joyce learned to adapt real geographies to his fictional storylines and how we as readers have been conditioned to respond with a thirst for order. We can think of Dublin as a symbol, a snare, and a narrative signpost, but for Joyce, it was also a place that he was constructing from maps and memory. Along the way, we will want to consider how Joyce's many Dublins reflect an awareness that geography in the Irish imagination and cartography in Irish history are always politically loaded and geographical narration, as Marjorie Howes has put it, is always about the nation.[9]

*

On September 1, 1905, Joyce wrote to his brother Stanislaus asking: "Is it not possible for a few persons of character and culture to make Dublin a capital such as Christiana has become?" (*Letters II* 105) Though uncertain of Dublin's future rise as a capital city equal to that of Christiana, a month later he would write to remind Grant Richards of its more triumphant record in the past: "I do not think that any writer has yet presented Dublin to the world. It has been a capital of Europe for thousands of years, it is supposed to be the 'second' city of the British Empire and it is nearly three times as big as Venice" (*Letters II* 122). It is clear from such pronouncements, written as they were at a time when Joyce was unsuccessfully soliciting publishers for *Dubliners*, that he had big plans for his native city. He was not content with the more modest project of publishing his stories with Dublin in the background as a kind of urban window dressing. Rather, he wanted to put Dublin on the map and make it a capital city like the London of Dickens and the Paris of Balzac, Flaubert, and Zola. To realize his goal, he knew that in addition to capturing the reality of Dublin life, he would have to make Dublin somehow visible to his audience with, what Terence Brown calls, "Ibsenite zeal" – a zeal clearly present in his unflinching attention to all kinds of geographical details.[10] This was a two-pronged objective that he would meet with each of his works: make your place-names as precise as possible so that your Dubliner cannot fault you and your non-Dubliner can not easily follow you.

Though set in the same city, the 15 stories in *Dubliners* are not, as one might expect, united by their geography. There is some overlap in the movement of characters, usually when they are in transit from one place to another, but each story is more or less organized around a single location. While bringing readers inside the closed space of pubs, offices, restaurants, churches, private residences, and shops, the public space of the city emerges during moments of transition as his Dubliners move around.

Let us start by considering more closely "An Encounter" where the itinerary of Mahoney and the narrator is mapped out before they actually embark for the Pigeon House at Ringsend: "We were to meet at ten in the morning on the Canal Bridge … . We arranged to go along the Wharf Road until we came to the ships, then to cross in the ferryboat and walk out to see the Pigeon House" (*D* 13). The route is simple enough and whether or not readers really know the exact location of these places, there is a progressive narrative sense of a beginning, middle, and an end: Canal Bridge, Wharf Road, Pigeon House. When the trip is finally underway the following morning, the boys' arrival at each of the signposts is slowed down by the extended descriptions (indicated by ellipses in the following quotation) of what actually passes in between:

We walked along the North Strand Road till we came to the Vitriol Works and then turned to the right along the Wharf Road … . When we came to the Smoothing Iron we arranged a siege … We came then near the river. We spent a long time walking about the noisy streets flanked by high stone walls … It was noon when we reached the quays … We crossed the Liffey in the ferryboat … When we wandered slowly into Ringsend … (*D* 14–15)

What began as a more spartan itinerary of two sentences grew centripetally into a two-page account of their journey. Within these orientational markers, there is a careful balance of concrete details and familiar landmarks, and the leaps in between have been colored in with descriptions of the sights they see, the people they encounter, the games they play, and the snippets of conversation they exchange. But in this second more descriptive itinerary, we also notice that "North Strand Road" has been added to accurately identify the road that connects the Canal Bridge to Wharf Road, the direction of the turn onto Wharf Road, the jagged turn around the Smoothing Iron, their dally along the high stone walls, and their arrival at the quay for the ferryboat. Joyce's imagination is always anchored in material reality, and this brief example provides a useful way for understanding how he weaves real geographies and fictional stories together. He begins with a crude skeleton map of an area in Dublin, most likely provided by his memory, a real map, or *Thom's Directory*, and proceeds to plot out the movement of his characters and develop the necessary themes and storylines in the process.

The plotting technique evidenced in "An Encounter" receives a more extensive application in later stories like "The Two Gallants." In many ways this story, written in sequence with "A Little Cloud" in 1906, anticipates in miniaturized form the topographical method he would use in *Ulysses*. In "The Two Gallants" we cover the widest expanse of central Dublin and encounter more than 30 passing references to real streets and place-names. The story is roughly divided into two parts: Lenehan and Corley together and Lenehan and Corley apart with the wandering eye of the narrator tagging Lenehan. Once left alone, Lenehan is trying to kill time before his appointed reunion with Corley at 10.30 on the corner of Merrion Street. While the reader unacquainted with Dublin's topography will nevertheless notice Lenehan's peripatetic listlessness, stopping only once for a plate of peas and a ginger beer, some knowledge of the city's layout will reveal a more interesting subtext.

In *The Joycean Way: A Topographical Guide to "Dubliners" and "A Portrait of the Artist as a Young Man,"* Bruce Bidwell and Linda Heffer discovered that when placed on a map, Lenehan's movements trace a pattern of three circles: "Lenehan's walk describes three complete circles, one around Stephen's Green, one bounded by Grafton, Nassau, Kildare and Stephen's Green north, and the large circle formed by Sackville, Great Britain and Capel Streets on the east, north, and west by Dame, Exchequer, and Wicklow Streets on the south."[11] These concentric symbols do not necessarily change the way that we read the story, but when known they do contribute to our understanding of how Joyce himself was structuring his narrative and arranging his characters. The so-called gallant Lenehan is stuck in the web of Dublin's streets and unable to extricate himself. After he reunites with Corley near Baggot Street, the theme of paralysis is subtly reinforced with their climactic turn into Ely Place: on the map, one sees that it is a cul-de-sac, or dead end, with no way out but back for either of them.

Despite the accurate itineraries in "An Encounter" and "The Two Gallants," there are other stories in *Dubliners* where Joyce lapses into ambiguity and relies on his imagination. After reading *Dubliners* with a copy of *Thom's* by his side, Clive Hart noticed that the names of some places mentioned in Dublin never even existed: "The 'Liffey Loan Bank' (*D* 159.28) and Callan's of Fowne's Street (*D* 93.27) appear to be imaginary, and so also, as far as we can tell, is the office of Crosbie and Alleyne, where Farrington works in 'Counterparts'" (*D* 87.26). Hart continues:

> Although in *Ulysses* Joyce would almost certainly have preferred to name real places wherever possible, the difference in method is not in this respect of much consequence. A more significant effect on the texture of the writing and on the relationship of the book to reality is created by Joyce's occasional failure in *Dubliners* to be precise. When he was writing *Ulysses* he would no longer have allowed Mr Duffy to meet Mrs Sinico in "a little cakeshop near the Parkgate" (*D* 112.3), but would have told us which of the three or four likely establishments he had in mind. One might object that he probably had no particular one of them in mind; that is precisely the point of difference. Those parts of *Ulysses* which have a firm base in realism are almost invariably given a sharp focus, Joyce having imagined both the scene and the events with the utmost clarity.[12]

Hart's distinction between the degrees of Joyce's geographical precision shows us that it is not always enough to name "a" place in Dublin; as Joyce's work continues, he must name "the" place to achieve the intended reality effect.

Ironically enough, it was the use of "the" place that would get Joyce into trouble in 1912 with his second publisher, George Roberts, who wanted him to substitute fictitious names for the public houses in "Counterparts" and four other places (*JJ II* 382). After he was unable to finalize a contract for *Dubliners*, Joyce drafted a satirical broadside, "Gas from a Burner," in which he lambasted Roberts for cowering to the threat that the real place names in *Dubliners* would be grounds enough for libel. In "Gas from a Burner" the imagined voice of Roberts rages:

> Shite and onions! Do you think I'll print
> The name of the Wellington Monument,
> Sydney Parade and Sandymount tram,
> Downes's cakeshop and Williams's jam?
> I'm damned if I do – I'm damned to blazes!
> Talk about the *Irish Names of Places!* (*JJ II* 382)[13]

Once contract negotiations between Joyce and Roberts collapsed, he would, of course, keep the Irish names in their proper places. He would also pay Roberts a little tribute years later when writing *Ulysses*; it is a novel, if one is fond of counting, with over 220 real addresses.

*

By the time Joyce came to write *A Portrait*, he had been away from Dublin for ten years with only two return visits, one in 1909 the other in 1912. This prolonged temporal and geographical distance greatly influenced his method for evoking Dublin, and we notice that something about the city has changed. Instead of emerging as an objective, concrete urban landscape, Dublin filters through Stephen's consciousness as something for him to create out of language: "And that was life. The letters of the name of Dublin lay heavily upon his mind, pushing one another surlily hither and thither with slow boorish insistence" (*P* 119). In reference to the Dublin of *A Portrait*, Seamus Deane suggests that it "is a place, a site of linguistic self-consciousness and a point on a map of the modern world that may be only a projection of our desire to give our knowledge a shape that is foreign to or other than it. Above all, it is a place that is named" (*P* xii). For Stephen, as well as Joyce, Dublin is no longer "out there" in the world but inside his imagination, something that he is free to name, order, and give shape to.

But geography, like language, is something that one needs to learn, and the entire novel charts Stephen's gradual control over his external reality. One of his earliest childhood memories is the geography lesson given to him by his aunt Dante: "She had taught him where the Mozambique Channel was and what was the longest river in America and what was the name of the highest mountain in the moon" (*P* 7). The gradual process of learning the chain of names and locations of places around the globe and beyond reinforces the young Stephen's awareness that he is in Dublin. One learns geography through a series of hierarchical spatial scales ordered by and large around the greatness of the universe and the minuteness of the individual. Frustrated by his inability to learn the extended list of American places-names in school, Stephen's mind reels: "They were all in different countries and the countries were in continents and the continents were in the world and the world was in the universe" (P 12). The sequence of countries, continents, the world, and the universe is one way to organize what is really an abstract epistemological vastness. But for Stephen, the act of creating spatial scales is one way of bringing order to his world and making familiar that which is foreign and threatening.

When Stephen sketches his own spatial scale on the flyleaf of a geography book, we notice that geographical scales are not simply timeless and absolute but determined by specific national histories and ideologies:

> *Stephen Dedalus*
> *Class of Elements*
> *Clongowes Wood College*
> *Sallins*
> *County Kildare*
> *Ireland*
> *Europe*
> *The World*
> *The Universe (P 12)*

On Stephen's flyleaf there is the conspicuous absence of "The United Kingdom" between Ireland and Europe, an absence with a subtle political message. Ireland, in Stephen's list, does not belong to the British Empire (as confirmed by the 1801 Act of Union) but to Europe and the world: an error which Jason Mezey argues should be read as a rejection of Ireland's colonial geography and history.[14]

Stephen's artistic awakening throughout the novel is tied up as much with his gradual mastery of the city as it is with his rejection of the Catholic Church. After the Dedalus family moves from suburban Blackrock to Dublin, he creates a skeleton-map of the city to orient himself:

In the beginning he contented himself with circling timidly round the neighbouring square or, at most, going half way down one side of the side streets: but when he had made a skeleton map of the city in his mind he followed boldly one of its central lines until he reached the customhouse. He passed unchallenged among the docks and along the quays wondering at the multitude of corks that lay bobbing on the surface of the water in a thick yellow scum, at the crowds of quay porters and the rumbling carts and the illdressed bearded policeman ...[15]

Stephen's independent wanderings enable his eventual untangling from the nets of home, school, and country. From this point on, Dublin is his to control and it simultaneously represents a site of freedom and a potential snare. The "new and complex sensation" of discovery that bedazzled him in the beginning quickly transforms into disgust as Stephen begins to explore the seamier side of Dublin with its docks, dirty river, illbearded policeman, and prostitutes. Potential sins and snares seem to be waiting around every corner and he structures his many walks to find and elude them. The description of Dublin therefore depends on the state of Stephen's soul and his move outside the protective confines of Belvedere and Clongowes into the world of the city: when his conscience is heavy the streets are slimy, dark, ill-lit, when he repents they are organic and muddy, and when he has chosen to reject the priesthood and pursue his life as an artist they are without adjectives, simply named or unnamed streets.[16]

By carefully learning the layout of Dublin's geography first-hand, Stephen prepared himself for an artistic life abroad. In his final walk with Cranly, a walk that marks the end of their friendship, Joyce weaves a topographical pattern – not unlike the one in "Two Gallants" – that reflects the novel's twin themes of paralysis and escape. As they move from the quadrangle of the National Library towards the township of Pembroke in the south, their conversation touches on Stephen's loss of faith, his embrace of an artistic vocation, and his vow to escape. Though it might seem as though they are lost in conversation, the route of their walk has been carefully plotted out. When Stephen's rant for independence reaches full pitch and he promises to use "silence, cunning, and exile" as the arms he will raise against Ireland, they are moving in an easterly direction, the "tarry easty" or Trieste, symbolic of exile. Unwilling to allow Stephen's symbolic escape before the actual one, Cranly seizes his arm – an ironic touch indeed – and steers "him round so as to head back towards Leeson Park" (P 269): that is, to the north and west commonly associated in Joyce's symbolism with death. In this final glimpse of Dublin, the streets morph into a threatening maze that evokes the labyrinth of the original Dedalus myth and acts as one of the novel's many subtle thematic *topoi* that reflects on events in the story.

*

In *Ulysses*, Joyce's third look at Dublin, he still performs many of the same topographical tricks, but here the streets have become more gnarly and navigation more complicated. Dublin is more maze-like with an inordinate amount of passing street-signs and place-names that chart the movements of characters, their chance encounters, near hits and misses, and deliberate detours. But even when you might think that characters have been lost somewhere in the fabric of the city, you realize that Joyce has been shadowing them the entire time.

The Dublin of *Ulysses* is massive and sprawling with the potential to overwhelm readers, and in critical assessments it has been characterized as a city whose topographical precision is meant to welcome Dubliners and non-Dubliners alike. If this was in fact a welcoming gesture on Joyce's behalf, a very polite but questionable proposition, it was one that has produced a rather long line of confused readers who have rigorously consulted and drafted maps to find their way around. It is precisely the experience that readers have had with maps of Dublin that we get a more refined sense of how Joyce was actually using them to orchestrate and stitch together his novel. Such an approach, in turn, enables us to understand that the real geography of *Ulysses* was a fiction from the start. Joyce wanted to recreate Dublin as it was in 1904, but he needed maps and directories between 1914 and 1921 to build it. Maps inspired the gaze of the exile and they continue to enlighten the alienated reader trying to get close to an outdated urban experience.

Let us start with Joyce's own bold claim that *Ulysses* is itself a blueprint of the city of Dublin. While walking down a street in Zurich, Joyce told Budgen, "One important personality that emerges out of the contacts of many people is that of the city of Dublin." Joyce added that he wanted "to give a picture of Dublin so complete that if the city one day disappeared from the earth it could be reconstructed from my book."[17] If an urban plan was a real goal in the structure of *Ulysses*, however, it was marred from the start. Though streets and places are named they are rarely described, and while we may have a vast collection of over 200 street addresses, it is oftentimes difficult to understand their relative location. The blueprint might not be a particularly useful way for making sense of the geography of *Ulysses*, but the distinction that Budgen makes between description and naming is. Budgen was quick to notice that one of the main differences between *Dubliners* and *Ulysses* is the lack of descriptive detail and the almost casual habit of naming. In his estimation, this technique of naming places without describing them is one way to treat readers as familiars and not foreigners. Though Budgen's distinction is certainly valid, say for the realism of Balzac or Dickens, it is anchored in a nineteenth-century conception that a concrete, though sparsely described, "setting" or "milieu," creates an organic unity between characters, readers, and their worlds. Such a distinction is not only outdated for Joyce's novel, but completely unable to account for the paradox that he would treat readers as familiars knowing that most of them would have a vague conception, if any, of Dublin's geography.

Before moving on to the topographical studies of *Ulysses*, I would like to focus on a moment in 1912 (two years before the first line of *Ulysses* was written) when Joyce visited the West of Ireland and wrote two articles for the Triestine newspaper *Il Piccolo della Sera*. In each of these articles, maps occasion some reflection on Ireland's prosperous past and its impoverished, colonial present and he carefully decodes them for his unknowing Triestine audience. Immediately striking is Joyce's fascination with the various topographical themes that are interwoven with the respective historical and political contexts of each map. As the Irish representative, Joyce wants to convince his audience that Ireland's independence is contingent on its economic prosperity and in reading these maps he offers some indication of what he had in mind when he engaged in his own map-making enterprise.

In "The City of the Tribes," Joyce draws the reader's attention to a well-known seventeenth-century map of Galway, which he designates as "the strangest and most interesting historical document in the city archives" (*CW* 23).[18] Using Richard Hardiman's 1820 study of Galway, *The History of the Town and County of Galway*, he explains the historical conditions under which the map was drafted: "made for the Duke of Lorraine in the seventeenth century, when His Highness wished to be assured of the city's greatness on the occasion of a loan requested of him by his English confrère, the happy monarch."[19] "The Pictorial Map of Galway," as it was known, was commissioned in 1651 to formalize the commercial and political transaction between the French Duke of Lorraine and the Marquis of Clanricarde, then Lord Deputy of the kingdom.[20] In their contract it was agreed that a £20,000 loan from the Duke of Lorraine would be repaid through the wealth of cities like Limerick and Galway. As an added security confirming the commercial eminence of Galway's ports, the map, dedicated to King Charles II, was subsequently given as security to the Duke of Lorraine.

After pointing out the political and economic motivations for the map, Joyce begins to decode the "symbolic expressions and engravings" superimposed over the layout of the town:

> All the margins of the parchment are heavy with the heraldic arms of the tribes, and the map itself is little more than a topographical symphony on the theme of the number of the tribes. Thus, the map maker enumerates and depicts fourteen bastions, fourteen towers on the wall, fourteen principal streets, fourteen narrow streets, and then, sliding down into a minor mode, seven gardens, seven altars for the procession of Corpus Domini, seven markets, and seven other wonders. (CW 231)

The numerical arrangement so carefully listed is considerably more difficult to decipher than Joyce would have his readers believe since the towers, bastions, gardens, and streets are engraved without any obvious spatial logic. To pick up on the "topographical symphony" of this heavily ornamented map, Joyce would have needed to refer to the two legends written in Latin and included along the bottom: each site on the map is accompanied by a number or letter which corresponds, in turn, to a description in one of the legends below. Describing the map as "little more than a topographical symphony on the theme of the number of the tribes," he includes the litotes, "little more than," to highlight the disparity between the layout of Galway as it might have actually been in the seventeenth century and the symbolic meaning assigned to it by the motif of the 14 tribes; the map was meant after all to assure the Duke of Lorraine that Galway was prosperous enough to repay its debts.

A topographical symbolism similar to that of "The Pictorial Map of Galway" recurs in *Ulysses* when Joyce assumed the role of cartographer conducting his own "topographical symphony" for "Wandering Rocks." In his bathymetric reading of "Wandering Rocks," Leo Knuth uncovered one of the more exquisite topographical puzzles whose clue was planted in Budgen's *Making of Ulysses* and most probably passed along by Joyce himself. By tracing the paths of Father Conmee, representative of the Holy Roman Catholic Church, from Mountjoy Square in the direction of Howth Head, and the Viceregal procession crossing the Royal Canal in Pembroke, Knuth discovered that an "X" is formed symbolizing both the tenth episode of the novel and the Christian Cross.[21] Few would argue that this superimposed topographical design marks one of Joyce's finest narrative feats. In a style reminiscent of the number of the 14 tribes depicted in "The Pictorial Map of Galway," the "X" in "Wandering Rocks" depends on a calculated measure of cartographic precision, not to mention timing. But, more importantly, the geographical realism matched with a narrative symbolism emphasizes above all who orders the space and the souls of Dublin: the British Empire and the Catholic Church.

In his second article, "The Mirage of the Fisherman of Aran," Joyce turns his attention to a more modern Irish map outlining the transatlantic trek between Galway and North America. The construction of a transatlantic port, part of a doomed project known as the Galway harbor scheme, had been in the works since the mid-nineteenth century and failed on several attempts. In yet another push around 1912, proponents for the Galway harbor scheme were arguing that the port of Galway could be used for strategic military purposes while allowing Britain to counteract the American monopoly of many Atlantic shipping lanes.[22] As Joyce describes his own ferry leaving Galway's harbor in the direction of Aranmor, his companion opens the map outlining the trek:

A border of white sand on the right indicates the place where the new transatlantic port is, perhaps, destined to rise. My companion spreads out a large map on which the projected lines curve, ramify, and cross each other from Galway to the great Canadian ports. The voyage from Europe to America will take less than three days, according to the figures. From Galway, the last port in Europe, to Saint John, Newfoundland, a steamship will take two days and sixteen hours, and from Galway to Halifax, the first port in Canada, three days and ten hours. The text of the booklet attached to the map bristles with figures, estimates of cost, and oceanographic pictures. (*CW* 235)

Reading the map and the figures together, this passage resembles a ferry brochure complete with routes and timetables. This information, however, has a necessary motivation. The concrete times and destinations that define the various routes are meant to emphasize the practical side of such an enterprise leading up to Joyce's dramatic exhortation: "The old decadent city would rise again. From the new world, wealth and vital energy would run through this new artery of an Ireland drained of blood" (*CW* 235). In this crescendo, the shipping lines are veins with life-giving potential capable of resuscitating Ireland's economy.

As he presents the commercial and military benefits of a transatlantic port, Joyce's argument indeed appears even-handed and optimistic. But as the article continues with the celebration of Aran's "bygone civilization" he begins veering towards a nationalistic lament of Ireland's degradation. Boarding the ferry back to Galway, an encounter with three Danish sailors occasions the following remark about their bemused silence: " ... they seem to be thinking of the Danish hordes who burned the city of Galway in the eighth century, of the Irish lands which are included in the dowries of the girls of Denmark, according to legend, and to which they dream of reconquering" (*CW* 237). The absurd surmising of another Scandinavian invasion certainly seems out of place. But this thematic shift to Ireland's territorial losses leads him back to the map upon which he first espoused Galway's economic rejuvenation: " ... we again open the map. In the twilight the names of the ports cannot be distinguished, but the line that leaves Galway and ramifies and spreads out recalls the motto placed near the crest of his native city by a mystic and perhaps even prophetic head of a monastery: *Quasi Lilium germinans germinabit / et quasi terebinthus extendens ramos suos* [It will grow like a sprouting lily, stretching out its branches like the terebinth tree]" (*CW* 237). Echoing the first description of the map in which the lines "curve, ramify, and cross each other," Joyce transforms their original signification as shipping lines (and metaphorical veins) across the Atlantic and back to an ancient origin filled with symbolic potential for an unrealized future. The "line" that extends outward from Galway on the map brings to mind the visual fulfillment of the "motto" ("it will grow like a sprouting lily") said to have issued from the mouth of an anonymous mystic.[23] Though Joyce played up the belief that Galway could be a "safety valve" for England in the case of war at the beginning of the article, the correspondence drawn between the lines on the map and the fabricated lines of the mystic reflect his own nationalist interest in the economic salvation of Galway all along. Despite the British intrusion that continues to keep the Western seaports impoverished, Galway has its own prophecies to fulfill.

Evidenced in Joyce's journalistic use of maps is his ability to transform visual lines into a more metaphorically oriented byline intended to contrast Ireland's past and present. If "The Pictorial Map of Galway" offered an example of the symbolic potential of cartography with its grandiose numerology superimposed over a more standardized representation, the transatlantic map, then, is evidence of the capacity to fuse the concrete detail with a more deeply rooted message. This type of cartographic effort to cast a concrete geography over an historical event surfaces in *Ulysses* when Joyce incorporates the sensational story of the journalist Ignatius Gallaher in "Aeolus." Myles Crawford recounts that in order to get the story of the Phoenix Park murders out of Ireland to *The New York World*, "the great Gallaher" narrated the events by telegraphing the movements of the Invincibles before and after the murder using an advertisement for Bransome's coffee from a back issue of *Freeman's Journal* (March 17, 1881) that could then be overlaid onto a map of Dublin:

> B is Parkgate. Good. ... His finger leaped and struck point after point, vibrating. T is viceregal lodge. C is where the murder took place. K is Knockmaroon gate ... . F to P is the route Skin-the-Goat drove the car for an alibi, Inichore, Roundtown, Windy Arbour, Palmerston Park, Ranelagh. F.A.B.P. Got that? X is Davy's publichouse in upper Leeson street ... Gave it to them on a hot plate, Myles Crawford said, the whole bloody history. (*U* 7:658–77)

The place-names track the escape route of the Invincibles from the scene of the murder (Phoenix Park) to the "X" (Davy's public house) where they then convened for a celebratory drink. By including the story of Ignatius Gallaher in "Aeolus" as an example of the "smartest piece of journalism ever known," Joyce draws our attention to the association between the journalist and the amateur historian whose clever mode of narration depends on the careful distribution of real sites across a map; it is the "whole bloody *history*" not just the bloody story Gallaher was transmitting. Both in Gallaher's telegraphic map of the Phoenix Park murders and, in a more modest way, in Joyce's maps from 1912 the current of Irish historical events runs steadily beneath the curving lines.

In *Ulysses*, the real geography of Dublin miniaturized and abstracted on a map is one of the many elaborate frames that Joyce used to keep his plot intact and readers have followed suit. It no longer seems possible, or critically responsible for that matter, to ignore the geography. Even Vladimir Nabokov, who derided the "professors of literature" for scouring through *Thom's Directory* to astound their colleagues with prized tidbits, encouraged his students to study the map of Dublin for *Ulysses* and sketched his own maps to prepare for his lectures.[24]

Though readers began mapping out sections of *Ulysses* early on, it was not until 1975 with the publication of Clive Hart and Leo Knuth's *Topographical Guide to Ulysses* that this novel would receive its first systematic mapping. By plotting out every geographical reference they allowed readers to visualize in elaborate detail where the action takes place.[25] The 18 maps they compiled were then accompanied by a separate book of critical commentary on each of the episodes with the address, time, location on the map grid, and a brief analysis of the character routes. By checking *Ulysses* against various maps from 1904 and the appropriate copies of *Thom's*, they demonstrated how central the topography of Dublin was for Joyce in the novel's conception, organization, and execution. They collected numerous examples to show just how accurately Joyce wanted the time and space of the novel to correspond with a verifiable physical reality.[26]

Their effort to organize Joyce's geography was not limited to cartographic and guidebook citations alone. They uncovered many narrative absences, omissions, lapses, and imaginative reworkings that reveal just how much the act of plotting for Joyce was motivated by maps. In Bloom's wanderings, for example, they uncovered patterns around the city that would go largely unnoticed by the reader without any topographical knowledge. Therefore, when "Lotuseaters" opens, a chapter in which very little of the urban landscape is revealed directly, and we find Bloom walking along Sir John Rogerson's Quay, Hart and Knuth, and after them Gunn and Hart, having deduced that he went by foot, suggest that the simplest route would have been "across Hardwicke Place, past St George's Church, down North Temple Street, Gardiner Place, Mountjoy Square West, Gardiner Street, Beresford Place, and across Butt Bridge."[27] Though absent from the chapter itself, this route "happens" behind the scenes and will pop up again in "Ithaca" in an inverted form when Stephen and Bloom walk to Eccles Street from Beresford Place: an inverted route in fact that unites "in perfect symmetry" the initial and final parts of the odyssey.

Bloom's meandering in "Lotuseaters" is appropriate to the action because he is trying to get to the Westland Row post office to pick up a letter from his epistolary mistress, Martha Clifford, without being seen by his fellow Dubliners. Though he seems more absent-minded than usual, Bloom's roundabout route is carefully calculated and reveals yet another topographical symbol. By the time Bloom actually reaches the Oriental Tea Company opposite the post office, his "wanderings describe the shape of a question mark," and after he picks up the letter and walks back up Westland Row his movements trace a complete circle.[28] In their topographical research, the work of Hart and Knuth has had a profound impact on our understanding of the creative process by which Joyce imagined and remapped his native city.

Published immediately after the *Topographical Guide*, Michael Seidel's *Epic Geography* uncovered another more ancient narrative layer in *Ulysses*. In his meticulous study, Seidel traced an entire network of character movements that mirror the larger directional scheme of Homer's *Odyssey* catalogued in Victor Bérard's *Les Phéniciens et l'Odyssée* (1902–03).[29] Seidel writes: "In *Ulysses*, Joyce does not have Homer's spaces at his disposal, but he has an angle of vision on Homer's plot that can open up another kind of narrative space – a comic overlap."[30] In his two-volume study, Bérard had mapped out Odysseus's epic voyage and determined many of the concrete locations for the major episodes in *The Odyssey* across the Mediterranean. Bérard's objective was to illustrate that *The Odyssey* was in fact a Semitic-Greek poem rooted in the voyages of the Phoenician navigators. It is suspected that Joyce came across Bérard's work for the second or third time around 1918, a critical period in the revision of the novel's scope as Michael Groden has shown with "Aeolus," and used the epic geography to reorient both the finished and unfinished chapters.[31] For Joyce, Bérard's book conveniently provided an epic based narrative logic for the itineraries, directions, and positions of Bloom and Stephen while also drawing consistent parallels between the themes of exile, migration, and homecoming. In addition, Seidel discovered that the southeast–northwest axis that characterizes Bloom's movements around Dublin mirrors the orientational axis of Odysseus in the Mediterranean as he moves from known to unknown lands.

The provocative topographical research of Hart, Knuth, and Seidel has shown us that geography is an active historical, narrative, and fictional force with the power to determine the direction, but also the fate, of the characters moving within it. Not content to allow his Dubliners to travel just anywhere, Joyce superimposed concrete routes with ancient topographies: yet another example of what T.S. Eliot called his mythic method to manipulate "a continuous parallel between contemporaneity and antiquity."[32] The 50-year delay between the publication of *Ulysses* and the arrival of these studies suggests that these superimposed topographies were always there to be read, but the map-readers trained to appreciate them had not yet arrived. More recently, critics like Marjorie Howes and Enda Duffy have returned to Joyce's geographies to explain how the image of Dublin in his texts challenges our understanding of Irish nationalism and national identity.[33] If, on the one hand, Joyce's Dublin presents viable alternatives to and arguments against land-based notions of national identity and the monolithic nation, he also used it to question how individuals attach themselves to the "imagined community" of the nation in the first place. For Joyce the exile, the map that demarcates borders and miniaturizes nations is also the place the includes some citizens while excluding others. Joyce, it seems, devised all kinds of tactics to return to Ireland, and in each of his novels we can sense his powerful longing for an Ireland that he can never return to.

It is impossible to know how many historical, social, and political maps it would take to exhaust every detail and context of Joyce's Dublin. But it is worth considering, I think, how naturalized the act of reading Joyce with a map has become for so many of his readers. And this is especially true for the seasoned veteran, who cannot help but imagine Dublin in cartographic terms. With such a prosperous topographical tradition in place, we might now want to "judge Joyce," as Derek Attridge has recommended, and consider some of the possible negative effects that this deceptively totalizing image of Dublin has had on the experience of reading. By descending from the more habitual bird's-eye view to street level, Dublin looks quite different, but it can arouse our interest in the ways that the city both enables and resists coming into focus. Such an experience, in turn, allows us to concentrate on the ways that reading *Ulysses* is and is not like navigating a real city as well as the mental reactions that derive from the feeling of being attracted to and distracted by unfamiliar streets. This is not a plea to jettison our maps but to recover some of the strangeness of the geography that Joyce has given us. It is ironic that we have ended up mimicking, through some kind of knee-jerk reflex, Joyce's own method for seeing Dublin *as if* on a map. Though we have a strong desire for narrative order and a refined taste for topographical design, we need to understand that this is one way, *not the only way*, of reading and making sense of Dublin. In developing alternative ways of reading Joyce's geography in the future, we might want to remember the case of Walter Benjamin, who finally found his way around his native city of Berlin at the age of 30 by deliberately getting lost and learning "the art of reading a street map."[34] But this is a practice, he confessed, that "calls for quite a different schooling."[35]

notes

1. James Joyce, *A Portrait of the Artist as a Young Man* (New York: Penguin, 1992). Subsequent references are to this edition.
2. See *Joyce and the City: The Significance of Place*, ed. Michael Begnal (Syracuse: Syracuse University Press, 2002). For an expert account of topolological history in Joyce, see "Naming and Claiming: Irish Topological History in *Finnegans Wake*" in Thomas Hofheinz's *Joyce and the Invention of Irish History*:

Finnegans Wake in Context (Cambridge: Cambridge University Press, 1995), pp. 69–105.

3. For some useful historical accounts of Dublin, see Samuel A. Ossory Fitzpatrick, *Dublin, A Historical and Topographical Account of the City* (London: Methuen, 1907); Patricia Hutchins, *James Joyce's Dublin* (London: Grey Walls Press, 1950); Cyril Pearl, *Dublin in Bloomtime: The City James Joyce Knew* (London: Angus and Robertson, 1969); Kieran and Des Hickey, *Faithful Departed: The Dublin of James Joyce's 'Ulysses'* (Dublin: Ward River Press, 1982); Jack McCarthy and Danis Rose, *Joyce's Dublin, A Walking Guide to 'Ulysses'*, revised edn (Dublin: Wolfhound Press, 1986, 1988).

4. Frank Budgen, *James Joyce and the Making of Ulysses* (Bloomington: Indiana University Press, 1960), p. 122.

5. Richard Kain, *Fabulous Voyager: James Joyce's Ulysses* (Chicago: University of Chicago Press, 1947), p. 122.

6. Robert Adams, *Surface and Symbol: The Consistency of James Joyce's Ulysses* (Oxford: Oxford University Press, 1962), p. xvii.

7. F.S.L. Lyons, "James Joyce's Dublin," *Twentieth Century Studies* 4 (1970), pp. 6–25. For a similar assessment, see J.C.C. Mays's "Some Comments on the Dublin of *Ulysses*," ed. L. Bonnerot, in Ulysses *Cinquante ans Après* (Paris: Didier, 1974), pp. 83–98.

8. Shari Benstock suggests that the eleven-year gap between when *Ulysses* was written (1914–22) and when it was set (1904) precludes the possibility that the Dublin of the text could be anything but a series of disjunctions between real and imagined worlds: Dublin is less an objective interpretive framework than a personalized narrative space that challenges readers (natives and non-natives alike) to follow with maps, stopwatches, and compasses. See Shari Benstock, "City Spaces and Women's Places in Joyce's Dublin," in *James Joyce: The Augmented Ninth* (Syracuse: Syracuse University Press, 1988), pp. 293–307.

9. Marjorie Howes, "'Goodbye Ireland I'm going to Gort': Geography, Scale and Narrating the Nation," in eds. Derek Attridge and Marjorie Howes, *Semicolonial Joyce* (Cambridge: Cambridge University Press, 2000), pp. 58–77.

10. Terence Brown, "Introduction," in *Dubliners* (New York: Penguin, 1992), p. xv. Subsequent references are to this edition.

11. Bruce Bidwell and Linda Heffer, *The Joycean Way: A Topographic Guide to "Dubliners" and "A Portrait of the Artist as a Young Man"* (Dublin: Wolfhound Press, 1981), p. 84. In *Joyce Annotated: Notes for Dubliners and A Portrait of the Artist as a Young Man* (Los Angeles: University of California Press, 1982), Don Gifford also makes a similar discovery (p. 55).

12. Ian Gunn and Clive Hart, with Harold Beck, *James Joyce's Dublin: A Topographical Guide to the Dublin of Ulysses* (London: Thames and Hudson, 2004), p. 18.

13. The Dubliners for whom Joyce intended "Gas from a Burner" would have known that the italicized "Irish Names of Places" referred to P.W. Joyce's book by the same name (1869): a book that was written to recover the "original" Irish place-names lost during the centuries of British colonization.

14. Jason Howard Mezey, "Ireland, Europe, the World: Political Geography in *A Portrait of the Artist as a Young Man*," *Journal of Modern Literature* 22:2 (1999), p. 348.

15. Ibid., p. 69.
16. Ibid., pp. 106, 150, 151, 154, 157.
17. Budgen, *James Joyce*, pp. 67–8.
18. The following discussion of "The Pictorial Map of Galway" and the transatlantic map has been adapted from my article "Joyce's Geodesy" in the *Journal of Modern Literature* 25:2 (2001–02), pp. 84–90.
19. Ibid. The original map is in Trinity College, Dublin. I referred to a facsimile edition in the Map Division of the New York Public Library.
20. See Richard Hardiman's *The History of the Town and County of Galway* (Dublin: W. Folds, 1820, reprinted 1958) for a discussion of the map and this transaction, pp. 25–34.
21. Leo Knuth, "A Bathymetric Reading of Joyce's *Ulysses*, Chapter X," *James Joyce Quarterly* 4:4 (1972).
22. In the newly published collection *James Joyce: Occasional, Critical, and Political Writings* (Oxford: Oxford University Press, 2001), Kevin Barry has identified the booklet (with map attached) as *Galway as a Transatlantic Port* (n.d. [1912]).
23. The words that Joyce quotes, however, are a complete invention as are the prophet and the motto supposedly placed near the crest of Galway. "*Quasi Lilium germinans germinabit / et quasi terebinthus extendens ramos suos*" is a combination of two separate quotations that are to be found on the top border of "The Pictorial Map of Galway": "*Quasi terebinthus extendens ramos suos*" and "*Quasi Lilium germinans germinabit, et laetabuntur deserta et invia.*" Such a deviation from the original was intended to emphasize the greatness of a lost Irish civilization whose potential is still realizable in the tenuous transatlantic shipping routes.
24. Vladimir Nabokov, *Lectures on Literature*, ed. Fredson Bowers (New York: Harcourt Brace & Company, 1980), p. 285.
25. Ian Gunn and Clive Hart are currently in the process of updating the information with period maps and a revised commentary.
26. Clive Hart actually followed the routes of the characters timing the various trams in the process, to prove that this episode is "constructed so as to be, in terms of timing, realistically exact. There is, here, no intentional distorting, no grotesquerie, no 'fractured surface', of the kind to be found in 'Cyclops' and 'Ithaca'. The characters move at rates consistent with physical life in Dublin in 1904." *James Joyce's Ulysses: Critical Essays*, eds. Clive Hart and David Hayman (Berkeley: University of California Press, 1974), pp. 200–1.
27. Gunn and Hart, *Topographical Guide*, p. 34.
28. Ibid., p. 35.
29. Michael Seidel, *Epic Geography: James Joyce's Ulysses* (Princeton: Princeton University Press, 1976).
30. Ibid., p. 91.
31. Michael Groden, *Ulysses in Progress* (Princeton: Princeton University Press, 1977), pp. 81–91.
32. T.S. Eliot, "*Ulysses*, Order, and Myth," in *Selected Prose of T.S. Eliot*, ed. Frank Kermode (New York: Harcourt, Brace, & Company, 1975), p. 177.
33. See Marjorie Howes, "'Goodbye Ireland I'm Going to Gort': Geography, Scale, and Narrating the Nation" and Enda Duffy's "Disappearing Dublin:

Ulysses, Postcoloniality, and the Politics of Space" in *Semi-Colonial Joyce*, ed. Derek Attridge and Marjorie Howes (Cambridge: Cambridge University Press, 2000).

34. Walter Benjamin, *Reflections: Essays, Aphorisms, Autobiographical Writings*, ed. Peter Demetz, trans. Edmund Jephcott (New York: Schocken Books, 1978), p. 4.

35. Ibid., p. 8.

4

joyce's politics: race, nation, and transnationalism

joseph valente

Over the last decade, several major Irish writers have been vigorously post-colonialized, none more so than James Joyce.[1] In keeping with orthodox historicist principles, according to which the unconscious conditioning force of an author's sociocultural inscription radiates throughout his literary praxis, this entirely welcome reconstruction of James Joyce has inspired a general re-evaluation of his geopolitical vision as well. Joyce the acerbic anti-nationalist cosmopolitan has largely receded before a Joyce whose alleged cultural nationalism better suits his downclassed Irish Catholic status. A steady run of recent studies connect Joyce with those movements that continue the romantic nationalist tradition of asserting the properly organic relationship between the ethnicity of a people and their language, culture and/or political framework.[2]

Taking account of both sides of the equation, this chapter proposes to show that the undeniable anti-nationalism of Joyce's Irish years and the budding nationalism of his early period in Italy dialectically resolved themselves into an idiosyncratic cultural *transnationalism*, in which the localized attachments of and to the ethnos coincide, productively, with their cosmopolitan negation.

As with any properly Hegelian dialectic, the relationship between the constituent terms is not additive but transformative. Joyce's cultural transnationalism, in other words, is not something over and above his expatriate nationalism; it is the *form* that nationalism took in sublating the principles of his anti-nationalism. That is to say, the roots of Joyce's post-exilic cultural transnationalism lie in the *specific nature* of the counter-national discourse found in his early writings. Moreover, as we shall see, the dimensions of that (trans)nationalism are already discernible there in reverse form, rather like a photographic negative. It is the business of this chapter to reconstruct the elements of Joyce's initial quarrel with nationalism in order to contextualize his later transnational turn.

As a young man, Joyce affected a fiercely anti-patriotic posture that became a byword among his college peers, most of whose sympathies were apportioned between the two leading species of Irish-Irelandism: the politically centered variety of Arthur Griffith's Sinn Fein movement (which remained on congenial terms with an as yet dormant Fenianism, as well as with Douglas Hyde's officially neutral Gaelic League), and the culturally centered variety espoused in D.P. Moran's newspaper, *The Leader*, which supplemented its own ties to the Gaelic League with strong allegiance to the Catholic hierarchy. Joyce's initial address to his "Literary and Historical Society" was received by his fellows as an exercise in "renegade ... cosmopolitanism" (*SH* 103). Joyce's second such effort, "James Clarence Mangan" was notable for celebrating the pre-eminent voice of young Ireland while judging him to be "little of a patriot" (*CW* 76). In between these public performances, Joyce privately published and circulated "The Day of the Rabblement," an equal opportunity assault on Irish nationalist culture, which charges the gentrified Anglo-Protestant Irish literary theatre with moral feebleness in capitulating to the demands of mainly middle-class Catholic "trolls" for popular nativist fare. In fact, Joyce goes so far as to admonish the leaders of the dramatic movement that in treating with the Irish people nation itself, "the most belated race in Europe," they had cut their enterprise "adrift from the line of advancement" (*CW* 71). That line, Joyce leaves no doubt, extended from one continental metropolis, one continental author, to another. Where "Drama and Life" elicited accusations of disloyalty to the nationalist cause, "The Day of the Rabblement" flamboyantly solicited them.

The rationale underpinning Joyce's youthful anti-nationalism provides the key to understanding its later evolution. Over the course of the nineteenth century and into the twentieth, the Irish nationalist movement had come to be dominated by the long-stymied Catholic middle classes. As a result, the hostility to British rule and the always related ethnic and sectarian antagonisms within Ireland itself coalesced in a new amalgam of political aims and demands. The Irish nation as a political entity seeking formal self-determination and autonomy under the aegis of Home Rule was supplanted by the Irish nation as a Catholic-identified spiritual and cultural entity seeking substantive self-definition under the rubric of an Irish-Ireland. It was precisely this new dispensation to which Joyce bore strong objection, despite being of the very social group that most stood to benefit. The obvious and most frequently raised explanation for Joyce's vigorous dissent involves what F.S.L. Lyons has called his "arrested Parnellism," his stubborn inherited allegiance to the great Home Rule architect, Charles Stewart Parnell, whose fall from grace exemplified, to Joyce's mind, the Irish propensity for self-betrayal.[3]

In its most sophisticated form, this thesis glosses Joyce's participation in the "cult of personality" surrounding the martyred "Chief" as a mode of transferential identification, whereby Joyce gives a national dimension to the similarly messianic cult of personality that he was fashioning for himself. His contempt for the new nationalism was, accordingly, vital to his romanticized self-image as a repudiated prophet in the making. But in reckoning, as we must, with Joyce's prodigious capacity for enabling self-mythification, we must not underestimate his countervailing proficiency at holding his analytic faculty in reserve, unstultified by his own typological embellishment of his life narrative. Whatever Joyce's personal investment in the legend of Parnell's leadership and the drama of his betrayal, his skeptical assessment of the eclipse of Home Rule by Gaelo-Catholic identity politics never lost sight of the fundamental principles at stake – most saliently, the delegitimization of sociocultural forces, practices and attitudes that did not conform to the notional yet narrowing canon of authentic Irishness.

At the extreme, the philosophy of Gaelic exclusivism – whether in the form of Sinn Fein ("ourselves alone") or an ultramontane Irish-Ireland – met with the young Joyce's disapproval for subordinating all cultural standards to those promoting ethnonational identity. Thus, Stephen complains to Madden, "It seems to me you do not care what banality a man expresses so long as he expresses it in Irish" (*SH* 54), an allusion to an article advancing precisely that thesis in Arthur Griffith's *United Irishman*, which Joyce regularly perused. The anti-imperialist motive of a program could not in itself justify the abdication of critical intelligence.

The symbolic centerpiece of Griffith's Sinn Fein movement, the Hungarian analogy, displays the need and occasions the exercise of such intelligence in *Stephen Hero*. The "irreconcilable" party at University College regularly invokes Hungary as "a glowing example for Ireland ... of a long-suffering minority, entitled by the right of race and justice to a separate freedom, finally emancipating itself" (*SH* 62). But in their Hibernocentric search for historical precedents, these "patriots" conveniently overlook some of the more unsavory aspects of "the case," which the "young sceptic" Dedalus supplies, noting "the capable aggressions of the

Magyars upon the Latin and Slav and Teutonic populations" (*SH* 62). The nationalist consensus of a "long-suffering minority," Stephen's analysis suggests, can easily breed minoritizing intolerance and coercion in its turn. Having "conflicted murderously ... with whacking hurley-sticks," the patriots' bodies were "set aflame with indignation" at this caveat, thereby illustrating its immediate pertinence (*SH* 62). The conceptual rhyme of "glowing" with "aflame," linked in either case with a form of "capable aggression," insinuates that Hungary might indeed prove an "example" of how Ireland, given over to a philosophy of "ourselves alone," would deal with its social, racial, and ideological "others." Joyce returned to this question, of course, in *Ulysses*: Leopold Bloom, a Hungarian-Irish baptized Jew, the very image of Ireland's unacknowledged ethnocultural hybridity, is at once the rumored author of Sinn Fein's politico-economic platform and the present victim of its appeal to, in Joyce's words, "the old pap of racial hatred" (*Letters II* 167).

Joyce's suspicion of the divisive undercurrents of Irish identity-politics ties in with a deeper dissent. Joyce did not regard himself as inhabiting the sort of Gaelic nation that the revivalists believed to exist just beneath the distorting sociocultural gravity of colonial dominion. The surmise of an underlying continuity between modern Ireland and the organic community of its pre-colonial forbears simply amounted to a denial of history so far as Joyce was concerned. As he proclaims in "Ireland, Isle of Saints and Sages," no survey uncolored by political enthusiasm could fail to register that "Just as ancient Egypt is dead, so is ancient Ireland ... the national spirit that spoke through the centuries ... has vanished from the world" (*CW* 173). Moreover, as Joyce knew from his own bloodlines, the long assimilative layering of foreign settlement and influence had not only consigned the aboriginal Gaelic spirit to an irreclaimable past, but muddied the genealogy of its descent beyond recognition. To begin with, continental missionaries not only Christianized Ireland but, in the event, ushered in the permanent hegemony of Roman Catholicism, which was so powerful that this imported faith became inextricably identified with the native Gaelic spirit. This development in turn bore direct consequences for Joyce's patrilineal forebears: the Anglo-Normans were the original colonial-settler class in Ireland, but owing to all the subsequent colonial depredations of a more sectarian tinge, they came to *count* as members of the indigenous people-nation – to share their afflictions, their ethnocultural identifications and their anti-imperialist attitudes. Subsequent waves of invaders also became "*Hibernis Hiberniores*, more Irish than the Irish themselves," and in consequence, Joyce writes, "a new Celtic race was compounded of the old Celtic stock and the Scandinavian, Anglo-Saxon and Norman races. Another national temperament rose on the foundation of the old one, with the various elements mingling and renewing the ancient body" (CW 161). In other words, the death of "ancient Ireland" was not, for Joyce, an unmitigated loss or an incurable trauma, but part of a Nietzschean creative-destructive process, the "foundation" of a new body politic. Joyce's famous barb, that the Irish value the dead above the living, carries a cultural point of reference as well, aimed at the whole range of recovery nationalisms.

For related historical reasons, Joyce also did not regard himself as inhabiting or giving voice to the sort of unequivocally colonial society to which recent trends in Joyce and Irish studies have typically assigned him. Dating back to that Anglo-Norman invasion, Ireland had sporadically participated in her own colonial subjacency, both political and religious. In the same lecture, Joyce describes how the Irish invited Henry II to impose foreign and, proleptically, colonial rule, and he remarks on their similarly voluntary cession of mind and spirit to the Roman imperium: "I do not see what good it does to fulminate against the English tyranny while the Roman tyranny occupies the palace of the soul" (CW 173). Finally, with the Act of Union – "passed not in Westminster but in Dublin" by "an Irish Parliament" (CW 162) – the newest addition to the United Kingdom became a fully metro-colonial space, a border zone at once joining and dividing the Anglo-Protestant and Gaelo-Catholic orders.

The resulting cultural and political ambivalence crystallized in Joyce's Dublin, at once the capital of the Irish people-nation, the heart of the English pale, and the second city of the British Empire. The Dubliners themselves epitomized the metro-colonial estate, and as bearers of its split ethno-national status or inscription, they were the subjects of a similarly split cultural interpellation or mandate. That is to say, they found themselves both authorized and constrained by the agonistic interpenetration of ethnically marked, politically charged discourses, ideologies and forms of life. They were summoned both to a sense of racial entitlement vis-à-vis other colonized groups and to a sense of racial subdominance vis-à-vis more decisively metropolitan peoples; to support for the British civilizing mission abroad and to intransigence toward that same mission at home; to a fluctuating acceptance and resistance to foreign influence (Roman, British, continental); to a cosmopolitan, Eurocentric view of the world and a provincial, Hibernocentric view; and finally to both an affirmation and a rejection of disparate assumptions, values, beliefs, forms of desire and expression, alternately marked by alien or native, dominant or subaltern, elite or popular.

Joyce's own verbal association of Dublin with doubling reflects upon the significance of this curved space of split identification to any account of Ireland and its capital. He begins *Finnegans Wake* by connecting the invasion of Dublin by foreign powers ("Sir Tristam ... fr'over the short sea ... rearrived from North Armorica" [*FW* 3.4–5]) to Dublin's imperial reproduction in foreign lands, like North America ("exaggerated themselves to Laurens County's giorgios" [*FW* 3.7–8]). The geopolitical transaction engenders a dual yet divided and thus uncertain identity that mimics the abject narcissism of the infant's dyadic relation to the mother ("doublin their mumper all the time" [*FW* 3.8–9]). This uncomfortable dehiscence of the metro-colonial psyche, a doppelganger to itself ("doublin"-er), finds subsequent expression in the paranoiac pun "Dyoublong" (*FW* 13.4): Dublin, doubling, do you belong?, expressing a distinctively Irish anxiety of national affiliation.

Reading *Dubliners*, Joyce's only major work begun in Ireland, one is struck by how far its narrative and stylistic methods justify treating the title as a pun (Dubliners as doubliner as dyoublonger) indexing the social topography of its world. At the narrative level, Joyce carefully situates almost every participant at the crux of a double-divisive interpellation, embodied in clashing authorities of various types: commanding figures, prevalent discourses, social institutions and customs, received ideas. As the volume progresses, the conflicts attendant to the metrocolonial estate rise to the surface. In "An Encounter," Roman history occupies a central place in the school curriculum, a privilege it enjoys by reason of the Roman Empire being an antitype of both the spiritual empire of Roman Catholicism and the temporal empire of Great Britain. By "Araby," the boy finds himself solicited by an ostensibly native species of chivalric romanticism, attached to the aptly named Mangan's sister, and by the English-accented, orientalizing and commodified romanticism of the bazaar. In "Two Gallants," Lenehan enacts a more vulgar brand of the same ambivalence, responding both to a feminized harp, a symbol of downtrodden Ireland, and to the venal, predatory cynicism of Corley, the English-identified police informer, whose latest female victim represents an analogous symbol of her country. Little Chandler's envious identification with the cosmopolitan brio of his expatriate "orange" friend, Gallaher, confounds his phantasmatic identification with the delicate, spiritualized languor of the Celtic Twilight bard. In the stories of public life, what we might call the characters' "Dublinscription" materializes in institutional presences and official ideologies: the national self-respect interred with Parnell versus the imported capital promised by "King Eddie" in "Ivy Day"; the patriotic call to Irish art versus the stereotypically British contractual legalism in "A Mother," grace as divine mystery versus grace as mundane respectability in "Grace."

Joyce's stylistic method in *Dubliners* supplements his narrative method by elaborating the relationship between the discursive and institutional constraints on the characters and their projected interiority as subjects. On one hand, Joyce systematically modulates his indirect free style into the distinctive idiolects of the protagonists.[4] On the other, and so less importantly, Joyce ventriloquizes these idiolects so as to render them pastiches of conflicting elements in the larger sociolect, the dialogized voices of Irish culture. Through this syncopated inflection of recognizable social codes with individuating stylistic accents, Joyce shows how the subjectivity of his Dubliners takes shape under and through the pressure of manifold discursive summons, at the point of their interaction and conflict.[5]

The political tenor of Joyce's youthful double-vision of Ireland can be usefully gauged by comparison with its most influential contemporary intertext, D.P. Moran's screed, "The Battle of Two Civilizations."[6] In what was an enormously popular piece of nationalist agitprop, especially among young middle-class Catholic intelligentsia like Joyce's classmates, Moran contended that the Gaelo-Catholic and Anglo-Protestant cultures or "civilization" of the island were locked in a life and death struggle, in which either the native order would win through to reclaim its authenticity and authority or the colonial order would establish a permanent, culturally genocidal hegemony at its expense. Moran and Joyce concurred in finding an imposed cultural scission at the heart of Irish society, and Moran echoed, in a different register, certain of Joyce's most cherished political beliefs. He judged the greatest impediment to Gaelo-Catholic regeneration to be the Irish proclivity for self-betrayal, which he identified with Seisinism, the internalization of Anglified tastes, priorities and standards of distinction. He further supposed the surest remedy for this plague of cultural perfidy to lay in the vigilant exercise of Irish self-criticism, which was precisely the function that Joyce liked to claim for *Dubliners*: "I seriously believe the cause of *civilization* in Ireland will be retarded if the Irish people are not given the opportunity to take one good look at themselves in my nicely polished looking glass" (*SL* 264, my emphasis).

But far from signifying some basic alignment of Joyce's culture critique with that of Moran, the manifest parallels between the social problematic informing *Dubliners* and Moran's "philosophy of Irish Ireland" only sets off their more substantive underlying differences. In fact, given the currency of Moran's polemics at the time Joyce was beginning *Dubliners*, the stories might be plausibly read as mounting an imminent critique thereof. They subject the broad premises of Moran's doctrine to a more sophisticated narrative logic, from which different consequences must be deduced. In the first place, even as he teased out the competing strains in Irish culture and society, Joyce did not see them as neatly opposable "civilizations." To the contrary, the characteristic drift of the stories in *Dubliners* is to epiphanize the concealed structural complicity between the avowedly antagonistic vehicles of metropolitan and nativist interpellation. In both "Araby" and "A Mother," for instance, nationalist, collectivist Irish culture embraces the English-identified entrepreneurial commodification that simultaneously promulgates and appropriates it; in "Grace," mundane respectability itself functions as the master signifier of the spiritual operations it deflects and co-opts; in "Ivy Day," sanctifying Parnell's memory as the personification of national self-respect entails fitting him to the distinctively British type of the "gentleman" and thereby validating that type in turn. In this fashion, Joyce recontours Moran's cultural battlefield along *internal* fault lines. Instead of discrete warring civilizations, Joyce portrays a civilization wrought of unevenly empowered component strands, unevenly abrasive and supportive of one another, symbiotic in their very antagonisms. Moran's famous dictate that "the Gael must be the element that absorbs" has no purchase on a social field understood in this fashion.[7]

While Moran diagnosed in his countrymen something akin to the collective psychomachia anatomized in *Dubliners*, he imputed it to their lapse from the native Gaelic spirit and tradition. A social problem, rooted in colonial politics, this psychomachia nevertheless bore a predominantly moral cast for Moran and indicated a correspondingly moralistic solution: the purgation of all metropolitan adherences and identifications and a return to a more authentic Irishness. His position was grounded in an onto-theological understanding of Irishness, for which the Anglified attachments of his compatriots bore a privative rather than positive reality. They were the colonially inflicted infirmities of an essentialized and ultimately incorruptible national soul. Thus, in "The Battle of Two Civilizations," Moran prophetically represents the native heart and soul as giving off an incantational refrain, the biblical commandment, "Thou shalt be Irish," the inescapability of which serves to explain the anomie of the present and to point the way to future redemption.

The complex social logic *underlying* the psychomachia in *Dubliners* implies a correspondingly complex social ontology of the Irish subject, which necessarily runs athwart the Irish Ireland agenda. In the early essay, "A Portrait of the Artist," Joyce eschews the stock conception of personality as a stable medium of experience, whether fixed permanently or in the moment, treating it instead as a developmental trajectory, "the curve of an emotion" (*P* 258). So too with what he would call the "national temperament" (*CW* 166). Rather than an essentialized medium of collective historical experience, the Irish character in *Dubliners* is an historically engaged construct, the form or logic of a developing, internally varied experience, at once *constraining and contingent*. The "national temperament" is not some collective depth upon which history plays itself out, it is flush with the historical reality inasmuch as that idea necessarily includes the experiential dimension – inasmuch as it is, in phenomenological terms, subject as well as substance. The Dubliners he depicts, accordingly, are not merely subject to but constituted through the embroiled lines of metro-colonial interpellation. By the same token, the foreign or metropolitan adherences that Moran would have purged from the true Irish character represent in Joyce defining as well as hybridizing properties of the Irish soul in its historical being. On his account, the perceived necessity of de-Anglicizing the Irish mind, the founding dictum of the Gaelic League, presupposed a "national temperament" so deeply informed by its assimilative struggle with English culture that the attempt to reverse or eradicate the involuted relationship thus forged could only sustain it on other terms.

The particular ethno-national interpellations staged in *Dubliners* remain indissociable from the character of the subjects they mobilize precisely insofar as they remain indissociable from one another. That is to say, the warring symbolic demands made on an Eveline Hill or a Jimmy Doyle do not merely cohabitate in the fabric of the individual psyche, but are *knotted together* there inextricably. The accession to one social mandate and its answering modes of desire entails some kind of accession, often unconscious, to its negating, corrupting or frustrating other. No sooner, for example, does Jimmy Doyle successfully answer his parvenu family's call to gain them entrée to an elite, metropolitan circle of social distinction, through a program of conspicuous consumption and display, than he winds up pushing his cavalier expenditure to a ruinous extreme, in part to convey some vaguely nationalist sense of his own Irishness to that elite circle. A subject like Jimmy Doyle, in fact, only emerges at the point where the discourses galvanizing him into consciousness interesect and jostle with one another, where each comes to exert its force through the specific resistance of the others. Here then is the matrix of that concealed structural complicity between apparently antagonistic "metro" and "colonial" imperatives.

For Joyce, Irish self-betrayal may have been a source of some moral outrage, but it was the effect of a vexed sociopolitical condition, and while it needed to be addressed from the self-critical posture in which he and Moran joined, it was not susceptible of a dogmatic or prescriptive antidote. From Joyce's perspective, Moran's nativist *ascesis* could not possibly restore the true Irish spirit now sadly betrayed – that spirit lived only as a nostalgia-effect – it could only betray whatever potential for richness and integrity that Irish culture consciousness still enjoyed, and it could do so in a variety of ways.

Most obviously, Moran's "philosophy of Irish Ireland" exhorted Irishmen and women to abnegate their own evolved frameworks of taste in favor of some notional, racially normative touchstone of cultural authenticity. In its form, such programmatic self-denial could not fail to remind Joyce of the Irish Catholic strictures on independent thought and individual desire. In its function, this programmatic self-denial did in fact have a strongly religious dimension, to which Joyce also objected. As Stephen argues, "they encourage the study of Irish that their flocks may be more safely protected from the wolves of disbelief; they consider it an opportunity to withdraw the people into a past of literal implicit faith" (*SH* 54). In this, Stephen is merely reading from the Irish-Ireland psalmody: "There is enmity between the Irish language and infidelity," one sermon had it.[8] Conversely, the appropriation of Irish-Ireland for religious purposes nurtured the illusion that the culture of Catholicism was itself a native growth and thus, in Joyce's words, "a phase of nationalism." In its content, finally, this Gaelocentrism offended Joyce in its insistence on throwing out the English-language and letters baby with the Anglo-imperialist bath water. He is said to have quit a Gaelic class because its instructor, Patrick Pearse, saw fit to belittle the English tongue as a part of his tuition, a scenario fractionally reproduced in *Stephen Hero*. Developing this theme further, Joyce has Madden, "the spokesman for the patriot party" (*SH* 54), give voice to an especially sweeping, uncritical version of such cultural anglophobia: "But really, our peasant has nothing to gain from English literature ... We want to have nothing of this English civilization" (*SH* 54). Stephen replies to this

"Rubbish" by defending English as "the medium of the content"(*SH* 54). But the remainder of the novel evinces the special autonomous value that the English culture itself bears for the aspiring Irish artist.

Like Joyce, for example, Stephen cherishes not only the lyrics of Jonson and the drama of Shakespeare but "the old country songs of England and the elegant songs of the Elizabethans" (*SH* 43).[9] He played these songs, which "were, for him at least really beautiful" (*SH* 43), to the polite appreciation of his social group at the University. In attendance on one occasion, however, is Emma Clery, whose Irish education proceeds under the supervision of the signally named "vulgarian," Father Moran. Having asked Stephen to sing, she rather ungraciously greets a lyric of Dowland not with applause but with a quizzical request for something Irish. His ensuing performance of "My Love She was Born in the North Countree" incites her to loud applause and dreamy rapture: "'I love the Irish music,' she said a few minutes afterward ... 'it is so soul-stirring'" (*SH* 155). At precisely this moment, Stephen "remembered almost every word she had said ... and strove to recall any word which revealed the principle in her worthy of so significant a name as soul" (*SH* 156). Miss Clery evidently takes aesthetic expression not at face-value but at ideological sign-value, and in thus submitting her experience of the piece entirely to the power of its ethnic associations, she forfeits all integrity of response and judgment, a principle not unworthy of the name "soul."

Emma's attitude anticipates both sides of the culture clash between Gabriel and Molly in "The Dead" and thereby casts significant light on the structure of that encounter and the cultural critique it advances. While the penchant of scholars for taking sides in Gabriel's dispute with Miss Ivors has only sharpened since the construction of "Joyce the nationalist," there has arisen some healthy bemusement that the position presumably authorized by subsequent events, Miss Ivor's Western bound nativism, does not receive a more sympathetic portrayal.[10] Like many of the adversarial pairs in *Dubliners*, Gabriel and Molly turn out to be ideological "counterparts" under the skin of their bruising political dispute. Both affect their cultural preferences as badges of the superiority of their respective sociological investments: his in cosmopolitan sophistication and a Europeanized Irishness, hers in nationalist zeal and commitment, and a Gaelicized Irishness. With these exclusionary gestures, both squander the opportunity to engage with the full scope and complexity of their shared cultural heritage in favor of a highly mystified, self-congratulatory synechdoche thereof. As if to underline this point, Joyce puts this scope and complexity on abundant display all around them:

from the performances of the operatic "Arrayed for the Bridal" and the folk ballad "The Lass of Aughrim," to the pictures of Romeo and Juliet and the princes in the tower, to waltzes, quadrilles and lancers, to wide-ranging discussion of opera and theatre, to debates over Church choirs and Cistercian customs, to Molly Ivor's own Irish brooch and Gabriel's allusion to Browning.

As Gabriel discovers, however, with the apparition of Michael Furey, the contradictory alloy of metro-colonial desire and attachment continues to insist at the unconscious level despite, or because, of consciously motivated attempts to privilege certain elements and disavow others. In enjoining this sort of selective/repressive endeavor, the revivalist agenda of "de-Anglicization" laid the groundwork for another species of self-betrayal on the part of its exponents. Writing of the sexual ethics in Joyce's *Exiles*, Vicki Mahaffey has astutely observed, "betrayal is only meaningful in response to a prior expectation."[11] In this instance, the prior expectation not only lends the betrayal its meaning, but brings it into existence as such. For it is only under the expectations inculcated by the cultural purity movements that an Irish subject's enactment of the real social and affective contradictions animating his/her being in the world – the process carefully charted in *Dubliners* – could entail a betrayal of some reified Irish authenticity that s/he is presumed to possess. In setting a standard of collective integrity at wide variance with the "national temperament" to be restored, the morality of Irish cultural exclusivism transformed an inevitable, and inevitably ambivalent form of self-externalization into a tacitly culpable form of self-betrayal. Moreover, because the guiding cultural expectations of Irish-Ireland are cast as matters of individual commitment and responsibility, something requiring little more than good faith and sufficient will, their disciples incur a certain blindness to their ongoing structural complicity with the ideological forms and institutional forces they oppose. In another twist of this "treacherous" dialectic, a single-minded devotion to promoting the cause of an essentially Irish culture leaves the cultural nationalist unwitting hostage to the effects of metro-colonial self-division.

Regarding Molly Ivors, for example, her discussion of her upcoming "excursion" bespeaks a tourist no less than a nationalist mentality.[12] She envisions the vestigial space of indigenous Irish culture as at once the true homeland ("your own land ... your own people ... your own country ..."), a foreign territory ("that you know nothing of"), and a vacation retreat ("It will be splendid out in the Atlantic" [*D* 189–90]). In this respect, she typifies the autoexoticizing impetus of the revivalist folklore generally: the well-known propensity of urbane Irishmen to take the politically authorized search for their own racial heritage as an occasion to enjoy unfamiliar climes and customs, primitive conditions and styles of life, all from a safe and superior psychosocial distance. But that is precisely to say that such Gaelic revivalism was, at least in part, a compromise formation designed to satisfy the warring interpellations and the polarized investments characteristic of the metro-colonial condition. Excursions of the type Miss Ivors contemplates were motivated by the wish to *be* the idealized aboriginal peasant, to identify with that subject as a gesture of colonial resistance or "De Anglicization," and by the wish to *see* the natives, to subject them to the empowered gaze of the Revivalist qua civilized metropolitan observer.

Dedalus gibes the "patriotic party" in *Stephen Hero* for just this structural complicity, which he terms "systematic compensation" (*SH* 63). Jousting with Madden, he exposes the college ideologues of an Irish-Ireland as strikingly West British in their practice. Thus, Hughes "sneers at the Parliamentary Party for taking the oath of allegiance" even as he prepares to be "a barrister, a Q.C. [Queen's Counsel], perhaps even a judge," all of which require the same expression of loyalty. The hypocrisy of his fiery separatist beliefs sitting cheek by jowl with his governmentally authorized and affiliated course of action is replicated over and again in the "many … Gaelic Leaguers … sitting for the Second Division and looking for advancement in the Civil Service" (*SH* 63). Over Madden's weak objections, Stephen notes that they too are to be "pledged to the government and paid by the government." In the context of the larger conversation, Stephen is clearly accusing his nationalist peers of stooping to the moral, and yes the material, equivalent of "taking the Saxon shillin'," a catchphrase for joining the British Army, a typically lower-class concession to financial necessity that bourgeois Irish patriots reviled as unpardonable perfidy.

Madden's rather unsteady effort to distinguish the two cases only serves to reveal how easily institutional dependency and cooperation can slip into ideological misrecognition and collaboration. He begins by staking out a far more metro/cosmopolitan position than any the "renegade" Dedalus has articulated: "Law is law the world over – there must be someone to administer it" (*SH* 63). Such a blasé elision of cultural difference in the formation of judicial systems reflects the expansive imperialist hegemony of one system in particular and validates, by naturalizing, its universal designs. Insisting as it does on the locality of the law in question, Stephen's retort – "I do not quite follow the distinction you make between administering English law and administering English bullets" (*SH* 63) – touches on this point of complicity, and the response it elicits is, for that reason, especially telling: "Any how it is better for a man to follow a line of life which civilization regards as humane. Better be a barrister than a redcoat" (*SH* 64). With its echo of D.P. Moran's well-known essay title, "The Battle of Two Civilizations," Madden's appeal to a universal "civilization" is clearly to be read as a voiding of cultural difference in the name of the very cultural nationalism that cherished it. During the exact period that Moran's controversial essays proclaiming the Anglo-Gaelic culture wars were appearing serially in the *New Ireland Review*, the most extreme "patriot" at University College can still posit, for Ireland, England and the world, some zero-degree of "civilization," in which the "barrister," a term and an office distinctive of British common law, earns well-deserved moral esteem. What civilization could this possibly be if not the British Empire as it existed in the British Imaginary?

Madden's denigration of "the profession of arms" (*SH* 63) further manifests his entanglement with the colonial ideology he is attacking. It does so not only because his disdain for the British aggressor belies his fervent participation in an enterprise, the Gaelic Athletic Association, whose celebration of revolutionary violence under the sign of manliness entails an identification with the aggressor *in* his aggression. More importantly, it does so in the very distinction it imagines between the coercive foundations of British sovereignty, implemented by the odious "redcoat," and the juridical edifice which, being implemented by the "humane barrister, Q.C., perhaps … judge," cannot fail to legitimate that sovereignty to a degree. On the one hand, this viewpoint inadvertently tallies with Matthew Arnold's famous apology for the policy of conquest: "might until Right is ready." On the other, Madden's attitude perfectly captures the unconscious ambivalence, which is also to say the structural self-division, plaguing metro-colonial nationalism. Madden's attempt to compartmentalize soldiering and the law, the most deeply imbricated and closely interactive tools of colonial domination, encapsulates the simultaneous rejection and respectful accommodation of empire.

In "The Necessity of De-Anglicizing Ireland," the address which launched the Gaelic League, Douglas Hyde sets forth his cultural nationalist agenda as a corrective to a communal ambivalence not unrelated to the metro-colonial condition that I have been charting. He argues that "Irish sentiment sticks in a half-way house, hating and yet imitating the English," and urges his countrymen to vacate this "anomalous position" and "build up the Irish nation on Irish lines."[13] In both his diagnosis and his prescription for the Irish condition, Hyde provided the template on which Griffith's Sinn Fein and Moran's Irish-Ireland forged their contributions to cultural nationalism. Spending his last year in Ireland amid the enthusiasm that Hyde had kindled, the maturing Joyce initially rejected out of hand the ends sought by this broad church of revivalism. Thus his early essays argue for a cosmopolitan embrace of multifarious European influence. But he ended this phase of his career on a more significant note, accepting the premises but puncturing the logic that gave revivalist nationalism its catalyzing *raison d'être*. Thus his early fiction takes the ingrained Irish self-division, upon which he, Hyde and Moran could agree, and traces its operation in the spokesmen of cultural nationalism themselves and in their articulation and enactment of the patriotic line. The burden of this strategy is twofold:

1. Inasmuch as the "halfway house" of "Irish sentiment" is serious and endemic, it must impede the revivalist nationalism that it occasions. For the attempt to build the Irish nation along indigenous Gaelic lines remains haunted by those metropolitan preferences and identifications that the patriots themselves, as Irishmen, inevitably harbor. If Michael Furey represents the ghost of Ireland's folk culture possessing Gabriel Conroy with shame at his own continental affectations, then Ignatius Gallaher functions as a specter of Ireland's metropolitan ambitions possessing Little Chandler with an frustration at his own provisional confinement.
2. Revivalist nationalism of the Irish-Ireland type fails to mount a cohesive version of what Anderson calls the "imagined community" of nationhood because its overall program is false to the "national temperament" that it claims to express.[14] To "build the Irish nation on Irish lines," as Hyde proposes, is precisely *not* to build it on predominantly Gaelic, traditional lines, as he assumes. Irishness does not consist in the legacy of peasant culture and tribal myth, nor for that matter in Ireland's contemporary affiliation with hegemonic metropolitan culture, but at the charged intersection of these coordinates. To distill Irishness to a unitary essence, therefore, is to distort it unsustainably, as the embarrassment of Joyce's nationalists is meant to attest. Irishness is at once the sum and the denominator of its rifts and contestations and must be mobilized on that basis. In this regard, the metro-colonial community represents something of an inter-nation, a restricted economy of Joyce's coming transnationalism.

Virtually all of the contextual evidence of Joyce's burgeoning nationalist sympathy dates from his first Italian sojourn, which he punctuated with three return visits to Ireland. Joyce the nationalist, that is to say, is the construct of a strictly delimited period, between the time of his Dublin upbringing and the final schism of permanent self-exile following the collapse of his contract for *Dubliners*. It was during this interval that certain of Joyce's letters to Stanislaus offer a highly qualified defense of Arthur Griffith's attempt "to revive the separatist idea along modern lines" (*SL* 110); it was during this interval that Joyce, inspired by Griffith's attempt "to inaugurate some commercial life for Ireland"(*SL* 111), fashioned himself an agent marketing Irish tweeds in Italy; it was during this interval that Joyce represented the case of his colonized homeland at the "bar of Europe," both in the Trieste lecture "Ireland, Isle of Saints and Sages," and in articles for the irredentist paper *Il Piccolo della Sera*; it was during this interval, finally, that Joyce sent *Il Piccolo* travelogues from the aboriginal West of Ireland, emphasizing its intimate connection with the ongoing history of metropolitan Europe.

As the last item presses home, the remarkable thing about this burst of nationalist fervor is that it occurred at the juncture when Joyce was no longer a native and not fully an exile, but rather a transnational in the contemporary post-colonial sense of the word, that is, a diasporic subject who imagines himself a member of his distant community of ethnic origin as well as his more proximate community of national residence. Joyce was a transnational before he became a nationalist. What is more, since Joyce's expatriation partly responded to aversive intellectual and cultural milieus that Irish-Ireland, broadly construed, had helped to foster, it would seem that he was a *transnationalist* before he became a nationalist, that he could only promote the culture of Ireland once its ecumenical possibilities came more distinctly into focus.

As a result, the parameters of Joyce's fledgling nationalism were, to say the least, expansive. Commenting on the timing of Joyce's political conversion, Willard Potts writes that it "appear[s] to demonstrate the truism that nothing turns people into patriots more quickly than living in a foreign country."[15] Now the point of the truism seems to be that the alienating exposure to different customs and life-conditions tends to nourish a more single-minded attachment to the familiar terrain of one's homeland and a stronger belief in the singularity of merits – in sum, patriotic sentiments of a phobic and so chauvinistic variety. If so, Potts's commentary would have things exactly backward in this case. Living in Trieste, an extraordinarily rich nexus of different languages, ethnicities and customs, Joyce not only appreciated certain metonymic connections between his native and adopted dwelling place, but he also grasped a more global likeness of the two as, in John McCourt's phrase, "living encyclopedia of the cultures ... [they] had assimilated."[16]

As if to advertise this transnational kinship between his community of origin and his community of residence, "Ireland Isle of Saints and Sages" lays extraordinary emphasis on the multiethnic, multicultural cast of Ireland, its historical status as a crossroads of and beyond Europe, a sort of Trieste West. Its rhetorical structure images forth the thoroughly transient history that it surveys, unfolding in a series of movements pegged to distinct phases of the island's ongoing assimilation, hybridization and exportation of racial and cultural groups: (1) the mythic prehistory of Phoenician influence, (2) the "invasions of the Spanish and Gaelic Tribes" (*CW* 156), (3) the early Church history of Irish missionary exchange with the Continent, (4) the invasions of the Scandinavian tribes, (5) the "Anglo-Saxon and Norman invasions" (*CW* 162), (6) the emigration of Irish writers during the colonial period, the political "flight of the wild geese" (*CW* 172) and the continuing economic emigration to America. At each of the latter stages, Joyce is careful to italicize the profound intermixture of racial temperaments and cultural attitudes that have ensued.

> The Scandinavians ... were gradually assimilated into the community, a fact that we must keep in mind if we want to understand the curious character of the modern Irishman. (*CW* 161)

> A new Celtic race was compounded of the old Celtic stock and the Scandinavian, Anglo-Saxon and Norman races. (*CW* 161)

> Our civilization is a vast fabric, in which the Nordic aggressiveness and Roman law, the new bourgeois conventions and the remnant of a Syriac religion are reconciled. In such a fabric, it is useless to look for a thread that may have remained pure and virgin. (*CW* 165)

> What race, what language ... can boast of being pure today? And *no* race has less right to utter such a boast than the race now living in Ireland. (*CW* 165)

> Do we not see that in Ireland the Danes, the Firbolgs, the Milesians from Spain, the Norman invaders and the Anglo-Saxon settlers have united to form a new entity. (*CW* 166)

With these entries, Joyce deliberately freights the parallelism between his old and new habitat with an implicit yet pointed critique of the more uncompromising form of revivalist nationalism – a Triestine Ireland is not, cannot, be an "Irish Ireland."

Trieste was, to be sure, a more diverse, robust and fully realized entrepôt than Dublin, or Ireland at large, but that very disparity only sharpened the outlines of the peculiar brand of nationalism that Joyce had begun to entertain. For Ireland to become a cosmopolitan European society, as Joyce had advocated back home, now meant that Ireland was to become what it already was, in the strong Nietzschean sense of that injunction, that is, to transvalue the present state of ambivalence and self-division into a constructive cultural perspectivism by refuting all romantic fictions, unionist or separatist, that predicated Irish well-being on a collective "unity of being" or staked the prospect of Irish self-determination on the consolidation of Irish self-identity. For Ireland "to write the history of the future" (*CW* 173) (in Joyce's own unmistakably Nietzschean catchphrase) – that is, for Ireland to invent a future that is answerable to her history, both as reflection and redress – it needed to recalibrate its metro-colonial condition on an inside-out basis. Ireland had been, to Joyce's mind, a liminal nation, defined in terms of pre-modern organic wholeness she had never enjoyed and could never achieve. But the same social elements, molded by the same historical dynamics, had prepared Ireland to become a modern trans-nation, characterized by cultural inmixing within its borders ("a bilingual republic" [*CW* 173]) and vibrant socioeconomic intercourse beyond them (carried out by "its own commercial fleet and its own counsels in every port of the world" [*CW* 173]).

At this point, it should be clear that Joyce's "new nationalism" did not evolve at the extinction of his early cosmopolitan anti-nationalism, but rather as a continuation of that critical stance in a more Irish-affirmative mode. And therein lies its complexity and eccentricity. For to celebrate, as Joyce does, the nomadic quality of Irish culture, both its migratory matrix and its resulting divagation from any ethnically marked center or norm, is in itself to attack the more uncompromising forms of cultural nationalism *in the name of the Irish nation*, the strengths, virtues and possibilities lodged in its inveterate errancy. Joyce thus came to espouse an Irish exceptionalism grounded not, as in revivalist doctrine, on a unique collective identity, but rather on a singular degree of collective self-alterity.

To make matters more slippery, Joyce appears to have linked his contrarian form of Irish exceptionalism with a revised estimate of Sinn

Fein. To avoid confusion on this point, we need to consider how his updated, aggressively selective reading of Arthur Griffith's agenda, amounting almost to a hostile appropriation, rehearses his general trans-lation of nationalist principles. Joyce's apologies for Sinn Fein focus mainly on its political and economic strategies, a number of which were direct extensions of Parnellism (plans for parliamentary withdrawal, based on the Hungarian model, had not only been considered by Parnell but merged the Chief's signature tactics of obstructionism and boycott). In the cultural domain, Joyce confined his defense of Sinn Fein to the Catholic Griffith's anti-sectarian willingness to challenge the authority of the Church in political affairs and so, implicitly, the role of Catholicism as a criterion of Irishness or nationalist legitimacy. This too was something of a Parnellite legacy. Where Griffith proposes more restrictive grounds of national belonging or privileges certain markers of Irish identity, Joyce dismisses him out of hand. As we have seen, he renounced Griffith's race-baiting, and he demurred as well at Griffith's support for the Gaelic revival – "If the Irish programme did not insist on the Irish language I suppose I could call myself a nationalist" (*SL* 125). Joyce's pattern was to favor Sinn Fein insofar as it proved itself an impure or improper mode of Irish cultural nationalism, and to disapprove Sinn Fein insofar as it remained a recognizably proper mode, dedicated to essentialist orthodoxies, like the inherence of the Gaelic language to the Irish spirit. In this regard, Joyce doubtless felt he was being faithful to the logic of a movement that had imported the ideas underpinning its nominally closed society ("ourselves alone") from a foreign community. (Indeed, Bloom's dual status as a Sinn Fein exponent/victim is itself but a parodic reflection of the constitutive duality of Sinn Fein.) More importantly, since romantic or revivalist nationalism centered on determining what was proper or improper to the "imagined community," Joyce's endorsement of Sinn Fein as a means of subverting that binary consists perfectly with his larger transnationalist objective of opening the borders of national(ist) identity in a nonetheless Irish-affirmative mode. The slogan "ourselves alone," with an emphasis on the multiplicity of selves, comes to name an Irish exceptionalism based on Ireland/Irishness as exceptions to themselves.

To see how this transvaluation of the metro-colonial double-bind operates, we might return to "The Dead," Joyce's first song of transnationalism. As Joyce began the story, he wrote to Stanislaus that he thought the previous tales in *Dubliners* had been too stinting in their representation of the positive aspects of Dublin society, in particular, its "hospitality," which he promised to feature prominently in the coda

(*SL* 110). His comments, together with the climactic evocation of Michael Furey as the deeply mourned ghost of an expired native life world, has lent "The Dead" a critical reputation as a prime testament of Joyce's developing cultural patriotism. What is striking, however, is the irreconcilability of the two pieces of evidence for any standard nationalist reading of the story.

In the first place, the generous "hospitality" on display at the Morkan's holiday party shows "a preference," as Potts observes, "for non-Irish music, dance, and art," so that "any Irish-Irelander would have dismissed the affair as West British."[17] For its part, the West of Ireland, that vestigial Gaelic space, is not really associated with Irish hospitality, except as its recipient: the figure of Michael Furey is hosted first in the bereaved memory of the transplanted Gretta and then in the besieged imagination of the "West Briton" Gabriel. If we look at these salient instances of hospitality – the social and the psychic, the material and the spiritual – the cardinal virtue of Joyce's Dublin appears altogether too accommodating for nationalist purposes: at different moments it embraces, non-exclusively, indigenous folkways and imperialist culture.

Because Gretta's shattering revelation and Gabriel's final epiphany might create the impression that the narrative is designed to harness the promiscuously metro-colonial "virtue" of hospitality to the elements and the ends of "the Irish programme," it is crucial to note that the Conroy's joint construction of Michael Furey is multiply, or rather multiculturally filtered. It is mediated by "The Lass of Aughrim," a Celtic folk ballad, which triggers Gretta's memory of Michael and has contributed to his subsequent iconicity as the feminized "native." Their construction is also framed by Shakespeare's *Romeo and Juliet*, an English tragedy of tribal antagonism, based on Italian materials. The famous balcony scene, a picture of which contributes to the West-Britonish atmosphere of the Morkan's parlor, finds a clear echo in the final fatal encounter of Gretta and her country lover. It is mediated as well by W.B. Yeats's revivalist classic, *Cathleen Ni Houlihan*: in informing Gabriel "I think he died for me" (*D* 221), Gretta unconsciously cites the summons to patriotic blood sacrifice issued by the allegorical figure of Ireland. The phrasing of Gretta's surmise suggests that Furey acquires his emblematic status as authentic Irishman in part through her diffuse inculcation into current nationalist mythology.[18]

The latter possibility becomes all the more conspicuous owing to another of the mediating frames, the class discourse of modern industrial relations. Gabriel summarizes Michael Furey's identity in the phrase, "a boy in the gasworks," and however condescending a character they supply, his words do remind us that we should not conceive Michael Furey strictly as the iconic Irish peasant of romantic imagination, "pass[ing] boldly into that other world, in the full glory of some passion" (*D* 224), but must see him too as a sadly displaced and debilitated modern laborer, passing weakly of an industrially induced or exacerbated disease. A strange and important phenomenon occurs when Gabriel begins his mental "journey westward" to meet Furey on his own sacred aboriginal ground: the ground reveals that the ruptures of the metro-colonial condition, so pronounced in the capital, have spread all the way to "the dark mutinous Shannon waves" (*D* 225). As far west as Galway, the pre-modern world undergoes the imprinting of transnational modernity; ancient local customs ("we used to go out walking, you know, Gabriel, the way they do in the country" [*D* 222]) engage factory laborers whose energies are alienated in and by an economic framework that extends well beyond their experiential horizons; the robust "glory of some passion" (*D* 225) identified with the unspoiled rustic world of the Irish peasant coincides with the specter of degeneration identified with increasingly industrialized and urban forms of life. At the denouement of "The Dead," it becomes apparent that "doublin," like the snow, "was general all over Ireland" (*D* 225). Paradoxically, the complex figure that Furey cuts at the end of "The Dead," read against the panorama of self-division marking the collection as a whole, only *confirms* D(o)ublin in its role as the archetypal instance of the Irish condition – and this against the current of ("Fureyite") Irish-Irelanders who deplored the capital as a West British anomaly.

In one of his more widely quoted remarks, Joyce translated the immanent universalism of William Blake's "Auguries of Innocence" ("to see the world in a grain of sand … and eternity in an hour") from the natural, cosmic dimension to a social and cultural register: "If I can get to the heart of Dublin, I can get to the heart of all cities in the world. In the particular is contained the universal" (*JJ II* 505). What facilitated this translation was Joyce's transnationalist apprehension of the many historically accumulated cultural strains interanimating to form his city and his country. The particularity of Dublin *is* this constitutive diversity, which resists the imposition of political or ideological universals but offers itself as a concrete aesthetic universal. The transnationalist optic thus conjoins Joyce's aesthetic method and social analytic in a fully synthesized or "binocular" vision. Without this "doublin," without the impacting of multiple, nationally inflected discourses within a contested space of Irishness, the narrative of "The Dead" would lose at a single blow its critical incisiveness and its affective nuance, its power to illuminate and to move.

The final tableau of "The Dead" is an object-lesson in the poignant doubling of the national and the transnational, especially when viewed in the light of Benedict Anderson's influential theory of nationhood. For Anderson, the birth of the modern nation could only take place with the waning of the religious communities of the pre-Enlightenment era. Linked by a sacred language and the idea of membership it implied, such communities understood themselves as being "coterminous with mankind."[19] The modern nation substituted "horizontal-secular" bonds of comradeship, held together by a vernacular language that was identified with a *finite* group of people and circulated through print culture. This national community is by definition bounded; it presumes other distinct communities of the same order. Whereas the former involved a community of belief, in which a sense of mutual belonging is forged on the anvil of ritualized dedication to something *beyond* the community, the modern nation is a community of the empirical imagination, in which social activity is so structured as to allow members to envisage all of the others undertaking the same cultural engagements in comparable ways within the same time frame.[20] Hence the importance to Anderson's scheme of the daily newspaper, which trains innumerable eyeballs simultaneously on the same cultural materials.

As Emer Nolan has remarked,[21] Joyce evokes something like this imagined community in anonymity in Gabriel's closing meditation: "Yes, the newspapers were right: the snow was general all over Ireland" (*D* 225). Here print culture not only delivers information, but instills a feeling of national coexistence. That sense, however, is so fragile as to be virtually unwritten and rewritten otherwise at the moment of its articulation. For one thing, Gabriel does not think in singular terms, "the newspaper," as one might expect, to reference a uniform consensus on an uncontroversial topic. In the wake of his quarrel with Miss Ivors over his writing in the "wrong" newspaper, he cannot assume the existence of a unanimous or representative journalistic voice. In other words, the papers of Ireland, indeed of Dublin, are too various and too fractious to sustain the baseline consensus necessary to create the mass intuition of synchronic cultural engagement that Anderson supposes. The point of consensus here, the weather, only confirms as much *via negativa*. Far more often construed as a natural phenomenon or a divine dispensation than a cultural datum, the weather is an experience people always share, but not as specifically ethnonational subjects. The weather, unlike say the climate, conforms neither to national boundaries nor self-conceptions. It possesses an irreducibly cosmic aspect, something beyond the social world it affects. Hence, Gabriel's invocation of the Irish nation, responding to the pressure of its internal fissures, comes to rest in a dimension in and yet beyond the nation, literally a trans-national space.

Joyce emphasizes and elaborates upon this dynamic by symbolically transfiguring elements of the snowscape into motifs of Christ's Passion: "It lay thickly drifted on the crooked crosses and headstones, on the spears of the little gate, on the barren thorns" (D 225). With this, Gabriel's invocation of Ireland swerves away from the nation-state and toward one of those "classical" religious communities, Christendom, that both predates and exceeds it, being "coterminous with mankind" or, in Joyce's words, "all the living and the dead" (D 225). And yet beneath the universalizing rhetoric of Christendom lurks its sectarian differences of interpretation that have asserted themselves as a primary variant of Ireland's metro-colonial self-division. The former is objectified in the leveling, all-embracing snow, the latter is negatively objectified in those "crooked crosses," whose shape and sectarian inflection are deliberately shrouded in white (are they [pre-Reformation] Celtic crosses, Catholic crucifixes, plain crosses acceptable to Protestantism?) In this relation between the positive image of blank abstract unity and the negative of a substantive, antagonistic multiplicity beneath glimmers the exquisite difficulty of Joyce's aesthetic project: to transcend the ideological limits of so-called national culture or art, unfolding the hybrid and contradictory elements of Irish life in ever more capacious designs, but to contrive against losing the local and, yes, the national particularity of those elements in elevating them to the dignity of the universal. Between this Scylla and Charybdis lies the transnational space Joyce enters in "The Dead" and explores ever more ambitiously thereafter, the locus where this difficulty achieves not its resolution, but its epiphany.

notes

1. For other examples, see Davis Coakley, *Oscar Wilde: The Importance of Being Irish* (Dublin: Town House, 1994); Marjorie Howes, *Yeats's Nations* (Cambridge: Cambridge University Press, 1996); Andrew Bennett and Nicholas Royle, *Elizabeth Bowen and the Dissolution of the Novel* (New York: St. Martin's Press, 1994); Joseph Valente, *Dracula's Crypt: Bram Stoker, Irishness, and the Question of Blood* (Urbana: University of Illinois Press, 2002).
2. Willard Potts, *Joyce and the Two Irelands* (Austin: University of Texas Press, 2000), pp. 60–1; Emer Nolan, *Joyce and Nationalism* (New York: Routledge, 1995), pp. 47–54; Len Platt, *Joyce and the Anglo-Irish* (Amsterdam: Rodolphi,

1998), pp. 18–47; Gregory Castle, *Modernism and the Celtic Revival* (Cambridge: Cambridge University Press, 2001), pp. 173–4; Pericles Lewis, *Modernism, Nationalism and the Novel* (Cambridge: Cambridge University Press, 2000), pp. 42–50.

3. F.S.L. Lyons, "James Joyce's Dublin," *Twentieth Century Studies* 4 (1970), pp. 6–35.

4. Hugh Kenner, *Joyce's Voices* (Berkeley: University of California Press, 1978), p. 15.

5. For a fuller account, see Joseph Valente, "Between Resistance and Complicity: Metro-Colonial Tactics in Joyce's *Dubliners*," *Narrative* 6.3 (1998), pp. 325–40.

6. D.P. Moran, "The Battle of Two Civilizations," *New Ireland Review* 13 (1900), pp. 323–6.

7. Moran, "Battle of Two Civilizations," p. 326.

8. Quoted in Philip O'Leary, *The Prose Literature of the Gaelic Revival, 1881–1921* (Pennsylvania University Park: Pennsylvania State University Press, 1994), p. 20. O'Leary goes on to note, "And this defensive metaphor recurs again and again in the jeremiads of the many proponents of the Revival."

9. The aesthetic value of the English verse and ballad tradition to Joyce himself is intriguingly documented in Padraic and Mary Colum, *Our Friend James Joyce* (Garden City, N.Y.: Doubleday, 1958), p. 84: "Joyce used to play and sing English songs, Elizabethan and Jacobean. 'They are ample,' he would say, contrasting their full-blooded gaiety with the mournfulness of Irish melodies. It may be because he was so possessed by this musical tradition that the poems he wrote are without a trace of Irish influence ... ."

10. See for example, Elizabeth Cullingford, "Phoenician Genealogies: Joyce, Language, and Race," in *Semicolonial Joyce*, eds. Derek Attridge and Marjorie Howes (Cambridge: Cambridge University Press, 2000), pp. 225–8.

11. Vicki Mahaffey, "Joyce's Shorter Works," in *The Cambridge Companion to James Joyce*, ed. Derek Attridge (Cambridge: Cambridge University Press, 1991), p. 201.

12. Cullingford, "Phoenician Genealogies," p. 227.

13. Douglas Hyde, "The Necessity of Deanglicizing Ireland," in *Ideals in Ireland*, ed. Lady Gregory (London: Unicorn, 1901), pp. 117–61.

14. The definition of the modern nation as an imagined community comes from Benedict Anderson, *Imagined Communities* (London: Verso, 1991). I will be discussing his conception in some detail further on.

15. Potts, *Joyce and the Two Irelands*, p. 48.

16. John McCourt, *The Years of Bloom* (Madison: University of Wisconsin Press, 2000), pp. 52, 78–121.

17. Potts, *Joyce and the Two Irelands*, p. 92.

18. For a fuller account, see Joseph Valente, "James Joyce and the Cosmopolitan Sublime: Imagining Ireland Otherwise," in *James Joyce and the Subject of History*, eds. Mark Wollaeger, et al. (Ann Arbor: University of Michigan Press, 1997), pp. 69–73.

19. Anderson, *Imagined Communities*, p. 7.

20. Ibid., pp. 15–23.

21. Nolan, *Joyce and Nationalism*, p. 35.

5
joyce, genre, and the authority of form

marian eide

James Joyce's first cosmopolitan readers and critics praised his art in part by claiming his works to be so innovative as to defy genre; contemporary readers might argue that his attention to genre and his stitching together of varied generic forms in each of his works were precisely the markers of Joyce's innovation. Joyce was invested in the idea of genre and equally in the constraints it presented to the writer; he was attentive to the ways in which genre divides literature into categories of high and low, lasting and ephemeral. Interested in the authority of form (as he was in authorities of various other kinds),[1] he suggested that genre conventions shape actual experience, that reality imitates fiction. While a great deal of attention has been paid to Joyce's generic revision of the literary tradition throughout his writings, I would like to attend equally to his fascination with genre fiction, popular literature, and the accessible arts.

Joyce's mingling of genres parallels the work of modernist painters such as Pablo Picasso and Georges Braque, who incorporated newspaper clippings and sections of corrugated cardboard in their collages, Joseph Cornell whose box assemblages turned ordinary objects into gems, or Marcel Duchamp, whose "ready-mades" chided high art expectations while at the same time reassessing the aesthetic forms of everyday objects. Joyce revitalized stable literary genres by placing them in new contexts, just as the common urinal was altered when Marcel Duchamp gave one a title ("Fountain") and placed it in the unlikely context of an art exhibition. Like the fountain, for example, the western story of battle between "cowboys and Indians" has new effects when placed in Joyce's "An Encounter" where it is read and incorporated in play by Irish boys whose colonial experience suggests an unconventional identification with embattled natives.[2] By mimicking genre conventions while placing

97

those genres in unexpected contexts, Joyce produces a new effect on the reader, a mediate effect between his intentions and the reader's existing expectations. This mediation allows a reader to see genre conventions in relation to various forms of social and cultural authority.

Joyce wrote in all the major literary genres, many of the minor ones, and he invented several genres as well. He composed poetry, short stories, essays, a play, a novel, and an epic. He invented the epiphanies and whatever it is that *Finnegans Wake* might be classified as. Though he didn't plan their publication, he also wrote letters and the notebook experiment we call *Giacomo Joyce*. Within each of these genres he included other forms: *Portrait of the Artist as a Young Man* contains a poem and a diary; *Ulysses* offers newspaper headlines, epic catalogues, advertising slogans, and a play; *Finnegans Wake* contains nursery rhymes, primer lessons, prayers, and a mime. More than any other writer of the formally experimental modernist period, Joyce explored the varieties of generic structure. In genre conventions he found the constraints of aesthetic precedent and reader expectation that would enable his own creative resistance.

As his Paris Notebooks reveal, at the beginning of his career, Joyce thought extensively about the role of form in producing literature; he focused primarily on reception in developing a working theory of genre. In *Portrait* he repeated the meditations from his notebooks in the voice of his young writer, Stephen Dedalus, emphasizing once again the extent to which reception determines genre and at the same time recontextualizing his aesthetic theory in the casual discourse of two city strollers. Stephen locates genre categories between the production and consumption of art, between the conventions writers follow and the expectations readers have when they turn to a particular form. He argues that the consumer of beauty will apprehend an image as beautiful both "by the art itself and by the form of that art. The image, it is clear, must be set between the mind or senses of the artist himself and the mind or sense of others" (P 213). This image as contained in a work of literary art succeeds as beautiful between two subjects, between writer and reader, between intention and apprehension, rather than in the singular place of either production or consumption. Stephen's emphasis on reception is an initial indication of his response to earlier aesthetic theories. Aristotle, in the *Poetics*, emphasizes that catering to audience expectations lessens the quality of tragedy.[3] While neither Stephen nor his author would be seen as pandering to mass tastes, the emphasis, both in Stephen's phrasing and in Joyce's placement of the theory within a dialogue, is on reception.

For this reason Stephen's generic or formal classificatory system is based on the mediation between writer and reader rather than on the more taxonomic codes of genre criticism which rely on distinctions within the text itself and on resemblance between texts of a particular genre. Instead of describing the lyric as a short poem with a musical inflection, then, he emphasizes the subjective or personal tone of the lyric poem, defining it as the form most proximate to the writer, in "immediate relation to himself" (*P* 214). (Stephen's definition is similar to Goethe's: he defined the lyric as a "burst of rapture.") The lyric may be the most self-revelatory of the three major genres Stephen discusses – the form in which the author's imprint can be clearly seen – but it may also be the least immediately accessible to the reader.

According to Stephen's definition, the dramatic form is nearly the opposite of the lyric in that it presents itself in "immediate relation to others" (*P* 214). Drama attempts to anticipate how an image might be apprehended by its audience, its focus is on reader expectation and response. Stephen uses the noun "relation" in this context, shifting the focus, at least temporarily to connections or relations between people.

The epic form compromises between the lyric and dramatic. According to Stephen, epic is the "form wherein [the artist] presents his image in mediate relation to himself and to others" (*P* 214). Epic as a mediating form is concerned both with the artist's self-expression and with an anticipated reader's response, expectations and desires. This mediation presents an artist with his or her greatest formal challenges, yet it is possible to see that in each of his works, from *Portrait* onward, Joyce attempted the intricacy of epic mediation.

Categorizing literature in these three genres, Stephen associates himself with the German Romantic school which congregated at the University of Jena and drew on Immanuel Kant's aesthetic. The German Romantics claimed a *natural* division of literary arts into three essential modes: the lyric, the epic, and the dramatic. Cyrus Hamlin describes the aesthetic theories developed at Jena and notes that however innovative or singular a particular literary work, a text was understood by these theorists to "manifest the generic form which is inherent to its own identity."[4] Goethe, in particular theorized genre as *natural*, arguing that it "constitutes a naturalization of art, where the realization of the work of art as form is essentially the same as that achieved by a plant in its process of growth." Of interest in this regard is the fact that Goethe, in his notes to the *West-östlicher Divan* (published in 1819), speaks of the "'natural forms of poetry' ... as *Epos, Lyrik*, and *Drama*".[5] Unlike

Aristotle, whose generic system is static, theorists such as Schlegel, Schiller, and Goethe understood genre as dynamic. In arguing for genre as natural to literature, however, the Romantics echoed Aristotle's idea that generic qualities are essential to literary expression rather than an artificial classification imposed from without. The question of whether genre is an artificial system of classification and a historical convenience necessary to critical reception or a formal distinction intrinsic in the text has persisted in the twentieth century. J. Hillis Miller, for example, cites the case of the elegy, asking whether the poetry of mourning has an intrinsic rhythm or whether the stateliness of this genre is an outcome of historical precedence. "If it is true that the process of mourning has a kind of intrinsic rhythm, then the structure of the elegy is not just a historical accident, but is something deeper which has a different sort of ground ... ."[6]

Two approaches to genre suggested in Aristotle's *Poetics* have been of crucial interest in twentieth-century theories: genre as heuristic for interpretation and genre as method for generating text. Aristotle's *Poetics*, though explicitly a taxonomic system, reads in part as a writer's handbook, as for example, when he cautions against the capricious use of the *deus ex machina*. In his discussion of the marvelous, Aristotle offers writers a menu of plot devices and their proper sequencing.[7] At that same time, his taxonomy provides the ground for an aesthetic of value, a systematic procedure for determining literary worth.

Joyce's approach, while relying on the taxonomy produced by the German Romantics, seems more in sympathy with the extrinsic approach to genre as a method for textual generation and a cue for interpretation. Like many literary theorists of the twentieth century, Joyce approaches genre in social, situational, and dynamic terms, responding to dominant cultural assumptions and social demands.

Stephen's theory is akin to Aristotle's in his approach to narrative voice, however. Like Aristotle who suggests that poets mask the personal voice, for Stephen, the artist "like the God of the creation, remains within or behind or beyond or above his handiwork, invisible, refined out of existence, indifferent, paring his fingernails." To which Stephen's interlocutor, Lynch, responds, " .– Trying to refine them also out of existence" (*P* 215), immediately deflating the potential arrogance of Stephen's comparison. Refining a personal voice from the text, the author cedes control over meaning and produces an epic effect of mediation. Unlike the lyric in which the reader is bound to the outpouring of self implied by the form and must gauge the author's experience or emotion to decipher the text, and the dramatic form in which Joyce anticipates Barthes's "death of the author," the epic form gives precedence to the mediation between intention and reception.

In *Portrait*, Joyce emphasizes reception as a determinant of form. Increasingly in his writing, Joyce re-examines those readerly expectations. By mingling genres, incorporating aesthetically marginal advertising slogans in the culturally accredited epic, for example, Joyce anticipates a reader's assumptions and consistently surprises them. These reversals serve two purposes: to revitalize degraded or neglected genres precisely because they anticipate certain readerly needs and to indicate the extent to which genre courts convention. Joyce surprises his readers by indicating the authority of form and then using that authority to serve unexpected ends.

To illustrate this point in miniature: *Exiles*, though clearly written in the dramatic form, has been consistently interpreted as lyric: as an expression of Joyce's own quarrels with marital conventions and his investment in the ideas of national service to Ireland. Perhaps as a consequence of the lyrical approach to this drama, *Exiles* has been read as Joyce's conspicuously failed text. If read as a drama, as its generic cues indicate, the play may have less to do with Joyce's preoccupations and more to do with an audience's discomfort with any deviations from the conventional love narrative, whether marital or national. *Portrait*, however, is presented as a lyrical text according to Stephen's taxonomy of form: the book draws on Joyce's own experiences for its plot. This adaptation of the *Künstlerroman* genre leads a reader to expect what Alistair Fowler calls "*poioumenon*," a work-in-progress novel like Proust's *A la recherche du temps perdu* which presents a character or narrator in the process of writing the text itself.[8] The *Künstlerroman* is often as concerned with poetics as *Portrait*'s fifth chapter is. Additionally, as the book drifts to its end with diary entries, a lyric intention might be intuited. The text culminates, however, with the statement of dramatic intentions: the forging of an uncreated conscience for the Irish "race."

The gravity of Stephen's exploration of form is undercut by its own heuristic; while his conclusions are abstract and scholarly, his means of getting to those abstractions may strike the reader as engagingly silly. He poses a series of comical/serious questions about formal classification and the production of art: "*Is a chair finely made tragic or comic? Is the portrait of Mona Lisa good if I desire to see it? Is the bust of Sir Philip Crampton lyrical, epical or dramatic? Can excrement or a child or a louse be a work of art? If not, why not?*" (P 214). Set apart by a laughing response from his friend and interlocutor, Lynch, is a final question: "*If a man hacking in fury at a block of wood ... make there an image of a cow, is that image a work of art? If not, why not?*" (*P* 214). An intuitive response to this final question might be that the resulting cow is not a work of art because the final image was not intended when the angry man began to hack. But the theory Stephen develops in response to these questions would militate against the primacy of intention in either classifying or apprehending the work of art. The cow might be understood to be lyrical because it embodies the immediate anger of the artist in making the work. If the contours of the cow communicate that anger readily to a viewer – perhaps by a jagged execution, perhaps by the retention of the hacking instrument in the final work – the sculpture might be apprehended as dramatic, communicating, in immediate relation to the audience, the experience of anger.[9] Joyce's cow is always Trojan: its hollow form implies one set of meanings but carries unexpected and even contradictory cargo, much as the soldiers in the Trojan horse contradicted the form of the peace offering in which they hid themselves before laying siege to the city. Joyce relies on the familiarity of genre to import forces that militate against convention and expectation.

Stephen indicates the extent to which genre is habitually recognizable and authoritative. Consistently using the term "form" in his aesthetic discussion with Lynch, when conversing with Cranly later in the same chapter, he uses "form" in relation to religious authority.[10] Cranly has been attempting to convince Stephen of the importance of his mother's love and the debt of kindness he owes her in return.[11] Knowing May Dedalus worries over Stephen's disaffection with the Catholic Church, Cranly tries to convince his friend that receiving the Eucharist would perform a kindness to his mother that would cost the son little. "It is a form: nothing else. And you will set her mind at rest" (*P* 241). Stephen is intimidated by the power of form and admits that he fears "the chemical action which would be set up in my soul by false homage to a symbol behind which are massed twenty centuries of authority and veneration" (*P* 243). If I might draw, as Stephen often does, on the religious precedent in understanding aesthetic practice (the fallen angel, Lucifer, is his exemplar for the role of the artist who refuses to serve), I would argue that a generic form, such as the epic, has centuries of accumulated practice and veneration attached to it, and may, like the Eucharist, make certain authoritative demands of obedience on practitioners and readers.[12]

Why then would Joyce begin to describe *Ulysses* as an epic (rather than a novel) precisely at the moment when he began most concentratedly to experiment with form?[13] Why does he abandon the term, "novel," a newer and more elastic form whose appellation in itself indicates innovation, in favor of a form that retains centuries of veneration and demands a particular obedience? A. Walton Litz, in his definitive 1974 essay on Joyce and genre, argues that *Ulysses* "lends itself easily to categories and classifications that give so little in return. Indeed the current trends in generic criticism may pose a threat to the whole pluralistic world in which the masterpieces of modern art developed, smoothing away the irregular achievements of Joyce's generation."[14] Litz argues that "neither Joyce, nor the most acute of his early readers, were much concerned with defining the genre of *Ulysses*."[15] Yet, as Litz himself indicates, Joyce gave the work two generic classifications – epic and encyclopedic – in a single letter to Carlo Linati.[16] Eliot, in his ground-breaking essay "*Ulysses*, Order, and Myth," claims that "novel" is an obsolete term and to define *Ulysses* as such is to reduce it; he dismisses also Joyce's chosen term, epic. Myth as genre, however, serves Eliot's interpretation of *Ulysses*. Pound gave *Ulysses* the generic classification of sonata. While all three modernists sought to eschew the obvious category of the novel (assuming this generic classification would reduce the complex form of the work) they seem also to be concerned that the text be labeled with *some* genre. The work of classification, which draws attention to conventions and limitations, was used by Pound to indicate the degree of *Ulysses'* innovation. While genre was being conceived as itself conservative and reductive, an unexpected classification such as sonata (which might have drawn restrictive limits around a musical composition) indicated progressive revolutions in form.

Genre implies taxonomy or a reliable classificatory system whereby structural and formal features of the text will define and group it with other texts of similar type. Readers might expect genre to have significance to their understanding of the content of the text, to guide response or interpretation according to inherent qualities. However, Philippe Lacoue-Labarthe and Jean-Luc Nancy speculate that "the inability to be defined or delimited probably belongs to the very essence of genre."[17] The most lucid system requires the marking of genre with labels that fall outside the text itself (Emily Brontë subtitled *Wuthering Heights* with the generic tag "A Novel by Ellis Bell," an editorial reveals its genre by its placement at the back of the first section of a newspaper). The marks that indicate belonging to a genre do not themselves belong. Within the text, genre asserts itself only by the repetition of conventions established by earlier texts in the mode. But while genre as a concept, as

Jacques Derrida notes in "The Law of Genre," asserts norms of purity and consistency, repetition threatens that purity with the contamination of other genres. Derrida speculates, "What if it were impossible *not* to mix genres. What if at the heart of the law of genre there were lodged a law of impurity or contamination?"[18] Joyce's texts consistently demonstrate this contamination; in their repetition of classical precedents, they call forth and embody a variety of mutually contaminating forms.

Mary Eagleton has pointed out that genres are neither neutral nor impartial formal categories. Rather, they bear the weight of ideological associations and are arranged according to loosely hierarchical valuations.[19] She indicates a tendency to classify the genres more often used by women – letters or journals – below those historically more often written by men – epic or drama, for example.[20] I would add that genres more often enjoyed by mass audiences and the culturally disenfranchised – westerns, romance, mystery, and true crime – are consistently ranked below those consumed by elite and privileged readers – poetry or performance art, to name only two. The attempt to disengage *Ulysses* from an appellation associated with mass popularity, the novel, may be a fleeting indication of the author's, and his early supporters', bid for elite status. But that bid seems to me at odds with Joyce's own artistic practice.[21] While he drew from his rich education in elite and classical literary forms, hanging *Ulysses* in the frames provided by the *Odyssey* and *Hamlet*, he also took inspiration and example from popular forms such as the ballad, detective fiction, and journalism. Stephen may try his hand at the complex form of the villanelle in *Portrait*, but he also writes in the neglected form of the diary entry. While the elite villanelle form produces the hackneyed sentiments of ambivalent courtship, the diary allows Stephen fresh insights about friendship, artistic responsibility, nation, and language.[22] These diary passages have become so familiar and often quoted as to have lost some of the revolutionary value they must have had on original publication. Yet we can still see a remarkable difference between the villanelle's sentiment – "*Your eyes have set man's heart ablaze*" (*P* 223) – and the equally chauvinist but far more unexpected diary entry: "certainly she remembers the past. Lynch says all women do … . Statues of women, if Lynch be right, should always be fully draped, one hand of the woman feeling regretfully her own hinder part" (*P* 251). After Joyce's own early experiments in poetic form, so cruelly slighted by W.B. Yeats,[23] he turned to the short story which, as Mary Eagleton indicates, was a relatively new form at the turn of the century and generally considered beneath critical consideration. Like many others working in this form, Joyce populated his stories with figures rejected by or outside the mainstream. *Dubliners* follows the occupations and preoccupations of gamblers and children, spinsters and suicides, of shirkers, abusers, and schemers, of the disappointed and the disabled. While elite form provided Joyce with structure, popular form often allowed him, like Stephen, his greatest insights.

Given that his insistence on the appellation epic for *Ulysses* cannot be read solely as a bid for elite status, this genre classification might more accurately be understood in the light of Stephen's definition of the epic as "in mediate relation" to the artist and his or her readers. *Ulysses* is a project that attempts to navigate between lyric self-expression and dramatic anticipation of audience response. It draws on convention in order to bring the expectant reader to a fresh insight about his or her condition.

Joyce often relies on the voracious readers within his texts to model interpretive possibilities for his anticipated readers in the real. Stephen is the most familiar of these readers and the most carefully educated. But several other figures in *Ulysses* from Dilly Dedalus to Molly Bloom love books and rehearse the ambitions and comforts of reading. One of Joyce's most avid and precise readers is the autodidact Gerty MacDowell, whose episode, "Nausicaa," has been among the most entrancing in Joyce's epic of seduction and resistance.

First-time readers sigh with relief as *Ulysses* descends from the virtuoso rhetorical experiments of the "Cyclops" episode with its epic catalogs, political debates, legal phrasing, and elegiac reference, to the comforts of "Nausicaa" with its familiar, even reassuring sentimental form. That ease may convince a critic temporarily that "Nausicaa" is a break from the real innovations and challenges of the text, that in effect with "Nausicaa" a weary reader, like the tired Odysseus, gets a warm bath and a hot meal. But drawing on sentimental romances with their conventional descriptions and hackneyed plotting and on ladies' journals with their tidbits of advice and outlines for daily practice, Joyce produces some of the most lyrical prose of his career and suggests an impressive array of insights about power, desire, and belief. Working within the constraints of sentimental romance allows Joyce to imagine what readers desire that they find in such fictions, and what prohibitions these fictions both assuage and enforce.

On a rudimentary level "Nausicaa" rehearses the romantic plot of a young woman's desire for courtship and for an enduring love in marriage that will transcend ordinary experience. But it also informs the reader about the disappointments this story caters to. So many Irish women of Gerty's time were excluded from eligibility in this plot, and Gerty with her marked disability embodies them as she limps away from her romantic lead, Leopold Bloom. The romance plot may assuage the hardship of many marriages – domestic management, child-rearing, and spousal incompatibilities – at the same that it produces the fantasies of enjoyment and exaltation that would enforce the marital conventions much as genre fiction enforces the marriage plot. The narrative habit, however, renders the realities of marriage even more difficult by stark contrast with the printed ideal.

Fantasizing in the language of sentimental novels, Gerty embraces equally their goals. For Joyce, however, those generic restrictions allow him to imagine a counter-narrative. What if, he asks, the story happily ends with marriage to a man like Gerty's father who, outside the frame of a sentimental novel, drinks to excess and has, on occasion, been violent?[24] Or what if the object of desire is by definition unavailable, married like Bloom or of another religion like the boy on the bicycle, Reggie Wylie? Or what if marital bliss also looks like constant labor and physical hardship in child-bearing, as it does for Mina Purefoy? Gerty's desire for conventional happiness makes her vulnerable to mistreatment, exposing herself to Bloom's exploitative gaze as she leans back like so many other girls have done before her.[25] The conventions that assuage and discipline her as a reader are constantly at odds.

Joyce addresses questions of cultural authority according to the assumptions of genre, considering the role reception plays in the contradictory forms of popular women's literature. The heroine of genre romance fiction is never aware of her own charms. Her attractions are written as artless and natural. The form is didactic in its intent – attempting to produce a marriageable, virtuous woman – when Gerty reads fashion magazines or Marie Cummins's sentimental novel *The Lamplighter* she is meant to imitate their ideals. However, by imitating the ideal, the reader becomes an artful production, as Suzette Henke notes, "doomed to construct a media-controlled self-image."[26] This media induction contradicts its own ideal. To achieve the desired effect the reader must want to be like the heroine of the novel or the subject of magazine instructions. At the same time these texts describe as ideal a woman who is utterly unself-conscious, whose effects are naturally wrought, without effort of external discipline, the heroine is naturally good and even more artlessly beautiful.[27] As a result the attempt to imitate her is inherently doomed: by imitating, the reader must be both artful and conscious of her moral good and physical appeal. As Kimberly Devlin argues, Joyce mocks the sentimental ideal and Gerty herself strays from the models provided by her reading of sentimental fiction in her disdain for the twin children at play on the beach, her envy of her friends, and her conscious courting of Bloom's sexual attention. Gerty wishes to be *seen* as a living embodiment of the sentimental ideal as much as she wishes to harvest the benefits and pleasures Cummins's characters enjoy. In search of that enjoyment, Gerty breaks all the idealizing rules while at the same time describing her actions to herself in the generic language of sentiment and virtue.

> ... her face was suffused with a divine, an entrancing blush from straining back and he [Bloom] could see her other things too, nainsook knickers, the fabric that caresses the skin ... and she saw that he saw and then it went so high it went out of sight a comet and she was trembling in every limb ... (*U* 13.724–8)

Oscillating between the practical advice of ladies' journals on the purchase or manufacture of women's "smalls" and the sentimental novel's exalted expression of romantic love, Gerty narrates her pleasure in reclining, with the excuse of viewing the bursting fireworks above the beach, revealing herself to Bloom and taking physical pleasure in his appreciative gaze.

Constrained by class and gender, Gerty has access only to a limited range of reading material.[28] This reading produces what Jean-François Lyotard might call a master narrative, a story the reader sees repeated over and over which allows her to understand lived experience according to received forms and which in return disciplines her according to its narrative demands. However, Joyce emphasizes that Gerty's reading material fails to produce the expected docile woman. Her apparent failure is produced by Joyce's contamination of the purity of the sentimental form with the licenses of erotica, his inscription of sexual pleasure into a new narrative possibility of young women's *Bildungsroman*.

Why would Joyce engage the most degraded and despised of pulp fiction forms to write this lyrical episode? Precisely because the episode is not only lyric but also dramatic. A section that presents itself as a *tableau vivant* also describes a dramatic interaction and silently staged dialogue between two main characters and a cast of background figures. Perhaps more important, like the sentimental novels it quotes, the episode engages the reader in an immediate relation. Drawing on the romance genre which inspires identification fantasies (as Gerty demonstrates), the chapter engages the reader directly using romance to implicate the reader's desires and pleasures as much as, or perhaps more than, those of his ostensible subjects, Gerty MacDowell and Leopold Bloom.

Joyce was not entirely optimistic about the use of the sentimental romance plot. He understood the tyranny of these generic conventions, and also understood their potency. Rather than eschewing pulp fiction altogether as beneath his aesthetic notice, Joyce worked creatively within the constraints of the genre, trying to imagine how its authority might be used to narrate another life story with room for the kind of characters who people his own texts.[29] Interested in how a young woman with few cultural or financial privileges might understand her own context, Joyce drew on the reading materials available to women of her class and experience to create Gerty's voice. Women's magazines and popular fiction gave him the language and perspective through which to make such a figure come alive on the page. Resisting the elitism of his own high modernist form, Joyce drew on genre fiction to produce a sympathetic reception for characters like Gerty who are often excluded from the pages of elite culture.

Like Gerty MacDowell, Molly Bloom is a consumer of genre fiction, though her tastes are more risqué. The morning on which the novel begins, she has just finished reading *Ruby: Pride of the Ring*, and later in the day Bloom will purchase *Sweets of Sin* for her. While Mary Power has argued for Molly's virtue (" ... Molly is quite right in defending the book – 'there's nothing smutty in it'"),[30] I would respond that Molly's motivation for reading *Ruby* and the other books her husband buys her is precisely their erotic appeal. She disdains *Ruby* because there's "nothing smutty in it" and because the lead character has been in love with the same man throughout the story.[31] Bloom anticipates that she'll prefer *Sweets of Sin* when he fastens on an adulterous scene featuring a beautiful woman's "heaving embonpoint" (*U* 10.616). It is clear from Bloom's purchase – he turns back a book Molly has already read – and from Molly's request for another Paul de Kock (an author's name becomes something like a brand here, a measure of content and consistency) – that she has read many novels in this genre already. Why does she read them? We might speculate that the erotica fills a void left by the celibacy in her marriage, or that it licenses her own transgression with Blazes Boylan. But while both explanations seem plausible, they are also contradictory. If the novels assuage a lack in the marriage, how would they also motivate adultery?

Molly's erotic reading, which she apparently shares with her husband, features as a form of fidelity in her marriage. Her question about metempsychosis is motivated by a particular enjoyment in Bloom's unusual intellect: she likes to explore his odd encyclopedia of information that mingles the accurate with the imaginative, degraded and erudite sources: "still he knows a lot of mixedup things especially about the body and the inside I often wanted to study up that myself" (*U* 18.179–81) and "if I only could remember the I half of the things and write a book out of it the works of Master Poldy" (*U* 18.579–80).[32] She takes pleasure in the predictable familiarity of erotica where the limits of social convention are tested by smut. While she doesn't seem to mind a little brutality in her fiction, in practice she is more cautious; she complains to herself of Boylan's rude behavior, which she finds demeaning, equating her with an ass or a horse ("I didn't like his slapping me behind going away so familiarly in the hall though I laughed Im not a horse or an ass am I" [*U* 18.122–4]). Erotica serves her as an alternative to reality. Though like all women, "whatever she does she knows where to stop" (*U* 18.1438–9), fiction and fantasy allow her to explore the other side of the proper place to stop without consequence.

Incorporating erotica in *Ulysses*, Joyce indicates the expectations this genre produces in its readers. Like Gerty, Molly is disappointed by the imitation of fiction in the real: Boylan's coy slap produces none of the wild excitement she might expect from her reading. But Joyce's motivation in producing this conflict is not to discipline his character (or his readers); her disappointment is not measured to enforce marital fidelity. Rather, his copy of erotica serves the same purpose as his duplicate of sentimental form. It indicates the extent to which a reader's expectations are constrained by the authority of form. By placing erotica in the context of epic, like hanging the urinal in the exhibition hall, he provides an alternative reception for the genre. *Ulysses* allows his contemporary reader to conceive of the erotic experience of a bourgeois woman without the disciplines of moral convention or the outrages of bloated expectation.

In her reading of another erotic genre, the love letter, Molly self-consciously insists on convention precisely for the effects produced by a proper adherence to genre. She particularly values Bloom's love letters during their courtship for their dramatic effects.

his mad crazy letters my Precious one everything connected with your glorious Body everything underlined that comes from it is a

thing of beauty and of joy for ever something he got out of some
nonsensical book that he had me always at myself 4 and 5 times a
day sometimes ... (U 18.1176–9)

Bloom adheres to the convention as Molly understands it: that the
epistle be focused on the receiver.[33] She indicates his letter's generic
conventionality by remembering his incorporation of a quotation from
Keats's "Endymion": "A thing of beauty is a joy for ever."

Roland Barthes compares the love letter to a musical composition that
having established a theme – "I am thinking of you" – sounds a number
of variations. The variations in the love letter voice the writer's desire
repeatedly while expressing anxiety about the genre itself. Because the
love letter is a habitual form, so often used, the question of authenticity
is rife. Thus the love letter engages in dialectic between the expressive
desires of the lover and the established codes of the genre: "both blank
(encoded) and expressive (charged with longing to signify desire)."[34]
While the lover may intend a fresh and wholly honest expression of love,
he or she is sentenced by an established form in which all the variations
have been sounded and have the effect of scripted or even hackneyed
discourse. From as early as the sixteenth century lovers have had recourse
to letter manuals that suggested the outline and variations of the form in
as precise and technical terms as instructions for a business letter.[35]

While the materiality of the love letter – secreted in a bodice or vest,
folded into hidden sections, enclosed in an envelope – indicates privacy and
interiority, it is equally a part of the social field of established conventions
and exchanges. Shilpa Raval, writing of Ovid's *Metamorphosis*, suggests
that love letters are a "repository of cultural conventions" and that the
practices of romantic love are "enactments of a script" first drafted in the
love letter.[36] Hélène Cixous notes of the lover, "Unknowingly he does
what the letter dictates. It writes him."[37] The experience of being in love
is constructed by the entrenched genre of the love letter, which is written
in the future anterior tense ("it will have been"); it struggles against the
rigid conventions of its form to bring an authentic love into being.

It is also possible to borrow strategically from the ancient script of
lovers to produce an effect. The *lover* does not intend to be strategic,
but the *correspondent* – to use Roland Barthes's terms – might employ
the codes of authenticity for the purposes of seduction. An amorous
correspondence is

a tactical enterprise to defend positions, make conquests; the enterprise must reconnoiter the positions (the subgroups) of the adverse group, i.e., must articulate the other's image in various points which the letter will try to touch ... . But for the lover the letter has no tactical value: it is purely *expressive* – at most, flattering (but here flattery is not a matter of self-interest, merely the language of devotion); what I engage in with the other is a *relation*, not a correspondence ... .[38]

While she may have been naively susceptible to the amorous forms inscribed in her first suitor's letter in Gibraltar, years later Molly is keenly aware of the tactical advantages of correspondence. She critiques her friend Atty Dillon's practice of the form for its strategic failure in an amorous foray.

those long crossed letters Atty Dillon used to write to the fellow that was something in the four courts that jilted her after out of the ladies letterwriter when I told her to say a few simple words he could twist how he liked. (*U* 18.740–4)

Atty Dillon borrows from a published script in composing her carefully honest and expressive missive, but Molly notes that all the tactical advantages are to be gained from ambiguity.

As savvy as she is as an advisor, Molly struggles with the dialectic of authentic relation and tactical correspondence when she meditates on love letters she has received. She recognizes the letter as a form that can be practiced to greater and lesser effect, but equally she maintains the lover's attachment to those effects, and is disappointed in her current lover's poor composition.

his wasnt much and I told him he could write what he liked yours ever Hugh Boylan in old Madrid stuff silly women believe love is sighing I am dying still if he wrote it I suppose thered be some truth in it true or no it fills up your whole day and life always something to think about every moment and see it all round you like a new world I could write the answer in bed to let him imagine me short just a few words. (*U* 18.735–40)

Like the tactical correspondent, Molly advocates the dramatic form: aiming to fill the recipient with anticipatory thoughts of the lover. Imagining a letter to Boylan, she curtails its length in advance, believing her letter is most persuasive when it is least informative or specific. The one detail she settles on is a description of herself composing the letter in bed, a device to inspire Boylan's amorous imaginings.

According to Molly's standards, Anna Livia Plurabelle in *Finnegans Wake* is a confused practitioner of the ancient form. In *Finnegans Wake* readers are repeatedly reminded that ALP has written a love letter concerning her husband, Humphrey Chimpden Earwicker. ALP's letter is not addressed to HCE, rather it is a public document written to defend him in the face of accusations of misconduct ("So may the low forget him their trespasses" [*FW* 615.36]). Throughout Joyce's last book readers unearth various versions of ALP's letter which we are lead to believe was scratched out of a trash heap by a hen. The letter is long by Molly's standards and as detailed as Atty Dillon's ill-fated missive (one version of the letter runs to nearly five pages [*FW* 615–19]). Like Molly's favorite love letters, though, this one opens itself to multiple interpretations, not only because it is abstract, but also because it is over written. One reader describes the appearance of the letter: "One cannot help noticing that rather more than half of the lines run north-south ... while the others go west-east ... . These ruled barriers along which the traced words, run, march, halt, walk, stumble to have been drawn first of all in a pretty check with lampblack and blackthorn" (*FW* 114.2–11). The content of ALP's letter is as difficult to decipher as its haphazard form. Like so many of Joyce's texts, however, it struggles with generic expectations. If the love letter is a future anterior genre, designed to bring a great love into being, the loves they actually create do not always follow the dictates of the genre. ALP's own marriage is a complex affair characterized by ambivalence, betrayal, affection, persecution, and enjoyment. It could hardly be described in the genre of sentiment. Her epistle has none of the uncompromising assuredness of amorous correspondence, and yet it may be read in the future anterior: references to the phoenix and to other forms of resurrection indicate that ALP wishes to reconstruct her husband from his own scattered remains, a metaphor vividly expectant of renewal.

Resurrection is also a central concern for ALP's other written text, her manifesto. By the time Joyce drafted ALP's "mamafesta" titles in 1925, the manifesto was an established form among the European avant-garde. From Filippo Marinetti's 1909 Futurist Manifesto declaring "We will glorify war – the world's only hygiene – militarism, patriotism, the destructive gesture of freedom-bringers, beautiful ideas worth dying for, and scorn for women ... We will destroy museums, libraries, academies of every kind ..."[39] to André Breton's widely influential manifesto of 1924, in which he defined surrealism as "Psychic automatism in its pure state, by which one proposes to express – verbally, by means of the written word, or in any other manner – the actual functioning of thought. Dictated by thought in the absence of any control exercised by reason, exempt from any aesthetic or moral concern,"[40] the manifesto was initiating experimentation in a variety of art forms from sculpture to poetry to film. In fact the genre was well enough established as early as 1918 that Tristan Tzara was able to parody it in his own "Dada Manifesto" of that year, writing "To launch a manifesto you have to want: A, B, & C, and fulminate against 1, 2, & 3 ... ."[41]

Though varying throughout the modernist era, the manifesto form has had a number of generic markers. Described by Mary Ann Caws as a "loud genre," the manifesto is programmatic, often hortatory and authoritative in tone, a text designed to persuade or even convert readers for ideological or aesthetic purposes.[42] The manifesto is deliberately oppositional, describing the group of adherents to an artistic practice or political position and posing those adherents in opposition to outsiders who are described by implication as ignorant, unwitting, or simply passé. Designed to mark the beginning of a movement, the manifesto can nonetheless convey a commemorative tone or sensibility. As Janet Lyon notes, the term "manifesto" is "often used retroactively to identify a text's foundational status."[43] The manifesto declares its position and refuses dialogue as irrelevant; its tone is antagonistic and single-minded. Manifestos are "usually taken to be transparent public expressions of pure will," expressing the passionate views of participants.[44] Though it produces an avant-garde, bringing a new movement into being or radically reforming a political position, in itself the manifesto is not entirely revolutionary, it conforms to predictable generic conventions.

As with his use of more popular genres, Joyce employs the manifesto in *Finnegans Wake* in part as a convention within which to comment on his contemporary culture and in part as a set of restrictions that provide the occasion for his aesthetic innovation. In a genre of insistently secular and even atheist texts, Anna Livia Plurabelle's manifesto is written "memorialising the Mosthighest" (*FW* 104.4), the God of Abraham whom she often conflates with her husband. Though her manifesto is untitled and indeed unrecorded, it has enjoyed wide reception among the readers who populate *Finnegans Wake* and who have given it myriad informal titles. In a gesture that Stephen might call epic in its mediation between author and readers, these titles provide Joyce's readers with their only access to the content of the "mamafesta."[45] While the manifesto is conventionally a lyric form, expressing the demands of a writer in the face of opposition, this text is not accessible from ALP's singular point of view. The reader of *Finnegans Wake* can only access the content of this document through the rumor mill of her readers' imposed titles.

These titles indicate that ALP's crucial concerns are with sin, punishment, and redemption. Drawing primarily on the texts of Genesis – "*See the First Book of Jealesies Pessim*" (*FW* 106.13) – she considers God's punishments for repeated violations of his covenant with humans. Conflating her late husband and her God, she raises the possibility that God is also fallen, breaking covenant by administering punishments such as the great flood and the expulsion from Eden. She speculates also that God is dead and that his followers' religious celebrations allow his continued presence or resurrection.

The latter possibility is raised by the title "*Suppotes a Ventriliquorst Merries a Corpse*" (*FW* 105.20). Drawing on the popular song from which *Finnegans Wake* took its title, this phrase refers to the waking of Finnegan. In the popular song, mourners or revelers, depending on your perspective, spill whiskey or spirits on Finnegan's body, waking or resurrecting him in effect by giving him spirit. Throughout *Finnegans Wake*, ALP orchestrates any number of wakes to revive her husband. And in her letter written in his defense, she is a ventriloquist speaking for the corpse to whom she is married. As a secular bride of Christ, she plays the role of another kind of ventriloquist speaking for the crucified and resurrected Jesus as so many of his disciples have been called to do. The work of these disciples wakes their God by celebrating his life, mourning his death, and keeping him alive to his followers.

The double role of disciple and wife is suggested by another of the manifesto titles: "*I am Older northe Rogues among Whisht I slips and He Calls Me his Dual of Ayessha*" (*FW* 105.18–20). Aisha was the youngest wife, and according to many accounts, the favorite, of the Prophet Mohammed. On his death she took a prominent military and theological role in the establishment of Islam. For Aisha, as perhaps for ALP, her primary strength and her power came late in life, after the death of her husband when her role in waking him and in celebrating his works and his God gave her a voice, the voice of a ventriloquist married to a corpse.

Though a disciple as well as a widow, ALP is critical of the corpse she wakes. Her mortal husband expressed an insistent sexual curiosity manifested in various infidelities like his putative visits to prostitutes ("*Measley Ventures of Two Lice* [or prostitutes] *and the Fall of Fruit*" [*FW*

106.21]), but ALP herself is condemned for any break with convention. The most conspicuous of her lapses – eating the fruit of the tree of knowledge – is mentioned repeatedly in the manifesto titles: "*Seen Aples and Thin Dyed*" (*FW* 106.24) and "*A Nibble at Eve Will that Bowal Relieve*" (*FW* 106.29–30). Like the fall from Eden precipitated by that nibble, ALP suggests that the fall of God is also irremediable. She evokes Humpty Dumpty who cannot be put back together again because, according to the nursery rhyme riddle, he is an egg. An egg signifies the beginning of things, and like the God of creation, is the source of life. In the manifesto, that source is consistently located in a fall from grace, in loss, in an irremediable break with God.

ALP's manifesto is as revolutionary as those written by Marinetti, Breton, and Tzara. It is destructive in its departure from received assumptions about God and religion. Like so many moments in the *Wake* when creativity is scratched up out of the wreckage of destruction, the manifesto is a resurrection, calling for a new form of marital and spiritual faith based on the ruins of broken covenants.

ALP is Joyce's modern Prometheus, the human brave enough to explore the places forbidden by God and bring knowledge back to humans. It is by knowing the convention, clearly understanding the rules and then allowing herself to break them by tasting the apple, that Eve brings moral knowledge of the difference between good and evil to humankind. Joyce's characters, from Stephen and Gerty to Molly and ALP, follow Eve's example. They produce knowledge from sources forbidden by residing experts and authorities by reading fashion magazines and smut, erotica and sentimental novels, manifestos and nursery rhymes to produce a knowledge of their condition and an imagining of human desire at odds with conventional wisdom but suited to everyday experience.

notes

1. Vicki Mahaffey and Jean-Michel Rabaté both consider concepts of authority and authorization in Joyce's *oeuvre*. Vicki Mahaffey, *Reauthorizing Joyce* (Cambridge: Cambridge University Press, 1988); Jean-Michel Rabaté, *James Joyce, Authorized Reader* (Baltimore: Johns Hopkins University Press, 1991).
2. The boys, whose lives are otherwise disciplined and restrained, imagine themselves into hedonism and pleasure reading the forbidden numbers of *The Half Penny Marvel*. The stories there hold more sway in their imaginations than the assigned pages of Roman history, though the lessons of conflict and power may be similar in each text. The friends understand themselves in relation to their playful genre imitations. The narrator validates his studiousness and physical frailty by identifying with the detective whose adventures are sparked

by inquisitive intelligence and resolved through ingenuity and whose efforts are presumably rewarded by "unkempt fierce and beautiful girls" (*D* 20).

3. Aristotle, *Poetics*, trans. James Hutton (New York: W.W. Norton & Co., 1982).

4. Cyrus Hamlin, "The Origins of a Philosophical Genre Theory in German Romanticism," *European Romantic Review* 5:1 (Summer 1994), p. 10.

5. Schlegel refined this system as a historical and dialectical sequence and defined Romantic poetry as the culminating integration of the three genres. See ibid., p. 13.

6. Barbara Johnson, Louis Mackey, and J. Hillis Miller, "Marxism and Deconstruction: Symposium," in *Rhetoric and Form: Deconstruction at Yale*, ed. Robert Con Davis and Ronald Schleifer (Norman: University of Oklahoma Press, 1985), p. 97.

7. Philippe Lacoue-Labarthe and Jean-Luc Nancy in their discussion of the German Romantic theorists adopt this approach, describing genre as "the identifiable product of an engenderment or of a generation." Philippe Lacoue-Labarthe and Jean-Luc Nancy, *The Literary Absolute: The Theory of Literature in German Romanticism*, trans. Philip Barnard and Cheryl Lester (Albany: State University of New York Press, 1988), p. 91.

8. Christine Froula notes the gender privileges inherent in the literary tradition within which Joyce composed *Portrait*, the heritage of writing in this genre and the immediate authority it created for Joyce in writing his own artist's novel. "In Joyce's work, where transformation of genre always holds colloquy with the father's word and law, literary revolution could be contained within the limits of still recognizable kinds: autobiography, *Künstlerroman*, epic. If Joyce takes us 'past Eve and Adam's' (*FW* 3.1) still he circles round again, re-forming images that we have seen and see again; and the constraints of genre that he breaks through should not blind us to the tremendous endowment that the legacy of the male artist-story bequeaths him." See Christine Froula's "Gender and the Law of Genre," in *New Alliances in Joyce Studies*, ed. Bonnie Kime Scott (Newark: University of Delaware Press, 1988), p. 161.

9. I leave it to more sophisticated genre critics to determine how the cow might be understood to be epic.

10. Throughout this chapter I use *form* and *genre* as nearly interchangeable terms. In doing so, I follow a precedent in genre theory in which the two are often conflated. However, in the *Poetics*, form as such is only one of several characteristics that determine genre, including plot, rhythm, time, structure, subject, and issue. Aristotle argued, for example, that while epic may describe a lengthy period of time, tragedy should take place in the single span of a day. The subjects of a tragedy or epic should be of a "higher order" while comedy embraces the lowly. Bernard Bosanquet also distinguishes form, describing it as "outline, shape, general rule ... the meter in poetry." Form is comprised of "all the sets of gradations and variations and connections that make anything what it is – the life, soul, and movement of the object." However, while in theory "form and substance are one, like body and soul," in practice, "we continue to contrast them as we do soul and body." Bernard Bosanquet, *Three Lectures on Aesthetic*, ed. Ralph Ross (New York: Bobbs-Merrill, 1963), pp. 11–12.

11. This conversation is to haunt Stephen after her death when he remembers that love, now lost, his own desertion, and suffers a haunting memory of her death and a melancholic guilt.

> In a dream, silently, she had come to him, her wasted body within its loose graveclothes giving off an odour of wax and rosewood, her breath, bent over him with mute secret words, a faint odour of wetted ashes.
> Her glazing eyes, staring out of death, to shake and bend my soul. On me alone. The ghostcandle to light her agony. Ghostly light on the tortured face. Her hoarse loud breath rattling in horror, while all prayed on their knees. Her eyes on me to strike me down. *Liliata rutilantium te confessorum turma circumdet: iubilantium te virginum chorus excipiate.*
> Ghoul! Chewer of corpses!
> No, mother! Let me be and let me live.
>
> (*U* 1.270–9)

12. Paul de Man, writing about the autobiographical form, also makes a case for the extent to which form determines the story it contains. "We assume that life *produces* the autobiography as an act produces its consequences, but can we not suggest with equal justice, that the autobiographical project may itself produce and determine the life and that whatever the writer *does* is in fact governed by the technical demands of self-portraiture and thus determined, in all its aspects by the resources of the medium." See Paul de Man's "Autobiography as De-facement," *Modern Language Notes* 94:5 (1979), p. 920.

13. According to A. Walton Litz, Joyce "seldom if ever referred to *Ulysses* as a novel after mid-1918, a point in time which coincides almost exactly with that moment in the process of composition when *Ulysses* ceased to resemble a conventional novel of internal–external reality and Joyce began to pour his creative energy into the various expressive techniques of his *schema*." A. Walton Litz, "The Genre of *Ulysses*," reprinted in *James Joyce: A Collection of Critical Essays*, ed. Mary T. Reynolds (Englewood Cliffs, NJ: Prentice Hall, 1993), p. 110. 1918 may also represent the point at which Joyce conceived the work as a national project which, like the *Odyssey* or the *Aeneid*, would provide a history or mythic background against which the nation of Ireland might emerge and define itself.

14. Ibid., p. 117.

15. Ibid., p. 111.

16. Joyce wrote to Carlo Linati in September of 1920 that *Ulysses* was emerging as an "epic of two races (Israelite-Irish) … . It is also a sort of encyclopaedia," quoted in Litz, 'The Genre of *Ulysses*," p. 110.

17. Lacoue-Labarthe and Nancy, *The Literary Absolute*, p. 91.

18. See Jacques Derrida's "The Law of Genre," in *Acts of Literature*, ed. Derek Attridge (London: Routledge, 1992), p. 225.

19. Eagleton's is an approach often seen in genre theory especially since the 1980s when critics – under the influence of Mikhail Bakhtin – asked more insistently that genre be understood in relation to social interactions, conventions, and

discourses. This approach queried the "work" a genre does and to whose benefit it does that work.

20. Mary Eagleton, "Genre and Gender," in *Re-reading the Short Story*, ed. Clare Hanson (Basingstoke: Macmillan, 1989), pp. 56–68.

21. I would make the same claim for Eliot, who, in *The Waste Land*, for example, made reference not only to Shakespeare's *The Tempest*, Dante's *Inferno*, and Ovid's *Metamorphoses* among other classical texts, but also (as his own, odd annotations remark) to the Tarot deck of cards, an Australian ballad, and a Bill of Lading, along with the cadences of popular ragtime music (" O O O O that Shakespeherian Rag – / It's so elegant/So intelligent"). T.S. Eliot, *The Waste Land*, in *Collected Poems 1909–1962* (New York: Harcourt Brace, 1970).

22. I refer to familiar passages on his aesthetic objectives such as the: "I go to encounter for the millionth time the reality of experience and to forge in the smithy of my soul the uncreated conscience of my race" (*P* 252–3) and his oddly hostile insight into Cranly's family life: "Hence Cranly's despair of soul: the child of exhausted loins" (*P* 248).

23. Yeats wrote to him: "Perhaps I will make you angry when I say that it is the poetry of a young man, of a young man who is practicing his instrument, taking pleasure in the mere handling of the stops." Quoted in Richard Ellmann, *JJ* II, 114.

24. Gerty wishes her father had "avoided the clutches of the demon drink ... that vile decoction which has ruined so many hearths and homes had cast its shadow over her childhood days. Nay, she had even witnessed in the home circle deeds of violence caused by intemperance and had seen her own father, a prey to the fumes of intoxication, forget himself completely for if there was one thing of all things that Gerty knew it was the man who lifts his hand to a woman save in the way of kindness, deserves to be branded as the lowest of the low" (*U* 13.290–302).

25. Jane Heap, co-editor with Margaret Anderson of *The Little Review* in which *Ulysses* was initially published in serial form, defended this chapter from the charges of obscenity in court, saying: "Girls lean back everywhere, showing lace and silk stocking; wear low cut sleeveless blouses, breathless bathing suits; men think thoughts and have emotions about these things everywhere – seldom as delicately and imaginatively as Mr. Bloom – and no one is corrupted." See Edward de Grazia, *Girls Lean Back Everywhere: The Law of Obscenity and the Assault of Genius* (New York: Random House, 1992), p. 10.

26. Suzette Henke, *James Joyce and the Politics of Desire* (London: Routledge, 1990), p. 138.

27. Tania Modleski notes that the generic conventions of sentimental fiction dictate that the heroine must lack self-consciousness and to produce this effect, authors writing within the form must adopt the third-person narrative perspective. Tania Modleski, *Loving with a Vengeance: Mass-Produced Fantasies for Women* (Hamden, Conn.: Archon Books, 1982), p. 55. Devlin argues that while Gerty emulates these texts, her appearance and manner are presented as carefully calculated and self-consciously constructed. Kimberly Devlin, "The Romance Heroine Exposed: 'Nausicaa' and *The Lamplighter*," *James Joyce Quarterly* 22:4 (Summer 1985), p. 388. She also observes that far from "demanding female artlessness, the fetishistic Bloom demands female art"

(ibid., p. 394). Joyce also values female art and the self-consciousness it implies as allied to the artistic temperament which demands conscious engagement both for the artist, and as a result of the art, for the viewer or reader.

28. Margot Norris has also commented on Gerty's limited access to cultural texts, arguing that Joyce narrates through Gerty "faulty learning not as stupidity but as the thwarted, yet eager, desire for learnedness … the pathos of the modern age suffering not from spiritual bankruptcy but from cultural disqualification." Margot Norris, "Modernism, Myth, and Desire in 'Nausicaa'," *James Joyce Quarterly* 26:1 (Fall 1988), p. 39.

29. Patrick McGee makes an allied argument when he writes that the "free indirect style of 'Nausicaa' is Joyce's nausea: his incorporation into the body of literature of the writing that literature excludes, that falls below the standard of the *mot juste* … . He exposes literature as ideology by forcing into it (stuffing it with) the genre it excludes, and he disrupts the ideological *naiveté* of sentimental romance by reinvesting it with coded desire." Patrick McGee, "Joyce's Nausea: Style and Representation in 'Nausicaa'," *James Joyce Quarterly* 24:3 (Spring 1987), pp. 308–9.

30. Mary Power, "The Discovery of Ruby," *James Joyce Quarterly* 18:2 (1981), p. 120.

31. *Ruby* was probably a bad choice for Molly's purposes. The fictive title seems to have been based on an actual book by Amye Reade titled *Ruby. A Novel. Founded on the Life of a Circus Girl.* Bloom's passing interpretation – "Cruelty behind it all" (*U* 4.349) – is probably the closest to meeting the intentions of the book which was a reformer's novel written to expose the cruelty of circus practices and conditions.

32. Molly's imagined book is much like the one Stephen wishes Haines could compile from his sayings and also like his "epiphanies written on green oval leaves, deeply deep, copies to be sent if you died to all the great library of the world, including Alexandria" (*U* 3.141–3).

33. While Bloom's fetishist attachment to the products of her body may seem unusual, it plays a variation on themes found in many love letters. Roland Barthes notes that each "object touched by the loved being's body becomes part of that body, and the subject eagerly attaches himself to it." Roland Barthes, *A Lovers Discourse. Fragments*, trans. Richard Howard (New York: Hill and Wang, 1978), p. 172. Joyce's own youthful correspondence with Nora Barnacle displays this same conventional attachment to her objects, though readers have delighted themselves being scandalized by his interest in Nora's drawers.

34. Ibid., p. 157.

35. Angel Day's *The English Secretorie* of 1586 (Menston, England: The Scolar Press Limited, reprint 1967) provided samples of love letters and extensive commentary on their purposes and execution. Edward Phillips's *The Mysteries of Love and Eloquence* of 1658 (Menston, England: The Scolar Press Limited, reprint 1972) also provides samples of love letters to be imitated by suitors along with valuable proverbs for incorporation in such missives and a brief rhyming dictionary to facilitate the writing of romantic poetry.

36. Shilpa Raval, "A Lover's Discourse: Byblis in *Metamorphosis 9*," *Arethusa* 34:3 (2001), p. 286.

37. Hélène Cixous, "The Book as One of Its Own Characters," *New Literary History* 33:3 (2002), p. 420.
38. Barthes, *A Lovers Discourse*, p. 158.
39. Filippo Tommaso Marinetti, *Selected Writings*, ed. and trans. R.W. Flint (New York: Farrar, Straus, and Giroux, 1971), p. 41.
40. André Breton, "Manifesto of Surrealism," in *Manifestoes of Surrealism*, ed. and trans. Richard Seaver and Helen R. Lane (Ann Arbor: University of Michigan Press, 1969), p. 26.
41. *The Dada Almanac*, edn. Richard Huelsenbeck (1920), English ed. Malcolm Green (Channel Islands: Guernsey Press, 1993), p. 121.
42. Mary Ann Caws (ed.), *Manifesto: A Century of Isms* (Lincoln: University of Nebraska Press, 2001), p. xx.
43. Janet Lyon, *Manifestoes: Provocations of the Modern* (Ithaca: Cornell University Press, 1999), p. 12.
44. Ibid., p. 9.
45. It is also possible to conclude that the manifesto and the letter are the same text. While there is evidence for that assumption in Shaun's professorial lecture, which follows the list of titles, for generic purposes, I prefer to treat the two texts as separate.

6
joyce and gender
vicki mahaffey

When people challenge the arbitrariness of gender differences, when they object to the unwritten but powerful social directives about how they may feel, what activities they may pursue, and even what they are expected to wear, what is fundamentally at stake is what I am calling the unlived life. We lack sufficient choice about which lives we may live, and which ones – because of the accidents of birth or death – are forever unlivable. Critiques of the categories of class, race, nationality, age, and education all take issue with the insufficiency of choices available to individuals. Because our options depend upon the degree of privilege we enjoy in a subtly rigid social hierarchy, some highly desirable pursuits remain out of reach, and the loss of alternative possibilities often seems irredeemable. The girl who longs to be a bomber pilot or president of the United States, the boy who dreams of bearing or nurturing children, the woman in a burqua who wants to study microbiology or Brehon law: these people are yearning for lives that are probably unlivable. More disturbing, however, is the phenomenon created by this unlikelihood: not only will people fail to live implausible lives, most will despair even of imagining them, which cuts creative or novel conceptions off at the source.

Dreams of transcending one's social or sexual category are the future counterparts of dead historical possibilities, such as the ones that Stephen contemplates in "Nestor": what if Pyrrhus had not been killed in Argos "or Julius Caesar not been knifed to death"? Stephen considers not only events that might have happened, but also those that did occur, acknowledging the precedence of historical facts as "not to be thought away. Time has branded them and fettered they are lodged in the room of the infinite possibilities they have ousted. But can these be possible seeing that they never were?" (*U* 2.48–52). Such purely virtual possibilities are unlived, perhaps unlivable: does that undermine their status as possible? In addition to interrogating whether eventualities that were never realized were ever really possible in the first place – an impossibility that renders them "fictional" – we should also explore the relation between such possibilities and memory, a fiction based on historical reality but not isomorphic with it. Although Stephen, while teaching history, characterizes his subject as "Fabled by the daughters of memory," he also knows that a given event – say the battle of Asculum – "*was* in some way if not as memory fabled it" (*U* 2.7–8, my emphasis). Except through its irreversible consequences, the past in all its complexity is unknowable; however, we have limited access to the past through memory, which fictively rearranges or re-members it. Both past and future, then, are unavailable to us except through the comparable "fictions" of memory and desire. A future-directed model of virtual experience is crucial to a discussion of gender because gender theory – by characterizing history as dystopian and the future as utopian – tends to polarize past and future in ways that are ultimately too simplistic. If, however, we view both the past and the future as fictions mediated by psychic needs as well as systems overdetermined by social forces, we gain more leverage for possible interventions.

Joyce, like Stephen, was less interested in the past than the future. In *A Portrait of the Artist as a Young Man*, when Stephen thinks of Yeats's poem "He [Michael Robartes] Remembers Forgotten Beauty," he defines himself in contrast to the persona of the poem: unlike Michael Robartes, who "presses in his arms the loveliness which has long faded from the world," Stephen yearns for the beauty that "has not yet come into the world" (*P* 251). What happens, then, if we too shift our attention from the past to the future, from history to desire? Is a man's longing to experience life as a woman impossible, seeing that – short of surgical intervention or highly plausible changes of dress and physical presentation – it never can be? To put the question another way, was Joyce sensitive or arrogant to shock his protagonist in "The Dead" into a sudden apperception of his wife's point of view, or unexpectedly to conclude *Ulysses* and *Finnegans Wake* in the voices of women? Can the boundaries of sex and gender legitimately be crossed through the exercise of imagination, and if so, how?

I propose to test these questions against the pressure exerted by Joyce's *oeuvre*: what is the experiential status of the unlived life, the unlivable "possibility"? If even personal experience and collective history are "fabled by the daughters of memory" (*U* 2.7), and are therefore constructions that rearrange or re-member the past, then our psychological experience is always a product of the continuous intercourse between fiction and fact. Fact is "not to be thought away," but we have access to it only through the fables woven by memory, through fiction. If this is so, when we direct such fabling toward the future by fantasizing, can hope be fabled by the mothers of desire? What effect, if any, does imagining or visualizing the unlikely or the impossible have upon the realities of loss and limitation? Can the exercise of imagination soothe the wounds inflicted by natural and social restrictions on individuals, or are such fantasies simply placebos, offering an illusion of wholeness we can never actually experience (or both)? To put the question another way, does a patriarchal social structure stimulate anemic fantasies of transgression as part of a psychic mechanism that sustains the status quo? Does the mere act of imagining bring the impossible into the realm of psychic possibility, making it a virtual experience that we experience as real even if it is factually untrue or impossible? Does it make a difference *how* we construct our visions of desirable possibilities? Finally, what happens to us if we *neglect* or *fail* to conjure up explicit visions of the unlivable possibilities we desire but cannot realize, or if we base our fantasies on stereotypical dreams instead of constructing more personal, fully con-cretized models of desire?

I would argue that the *way* we envision our desire is a crucial determinant of the experiential effect of our future-directed fictions.[1] Corroboration may be found in "Lines and Squares," a poem by A.A. Milne, that virtuoso of the enabling dream. In "Lines and Squares," Christopher Robin has envisioned that whenever he walks on a London street there are "masses of bears / Who wait at the corners all ready to eat" the people who walk on the lines of the street; so he steps in the squares. He imagines that "Some of the bigger bears try to pretend / They've gone round a corner to look for a friend. / They try to pretend that nobody *cares* / Whether you walk on the lines or the squares." Christopher Robin's fantasy is that it matters how he walks down the street, and if he walks carefully and with awareness, he will get to flaunt his success to the bears, whereas if he "is silly and steps on a line" the little bears will compete to eat him. Walking down the street with care serves as a metaphor for the *way* we construct our fantasies – our awareness of distinctions that seem meaningless to others, our consciousness of the artifice of the activity – and it matters greatly how we do it, and with what degree of self-awareness. Although the bears pretend that nobody cares whether you walk on the lines or the squares, "Only the sillies believe their talk. / It's *ever so portant* how you walk." In the writing of Joyce, this distinction between sloppy fantasies – which sustain paralysis – and healing ones, which allow for psychic movement, is best illustrated through the difference between the characters' standard fantasies in *Dubliners* and the much more idiosyncratic, artificial, impossible ones generated by the trinity of protagonists in *Ulysses* – Stephen, Bloom, and Molly – with Stephen's fantasies in *A Portrait of the Artist as a Young Man* serving as a bridge between the two.[2]

Dubliners demonstrates that the failure to fantasize in an energetic, original way, while maintaining an awareness of the unreality of one's dreams, produces a corresponding failure in sensory perception that predicts a corresponding failure to act. The characters of *Dubliners* are afflicted with metaphorical blindness, muteness, insensibility, deafness, and even paralysis as a consequence of indulging in the vague and hackneyed dreams marketed by popular culture, instead of designing more elaborate and impossible ones. In contrast, the capacity to visualize impossible realities, in all their uncompromised impossibility, as the flawed characters in *Ulysses* are nonetheless able to do, restores a wholeness in the subject that can never be realized in the world: I call this capacity the Rudy Principle. The Rudy Principle, as I hope to demonstrate, is a psychological, artistic response to the social divisions of gender, class, religion, and age, not a political one. A political response would aim to change the external, natural or social world, whereas the Rudy Principle works its changes only on the perceiver. Its effect, to paraphrase Stephen and to understand his words in a different way, is not to change the country or the world, but to change the subject (see Stephen's comment, "We can't change the country. Let us change the subject" [*U* 16.1171]).

The Rudy Principle is, of course, named after the Blooms' dead son, and specifically his phantasmagoric appearance at the end of the "Circe" episode. I chose this scene because it is clearly impossible for Rudy to appear at all (since he is dead), least of all at the age and in the guise he assumes at the end of "Circe." To set the stage: Bloom is standing over Stephen after he has been knocked out by Private Carr in a dispute in which politics and sex are closely intertwined. The British soldiers have accused Stephen of insulting Ireland in the unexpected guise of Cissy Caffrey, the virgin-cum-shilling whore who is being treated by the British Privates and therefore ironically insists on her (momentary) faithfulness to them (*U* 15.4382–3). In addition to insulting Ireland, Stephen is also seen as insulting Britain when he pacifistically taps his brow and proclaims, "in here it is I must kill the priest and the king" (*U* 15.1436–7). In this way, Stephen emerges as a poetic, intellectual, anti-violent representative of Ireland and avatar of the crucified Christ, fighting only with his mind against soldiers who deal physical blows for a woman-country who is at once naive and pure, on the one hand, and who sells herself cheaply, on the other (a virgin/whore hybrid, as opposed to the usual fiction that women are one or the other). Bloom tries to arouse the prostrate Stephen by calling his name, while Stephen, moving into the fetal position, recites bits of Yeats's poem "Who Goes with Fergus," which he sang for his dying mother. And as Stephen sings to his dead mother, reverting to infancy in his bodily attitude, Bloom sees the mother through the son: "Face reminds me of his poor mother" (*U* 15.4949). He stands guard, misunderstanding Stephen's murmured poetic fragments as evidence of a romantic attachment, and then his own dead son appears wondrously, impossibly before him:

> *Against the dark wall a figure appears slowly, a fairy boy of eleven, a changeling, kidnapped, dressed in an Eton suit with glass shoes and a little bronze helmet, holding a book in his hand. He reads from right to left inaudibly, smiling, kissing the page.* (*U* 15.4956–60)

When Bloom calls softly to him he "*gazes, unseeing, into Bloom's eyes and goes on reading, kissing, smiling. He has a delicate mauve face. On his suit he has diamond and ruby buttons. In his free left hand he holds a slim ivory cane with a violet bowknot. A white lambkin peeps out of his waistcoat pocket*" (*U* 15.4964–7). What has happened, silently, beautifully, is that for an instant Bloom and Stephen have psychically interlocked through their dead relatives: Bloom has become Stephen's mother (across the sexual divide), and Stephen has become Bloom's son Rudy, at the age he would have been had he lived (half Stephen's own age). This fragile, ephemeral bond has been created through a mutual fantasy (literally a "making visible") that is both real and unreal: at once a restoration and confirmation of loss.

Bloom's fantasy, told in the imagery of a waking dream, is that Rudy did not die, but was taken by fairies, where he learned to read Hebrew like a good Jewish son. Like both of his parents, in addition to being Jewish he is also Christian; he carries in his pocket a lambkin, token of Christ, the sacrificial lamb of God who taketh away the sins of the world, which is how Joyce read the story of any child's nativity.[3] The visual plays on his name operate through the proximity of Rudy to "ruddy" and "ruby"; instead of being "ruddy," or red with life, his face is the delicate mauve of death, as when the Blooms buried him, and his ruby buttons show that through a 180-degree twist of the "d" in his name he morphs into a red jewel who is also the circus-ring victim of the monster Maffei in Amye Reade's novel *Ruby: The Pride of the Ring*; at the same time, he is also the whore that Bloom himself became earlier in "Circe" when, as a woman, he took the name of Ruby Cohen (*U* 4.347–58; 15.2968). That Rudy is simultaneously Stephen is shown not only by his possession of a whitened equivalent of Stephen's ashplant, the "slim ivory cane," but also by his glass shoes, which connect him with a figure associated with a different kind of ash, Cinderella (again crossing the line of sexual difference). Like Cinderella, Stephen, and even Bloom, Rudy has lost his mother and is in a debased state, awaiting a magical, "impossible" transformation.

What makes these fantasies so different from those of the characters in *Dubliners*, for example, is their sheer unbelievability, their extravagant artifice. Paradoxically, it is the impossibility of the fantasy that mitigates its hopelessness, evening out the relation between loss and possibility. Rudy is a victim, like Stephen before the privates, like Bloom whose masochistic jouissance makes him long to be Molly-Bello's humiliated slave, like Ruby in the novel Molly just finished, naked and prostrate on the floor beneath a cruel Italian brandishing a carriage whip. But this victim has rearisen: impossibly, like the sacrificial lamb peeking from his pocket; or ordinarily, like the sun with which he shares a homonymic kinship. This private, hermetic and outrageous fantasy signifies something larger, that in the human race the dark horse will beat unfavorable odds to come from behind and finish first, before the golden favorite. Rudy will not literally return to life, but Bloom, through a half-conscious identification with him, Stephen, and Molly, and Ruby, will help them all rise to face another day.

Contrast this carefully wrought fantasy with the anemic, derivative ones that limply motivate the characters in *Dubliners*: the boy's desire to have a wild adventure like the ones he reads about in pulp westerns in "An Encounter"; Little Chandler's longing to see his name in print (T. Malone Chandler) as the author of a book of melancholy poems that strike the Celtic note; Maria's long-buried wish for a wedding ring; Eveline's frantic need to "escape," to be saved by an open and frank man instead of bullied by a drunken and abusive father; even Gabriel's fervent but utterly ordinary hope for a riotously poetic sexual encounter with his wife after a holiday party. The most Corley can hope for in "Two Gallants" is to extract money from the woman he is currently bedding instead of spending money on one who retains her "virtue"; the best aspiration Lenehan can devise is to settle down with some girl who has a little cash. Farrington's highest goal is to enter a pub, get drunk, and win a contest of strength against an Englishman (failing that, he will wrest his victory from his pitifully praying stripling son). The men ostensibly revering Parnell's memory on Ivy Day are only concerned about getting paid; the "nationalists" in "A Mother" care nothing for fairness to women, asking only that women preserve their ladylike decorum; the mother herself, in her zeal to protect her daughter's rights, never stops to wonder what her daughter herself desires. Mr. Kernan only needs enough "grace" not to fall down the lavatory stairs, and the redemption his associates conspire to attain for him amounts to little more than a business deal with a popularly pragmatic priest. Jimmy's idea of "seeing life" doesn't extend beyond fast cars and losing large sums of his father's money to the English and the French, whereas the priest in "The Sisters" passes an "idle chalice" to the boy he tutored, bequeathing to him an empty faith that the boy later translates into romantic terms as he carries it reverently through (and to) the marketplace in "Araby." The economic poverty of the Dubliners is lamentable, but it is less tragic (because more easily addressed) than the poverty of their imaginations.

With respect to the partitioning of experience by gender, class, race, or religion, *Dubliners* and *Ulysses* exist in an almost antiphonal relation to one another: *Dubliners* details the debilitating effects of social restrictions on individual subjects, whereas *Ulysses* celebrates imaginative means of partially recuperating lost experience (while never denying its loss). In both books, however, once again what is at stake is the quality of the unlived life: in *Dubliners* the quality of life (both lived and unlived) is poor, whereas in the more comic world of *Ulysses*, despite the fact that the real lives of the characters are haunted with grief and fear, the unlived life is quirky, vigorous, and remarkably varied. Ideally, a high-quality unlived life does not *replace* an unsatisfactory reality – that would make it merely escapist; instead, it unearths buried truths of desire, which are generative because they are inspirational: oddball fantasies, then, unexpectedly help reality to bloom. The possibility that reality may suddenly flower depends, however, on whether life is assigned the value of a continuously generative, inventive force, or whether life is seen as predominantly routine.

It cannot be too strongly stressed that Joyce, like Beckett after him, was decidedly part of the pro-generative, anti-habit school of thought; he was a passionate advocate of the importance of living fully – dynamically, intensely, and comprehensively; he had what Charlotte

Brontë once called the "rage for experience." As Stanislaus recorded in his diary in 1904,

> Jim wants to live. Life is his creed. He boasts of his power to live, and says, in his pseudo-medical phraseology, that it comes from his highly specialized nervous system. (13 August 1904)[4]

In *My Brother's Keeper*, Stanislaus reports that Joyce accused him – along with everyone else in Dublin – of fearing life, which he elsewhere associated with a complementary terror of death.[5] Joyce told his brother,

> What's the matter with you is that you're afraid to live. You and people like you. This city is suffering from hemiplegia of the will. I'm not afraid to live ... . I don't care if I never write another line. I want to live. I should be supported at the expense of the state because I am capable of enjoying life. (p. 248, quoted in *JJ II* 184)

Earlier, in 1902, the young Joyce penned an extraordinary prophecy: the time had come when "a man of timid courage" would proclaim "the praise of life ... and of death, the most beautiful form of life" (*JJ II* 95; compare the jibe Lynch's cap makes to Stephen in *Ulysses*: "Death is the highest form of life! Ba!" [*U* 15.2098]). Joyce's passion for life is important partly because it gave him the motivation to tolerate, even embrace, the difficulty of truth; as his student Amalia Popper once wrote, Joyce's goal was to be able to confront the Medusa of reality without being turned to stone by it (art, by implication, is the mirror through which this Medusa may be safely seen). Although he wrote fiction, Joyce was at war with the fictions individuals construct or accept to protect themselves against the real. Paradoxically, he wrote fiction because it has the capacity to encompass the various dimensions of reality more honestly than do most individuals, especially those determined to project attractive or respectable images.

Contrast Joyce's hunger for life with the nostalgic threnody for lost life that is *Dubliners*. In *Dubliners*, we are given a glimpse of every protagonist's desire for life, whether it is betrayed by a penchant for "eating a great deal of Turkish Delight in secret" (*D* 137), or by a repeatedly disappointed hope of getting the ring in a Halloween fortune-telling game. Eveline's short-lived frenzy to "Escape!" is fueled by the assurance that Frank "would give her life, perhaps love, too. But she wanted to live" (*D* 40). In "After the Race," Jimmy's prodigal, foolish gambling is a byproduct of his excited belief that the race "laid a magical finger on the genuine pulse of life" (*D* 45), that his subsequent drinking, dancing, and card-playing was "seeing life, at least" (*D* 47). Lenehan's hope for life in "Two Gallants" is more attenuated, less excitable. After he eats, he feels "less weary of his life, less vanquished in spirit. He might yet be able to settle down in some snug corner and live happily if he could only come across some good simple-minded girl with a little of the ready" (*D* 58). As *Dubliners* unfolds, the characters' vital signs grow fainter, more deeply shadowed by their failures. When Little Chandler thought of life "(as always when he thought of life) he became sad" (*D* 71). He dismisses the energy of children as "minute vermin-like life" (*D* 66), preferring to contemplate Gallaher's vision of Parisian vitality: "it's the life of Paris, that's the thing. Ah, there's no city like Paris for gaiety, movement, excitement ... "(*D* 71). "They [the Parisians] believe in enjoying life – and don't you think they're right?" (*D* 72). For Farrington in "Counterparts," vitality is to be found neither at work nor at home, but only in "the hot reeking public-house" (*D* 93). In "A Painful Case," life is famously celebrated as a feast, from which Mr. Duffy, having "gnawed the rectitude of his life," comes to see himself as outcast (*D* 113). For Jack the caretaker in "Ivy Day in the Committee Room," as for the men who wax nostalgic for Parnell, life is past; specifically, what life there is is locked in the years before Parnell died, before Jack's son became a drinking wastrel: "God be with them times! Said the old man. There was some life in it then" (*D* 119).

Not surprisingly, the question of what life is and where it resides is most insistent in "The Dead." The story poses the negative version of this question – about death rather than life – through the title: to whom does it refer? Who are the dead? Michael Furey and those like him, or the people at the party who think they are so alive and festive? This question gets bounced to Robert Browning via Gabriel's review of Browning's poems in the *Daily Express* (*D* 187–8) and the unidentified allusion to Browning that Gabriel decides to delete from his speech (*D* 179). In a story all about ghosts, the Browning poem that seems to haunt "The Dead" most poignantly is "A Toccata of Galuppi's," in which the ghost of a Venetian composer comes to a contemporary English scientist, speaking to him through music. This is of course what happens to Gretta in "The Dead" when Furey's ghost comes to her through Bartell d'Arcy's rendition of the song, "The Lass of Aughrim," and it also happens to Gabriel as well through vicarious participation in Gretta's experience. Eerily, in "A Toccata of Galuppi's" the living and the dead imperceptibly exchange places: the dead Venetians come alive, dance, murmur sweet nothings, and kiss, despite the scientist's complacent dismissal of them as dead and gone, whereas the living scientist unexpectedly comes to see himself as one of the dead when Galuppi, "like a ghostly cricket," begins mocking him for his assumption of immortality: "you know physics, something of geology, / Mathematics are your pastime; souls shall rise in their degree; / Butterflies may dread extinction – you'll not die, it cannot be!" And when Galuppi stops speaking through his "cold music," the scientist-narrator feels his own life-force ebb as he contemplates the paradoxical vitality of Galuppi's dead women: "Dear dead women, with such hair, too – what's become of all the gold / Used to hang and brush their bosoms? I feel chilly and grown old." Browning's poem could have been called "The Dead" too, because it asks the same question as Joyce's story: who are "the dead"? In what does life inhere, if people who are biologically alive can be spiritually dead? Who is the deadest: Michael Furey, who appropriately came alive again for Gretta on the night of the Epiphany, or Gabriel Conroy, who began the evening full of life, but ends it with his soul approaching that "region where dwell the vast hosts of the dead" (D 223)? Does the apprehension of "distant music" (D 210, 214) represent the sensation of life or death? The distant music that we hear from Joyce's story itself, is it a sign of Dublin's former vitality or a reminder of the many people and characters who never really existed because they became too habituated to routine, like Patrick Morkan's horse (D 207–8)?

"The Dead," like "A Toccata of Galuppi's," also interrogates the relation between life and love. Does vitality depend upon the capacity for love, and if so, how should we define love? Who is more loving: Michael Furey, who sacrificed his life to say goodbye to the girl he loved, or Gabriel Conroy, who has sacrificed nothing but lustily (and fruitlessly) longs to enjoy his wife's touch? If we privilege Michael Furey as the lover, how do we account for the pyrrhic quality of his victory (he is dead); alternatively, if we nominate Gabriel, how do we explain the abject failure of his fantasy? Life and love, by implication, happen somewhere between the beginning of time (its annunciation, presided over by the archangel Gabriel) and its end (Michael is the angel of the last judgment). Life is assured neither by verbal pronouncement (mere annunciation), nor a final judgment (evaluation), but flickers somewhere between the futility of death and the not-yet incarnate promise of new life.

To return to fantasy, though, let us look at what the threadbare fantasies of the characters in *Dubliners* produce: Gabriel's heated vision of a rekindling of his and his wife's "souls' tender fire" (D 214) ends, paradoxically, in darkness and cold, with snow tapping on the pane. Michael Furey impossibly takes shape before him – "the tears gathered more thickly in his eyes and in the partial darkness he imagined he saw the form of a young man standing under a dripping tree" (*D* 223) – and the world he thought to be solid begins to disintegrate: "His own identity was fading out into a grey impalpable world: the solid world itself which these dead had one time reared and lived in was dissolving and dwindling" (*D* 223). In short, every hope produces its opposite. "Grace" is equally ironic in its treatment of mundane fantasy. The fantasy in "Grace" is the fallacious assurance that manliness and salvation depend upon honest accounting and divine forgiveness of "debts." What makes this apparently pragmatic logic bankrupt is the characters' ignorance of the latent meaning of "debt"; like most readers, Mr. Kernan's would-be saviors, who are as debt-ridden as he, fail to realize that etymologically, "debt" is the opposite of "habit": "debt" comes from *debere*, to owe, or *de habere* (not to have), in contrast to "habit," which comes from the past participle of *habere*, to have. Both Mr. Kernan (in decline) and Mr. Power (whose social stock is rising) are saddled with debts (*D* 154) that compel them to seek salvation through closer accounting, when in fact it is habit (or having) that makes one resistant both to grace and to gratitude (which derives from the same root as "grace"). Note that Mr. Kernan drinks most heavily when he *has* money; his debt comes from *having*, not the reverse (*D* 154).[6] Mr. Kernan's drinking causes him both to fall and to bite his tongue; the fantasy is that he can rise again, achieve lost wholeness (the literal meaning of salvation), and become a new man through the Catholic "habit," or insistence on having, when habit is what caused his fall in the first place.

Mrs. Kearney's fantasy in "A Mother" is that her investment in the nationalist concert will be reciprocated in a just and nonsexist manner, whereas what happens in fact is that "Mrs Kearney's conduct was condemned on all hands: everyone approved of what the Committee had done" (*D* 149). Ironically, the self-identified patriots betray her and her daughter, whose name – Cathleen – evokes the representation of Ireland itself as Cathleen Ni Houlihan. In "Ivy Day," the fantasy is that the Irish will pay homage to Parnell less superficially and hypocritically, and in so doing will understand the meaning of liberty in a revolutionary new way. What is most interesting about the characters' fantasies in the earlier stories, however, is the way Joyce represents the effects of their failure: unlike "Ivy Day," "A Mother," and "Grace," which expose ironic inconsistencies at the heart of political and religious observances, the earlier stories dramatize what happens to individual characters when their vapid ideals are exposed as shabby and self-interested: the characters experience a temporary but symbolic loss of one or more of their senses. Mr. Duffy cannot feel or hear anything at the end of "A Painful Case," Maria has a memory lapse in "Clay" when she sings the first verse of "I dreamt I dwellt in marble halls" twice and Joe's tears interfere with his vision. "Counterparts" and "Araby" end in a darkness that underscores the protagonists' blindness, whereas "After the Race" climaxes in an ironic "daybreak," and "Two Gallants" concludes with the image of a gold sovereign in a pool of lamplight, signifying Corley's success at using kisses to effect betrayal. Eveline appears paralyzed and blind as she stalls at the railing while Frank moves onto the boat: "her eyes gave him no sign of love or farewell or recognition" (*D* 41), and even Polly Mooney loses the ability to see what is in front of her at the end of "The Boarding House": "Her hopes and visions were so intricate that she no longer saw the white pillows on which her gaze was fixed or remembered that she was waiting for anything" (*D* 68). Whether the characters are blinded by hope, folly, anger, vanity, principle, patriotism, or religion, after the first three stories all end up with less sensory and cognitive perceptiveness than they had at the outset, as the fantasies that inspired them – of love, victory, artistic success, adventure, justice, solvency – dissolve into disabling clichés. No one imagines changing his or her sex; on the contrary, the characters' routines are utterly predictable and standard. In the words of Wallace Stevens, everyone assumes a similar stance: "The houses are haunted / By white night-gowns ... / People are not going / To dream of baboons and periwinkles" ("Disillusionment of Ten O'Clock").

The fantasies of Stephen Dedalus are progressively more inventive than those of the protagonists of *Dubliners*, especially as he moves toward the garish extravaganza of "Circe." In *Stephen Hero*, Stephen's proposal to Emma Clery that they have a night of honest sex in her bedroom without expectation or commitment is shocking, even insulting to her and doubtless unusual within Stephen's Catholic, adolescent world, but because he presents it to her as a reasonable proposition and recommends that they act on it, it is not a fantasy that operates according to the Rudy Principle (*SH* 198). It is also more rebellious than creative: what adolescent boy *doesn't* wish for sexual freedom without consequences or anxiety, especially in the company of a desirable sexual partner? In *A Portrait of the Artist as a Young Man*, Stephen's fantasies begin with his childlike desire to be a savior-hero following the combined pattern of Parnell and Christ, but once again, this is a plausible – if challenging

– fantasy he tries to *live in the world* (with temporary success).[7] His next fantasy, although it begins conventionally enough as a derivation from the romantic subplot of *The Count of Monte Cristo*, and although it, too, is at least partially enacted, is more daring in that it violates his gender identity by subtly placing Stephen in the female erotic position. When he visits the prostitute at the end of chapter 2, he wants to be passive and receptive, not proactive: "He wanted to be held firmly in her arms, to be caressed slowly, slowly, slowly" (*P* 101). When the prostitute adopts the active role by kissing him, "He closed his eyes, surrendering himself to her, body and mind, conscious of nothing in the world but the dark pressure of her softly parting lips." She presses, he surrenders, and then she enters him, her gift affecting him as powerfully as spoken language: "[Her lips] pressed upon his brain as upon his lips as though they were the vehicle of a vague speech; and between them he felt an unknown and timid pressure, darker than the swoon of sin, softer than sound or odour" (*P* 101).

Stephen's fantasies in chapter 3 are, unsurprisingly given the Christian context, responsive ones; specifically, he is imaginatively reacting to the priest's carefully crafted, highly specific and sensual vision of hell. Stephen's hallucinations take the form of detailed visions of judgment, punishment, and forgiveness called forth by the priest's words,[8] and although they eventually produce an action – Stephen's confession – they initially emerge as purely imaginative exercises, which enhances their experiential impact. First, Stephen envisions his own death and judgment as "the preacher blew death into his soul" and he is coffined, buried, made to stand before God and ultimately experience the "bloodred" moon and falling stars of Doomsday (*P* 112–13); next, he imagines himself and Emma standing in a wide land under "the pale green sea of heaven" being forgiven by the Virgin Mother (*P* 116); subsequently, he endures hell with flames bursting out of his skull (*P* 125); finally, he is forced against his will to see the "hell reserved for his sins" in an evil-smelling weedy field crusted with dried dung:

Creatures were in the field; one, three, six; creatures were moving in the field, hither and thither. Goatish creatures with human faces, hornybrowed, lightly bearded and grey as indiarubber. The malice of evil glittered in their hard eyes, as they moved hither and thither, trailing their long tails behind them. A rictus of cruel malignity lit up greyly their old bony faces. One was clasping about his ribs a torn flannel waistcoat, another complained monotonously as his beard stuck in the tufted weeds ... They moved in slow circles, circling closer and closer to enclose, to enclose, soft language issuing from their lips, their long swishing tails besmeared with stale shite, thrusting upwards their terrific faces ... Help! (*P* 137–8).

This fantasy has the impact of actual experience for Stephen, inciting him to vomit "profusely in agony" at this God-given vision of "the hell reserved for his sins: stinking, bestial, malignant, a hell of lecherous goatish fiends. For him! For him!" These fantasies work by the Rudy Principle in the sense that they are sensually specific – evoking sight, smell, touch, and hearing – while remaining quite impossible. However, Stephen's visions are also responsively tied to someone else's language in a way that the characters' fantasies in *Ulysses* are not. Moreover, although their subject is Stephen's transgressions, they are not themselves transgressive; despite his belief to the contrary, Stephen himself doesn't undergo significant metamorphosis, even when his body imagines its own demise.

I do not mean to suggest that Stephen's experience of his own gender is simple or uninteresting. On the contrary, he identifies with both genders throughout the first four chapters, but in a conventional, biologically literal way: when he is in the active position, he experiences himself as male, but when he is receptive, he imagines himself as female. His "femaleness" is apparent erotically, when he lets himself be kissed by the prostitute at the end of chapter 2, as well as spiritually, when his soul surrenders to God in chapter 4. In the fourth chapter, his female soul even becomes metaphorically pregnant: after his soul had taken up again "her burden of pieties, masses and prayers and sacraments and mortifications," "only then for the first time since he had brooded on the great mystery of love did he feel within him a warm movement like that of some newly born life" (*P* 150). At times his soul is a yielding virgin, as when he visits the Blessed Sacrament and feels "dissolving moments of virginal selfsurrender" (*P* 152), and at other times, such as while praying, she is simply "humiliated and faint before her [male] Creator" (*P* 150). His (female) soul certainly experiences highly sensual, erotic moments; when Stephen is reading the "old neglected book written by Saint Alphonsus Liguori," he thinks in the language of the Song of Solomon,

An inaudible voice seemed to caress the soul, telling her names and glories, bidding her arise as for espousal and come away, bidding her look forth, a spouse, from Amana and from the mountains of the leopards; and the soul seemed to answer with the same inaudible voice, surrendering herself: *Inter ubera mea commorabitur* [he shall lie between my breasts]. (*P* 152)

However, that essentialist division between active, sinning males and passive, languorously receptive females begins to break down when Stephen has his famous vision of the bird-girl on the beach at the end of chapter 4. The crucial point to realize is that Stephen's desire for transformation has crossed bounds of gender as well as species: the bird-girl is not only a fantasy of what he desires to have, but also what he desires to *be*; moreover, she combines a ("male") capacity to act by transcending her immediate environment with a ("female") propensity to withdraw or escape, in that she is poised for flight.

To appreciate the fundamental change in Stephen's mind at the end of chapter 4, a change that ultimately makes him more fully androgynous or whole, we must first recall the setting: Stephen is walking from Clontarf along the Bull, a sea wall built in 1820 from Clontarf almost to the Poolbeg lighthouse that helped form a safe harbor for ships in Dublin Bay. His friends – all adolescent boys – are swimming in the sea: Ennis, Shuley, and Connolly – and are calling to him in Greek in a way that connects him to a garlanded ox or cow, an animal dressed for sacrifice: "Stephanos Dedalos! Bous Stephanoumenos! Bous Stephaneforos!" (*P* 168). The interplay that follows between their cries and Stephen's thoughts produces an ironic tension between Stephen's view of himself as Daedalus flying over the waves and the implication planted through their cries that he is more likely Icarus: "O, Cripes, I'm drownded!" After his ecstatic vision of himself as a classical genius, Stephen takes off his shoes and wades in a rivulet of water up the strand, asking, "Where was his boyhood now?" (*P* 171). Interestingly, the indirect answer is that his boyhood has mutated into girlhood; in place of the shouting boys before him earlier, he sees the "gayclad lightclad figures of children and girls and voices childish and girlish in the air," and then "A girl stood before him in midstream, alone and still, gazing out to sea. She seemed like one whom magic had changed into the likeness of a strange and beautiful seabird ... her long fair hair was girlish: and girlish, and touched with the wonder of mortal beauty, her face" (*P* 171). The bird-girl is Stephen-as-Daedalus' counterpart and mirror image; she is a hybrid figure: part woman/part girl, part human/part bird; part erotic object and part provocateur. She represents the promised embrace of the earth and the heavens that lulls Stephen to sleep: "He felt above him the vast indifferent dome and the calm processes of the heavenly bodies: and the earth beneath him, the earth that had borne him, had taken him to her breast" (*P* 172). It is only through his female, girlish bird-self that he experiences himself as at one with the world. One possible way of understanding this change is by reading Stephen against the story of another Daedalian invention recounted in Ovid's *Metamorphoses*: the invention of the cow that allows Queen Pasiphae to mate with the bull she desires. Stephen has been walking from Clontarf (which means the field of the bull) along the North Bull wall, and his friends have called him an ox or bull (*Bous*, although the Greek word is not gender-specific here). His problem lies in his alienation from this world of bullying, and he solves it by alternately recreating himself as "female," thus enabling himself to be at one with the Bull, to be pacified (to play on the English homonym for Pasiphae). Like Daedalus, he has invented a uterus to facilitate a union between the human and the natural, with the result that he can recognize himself as an artist. Also like Daedalus, his two inventions imitate the functions of cattle and birds, respectively, fostering a union and an escape. It should be clear that although Stephen's fantasies are still derivative, they are becoming more bizarre, specific, and outlandishly impossible.

The climax of Stephen's androgynous fantasies occurs in chapter 5 when he awakes at dawn to write his villanelle (most probably in the wake of a wet dream, since his first observation is that "His soul [sic] was all dewy wet" [*P* 217]). Here, the imagined erotic caresses of a woman and the inspirational caresses of the Holy Spirit merge, and he becomes both the passive instrument of a temptress/muse and the active scribe of the formal poem he scribbles on a cigarette packet. Like Mary, he has been impregnated by a word: "In the virgin womb of the imagination the word was made flesh," and the incarnation produces both erotic and poetic results. After a moment of compassion in which he empathizes with the pain caused by Emma's sexual maturation, "the strange humiliation of her nature" that he associates with his own experience of sin, "A glow of desire kindled again his soul and fired and fulfilled all his body" (*P* 222–3). The rhythm that fills him is again simultaneously sexual and prosodic, only here, at least part of the time he is the active, initiating partner and she the responsive one who yields to his desirous insistence and "enfolds him like water with a liquid life" as "the liquid letters of speech flowed forth over his brain" (*P* 223; at other times she is the temptress and he her victim). Fluidity of sex, spirit, language, and gender roles are crucial to Stephen's creative life, which retains its sharp precision while remaining dynamic, even sexual in its capacity for unexpected interchange.

The capacity for imaginative androgyny is crucial to the production of fantasies governed by the Rudy Principle. When Stephen relapses into priggishness at the end of *A Portrait*, that priggishness is accented by the withdrawal of his willingness to identify with women, coinciding with a determination to objectify them. This objectifying impulse is clear in the conversation between Stephen and Cranly, especially when they hear a servant singing *Rosie O'Grady* (*P* 244). Stephen immediately pictures "the figure of woman as she appears in the liturgy of the church," narcissistically annexing her as an extension of his own boyish singing when he sees her as "a white-robed figure, small and slender as a boy and with a falling girdle. Her voice, frail and high as a boy's, was heard intoning from a distant choir the first words of a woman which pierce the gloom and clamour of the first chanting of the passion" (*P* 244). In contrast, Cranly thinks of a real woman that a man looks forward to marrying, remarking that such a Rosie is "easy to find" and opining about the chorus, "There's real poetry for you ... There's real love" (*P* 244). Stephen looks at Cranly and registers the sharp difference between them with aggressive disdain: "He [Cranly] felt then the sufferings of women, the weaknesses of their bodies and souls; and would shield them with strong and resolute arm and bow his mind to them" (*P* 245). Stephen has temporarily set himself against feeling the sufferings of women, mockingly quoting two lines of Blake's "William Bond" without heeding its injunction to "Seek love in the pity of others' woe" (*P* 249). Like Gabriel in "The Dead," Stephen has unconsciously armed himself against imaginative identification with women by conceiving of himself as superior to others, a position that cracks briefly on April 15, when he records an encounter with Emma:

> I liked her today. A little or much? Don't know. I liked her and it seems a new feeling to me. Then, in that case, all the rest, all that I thought I thought and all that I felt I felt, all the rest before now, in fact ... O, give it up, old chap! Sleep it off! (*P* 252)[9]

Stephen's default position towards women is a defensive denial of their complexity, their vibrancy, their hopes and difficulties, which makes it as difficult for him to like them as it was for Gabriel in "The Dead" to love them. Stephen's fantasies of women, like those of the Bob Doran in "The Boarding House" or Little Chandler in "A Little Cloud," are little more than caricatures that reassure the men of their own greater importance and worth; they support thin, one-dimensional fantasies with little virtual power.

In *Ulysses*, Stephen and Bloom still struggle with a tendency to reductively diminish the rich and dynamic complexity of women by denying them a vulnerability comparable to their own. Stephen's mother appears to him a frightening ghoul who threatens to rob him of life, and Bloom most typically views Molly as a sadistic dominatrix in the style of Bello Cohen, a woman who wears trousers and flaunts her sexual and maternal power, not only when she was virginal but also now that she is an adulteress. It is vital for subjects to apply the Rudy Principle to their fantasies precisely because it interferes with this knee-jerk tendency to oversimplify the other in an unconsciously grandiose effort to humanize and win sympathy for the self. It disrupts gender binaries by virtue of the fact that it encourages imaginative identification (while discouraging projection) across the boundary of sexual difference; in a similar way, it also disrupts racial or ethnic polarities and hierarchies based on age or class. We see both Bloom and Stephen trying to prove manhood by idealizing or disdaining womanhood; we also see both trying to assert the superiority of their Irishness by denigrating Jews (Bloom is eager to diminish Reuben J. Dodd in "Hades" [*U* 6.262–91], and Stephen is quick to distance himself from Bloom's Jewishness in "Ithaca" by singing the anti-Semitic ballad of "Little Harry Hughes" [*U* 17.801–49).[10]

Where in *Ulysses*, then, do we see the Rudy Principle at work and what does it accomplish? First of all, we see it operating in Bloom as his defenses weaken with fatigue and distress, especially in "Circe" and "Ithaca," and he finds himself unconsciously in league with women. In "Circe," Bloom experiences himself by turns in the three different roles he has ascribed to Molly: first he is declared *"virgo intacta"* by "Dr. Mulligan" after a "pervaginal examination" (*U* 15.1784–6), which inspires Bloom with virginal modesty, as he "holds his high grade hat over his genital organs" (*U* 15.1787). Shortly afterwards, Dr. Dixon pleads clemency for Bloom on the grounds of Bloom's imminent motherhood: "He is about to have a baby," which provokes Bloom to exclaim, "O, I so want to be a mother" (*U* 15.1810, 1817). Finally, Bloom gains a first-hand experience of prostitution when Bello turns Bloom into a female pig-whore named Ruby Cohen: *"With a piercing epileptic cry she sinks on all fours, grunting, snuffling, rooting at his feet: then lies, shamming dead ..."* (*U* 15.2852–3). Bello accents the connection between a whore and livestock by detailing the various ways she will punish her property:

The nosering, the pliers, the bastinado, the hanging hook, the knout I'll make you kiss while the flutes play like the Nubian slave of old. You're in for it this time! ... I shall sit on your ottoman saddleback every morning after my thumping good breakfast of Matterson's fat hamrashers and a bottle of Guinness's porter ... Very possibly I shall have you slaughtered and skewered in my stables and enjoy a slice of you with crisp crackling from the baking tin basted and baked like sucking pig with rice and lemon or currant sauce. It will hurt you. (*U* 15.2891–902)

Bello cruelly extinguishes his cigar in his Bloom-whore's ear and rides him like a horse, telling him, "Henceforth you are unmanned and mine in earnest, a thing under the yoke. You will shed your male garments, you understand, Ruby Cohen? And don the shot silk luxuriously rustling over head and shoulders" (*U* 15.2966–9). Bloom's final punishment is to be dressed like a woman, "wigged, singed, perfumesprayed, ricepowdered, with smoothshaven armpits ... You will be laced with cruel force into vicelike corsets of soft dove coutille with whalebone busk to the diamondtrimmed pelvis" (*U* 15.2972–6). As inspiring and humiliating as Bloom's transformations are, however, they help him understand at last the many roles of women, which in turn enables him to recognize Bella as a mother as well as a whore, and to see Molly as multidimensional and needy as well as powerful and threatening, as we see when he confesses, "Moll! I forgot! Forgive! Moll ... " (*U* 15.3151).

Stephen undergoes a similar metamorphosis when, unconsciously employing the Rudy Principle, he goes in search of a goddess-cum-whore, Georgina Johnson (*la belle dame sans merci, ad deam qui laetificat iuventutem meam*, the beautiful lady without mercy, the goddess who gladdened the days of his youth who turns out to be "dead and married" [*U* 15.122–3, 3620]), and instead encounters his mother. The goddess who gladdened the days of his youth *is* his mother, and she is simultaneously a virgin (meaningfully buried in her wedding dress), a whore in that she valued herself too cheaply, and a ghoul and she pierces his heart with the claws of a crab (*U* 15.4220). Interestingly, like Bloom who learns what it is like to be sexually penetrated when he becomes a woman, Stephen learns to be penetrated by death in the form of the woman who gave him life. As in *Portrait*, he again assumes a receptive or biologically "female" position, at least until he lifts his ashplant to smash the chandelier (*U* 15.4243). Not only does Stephen become suddenly active when he tries to end death, by sparking "*Time's livid final flame*" (*U* 15.4244), but that flame is paradoxically produced by a mating of ash with ash (ashes to ashes, dust to dust) since he uses an ashplant to attack the dead woman with the "*ashen breath*" (*U* 15.4217). This is part of Stephen's Cinderella complex: his obsession with the death of his mother, expressed by a close association with ashes (which express grief).

Molly, too, uses the Rudy Principle to cross gender boundaries in her imaginative wanderings, as when she ruminates about being the man during intercourse with a woman. She is thinking about the attractiveness of her thighs: "I bet he never saw a better pair of thighs than that look how white they are the smoothest place is right there between this bit here how soft like a peach easy God I wouldnt mind being a man and get up on a lovely woman" (*U* 18.1144–7). Bloom, too, transforms her into a man when he dreams of her in Turkish trousers and that dream comes to life in "Circe" (*U* 15.297–302). Molly also feels free to think across generational lines when she thinks about Stephen with desire (*U* 18.1300–67). Whether Molly is admiring the "lovely little statue" of Narcissus that Bloom bought and feeling the urge to take "his lovely young cock" in her mouth "so clean and white he looks with his boyish face" (*U* 18.1349–54) or whether she is imagining sex with a priest, her fantasies stand in stark contrast to the vaguer, utterly conventional expectations of someone like Eveline or Polly Mooney. Bloom in Stephen's dream offers Stephen a ripe melon that we later come to realize signifies his wife's rump; contrast this with Corley's tawdry, plausible and predictable idea of convincing a slavey to fetch him a gold coin. The idiosyncratic specificity of Bloom's fantasies is apparent in the elaborate visions he rehearses in "Ithaca" of purchasing the bungalow he plans to call "Bloom Cottage" in Flowerville (*U* 17.1497–753). Stephen, not to be outdone, imagines a multitude of umbilical cords forming a telephone line back to Eve in Eden that he can access by dialing alpha, aleph and zeroes: "The cords of all link back, strandentwining cable of all flesh ... Hello! Kinch here. Put me on to Edenville. Aleph, alpha; nought, nought, one" (*U* 3.337–40). *Ulysses* is rich with examples of how its protagonists contemplate in detail possibilities that most people would consider unimaginable, unthinkable. These thoughts are clearly neither practical nor, in most cases, would they be desirable if they were realized in action, but the characters refuse to censor them for their implausibility or outrageousness. It is precisely this range of imaginative movement that gives the characters a vitality that threatens to burst from the pages (as Wilde writes in "The Decay of Lying," "The only real people are the people who never existed"). Such imaginative exercise produces possibilities only a fraction of which can (or should) be made real, but in so doing it creates an apprehension of infinitude to balance and highlight the stark limits of everyday life. It is precisely such perceptions of subjective infinitude that gender roles proscribe.

If, as I have suggested, the principle of accretion that drives Joyce's work towards an ever more specific and dynamic comprehensiveness is one of future-directed fantasy, a realization of the possible as possible (see *U* 2.67), then it is easier to appreciate the logic that finally produced that unwieldy, multilingual dream of human history and prospects, *Finnegans Wake*, and to see why gender divisions in that work have become as unstable and provisional as those of any "work in progress." As a "map of the soul's groupography" (*FW* 476.33), *Finnegans Wake* suggests that every soul is not only a place – with a geography – but it is also a group, a collection of parts, that are male and female, old and young, goy and Jew. This is also true of the mind, the Latin word for which is suggestively *mens*. In *Finnegans Wake* the mind (like the soul) is both finite and infinite, male and female: "Finight mens midinfinite true. The form masculine. The gender feminine" (*FW* 505.24–5; the gender of the Latin *mens* is indeed feminine). For *Finnegans Wake* is not just a replay of the past in all its jumbled chaos, but the dream of a future in which we have learned to embrace division and entertain the incomprehensible, so that "We are once amore as babes awondering in a wold made fresh where with the hen in the storyabout we start from scratch" (*FW* 336.16–18).

So, to quote the variation on Ecclesiastes found in *Finnegans Wake*, all is not vanity, but fantasy: "Fantasy! funtasy on fantasy, amnaes fintasies!" (*FW* 493.18). Moreover, fantasies must not be pure, for to be pure is to be young, in the sense of puerile; "You are pure. You are in your puerity" (*FW* 237.26). Maturity is a function of learning to see a possible if unlikely future through division, through fracture, which paradoxically becomes the only way we may apprehend wholeness. Joyce's model of growth might well be based on the division of cells, which in *Finnegans Wake* takes the form of divided words. Such division is indeed "genderous" (*FW* 268.25, both generous and based on gender), since it brought forth all "moodmoulded, cyclewheeling history" (*FW* 186.2). Not only should our fantasies be fun ("funtasy") and fractured, they must also seem extravagantly impossible, for the simple reason that the more flamboyant the artifice the less easily we can escape the realization that we aren't ever really sure what is real, or what is possible. The *Wake* enjoins us to rise and pray to "the cloud Incertitude" (*FW* 178.31–2), and to do so through wise play, or funtasy: "a wise and letters play of all you can ceive" (*FW* 237.19).

What prevents us from applying the Rudy Principle more regularly in our daily lives? Why doesn't everyone spend a percentage of time every day devising wild, detailed, surprising fantasies that disregard unspoken injunctions not to transgress the bounds of gender, age, religion, or nationality? Why do we tend to experience one such fantasy – *Finnegans Wake* – as daunting and insane rather than imaginatively liberating and inspiring? One answer has to do with a widespread reluctance to dissociate imagination from action.

We seem to want to realize in the mind only those things that might plausibly become real in the flesh. But to quote Browning's "Andrea del Sarto," "Ah, but a man's reach should exceed his grasp / Or what's a heaven for?" To achieve perfection – to capture the real – is a lesser accomplishment than to express desire for what eludes expression: the unknown and unknowable pulse of life. Del Sarto laments that his "low-pulsed forthright craftsman's hand" and his "perfect art" reflects only the subdued vitality, the grayness of what has already been realized in the city of Fiesole: "A common grayness silvers everything ... My youth, my hope, my art, being all toned down / To yonder sober pleasant Fiesole." Many of us yearn for perfection, purity (or puerity) instead of hearing the "adult" in "adulteration" and striving, with Lily Briscoe in Woolf's *To the Lighthouse*, to achieve that "razor's edge of balance between opposite forces." To do that, we must learn to be composite rather than pure, to comprehend or encompass divisions of gender, age, race, and creed, to apprehend the reality of loss as clearly and firmly as we envision impossible futures.

In his elegy "In Memory of W.B. Yeats," W.H. Auden famously insists that poetry is a kind of fantasy, in that "poetry makes nothing happen." By splitting poetry – or the imagination – from action, Auden takes it from the realm of politics into the sphere of ontology: "it survives, / A way of happening, a mouth." Poetry in general, and the poetry of Yeats in particular, gains its power from its "unconstraining voice," a voice that sings of dark truth and its contrapuntal relation to joy, thereby mitigating the realities of "intellectual disgrace," pitiless coldness, and helpless incarceration from which all "free" people suffer. This is also what the Rudy Principle illustrates: the vivid apprehension of a loss – here Rudy – restores the desire for wholeness by accenting its very impossibility. What we stand to gain by vividly picturing the unlived and unlivable lives that are barred to us "in the prison of [our] days" is a renewal of motivation, a rebirth of desire. This – together with his imaginative willingness to experience life as a woman – is what releases Bloom to go home, and what frees him to face a newly unknowable day.

notes

1. This argument has been influenced by Veronica Schanoes's work in progress on fantasy and feminist revisionism.

2. In "*Ulysses* and the End of Gender," I tried to argue that the characters of Stephen, Bloom and Molly were deliberately constructed in such a way as to violate standard expectations of gender and generational differences. See *Masculinities in Joyce: European Joyce Studies*, 10 (Amsterdam, 2001), pp. 137–62, and *A Companion to James Joyce's Ulysses*, ed. Margot Norris (New York: Bedford, 1998), pp. 151–68.

3. In the manuscript materials for his play *Exiles*, Joyce suggests that Archie, Richard Rowan's son, is the lamb of God who takes away the sins of the world; that is, like the baby Jesus, he brings new life to the world. The implication is that Christianity is ingenious in its celebration of the child.

4. Stanislaus Joyce, *The Complete Dublin Diary*, ed. George Healey (Ithaca: Cornell University Press, 1971), p. 51.

5. See 1902 essay on James Clarence Mangan (*CW* 73–83); also *JJ II* 99.

6. Mr. Cunningham, too, is saddled with debts because "he had married an unpresentable woman who was an incurable drunkard" and who pawns the furniture on him (*D* 156). Mrs. Kernan, in contrast, is defined less by her debts (or those of her husband) than by her habits: she has retained very few of her illusions, and "Religion for her was a habit" (*D* 156).

7. See Vicki Mahaffey, *Reauthorizing Joyce* (Cambridge: Cambridge University Press, 1988), and "The Janus Faces of Authority," in Mark Wollaeger, ed. *James Joyce's A Portrait of the Artist As a Young Man: A Casebook* (Oxford: Oxford University Press, 2003).

8. Some of these visions began as lyrical epiphanies, such as the vision of a goatish hell (*P* 137).

9. Compare Gabriel's analogous realization in "The Dead": "He had never felt like that himself towards any woman but he knew that such a feeling must be love" (*D* 223).

10. Femininity and Judaism are insidiously linked as undesirable characteristics in Otto Weininger's influential *Sex and Character* (1903) (trans. anon. 1906; reprinted New York: AMS Press, 1975).

7
joyce, language, and languages
laurent milesi

In the same way as Basil Bunting remarked about Pound's *Cantos* that, like the Alps, "you will have to go a long way round / if you want to avoid them,"[1] it would take an obstinate effort on the part of the aspiring Joyce scholar to sidestep a confrontation with the Irish writer's use of language throughout his work. Indeed, Joyce's attempts to harness the effects of language and, increasingly with time, languages, may be selected as the feature of his writing which mostly conditioned its technical transformations: from the failed poetic attempts of his youth to their redeployment into the epiphanic vignettes of *A Portrait of the Artist as a Young Man* and a full-blown poetics of sounds and rhythms as early as *Dubliners*; the rewriting of the verbose novel *Stephen Hero* into the more concise modernist *Portrait*; the readoption of an aesthetics of expansion half-way through *Ulysses* to supersede the earlier aesthetics of economy, and so on. His now time-sanctioned pronouncements on the subject, which could be paired to such key stages in his constant endeavor to reinvent literariness, especially in the later, more ambitious works, give an acute representation of the seriousness and centrality of Joyce's attritional war against the materiality and semantic oppressiveness of an inherited language of tradition:

[While writing *Ulysses*] I'd like a language which is above all languages … . I cannot express myself in English without enclosing myself in a tradition. (quoted in *JJ II* 397)

[To August Suter while composing *Work in Progress*] *Je suis au bout de l'anglais.* (quoted in *JJ II* 546)

[To another friend] I have put the language to sleep ... . (quoted in *JJ II* 546)

[To Max Eastman] When morning comes [at the end of *Finnegans Wake*] ... I'll give them back their English language. I'm not destroying it for good. (quoted in *JJ II* 546)

[In a letter to Harriet Shaw Weaver dated November 11, 1925] What the language will look like when I have finished I don't know. But having declared war I shall go on *jusqu'au bout*. (*Letters I* 237)

[Towards the end of the composition of *Work in Progress*:] I have discovered I can do anything with language I want. (quoted in *JJ II* 702)

At the critical intersection of poetics and politics, Joyce's relentless dusting up of (the English) literary language transcends both the earlier exegetical attempts by Joyce scholars to interpret the dense linguistic texture of *Finnegans Wake* for its own sake and the later assimilation of language-based critical approaches to a reactionary aesthetisization.[2]

joyce's linguistic (hi)story

Joyce's life in Dublin, where from an early age his ear was attuned to the pronunciations and turns of phrases of different idioms and sociolects, may have shaped his strong interest in the workings of language and the study of languages. History had given Ireland and its inhabitants a keen taste for witticisms (the well-famed Irish bull) coupled with a legendary garrulity epitomized by the Citizen in "Cyclops," the Hiberno-English – or, in Joyce's days, Anglo-Irish – dialect with its many local and provincial inflections which he will tap in his fiction on numerous occasions,[3] an archaic tongue (Irish Gaelic) which, in his own opinion, nationalists were artificially striving to revive, and various obscure cants like Shelta (tinkers' slang), Béarlagair Na Sáer ("vernacular of masons") or Bog Latin, which were to join the list of linguistic curios now gracing the preparatory holograph notebooks for *Work in Progress*.[4] The English language itself provided a ready enough model of historico-linguistic versatility, with the alliterative rhythms of old Anglo-Saxon verse, the Norman influence in its early shaping, its long-standing tradition of conceits, wordplay, and linguistic innovations of all kinds easily absorbed into the onomatopoetic fabric of its structure, long before school and university (where he learnt

Latin, Italian, French, a modicum of Gaelic – and Dano-Norwegian and German by himself) and his exiled life in Switzerland, Italy, Istria and France were to equip Joyce with the unprecedented polyglottism which will irradiate his fiction. In a letter to his brother Stanislaus, possibly dated March 1 1907, Joyce could thus rightly claim: "I know three languages [English, Italian, and French] very well and two others [German and Danish] passably well" (*SL* 153), to which he added Greek in a subsequent letter to Harriet Shaw Weaver: "I spoke or used to speak modern Greek not too badly ... and have spent a great deal of time with Greeks of all kinds from noblemen down to onionsellers, chiefly the latter" (*SL* 284, letter dated June 24, 1921). The composition of *Finnegans Wake* was naturally the occasion for researching new languages, often by compiling indexes of lexical entries and grammatical features from the relevant articles of the eleventh edition of the *Encyclopaedia Britannica*, but several trips or periods of forced inactivity due to his eye problems also allowed him to teach himself some Flemish (while he was in Ostend in September 1926) and, in 1928, Spanish and Russian,[5] to name but the most significant ones. Quite tellingly, Joyce wrote to Harriet Shaw Weaver on February 16 1931, about relinquishing four-fifths of his books, keeping only dictionaries and books of reference to facilitate his research (*Letters I* 299).

Joyce's linguistic bend can be "officially" traced back to the juvenile essay "The Study of Languages" (1898/99?),[6] which initially recalls that "grammar" (but also rhetoric) was one of the seven sciences for the ancients,[7] and asserts that the "study of language" is indeed a science since it pertains to a knowledge of Truth – what "etymo-logy" more specifically and etymologically means. In the less than accomplished style of this matriculation paper, the young Irish writer advocates the scholarly acquaintance with ancient languages, which allows for a better understanding of the history and etymology of one's own, and already manifests a keen awareness of the unicity of each of the world's interrelated idioms, the ensuing importance of translation and of the pivotal role of the writer as a custodian of a nation's language. Joyce's linguistic notetaking will later fully demonstrate his enduring fascination for the quaint turn of phrase in any language, and the poetics of "Wakese", which often cuts across semes and phonemes in several of the world's idioms, will jointly hold the premises ("keys") of its own intralinear translatability – what Atherton first referred to as the "trope" of translation[8] – as well as a structural resistance to translation. Of particular interest is the following observation, which already bears *in nuce* a significant range of literary-linguistic practices that will surface in *Ulysses* and will come to preside over the whole creation of *Finnegans Wake*:

> First, in the history of words there is much that indicates the history of men, and in comparing the speech of to-day with that of years ago, we have a useful illustration of the effect of external influences on the very words of a race.[9]

Joyce here adumbrates the thematic crux of "Oxen of the Sun," the chapter in the more mature second half of *Ulysses* which records his first systematic attempt at depleting and mimicking styles, idioms and idiolects in a carnival of linguistic vivisection and mimesis pitted against the fetus's growth, in which ontogeny (the development of the individual) recapitulates phylogeny (the evolution of the species).[10] More generally, and put in more linguistic terms, the indissociability of structure (synchrony) and history (diachrony) is prefigured and given a Vichian twist *avant la lettre*, as Joyce's analyses are implicitly already in tune with the Neapolitan philosopher's concept of a linguistic, more specifically poetic and imaginative, consciousness at the root of culture and mental activity, and his emphasis on the insights etymology can offer into historical processes such as colonization. Through systematic (yet arguably forced) linkages between the history and etymology of words and the evolution of nations, races and cultures, Vico's own "New Science" offered a comprehensive view of human societies across the three-plus-one Ages of his "Ideal Eternal History" to which Joyce returned time and again for inspiration in his later work, and whose mixture of philosophy, philology, history, anthropology, and social theory can already be extrapolated here. As we shall see, this outlook on the intertwinings between language, history, nation, and culture will provide the platform for the thematization of "families" of languages and characters in the xenolalic microcosm of *Finnegans Wake*.[11]

Steeped in nineteenth-century historical linguistics and the "popular philology"[12] already prevalent in his days of formation – like his fictional counterpart Stephen Dedalus, who "read Skeat's *Etymological Dictionary* by the hour" (*SH* 26) – Joyce often allowed his narrative, Bible-like, to acquire deeper symbolic resonance through a condensation of the etymological aura of a word (as in the cutting irony of "generous" and "general" which further undermines the moment of Gabriel's self-anagnorisis at the end of "The Dead"), and, especially in *Finnegans Wake*, a lexical element which strikes the reader as a foreignized coinage or nonce-word turns out, on closer scrutiny, to be an old forgotten English form palimpsestically excavated from the linguistic "midden" of Joyce's text.

But Joyce's wide-ranging interest did not stop at the diachronic studies, inventories and taxonomies of linguistic systems and families of the Humboldtian era. From the combination of the scant surviving evidence of his Paris library and, more reliably, his copious notetaking during the gestation of *Work in Progress*, we know that he kept up to date with the proliferation of contemporary trends and theories in what was becoming modern linguistics:[13] the work by Danish linguist Otto Jespersen on the nature of (the English) language and on an international idiom;[14] German linguist Fritz Mauthner's on metaphor in *Beiträge zur einer Kritik der Sprache* (1923 ed.);[15] Meillet and Cohen's timely publication of an encyclopaedic survey of *Les Langues du monde* (1924).[16] Towards the late 1920s, Joyce enthusiastically attended lectures on comparative phonetics and linguistics by the Jesuit Father Marcel Jousse, who also staged performances of the Gospel to demonstrate the gestural origin of language. In the riddle of the "Mime of Mick, Nick, and the Maggies" (*FW* II.1), the phonetic description of "heliotrope" mediates the return back to the visualization of the girls' underlying gestural pantomime of the consonants – a direct imitation of Father Jousse's own performing girls, who spoke words in Aramaic, a Semitic language, therefore based on consonantal roots – and testifies to the structural relevance of Jousse's theories and of his allegorical stagings for *Finnegans Wake*.[17] Used to strengthen the Vichian framework already in place, Jousse's rather eccentric teachings were soon bolstered up by Sir Richard Paget's two 1930 book publications: *Human Speech* and especially *Babel, or The Past, Present, and Future of Human Speech*, in which the Fellow of the Physical Society of London and of the Institute of Physics expounds a more scientific view of the gestural articulation of sound as an "etymological" basis for the constitution of oral language, and a "Gesture Theory of human speech" consonant with Jousse's.[18] Working away from his juvenile enthusiasm for the rhythmic "e-motive" epiphany and view of art as gesture in *Stephen Hero* or in his notetaking on rhythm and dance in the 1903 Paris Notebook,[19] Joyce took into uncharted territory the post-symbolist elevation of music as the paragon any art should aspire to, as he probed into language for its many rhythmical inflections, the play betweeen phonemes and graphemes, or even its dysfunctioning as entropic noise, culminating in the *Wake*'s ability to "tune in" to idioms and languages (whose clusters more often than not reflect preparatory notetaking in the Buffalo Notebooks) as one would to frequencies of radio stations in a polyphonic babel (for example, *FW* 500–1). As Stephen is made to say in "Circe": "gesture, not music not odour, would be a universal language, the gift of tongues rendering visible not the lay sense but the first entelechy, the structural rhythm."[20]

Also during these years of theoretical ferment, Joyce became acquainted with the work of C.K. Ogden – for whom he recorded the closing pages of the "Anna Livia Plurabelle" chapter at the Orthological Institute in August 1929 – in pragmatic linguistics and, with I.A. Richards, on *The Meaning of Meaning* (transformed by Joyce into "the maymeaminning of maimoomeining" [*FW* 267.03]). More specifically, Joyce took an interest in Ogden's project of a Basic English, yet another internationalist venture and artificial construction, which no doubt helped keep his own perilous Wakean enterprise on an even keel in those somber years of compositional stagnation plagued by eye and family troubles.

Faced with this vast array of sometimes conflicting linguistic theories, the critic may well wonder how Joyce related to them from a literary point of view. It is worth noting that, although Joyce's keen awareness of the literary potential of language's materiality stretches as far back as the very first lines of "The Sisters," with the uncanny signifiers of paralysis, gnomon and simony distilling their substance throughout the story, his more intensive research into etymology, structure, meaning, individual idioms as well as artificial universal constructs, corresponds with the ironic turn taken by his more mature novelistic production, from the "second half" of *Ulysses* onwards (1918–19). Joyce's no-nonsense approach to such a long-standing structural influence as Vico in the famous statement "I use his cycles as a trellis"[21] may be generalized as the key to the relativizing mixture of irony, detachment and pragmatism to which this variegated material was increasingly subjected. One salient instance of his leveling off of all such competing doctrines can be seen in *Finnegans Wake*, where, kicked off by "-mock Gramm's [Grimm's] laws," such silly-sounding names as the "pooh-pooh" and "bow-wow" theories of the origin of speech (culled from Jespersen's *Language*) provide the facile trigger for humorous dismissal as "outer nocense" (that is, utter nonsense), alongside a recall of the Vichian-Joussean tripartite scheme for the evolution of language: "In the buginning is the woid, in the muddle is the sounddance and thereinofter you're in the unbewised again, vund vulsyvolsy" (*FW* 378.29–31).[22] Joyce therefore both "used" (thematically reprocessed) and "mentioned" his material, and this explains why he gradually ventured into languages in which he was not "competent" or self-taught as "performance" was the aim: at two key points during his

16-year-long *Work in Progress* – soon after the initial structuration period (from late 1925 onwards) and during the final period of harmonization-revision (1937 onwards) – Joyce ransacked dictionaries, glossaries and encyclopedias more than ever before and in seemingly indiscriminate fashion in order to hoard raw elements from unknown foreign tongues for his babelian edifice.[23]

poetic synthesis versus political artificiality

Among the palette of the world's idioms which Joyce amassed for inclusion in what would become *Finnegans Wake*, the so-called "artificial languages" – which often appear clustered together in the final text – form a specific category. Alongside Japanese, Esperanto (the "language of hope") is one of the first languages of non-competence to have found its way into the drafts of *Work in Progress* (in October–November 1925, now in *FW* 565.25–8) – appropriately enough, in chapter III.4, heralding a new dawn – thus confirming how relevant such still fashionable ideals were to his own work "told in sounds in utter that, in signs so adds to, in universal, in polygluttural, in each auxiliary neutral idiom ... and anythongue athall" (*FW* 117.12–16). Earlier on, in one of its numerous self-reflexive, metafictional descriptions, the book had just advertised its "lingo" as "however basically English" (*FW* 116.25), and reminded us indirectly that its polyglottal web remained rooted in a recognisably English morphological substratum, a bedrock of "volupkabulary" (*FW* 419.12; vocabulary + Volapük, another artificial language) and grammar necessary to anchor and give shape to the literary experiment, "however apically Volapucky" (*FW* 116.31) the latter might be. It is as if the novel's newly found babelian impetus – the first tentative notebook entries on Babel date back to late 1923 early 1924 – could not have taken full swing without a move outside the circle of familiar Indo-European languages but also an incursion into artificial, experimental linguistic territory.

Yet although Joyce's "artificial tongue with a natural curl" (*FW* 169.15–16) seemingly shares with attempts at an international language like Volapük, Esperanto, Jespersen's own Novial (*FW* 351.15: "noviality"), Idiom Neutral (cf. *FW* 117.14) or Basic English,[24] a similar extraction of mainly West European idioms as the basis for its creation and viability, the ideological aims of "Wakese" and artificial universal languages are ultimately different, not to say diametrically opposed. Whereas Basic English and suchlike operate through forceful reduction, minimalism and simplification in order to survive as an instrumental communicational tool, Joyce's Wakean language evinced ever-increasing expansiveness and jubilatory excess as it grew in fluency and scope.[25] If artificial tongues were not notoriously known for intrinsically defeating poetic expression through such linguistic strictures, one could compare their inner workings rather with Joyce's earlier aesthetics – when he was condensing a prolix literary work into a terser modernist one – which he had relinquished and even "turned upside down" well before he embarked on the composition of *Finnegans Wake*. Besides, the "cosmopolitics" at work in Wakese is at variance with the imperialist nature of a universalist "Basic English," for instance, and Joyce's ideal desire to let every fragment of the *Wake* speak to any citizen of the world should not be misconstrued as the triumph of the communicative, let alone commercial, proselytizing function of literature but as that of the imaginative force of poetry in bridging the post-babelian linguistic gap, if only in a dream. What Joyce's dream of a universal language makes clear is that global communication is not achieved through the reduction of difference and meaning to a mythically common denominator but by multiplying and cross-fertilizing localisms. One should recall here the trajectory of Joyce's creative movement: from the particular to the universal, or, as he himself put it to Arthur Power in 1921, in a literary context which can be profitably appropriated here:

[The great writers] were national first … and it was the intensity of their own nationalism which made them international in the end … . For myself, I always write about Dublin, because if I can get to the heart of Dublin I can get to the heart of all the cities of the world. In the particular is contained the universal. (*JJ II* 505)

The radical extraction from a language, stripped of whatever is not strictly necessary to further its universalist vocation, of what would be a "purer" communicative kernel is also indirectly targeted in the *Wake*, where, if anything, "purity" is associated with the hybrid strains of the Anglo-Irish "vulgar" or vernacular rather than any linguistic streamlining.[26] More artistic than artificial, Joyce's ultimate literary brew of multilingual portmanteau words might best be called "synthetic" and aims to eschew both the excesses of the naturalization of the national and the depoeticized, "basic" aridity of universalist, auxiliary creations. In calling into question the (inter)nationalist ideology and politics at work in any linguistic identification and foregrounding the drama of representation and kinship, it ultimately forces the reader to rethink the relationship between "natural" and "artificial," national, international, and local idioms.

To assess the full literary potential of Joyce's *linguisteries*, one may consider the poetics of "father Dante," which offers the ready model of a syncretic, yet idiosyncratic idiom capable of driving a literary wedge into the heart of nationalism and parochialism alike. No doubt developing some of the lines Joyce himself had thrown to him, Samuel Beckett had already stressed the parallel between the *Wake's* international synthetic language and Dante's interregional construct exhumed after ruthlessly vivisecting municipal idioms and parlances in *De Vulgari eloquentia*.[27] If Dante's sifting of the pure Italian language or *vulgare illustre* from the multiplicity of coarse Italic dialects led him to a synthetic, utopian creation through a kind of "linguistic alchemy," its aim went beyond mere communication – language as vehicular for political and economic purposes – into the realm of literature (the later fashioning of the *Divine Comedy*) but also "religious politics": turning the universalizing of the *vulgare* into an illustrious redemption of Babel. It is quite fitting therefore that Joyce's ultimate artistic alter ego Shem the Penman, mainly in the chapter devoted to his scathing portrait by his twin brother Shaun, will concentrate the references to Dante's project of a synthetic linguistic composition and verbal echoes of *De Vulgari eloquentia*, after the significant mention of his "synthetic ink" (*FW* 185.7).[28]

Joyce's intimate knowledge of Dante enabled him to grasp the thematic continuity between the problematics of linguistic universality and Babel which went beyond the ideological strictures seen above into the sphere of mythopoetics. Scattered allusions throughout *De Vulgari eloquentia* and the *Divine Comedy* reveal Dante's discrimination between two stages in man's universal language: an original Adamic idiom, not yet tainted by the original sin; a fallen post-lapsarian, yet still unique language spoken by man after the expulsion from Paradise, before the linguistic counterpart to the sexual fall, Babel, and the post-babelian dispersion of the unique idiom into a myriad tongues estranged from one another. The narrative kernel of *Finnegans Wake* – the ceaselessly replayed linguistic-sexual misdemeanor of HCE, himself both Nimrod and the tower, dispersed into a numerous offspring – recalls such a distinction and its articulation to the confusion of tongues after God's destruction of the Tower of Babel, according to the various tasks of the assembled builders (cf. *De Vulgari eloquentia* I.vii.7).[29] In distilling the vulgar matter of Italy in search of the illustrious vernacular, ideally obtained through a process of synthetic refinement, Dante paved the way for Joyce's Wakean transposition of the drama of language since the dawn of humanity and the "original sinse" (sin + sense + since; *FW* 239.02): from untainted originality and unicity to perverted, hybrid multiplicity "since primal made alter in garden of Idem" (*FW* 263.20–1), with the attendant desire to abstract, synthesize and purify, return to the roots and/or palliate the loss of meaning through translation.

babel, pentecost and the *wake*'s language "families"

Contrary to "popular scholarly belief," Joyce did not conscript every single possible scrap of foreign idiom from the languages he came across into *Finnegans Wake* but left out a few in the notebooks (for example, Banda in VI.B.4 107 or Lapp in VI.B.41 96, 98; the latter is, however, mentioned and thematized in the novel, on account of its proximity with ALP) – nor, conversely, is the dubious list of 40-odd languages kept in the British Museum (MS 47488.180) an accurate record of the overall tally of foreign idioms in the finished text. While the element of chance to which Joyce's textual creations were increasingly intimately subjected cannot be ruled out, this discrepancy invites us to look for a possible numerological design behind the selection.

Through carefully interpreted notebook evidence, and with an awareness of the thematic role of diachronic difference for linguistic identification within Joyce's novel, the overall number of foreign idioms which at least once entered into the combinatory linguistics of *Finnegans Wake* can be made to oscillate between 70 and 80. On two occasions at least, drafted each time soon before a major stint at linguistic notetaking, Joyce's text points towards such a figure, in contexts reminiscent of post-babelian confusion (*FW* 54.5–19, especially "at sixes and seventies") or the dissipation of meaning: "So you need hardly spell me how every word will be bound over to carry three score and ten toptypsical readings throughout the book of Doublends Jined" (*FW* 20.13–16). The number 70 is endowed with a double symbolic significance in the division of languages according to Judeo-Christian exegesis. It is the traditional number of peoples said to have inhabited the earth, and the Talmud states that each commandment which issued from God's mouth in the gift of the Law on Mount Sinai was divided into 70 languages, so that each people could hear the divine revelation. But the series of the 70s (mainly 70 and 72) is also the most frequently cited number of "sibspeeches of all mankind [that] have foliated ... from the root of some funenr's stotter" (*FW* 96.30–1). While the former would suggest a Pentecostal concord as the proof of God's expiatory forgiveness, the latter can only be palliated by humankind's recourse to translation in order to restore semantic unity.

Whether from Babel to Pentecostal atonement (the gift of tongues) or to translation (from the father's punishment to the sons' rebellion), the *Wake* incessantly replays the drama of the evolution, corruption, multiplication and redemption of language as a creative *felix culpa* (happy fault) whose dynamic unit is the miscegenated portmanteau word, which aptly reconciles, as it were through a process of at-one-ment, estranged languages and the cultures they represent into a localized, transcultural synthesis, just as the whole encyclopedic universe is subsumed into the microcosmic Dublin family of the Earwickers.

From the quaint blend of popular beliefs and scientificity that presided over the nineteenth-century philological tradition, Joyce derived the highly thematizable notions of a language "character" and "family" and made them his own for fictional purposes.[30] The various intricate weavings of sigla (used in the notebooks to stylize facets of the *Wake*'s archetypal characters into interrelated universals), alphabetical letters or characters, voices, and idioms shape loose "linguistic families" in the work's "celtellenteutoslavzendlatinsoundscript" (*FW* 219.17), conjunctions and disjunctions that freely comply with or bypass and betray the stricter laws of historical kinship to fully exploit the range of thematic valencies offered by cultural, geographical, and so on, coincidences. These atomic families often intersect with the family nucleus of Wakean protagonists and provide a linguistic replica to the ever lurking presence of two and/ or three boys/girls in the work's polymorphous sin, whose quest thus doubles up as a linguistic quest. They also remind us of the Vichian equivalence between the history of families and institutions and the history of language(s), a topos that one may trace back to the alignment of idioms with the genealogies of peoples in the Bible and its exegetical traditions. Such cross-linguistic, "comparative" thematics only surface fully in the final text, in the various colorings, moods and tones an idiom may contribute to a given passage or throughout the work, but are revealed in a raw, more accessible form in the preliminary notebooks. For instance Italian, Romansch, Provençal are punningly interrelated as *romance* languages; *I*talian and *I*rish offer contrasted versions of multiple *i*dentity and political, psychoanalytical, linguistic split: irredent provinces and plurality of dialects (Italian), division of Ireland and P/K split (a philological phenomenon of inversion between the sound P and K) in Irish, and are often found in the vicinity of the schizophrenic girl *I*ssy;

Scandinavian and Slavonic languages stage one version of the linguistic drama of origins in the two central tales of *FW* II.3; Finnish, Scandinavian languages, Portuguese, Swahili partake of the fluvial vein of the work; Uralic languages are facetiously thematized as ur-aliens on account of their "exotic" agglutinative morphology; and Latin versus Greek, Russian (and other Slavonic languages) dramatize religious schism (especially in "The Mookse and the Gripes," *FW* I.6).[31] At once the giant builder and tower of Babel, Here Comes Everybody, with his versatile foreign origin as ur-alien, Scandinavian, Russian, and so on, before being assimilated as Irish, is the ultimate all-too-human anchoring point for this geolinguistics of ancient migrations and errancies, of linguistic and family genealogies set adrift on the riverrun of the *Wake*.

conclusion: avant-garde or reactionary linguistics?

As time went by and later generations of scholars as well as writers started questioning their modernist predecessors, these came under attack for the cultural elitism of their avant-garde experiments and the reactionary nature, or at best absence, of their politics. In that respect *Ulysses* and especially *Finnegans Wake* are the pinnacle of high modernism's revolutionary aesthetics and also therefore the epitome of elitist impenetrability in the eyes of their detractors. Even Pound himself, a steady admirer of Joyce's earlier writings, lost faith in his former protégé from the "Sirens" episode onwards and crudely stated, apropos of the Shaun book of the *Wake*, that "[n]othing so far as I make out, nothing short of divine vision or a new cure for the clapp [*sic*] can possibly be worth all the circumambient peripherization" (*Letters III* 145, letter from Ezra Pound dated November 15, 1926). And although Joyce's Wakean idiom, once held to be the acme of linguisticism, is being reappraised for its generous anti-nationalist geopolitics, it is worth asking in conclusion whether the fictional redeployment of Vico's somewhat antimodernist philosophy and philology is salvaged by the more progressive framework of ethics and humanity in his Dublin microcosm.

An obvious, though unsatisfactory answer would be to claim that Joyce's ironic distancing holds at bay the potential totalitarianism of the overall schemes which frame his last work, since this modernist trope par excellence – an avatar of the philosophically sanctioned romantic irony – would level off all positions as a way out of any objective engagement with the real issues of the outside world, not unlike Stephen sophistically unbinding himself from his debt to A.E. (George Russell) in "Scylla and

Charybdis." Indeed, no matter how Joyce grew out of his juvenile alter ego, self-centered aesthete and slight social misfit, his first reaction at the outbreak of World War II was to bemoan a historical conflict which would jeopardize the reception of his novel, also published in 1939. However, post-*Wake* notebooks reveal a cluster of entries related to the brave Finnish resistance against their Russian invaders in November 1939 (*JJ II* 730), in a typical double gesture which at once testified to Joyce's awareness of current world affairs as much as to his irrepressible drive to filter and reprocess them within the crucible of his art. The *Finnegans Wake* of literature became the annunciation of "the Finn again wakes" of History.

Joyce's unmistakable exposure, in several sections of *Ulysses* and *Finnegans Wake*, of the theoretical naivety of unqualified adherence to explanatory, analogical systems, etymologism as a foundation of linguistic truth, classifications into families, the lure of taxonomies, and of a belief in the organicity of language as a system, should not prevent us from inquiring into what is at stake behind the fictional glorification of a "root language" (*FW* 242.17) in this neo-Dantean universe. Here again, not only the reactionary drift of Pound himself, the increasingly gaping gulf between his high modernist aesthetics of the "make it new" and his totalitarian leanings, but also the specter of a Heidegger raking the ashes of the Germanic language in search of ancient forgotten roots through which to replenish semantically the national vocabulary, are alarmingly suggestive tokens of the divorce that can exist between "radical" philology and a not-so-radical politics when a modern(ist) project is reared on a nostalgic act of linguistic and cultural excavation. However, if Joyce's narrative often evinces an impulse towards the radical, its aim is far from the consolidation of an existing national idiom in a "gathering" gesture but rather to allow all languages, "major" or "minor," to interact and coexist within the versatile entity of the Wakean portmanteau. "*The abnihilisation of the etym*" (*FW* 353.22), which follows Buckley's long-delayed decision to shoot the imperialist Russian general (*FW* II.3), famously concentrates the dynamic tension between the annihilation of the atom or, in linguistics, the etymon as well as creation *ab nihilo* from both, and, rather than a Heideggerian *Destruktion* of metaphysics here applied to languages, offers the solace of a "poetic metaphysics" – to borrow a category from Vico himself – more akin to the positive work of deconstruction: no annihilation without a concomitant (re)creation *ab nihilo* as the ultimate synthetic gesture.

Perhaps the crux of the problem lies in the "movement" of the linguistic experiment, either from local to general (inductive, a posteriori) or the other way round (deductive, a priori), from the root to the derivation (thus following the drift of history) or back to the source (reverse or even regressive history). The *Wake* itself stages the issue in yet another self-dramatization: "(in the Nichtian glossery which purveys aprioric roots for aposteriorious tongues this is nat language in any sinse of the world ...)" (*FW* 83.10–12). Although the passage playfully reworks Jespersen's quoting of Dr. Sweet in *An International Language* – "the ideal way of constructing an *a posteriori* language would be to make the root words monosyllabic, and build up the whole vocabulary on them, without any borrowed words; and to make the grammar *a priori* in spirit as well as form – independent of European grammar and parts of speech, no concord, no verbs etc."[32] – the dismissive tone seems to leave little doubt as to Joyce's no-nonsense opinion on the arbitrariness of such a denaturalized construction: this is not language in any sense of the word/sinse of the world (that is, since the beginning of the world). But in the fictional, redemptive universe of the *Wake* and its generous laws of *coincidentia oppositorum*, it can also become a night (Dano-Norwegian *nat*) language in which *nichts* (nothing) and non-sense is turned into an affirmation of obscurity (night). Against radical etymologism (Heidegger), monolingual simplification or "debabelization" (Basic English)[33] but also selective synthetic universalism (Esperanto), and any steadfastly observed theory at all, Joyce's pliable Wakese promotes the commonality of roots through the intercultural "pollylogue" (*FW* 470.09) of its portmanteau idiom. Unlike his fellow modernists, Joyce managed to develop a viable mixture of poetics and politics in language, half-way between aesthetics (yet devoid of the empty aestheticism of Stephen Dedalus) and ethics.

notes

1. Basil Bunting, "On the Fly-Leaf of Pound's Cantos," *Collected Poems*, 2nd edn. (Oxford: Oxford University Press, 1978), p. 110.
2. The intense deciphering of those foreign elements Joyce worked into *Finnegans Wake*, which resulted in the lexical glossaries of *A Wake Newslitter* and book-length studies throughout the 1960s and 1970s, marks the "structuralist" acme of language-oriented approaches to the Joyce corpus, which the later post-structuralist vogue extended to more theoretical questions of language and textuality. Since the early 1990s, however, the focus has shifted from textuality to politics (gender, race, nation), aesthetics to ethics, while reductively relegating critical concerns with language to the isolated realm of the former, and only recently has the centrality of language, more broad-

mindedly placed at the crucial junction of several decades of theories and problematics, been rehabilitated in the scholarly community's ongoing attempt to assess the literary-critical impact of Joyce's *oeuvre*. For such a refocusing, see *James Joyce and the Difference of Language*, ed. Laurent Milesi (Cambridge: Cambridge University Press, 2003), especially "Introduction: Language(s) with a Difference," pp. 1–27.

3. For example, the Four Gospellers or "Mamalujo" in *Finnegans Wake* are associated with the four provinces of Ireland and their regional accents. See *SL* 297; letter to Harriet Shaw Weaver dated October 12, 1923.

4. See Danis Rose's edition of *The Index Manuscript. Finnegans Wake Holograph Workbook VI.B.46* (Colchester: A Wake Newslitter Press, 1978), pp. 144–58 ("Secret Speech").

5. The latter thanks to Paul Léon's brother-in-law – cf. the Anglo-Russian entry in Notebook VI.B.23 145: "Ponisovsky/spasibo thanks".

6. James Joyce, "The Study of Languages," in *CW* 25–30.

7. Ibid., p. 25. The trivium (grammar, rhetoric, and logic) and the quadrivium (arithmetic, geometry, astronomy, and music) will form the thematic backbone of the "Lessons" chapter in *Finnegans Wake* (hereafter *FW* with page and line identification), II.2 (cf. *FW* 306.12–13: "triv and quad"). See Laurent Milesi, "Toward a Female Grammar of Sexuality: The De/Recomposition of 'Storiella as she is syung'," *Modern Fiction Studies* 35:3 (Autumn 1989), pp. 569–85. The full title of the "Storiella" echoes that of a hilariously error-ridden Portuguese–English phrasebook authored by one Pedro Carolino: *English as She is Spoke*, indirectly mentioned in a letter to Valéry Larbaud dated July 30, 1929 (*SL* 345). Note also Joyce's celebrated retort to a critic: "some of the means I use are trivial – and some are quadrivial." Quoted in Eugene Jolas, "My Friend James Joyce," *James Joyce: Two Decades of Criticism*, ed. Seon Givens (New York: Vanguard, 1948), p. 24.

8. James S. Atherton, *The Books at the Wake: A Study of Literary Allusions in James Joyce's "Finnegans Wake"* (Mamaroneck, N.Y.: Paul P. Appel, 1974 [1959]), p. 203. For idiomaticity, see Jean-Michel Rabaté's chapter on "Idiolects, Idiolex" in his *James Joyce, Authorized Reader* (Baltimore and London: Johns Hopkins University Press, 1991), pp. 116–31.

9. Joyce, "The Study of Languages," p. 28.

10. Cf. Joyce's famous letter to Frank Budgen, dated March 20, 1920; *SL*, pp. 251–2.

11. The most serviceable studies on the relation between Vico's Ideal History and Joyce's language can be found in *Vico and Joyce*, ed. Donald Phillip Verene (Albany: State University of New York Press, 1987) and John Bishop's chapter on "Vico's 'Night of Darkness': *The New Science* and *Finnegans Wake*" in his *Joyce's Book of the Dark: Finnegans Wake* (Madison: University of Wisconsin Press, 1986), pp. 174–215.

12. See Hugh Kenner, "Joyce and the 19th Century Linguistics Explosion," *Atti del Third International James Joyce Symposium, Trieste 14–18 giugno 1971* (Trieste: Università degli Studi, 1974), pp. 45–60. More recently, Gregory M. Downing has undertaken a thorough reappraisal of the impact of popular philologists like Richard Chenevix Trench and Max Müller on Joyce's literary mindset: see "Richard Chenevix Trench and Joyce's Historical Study of Words," *Joyce*

Studies Annual 9, ed. Thomas F. Staley (Austin: University of Texas Press, 1998), pp. 37–68, and "Diverting Philology: Language and its Effects in Popularised Philology and Joyce's Work," *James Joyce: The Study of Languages*, ed. Dirk Van Hulle (Brussels: Peter Lang, 2002), pp. 121–66.

13. For a comparative approach, see Benoit Tadié, "'Cypherjugglers going the highroads': Joyce and Contemporary Linguistic Theories," in Milesi, *James Joyce and the Difference of Language*, pp. 43–57.

14. In particular *Language: Its Nature, Development and Origin* (1922) and *An International Language* (1928). See Roland McHugh, "Jespersen's *Language* in Notebooks VI.B.2 and VI.C.2," *A Finnegans Wake Circular* 2 (1987), pp. 61–71, and Erika Rosiers and Wim Van Mierlo, "Neutral Auxiliaries and Universal Idioms: Otto Jespersen in *Work in Progress*," in Van Hulle, *James Joyce: The Study of Languages*, pp. 55–70.

15. See Linda Ben-Zvi, "Mauthner's *Critique of Language*: A Forgotten Book at the *Wake*," *Comparative Literature Studies* 19:2 (1982), pp. 143–63, and Dirk Van Hulle, "Beckett-Mauthner-Zimmer-Joyce," *Joyce Studies Annual* 10, ed. Thomas F. Staley (Austin: University of Texas Press, 1999), pp. 143–83 and "'Out of Metaphor': Mauthner, Richards and the Development of Wakese," in Van Hulle, *James Joyce: The Study of Languages*, pp. 91–118.

16. See Vincent Deane, "*Les Langues du Monde* in VI.B.45," *A Finnegans Wake Circular* 3:4 (1988), pp. 61–74.

17. See Mary and Padraic Colum's often quoted account in *Our Friend James Joyce* (London: Victor Gollancz, 1959), pp. 130–1. Joyce's keen interest is reflected in a series of small clusters entered in VI.A 1 and in three contemporary notebooks: VI.B.18 262; VI.B.21 16–17, 20, 22, 24, 26; and VI.B.23 103. Jousse's most relevant works are "Le style oral rythmique et mnémotechnique chez les verbo-moteurs," *Archives de Philosophie* II:IV (1924), pp. 435–675, and *Mimisme humain et psychologie de la lecture* (Paris: Geuthner, 1935), although no direct notetaking has been recorded as yet. Critical studies of the impact of the Joussean system on the writing of *Finnegans Wake* include Lorraine Weir, "The Choreography of Gesture: Marcel Jousse and *Finnegans Wake*," *James Joyce Quarterly* 14:3 (Spring 1977), pp. 313–25, and Laurent Milesi, "Vico ... Jousse. Joyce.. Langue," *James Joyce 1: "Scribble" 1: Genèse des textes*, ed. Claude Jacquet (Paris: Lettres Modernes, 1988), pp. 143–62 (especially pp. 159–60).

18. For Paget, see Laurent Milesi, "Supplementing Babel: Paget in VI.B.32," in Van Hulle, *James Joyce: The Study of Languages*, pp. 77–91. Another prominent study, in Joyce's Paris library, on mental and linguistic rhythms which play such a subtly poetic role in *Finnegans Wake*, was Henri Goujon's *L'Expression du rythme mental dans la mélodie et la parole* (1907).

19. See *The Workshop of Dedalus: James Joyce and the Raw Materials for "A Portrait of the Artist as a Young Man*," ed. Robert Scholes and Richard M. Kain (Evanston, Ill.: Northwestern University Press, 1965).

20. *Ulysses: A Critical and Synoptic Edition*, ed. Hans Walter Gabler, with Wolfhard Steppe and Claus Melchior, 3 Vols. (New York: Garland, 1986), episode 15: 105–7.

21. Colum, *Our Friend James Joyce*, p. 122; also quoted in *JJ II* 554. Joyce's interest in Vico dates back to soon after 1911 at least, as is attested by the Cornell notes; see Andrew Treip, "The Cornell Notes on Vico," *James Joyce 3. "Scribble"*

3: Joyce et L'Italie, ed. Claude Jacquet and Jean-Michel Rabaté (Paris: Lettres Modernes, 1994), pp. 217–20.

22. See Carole Brown, "*FW* 378: Laughing at the Linguists," *A Wake Newslitter*, Occasional Paper No. 2 (1983), pp. 4–5.

23. See Laurent Milesi, "L'idiome babélien de *Finnegans Wake*: Recherches thématiques dans une perspective génétique," *Genèse de Babel: Joyce et la création*, ed. Claude Jacquet (Paris: CNRS, 1985), pp. 155–215 (especially pp. 166–71). It must be noted that Joyce composed more and more fluently in the newly devised portmanteau idiom as he advanced in the writing process and acquired some form of linguistic proficiency in this literary nonce-idiom.

24. A minor one is Webster Edgerly's *The Adam-man Tongue: The Universal Language of the Human Race* (1903), possibly alluded to in *FW* 267.18. See Clive Hart, "Adam-man," *A Finnegans Wake Circular* 2:3 (Spring 1987), pp. 41–5.

25. Cf. Ogden's own comment accompanying his joint effort at a translation from the "Anna Livia Plurabelle" passage: "the simplest and most complex languages of man are placed side by side"; quoted in Jean-Michel Rabaté, *James Joyce and the Politics of Egoism* (Cambridge: Cambridge University Press, 2001), p. 149. For a discussion of the convergence between Joyce's and Ogden's projects, including Joyce's collaboration to Ogden's rendering of Joyce's recorded extract into Basic English, see Susan Shaw Sailer, "Universalizing Languages: *Finnegans Wake* Meets Basic English," *James Joyce Quarterly* 36:4 (Summer 1999), pp. 853–68.

26. See Laurent Milesi, "The Perversions of 'Aerse' and the Anglo-Irish Middle Voice in *Finnegans Wake*," *Joyce Studies Annual* 4, ed. Thomas F. Staley (Austin: University of Texas Press, 1993), pp. 98–118. Interestingly, Joyce owned a tract from the *Society for Pure English* in his Paris library.

27. Samuel Beckett, "Dante … Bruno. Vico.. Joyce," *Our Exagmination Round His Factification for Incamination of Work in Progress*, ed. Samuel Beckett *et al.* (London: Faber, 1972 ed. [1929]), pp. 3–22. Cf. Joyce's well-known statement: "May father Dante forgive me but I took his technique of deformation as my point of departure in trying to achieve a harmony that vanquishes our intelligence as music does." Quoted in Mary T. Reynolds, *Joyce and Dante: The Shaping Imagination* (Princeton: Princeton University Press, 1981), pp. 203–4.

28. The Dantean echoes within Joyce's poetics of the synthetic have been analysed by Lucia Boldrini in *Joyce, Dante, and the Poetics of Literary Relations: Language and Meaning in "Finnegans Wake"* (Cambridge: Cambridge University Press, 2001), especially pp. 117–21 and *passim*, and in "*Ex sterco Dantis*: Dante's Post-Babelian Linguistics in the *Wake*," in Milesi, *James Joyce and the Difference of Language*, pp. 180–94. See also Laurent Milesi, "Italian Studies in Musical Grammar," in Jacquet and Rabaté *James Joyce 3. "Scribble" 3: Joyce et L'Italie*, pp. 105–53, about the inscription of Joyce's Dantean poetics within the context of his use of the musical vein of Italian in *Finnegans Wake*.

29. This schematic explanation for the division of languages finds a possible illustration in the episode of the Norwegian captain (*FW* II.3); the preterite form "said" modulates into "sagd" (Dano-Norwegian *sagde*), "sayd" and "sazd" when used by the Norwegian captain, the ship's husband, or Kersse the Dublin tailor respectively.

30. See for example Dennis Baron's *Grammar and Gender* (New Haven: Yale University Press, 1986) for a critical account of the nationalist ideologies behind the sexualization of languages throughout history, which also permeates the fictional thematics of the *Wake*.

31. Note John Bishop's conclusive remark to a lengthy footnote in his *Joyce's Book of the Dark*, pp. 460–1, n29 about Dutch, Swahili and Armenian, which is still relevant some 15 years after: "A great deal more work needs to be done ... on the 'states' that the languages of foreign states evoke in the *Wake*."

32. Otto Jespersen, *An International Language* (London: Allen, 1928), p. 41. First identified in Rose's edition of VI.B.46 (p. 136), and further discussed in Rosiers and Van Mierlo, "Neutral Auxiliaries and Universal Idioms," p. 67.

33. Cf. Ogden's *Debabelization with a Survey of Contemporary Opinions on the Problem of a Universal Language* (1931), which derides existing universal languages and proposes English as the likeliest contender to stem the tide of the "existing Babel." See Rabaté, *James Joyce and the Politics of Egoism*, for whom, however, "Ogden's project of the 'universalization of English' is not very different from Joyce's poetic experimentation with several languages" (pp. 149–50).

8
joyce and science

sam slote

What would an inquiry into Joyce's use of the scientific disciplines in *Ulysses* and *Finnegans Wake* entail? Is it a question of how Joyce appropriates (or misappropriates) scientific theories into his text? Or is it simply a question of how Joyce represents natural phenomena, that is, those things and data that fall under the purview of the natural sciences? Does Joyce's naturalism accord with a scientific understanding of the world that would have been current in his lifetime? Clearly in many cases it does, but there are some exceptions that point to a richer field of inquiry, a question of how Joyce deploys the languages (for these are plural) of the scientific disciplines (for these are also plural).[1] How does Joyce use and manipulate the language games of science and how are the languages of science inflected in *Ulysses* and *Finnegans Wake*?

At the close of the "Ithaca" episode of *Ulysses*, when Bloom is lying in bed next to his wife, facing her feet, their position and movement is described with a seemingly clinical precision:

In what state of rest or motion?

At rest relatively to themselves and to each other. In motion being each and both carried westward, forward and rereward respectively, by the proper perpetual motion of the earth through everchanging tracks of neverchanging space. (*U* 17.2306–10)

This passage apparently zooms away from the Blooms' bedroom on Eccles Street to comprehend the more cosmic perspective of the earth's motion in space. There is, however, a slight problem with such an objective reading, namely the fact that the earth rotates from west to east and thus one would expect Bloom and Molly to be carried eastward. There is reason to believe that "westward" was deliberate. In a letter to Frank Budgen from February 1921 Joyce wrote that in "Ithaca" "Bloom and Stephen thereby become heavenly bodies, wanderers like the stars at which they gaze" (*Letters I*: 160). If at the end of the episode Bloom and Molly are like stars, then, from the perspective of an observer on the surface of the earth, they would appear to be moving westward. Rather than describe an objective phenomenon (Bloom and Molly lying in a bed carried by the earth's movement in space), this passage effects a symbolic metamorphosis of Bloom and Molly into astral beings. Even if such a reading of a symbolic, astronomical transference is rejected, one still has to admit that much of the scientific data in *Ulysses* is, well, not scientific (at least not if one credits the scientific disciplines with some kind of basic accuracy). Perhaps overstating the case, Richard Madtes goes so far as to describe the scientific precision of "Ithaca" as being "about as authentic as the electrical pyrotechnics in a Hollywood production of *Frankenstein*."[2]

The representation of natural phenomena in *Ulysses* is not always inaccurate. The great efforts Joyce took in maintaining a large (but not complete) degree of verisimilitude in the representation of 1904 Dublin also extend towards the treatment of the natural world. For example, even the closing scene in "Nestor" is perfectly naturalistic: "On his wise shoulders through the checkerwork of leaves the sun flung spangles, dancing coins" (*U* 2.448–9). Considering the anti-Semitic Deasy's fondness for filthy lucre, this final, somewhat surreal image is typically read as being purely symbolic. Neil R. Davison writes that Stephen's "perception reveals again the materialist hatred behind Deasy's flimsy religiosity."[3] However, the image of the dancing coins is an entirely legitimate physical phenomenon in addition to any symbolic force that it carries.[4] Marcel Minnaert describes such an occurrence as being occasioned by the fact that the sun is not a single point of light but a disk. Any gap between the leaves of a tree allows for the projection of a sharp image of that disk and multiple gaps allow for multiple, displaced, and dappled sunlight spots, hence the dancing coins.[5] This passage is thus an inversion of what happens in the westward passage in "Ithaca"; here the language is symbolic while also being perfectly empirical.

Much of the science in *Ulysses* is filtered through Bloom, who is an enthusiast of popular science, as is illustrated by some of the books he owns (catalogued in "Ithaca" at 17.1362–407) as well as by his attempts at ratiocination throughout the day. To a large extent, his scientific curiosity is an extension of his empathy; as Ezra Pound remarked, "Il s'intéresse à tout, veut expliquer tout pour impressionner tout le monde [He is interested in everything and wants to explain everything in order to impress everyone]."[6] Furthermore, in being (or attempting to be) a "cultured allroundman" (*U* 10.581), Bloom exhibits many of the traits of the Victorian *bourgeois gentilhomme*. Before the Free State was established, scientific pursuits were very much tied to "the cultural aspirations of the ascendancy party in Ireland."[7] Indeed, Bloom's interest in astronomy provides a parallel to C.S. Parnell, who was, according to Katherine O'Shea, also an enthusiast of Robert Ball's writings.[8] However, Bloom's interest in scientific matters far exceeds his mastery of the subject. For example, he cannot accurately describe the phenomenon of black absorbing light and heat: "Black conducts, reflects, (refracts is it?), the heat" (*U* 4.79–80).[9] Bloom is not entirely fluent in the languages of science.

Although he is derided for this at Barney Kiernan's pub in "Cyclops," Bloom has eminent faith in the explanatory powers of science (*U* 12.464–5). As he states in "Circe," "Every phenomenon has a natural cause" (*U* 15.2795–6), that is, every phenomenon is always potentially explicable. These points are further articulated in the Thomas Huxley inset in "Oxen of the Sun" (*U* 14.1223–309): "Science, it cannot be too often repeated, deals with tangible phenomena. The man of science like the man in the street has to face hardheaded facts that cannot be blinked and explain them as best he can. There may be, it is true, some questions which science cannot answer – at present" (*U* 14.1226–30). Unsurprisingly, these propositions are quite congruent with Huxley, who defined the presuppositions of the physical sciences as "the objective existence of a material world ... [and] that nothing happens without a cause."[10] Huxley projects a futural dimension to the sciences: what cannot be explained presently will be resolvable in time.[11] This assumes that "science" is a unified body of knowledge that continually perfects itself so that ultimately, ideally, everything can be explained and understood. Such attitudes persist today in the ongoing attempts to articulate a Grand Unified Theory that would unite relativity and quantum mechanics and thus explain the universe on both a macro and a micro scale. But even such an ambitious "theory of everything" could not explain *every* thing. Indeed, the Grand Unified Theory only concerns physics and would not contribute to biology or geology. As Feyerabend and others have variously argued, no theory can be utterly comprehensive.[12] Hardheaded facts can be, and indeed are, blinked.

In a very generalized sense, the scientific disciplines are just as *discursive* as, say, the mystics Stephen contemplates on Sandymount strand. Indeed, by closing his eyes for a short time, Stephen is even engaged in trying to verify Aristotle's claims about perception through a kind of basic experimentation (*U* 3.10–28). The coda Stephen takes as a designation of his intellectual exercise, "Signatures of all things I am here to read" (*U* 3.02) – from the title of a seventeenth-century mystical tract by Jacob Boehme – could also easily apply to Bloom's various observations of Dublin and environs. Both Bloom and Stephen are hermeneuts, albeit with distinct temperaments, the scientific and the artistic (see *U* 17.559–60).[13] They each try to explain the world around them by using their different intellectual resources, which are partial and incomplete. They frequently misread the signatures of all things.

The superabundance of detail meted out in "Ithaca" obviously provides a good testing-ground for Joyce's treatment of the sciences in *Ulysses* (according to the Gilbert schema, the art of this episode is science). In "Ithaca" there is no one single scientific mode (of discourse and of enframing the world), but many, and these are merged with other discursive forms (economics, history, genealogy, bibliography, and so forth). Katie Wales precisely describes the Ithacan mode as "a result of register-mixing … a confluence or congregation of hundreds of prototypical technical terms from specific and prototypical scientific disciplines."[14] As well as discursive miscegenations, we also see in "Ithaca" the "fusion" of Bloom's and Stephen's perspectives, the artistic and the scientific: the languages of science meet those of art. Joyce's "theory of everything," at least for this episode, also includes ignorance, imperfection, superstition, and the psuedo-sciences.[15] The register-mixing Wales describes effectively serves as the vehicle for a kind of omni-science in *Ulysses*. As Derrida remarked in his counter-defense against John Searle, in a line that is quite apposite to *Ulysses* and *Finnegans Wake*: "as though literature, theater, deceit, infidelity, hypocrisy, infelicity, parasitism, and the simulation of real life were not part of real life!"[16]

John Barrow concludes his study on the possibility of a "theory of everything" by stating that "The prospective properties of things cannot be trammelled up within any logical Theory of Everything. No non-poetic account of reality can be complete."[17] From this perspective one could say that literary style (or rather styles) provides a not-insignificant component to Joyce's omni-science. The narrative voice in "Ithaca" exhibits a tendency to add poetic flourishes to supposedly dispassionate descriptions; for example, in the description of the different spectral classes of stars: "The various colours significant of various degrees of vitality (white, yellow, crimson, vermilion, cinnabar)" (*U* 17.1104–5).

The chemical properties of stars differ according to their age and energy output and these can be measured through spectroscopic observation. The scheme employed now, the Draper classification, was first devised in the 1890s at Harvard. Stars are classified according to the distribution of dark absorption lines in their spectra which indicate the presence of various elements. Stars of a certain class tend to be of a similar hue but a star's color is a secondary attribute of its spectral class.[18] Therefore colors do not directly indicate the "various degrees of vitality" of the stars, as this passage implies, although it is presumably easier to rhapsodize about colors than about spectral lines. However, the colors given here roughly approximate the colors and order indicated in the Draper system, although they are much less prosaic than the ones found in an astronomy textbook: "Stars of classes O and B (as most of the stars in Orion) are bluish-white; those of class A, white (Sirius, Vega); of class G, yellow (Capella, the sun); of class K, orange (Arcturus); of class M, red (Antares). Those of classes R and S are also red; and of class N, very red."[19] The more literary terms given in "Ithaca" are also somewhat less precise as descriptions, especially since cinnabar is equivalent to vermilion. The apparent precision of classification here is belied by a colorful language.

After a very clinical and seemingly detached account of Bloom and Stephen leaving Bloom's house to enter the back garden, the spectacle of the sky is described, in one of *Ulysses'* most memorable lines, as "The heaventree of stars hung with humid nightblue fruit" (*U* 17.1039). This highly metaphoric description of starlight organically growing from the dark sky is a concatenation of the final image in Dante's *Inferno*: "tanto ch'i' vidi de le cose belle / che porta 'l ciel, per un pertugio tondo. / E quindi uscimmo a riveder le stelle [so far that through a round opening I saw some of the beautiful things that Heaven bears; and thence we issued forth to see again the stars]."[20] This poetic image intrudes upon an apparently objective account of Bloom and Stephen's situation, as if the narrative voice borrowed from Stephen's artistic temperament a means of describing the heavens in this instance. In general, the Ithacan voice that describes astronomical matters follows, albeit not exclusively, from Bloom's predilections.

With what meditations did Bloom accompany his demonstration to his companion of various constellations?

Meditations of evolution increasingly vaster: of the moon invisible in incipient lunation, approaching perigee: of the infinite lattiginous scintillating uncondensed milky way, discernible by daylight by an observer placed at the lower end of a cylindrical vertical shaft 5000 ft deep sunk from the surface towards the centre of the earth: … of our system plunging towards the constellation of Hercules: of the parallax or parallactic drift of socalled fixed stars, in reality evermoving wanderers from immeasurably remote eons to infinitely remote futures in comparison with which the years, threescore and ten, of allotted human life formed a parenthesis of infinitesimal brevity. (*U* 17.1040–56)

Aristotle claimed in the *De Generatione Animalium* that stars can be seen in the daytime if an observer were placed at the bottom of a deep shaft or well (780b 21), although this has since been disproven, first by Robert Hooke in "An Attempt to Prove the Motion of the Earth from Observations" (1674). Besides the pseudo-scientific aspects to this claim, Mary Reynolds notes a further parallel to Dante here since Dante's Inferno is a vast inverted cone with its apex at the center of the earth.[21] Bloom's scientific meditation is thus also not immune to Dante. In any case, the "heaventree of stars" would be invisible from either the bottom of a well or the bottom of a hell.

This passage obliquely relates Bloom's attempts at impressing Stephen with "the story of the heavens," which is the title of a book by Sir Robert Ball that Bloom owns (*U* 17.1373).[22] While the account rendered in "Ithaca" appears in the form of a list, the peculiar style is not without its quirks. For example, the phrase "the infinite lattiginous scintillating uncondensed milky way" contains Joyce's neologism "lattiginous" (from the Italian *lattiginoso*, "milky"; and thus tautological when used in collocation with the English word "milky"). Furthermore, the narrative voice apparently cannot resist adding the word "uncondensed" to "milky way," thereby making a joke on condensed (that is, inferior) milk. Such whimsy undermines the accuracy of the line since the milky way "is composed almost entirely of faint stars, invisible to the naked eye … . In the richer regions the stars are very densely crowded."[23] The phrase "condensed milky way" would thus be more accurate, albeit less funny.

Bloom's final meditation in this passage proposes that an awareness of the vastness of the universe places "allotted human life" into a perspective of "infinitesimal brevity."[24] In other words, the universe as revealed by astronomy is not so much awe-inspiring as it is alienating. Indeed, Bloom's final thought on astronomy in *Ulysses* is his reflection on "the apathy of the stars" (*U* 17.2226).[25] Bloom's reflections then turn away from the vastness of the heavens towards the ever smaller, in a form of Zeno's paradox, "its universe of divisible component bodies of which each was again divisible in divisions of redivisible component bodies, dividends and divisors ever diminishing without actual division till, if the progress were carried far enough, nought nowhere was never reached" (*U* 17.1065–9). In other words, Bloom perceives futility at both macro and micro levels. Ultimately, the universe is away and apart and incommensurable with human endeavor.

Yet Bloom's realization of futility derives from a decent, if imperfect, scientific knowledge. In fact, the account of stellar parallax and the proper motion of stars is essentially accurate from an astronomical perspective. Bloom's thoughts on the vastness of the universe begin with the notion that our sun, along with our solar system, is not stationary but is moving, somewhat rapidly, in the general direction of the constellation of Hercules. This was first established by Sir William Herschel in the late eighteenth century.[26] Next, Bloom considers the phenomenon of stellar parallax, which is discussed in Ball's book and acts as both a motif and a narratological device in *Ulysses*. Stellar parallax is the measurement of the stellar distance using the parallax effect, which is the apparent alteration of an object's position against a fixed background caused by a change in the observer's position. For measuring stellar distance, a very large baseline, that is the separation between the two observation points, is needed and so the distance between the earth and the sun is used by observing a star at (typically) six-month intervals. Since the distance to the sun is known, the distance to the star is calculated by measuring its apparent deviation against the more distant stars that appear motionless. Since the sun is itself not stationary, its own motion, over time, contributes a further parallax effect, which is known as parallactic drift.[27] The apparent motion of a star through parallax and parallactic drift is thus an effect of both the earth's movement around the sun and the sun's own movement. But beyond the phenomenon of parallax, the so-called fixed stars themselves have their own proper motion, as was first discovered by Edmund Halley in 1718.[28] So the stars are also planets (*planétes*, Greek for "wanderer"), like our sun, like our earth, and like Bloom.

The measurement of stellar parallax was a burgeoning field in late nineteenth- early twentieth-century astronomy. In his book *"Ulysses,"* Hugh Kenner provides an admirable explication of how this phenomenon is deployed in *Ulysses*, but he misses a few salient examples. We first hear of parallax in the "Lestrygonians" episode when Bloom is walking past the Ballast Office:

Mr Bloom moved forward, raising his troubled eyes. Think no more about that. After one. Timeball on the ballastoffice is down. Dunsink time. Fascinating little book that is of sir Robert Ball's. Parallax. I never exactly understood. There's a priest could ask him. Par it's Greek: parallel, parallax. Met him pike hoses she called it till I told her about the transmigration. O rocks! (*U* 8.108–13)

This passage is rich with multiple layers of parallax. Even on the level of style we can register a kind of parallax as the perspective shifts from a third-person past tense, impersonal narrator in the first sentence to the first-person present tense of Bloom's interior monologue (Joyce called this technique the book's "initial style" [*Letters I* 129]).[29] Our sense of Bloom throughout the book derives from triangulating these shifting narrational perspectives. Here, Bloom notices that the time-ball atop the Ballast Office is down; this is lowered every day at 1 p.m. Greenwich Mean Time, which is 25 minutes ahead of Dublin time. The Ballast Office also has a clock that shows Dublin time as measured at Dunsink Observatory (hence "Dunsink time"), although from Bloom's perspective on the street he cannot see the clock.[30] Bloom's inference about the time on the basis of the lowered ball is thus not necessarily correct since it falls at 12.35 Dublin time (although he is actually correct since it is after 1.00 when he passes the Ballast Office). He realizes this discrepancy later when he passes by the shop Yeates and Son, which sells optical instruments: "Now that I come to think of it that ball falls at Greenwich time. It's the clock is worked by an electric wire from Dunsink" (*U* 8.571–2). As Kenner points out, Bloom's perspective on the time-ball (as either measuring Dublin time or Greenwich time) changes relative to his own position and is thus an example of parallax. Furthermore, the Ballast Office itself offers a parallactic presentation of time: one time (Dublin) for pedestrians via the clock and another (Greenwich) for mariners via the time-ball.[31]

So, the initial sighting of the lowered time-ball is enmeshed within parallactic readings and such parallaxes multiply within that passage. The time-ball reminds Bloom of Sir Robert Ball, both by the contiguity of the word "ball" but also by the fact that Sir Ball was Astronomer Royal of Ireland from 1874 to 1892 and thus had worked at Dunsink. Two different perspectives inform his appearance within Bloom's mind. While at Dunsink, Sir Ball worked extensively on the measurement of stellar parallax.[32] Here Bloom, ever the avid bourgeois reader of popular science, calls *The Story of the Heavens* a "Fascinating little book," even as he admits he does not fully understand it. In "Wandering Rocks,"

M'Coy remembers the day Bloom purchased this book although he is more impressed with the bargain Bloom enjoyed than with its actual contents (U 10.525–8). He then describes a winter's night when he was with Bloom who was recounting the "story of the heavens" to Molly and Chris Callinan. Although Bloom was in fine form, impressing his audience with his knowledge, Molly pointed to a star he could not identify. Callinan then made a joke at Bloom's expense: "*that's only what you might call a pinprick*" (U 10.573).

Bloom's less-than-stellar knowledge is further exposed in "Circe" when Chris Callinan appears in order to ask a preternaturally sophisticated question: "What is the parallax of the subsolar ecliptic of Aldebaran?" (U 15.1656). In effect, Callinan is asking what is the parallax of the star Aldebaran, that is, what is its apparent deviation in the sky when it is observed from opposite points of the earth's orbit around the sun. The qualifying phrase "subsolar ecliptic" is somewhat unusual. The ecliptic is the apparent orbit of the sun around the earth as observed from the earth, thus it is by definition subsolar.[33] Since the measurement of stellar distance is made through ascertaining the parallax of a star caused by the earth's orbit around the sun, the phrase "subsolar ecliptic" is redundant if not meaningless.[34]

The answer Bloom gives is incorrect on at least two levels: "Pleased to hear from you, Chris. K.11" (U 15.1658). In 1910 the parallax of Aldebaran was measured by the German astronomers Kapteyn and Weersma at 0.073 seconds of arc, which indicates a distance of approximately 44 light years.[35] Bloom's answer, K.11, appears instead to indicate the star's spectral class using the Draper classification scheme. In this scheme, the major class is indicated with a letter and its sub-class through a number. K.11 is an impossible designation since the sub-class only ranges from 1–10. Aldebaran is a class K.5 star, making it somewhat cooler than our own sun.[36] So, Bloom's answer is at least partially correct, albeit to a different question ("What is the spectral class of Aldebaran?"). As noted above, in "Ithaca" Bloom at least does know enough about astronomy to differentiate between spectral classes and parallax, although, characteristically, his ability to answer a technically specific question is far from certain. The answer he gives Callinan in fact derives from the advertisement he espied in "Lestrygonians" shortly before he saw the lowered time-ball at the Ballast Office: "*Kino's / 11/- / Trousers*" (U 8.90–2). Bloom's improvised answer to Callinan's question concerning parallax is thus itself parallactic, the result of a different perspective, one tinged by his ignorance.

So Bloom's initial musings on parallax and Sir Robert Ball in "Lestrygonians" are subtended by other perspectives, such as thrift, imposture, and his own imperfect pretensions to mastering a knowledge of the universe. Indeed, the reason why Joyce would not make a good astronomer is that rather than build a picture of one object from two distinct parallactic perspectives, he offers continually differentiating perspectives of different and ever-changing objects. In the "Lestrygonians" passage quoted above we see Bloom's perspective, at that time, of the time-ball, which is later corrected, and also one perspective on Sir Ball's book which is subsequently elaborated with different, partially incommensurable details, and so on. Parallax in *Ulysses* is nothing if not kaleidoscopic (as opposed to telescopic). In a broad context, the phenomenon of parallax suggests that each perspective yields a partial approximation of some ultimate truth beyond. In the strictly astronomical domain this "truth" (specifically stellar distance) can be inferred from the differential juxtaposition of these individual, partial perspectives (that is, by precisely measuring the difference in a star's position as recorded on different dates). In *Ulysses*, this possibility of strict measurement is not necessarily possible, no single unequivocal truth can be teased out of the differential perspectives that are offered. The differences can be neither reconciled nor sublated. No single perspective is the truth, the whole truth, and nothing but the truth: the truth is still somehow more than just some synthesis of those perspectives. (Furthermore, this particular thesis concerning the unattainability of a single truth amidst a proliferation of parallactic perspectives is itself partial and incomplete.)

In this way, the difference between Bloom's and Stephen's temperaments (scientific and artistic) is parallactically enmeshed within *Ulysses*. Both languages are spoken, both perspectives are granted, but even as they synthesize, they remain distinct and apart. In certain passages of *Ulysses*, Joyce *evokes* a scientific language (through a manipulation of certain key terms and facts), that is, he evokes different modes of representing or enframing the world (or universe) as nothing but a sub-set of that universe. In *Ulysses*, the world – the scientific representations of the world – is *not* all that is the case, there are other perspectives. With *Finnegans Wake*, Joyce expands the play of multiple perspectives that he had deployed in *Ulysses* to bring about a simultaneity of multiple perspectives, a "collideorscape" (*FW* 143.28) in "all flores of speech" (*FW* 143.04).

There is no doubt that while writing *Finnegans Wake* Joyce was well aware of the revolutionary developments then transpiring within the physical sciences, indeed it would have been almost impossible to ignore them. There are numerous clear references to contemporary scientific breakthroughs in the *Wake*, such as Edwin Hubble's discovery in 1929 of "a more and more almightily expanding universe" (*FW* 263.25–6).[37] One could even make analogies between Joyce's linguistic experimentation and the new physics: that Joyce deals with "*The abnihilisation of the etym*" (*FW* 353.22), the splitting up and recombination of basic (linguistic or physical) particles.[38] Joyce may have seen this analogy between splitting the atom and his own lexical "warping process" (*FW* 497.03), but this does not make it a fundamental process for his language games.[39] In a very provocative book, Donald Theall makes such a claim:

> Joyce extended the logic of flows and discontinuities and the paradoxes or serial order to language itself. He posits a quantum-like theory of the interplay of the synchronic-diachronic axes and the paradigmatic-syntactic axes of language, so that lexical units can be both identified as seeming to be particulate and as appearing to form the wave-like movement of a flow.[40]

While an analogy can exist between the dual nature of light (as both a wave and particle simultaneously) and the Wakean "parapolylogic" (*FW* 474.05), Theall's analysis perhaps overextends itself in that he assumes that the stylistic effects of the *Wake* were directly influenced, at least in part, by developments in physics.[41] Furthermore, the use of scientific and technological analogies to explicate Wakean language is not necessarily more compelling than a musicological or tropological frame.[42] Likewise, Wakean indeterminacy has little to do with Heisenberg's uncertainty principle.[43] Ultimately, such analogies would be less-than-helpful in that they would overstress superficial commonalities, such as complexity and counter-intuitiveness,[44] whilst minimizing key differences.

Much has been made of Joyce's "unification" of space and time in the *Wake*'s two fables, "The Mookse and the Gripes" and "The Ondt and the Gracehoper," and Einstein's theory of relativity. Indeed, the fables were drafted in response to Wyndham Lewis's accusation that the chronocentric Joyce "is very strictly of the school of Bergson-Einstein, Stein-Proust."[45] Elsewhere Lewis admits that while he is no fan of relativity, the subject of his critique is not Einstein per se, but rather his (pernicious and as yet undigested) effect or influence upon artists.[46] He attacks the metaphysics, and not the physics, of relativity. This is an important distinction since while there are references to Einstein in the fables (such as the opening of "The Mookse and the Gripes": "Eins within a space ... " [FW 152.18]), the Joycean treatment of space and time is not really articulated in Einsteinian terms.

For Einstein, space and time are united because the theory of relativity posits that there can be no absolute measurements of spatio-temporal location, only relative ones (space and time are united because they are equivalently relative).[47] For example, if a yardstick approached the speed of light, its length would tend towards infinity to an observer at rest, but if this observer were traveling in tandem with this most velocious yardstick, its length would be the same as if it were motionless. The theory of relativity has two key predicates: the invariance of the speed of light and the universal applicability of the laws of physics.[48] Without these, it's just relativity, not Einsteinian relativity. The Joycean conjunction of space and time makes little or no reference to these prerequisites. Instead, Joyce proposes a non-Hegelian synthesis of space and time. Both space and time "exist" interdependently without negating or sublating the other. For example, the Gracehoper's wastefulness is described as "Erething above ground, as his Book of Breathings bed him, so as everwhy, sham or shunner, zeemliangly to kick time" (FW 415.22–4). The word "zeemliangly" combines "seemingly" with the Russian zemlya, "land," and the Chinese liang, which commonly means two, but can also, depending upon the tone, mean light. As a verb liang means to measure and the phrase zemme liang means either "how to measure?" or "how bright it is!" (both senses are common). Also, zemme liang li means either "how do you measure reason?" or "how do you measure miles?" – both senses being pertinent to Joyce's response to Lewis's privileging of space.[49] The Gracehoper seemingly, spatially wastes time, perhaps by the action of measuring, but this seeming waste is (at least) doubled through the polyvalence of the Chinese word liang. If one accepts the sense of liang as light then one could see a reference to relativity here, but Joyce's liang-light is variable whereas Einstein's is constant. The synthesis between time and space is rendered through an excess of meaning in this one word "zeemliangly."

Einstein offers synthesis (through the invariance of the speed of light), whereas Joyce proffers coincidence through linguistic equivalence and differentiation. The "coincidence" between Joycean and Einsteinian space-time does not necessarily betoken similar theoretical underpinnings as Andrzej Duszenko has claimed.[50] While there are partial allusions, relativity is much less a factor in Finnegans Wake than parallax was in Ulysses. Unlike parallax in Ulysses, relativity does not appear to have exerted any structural influence on the *Wake*. This is not to say that there was no concerted attempt to incorporate Einstein into the *Wake*, but merely to point out that Wakean reference is somewhat diffuse. As Adaline Glasheen notes, "Any 'stone' ... in any language can name Einstein in FW."[51] Einstein is just one more dab of "local colour" (*FW* 109.23) that Joyce adds to the *Wake*.[52]

In writing the *Wake*, Joyce spent much time using his notebooks to compile phrases and expressions and facts from a wide variety of sources in order to fill his work with the local color and trivia of the world.[53] Any kind of verisimilitude evinced in the *Wake* results less from traditional modes of representation (as was the case with *Ulysses*), but rather from the recurrence of potentially recognizable linguistic titbits, such as, for example, the river names strewn throughout the ALP chapter and the city names deployed in "Haveth Childers Everywhere."[54] In other words, the representation of the world is figured linguistically and not phenomeno-logically. From this more delimited perspective of the "local colour" of science, one can see many references to science in *Finnegans Wake*.

If Einsteinian relativity does not play a large role in the *Wake*, Notebook VI.B.1 shows a previously unremarked conceptual correlation between relativity and the *Wake*. In May 1924 Joyce described III.1–2 as "written in the form of a *via crucis* of 14 stations but in reality it is only a barrel rolling down the river Liffey" (*Letters I* 214). VI.B.1 contains notes preparatory to this conception, including a cluster that derive from some as yet unidentified text on Einstein: "See history retrograde if / leave E[arth] faster than lux / ∴ cause produces effect" (VI.B.1: 165). A consequence of relativity is that from the perspective of an observer traveling faster than light, time outside his spaceship would appear to be moving in reverse (but, fortunately enough, within his craft things would appear normal).[55] Obviously this paradox meshes with Shaun's backward motion, but the final text bears no trace of this potential Einsteinian parallel and, indeed, ultimately III.1–2 does not rigorously follow Joyce's original plan of a reverse *via crucis*.[56]

Scientific allusions sometimes appear in the *Wake* as an indicator of pretension, usually Shaun's. For example, shortly after invoking the "where's hairs theories of Winestain" (*FW* 149.28), Shaun declares: "Talis is a word often abused by many passims (I am working on a quantum theory about it for it is really most tantumising state of affairs)" (*FW* 149.34–6). This particular quantum theory has less to do, at least directly, with quantum physics as it does with the liberal dispersal throughout this passage of Latin adjectives and adverbs such as *talis* ("such like"), *passim* ("here and there"), *quantum* ("as much as"), and *tantum* ("so much").

Joyce certainly used scientific terms and concepts in the *Wake* with a fair degree of precision. The following passage shows Joyce's familiarity with how television works: "(his dectroscophonious photosensition under suprasonic light control may be logged for by our none too distant futures as soon astone values can be turned out from Chromophilomos, Limited at a millicentime the microamp)" (*FW* 123.12–15). Fundamental to the function of television is the conversion of light into electrical signals. This was not possible until Einstein explained that light consists of quanta which release electrons upon striking the atoms in a metal.[57] While this passage does not describe the operation of a television in terms of quantum physics, it does use seemingly precise and technical terms: scophony is a "proprietary name for a television system employing an optical and mechanical method of picture scanning" first developed in 1932 by G.W. Walton (*OED* 2) and *dektos* is Greek for "receiver." Therefore, it is feasible, if bizarrely verbose and not entirely accurate, to describe the operation of a television as "dectroscophonious photosensition under suprasonic light control."[58] However, while this passage evinces some technical awareness, there is little here beyond linguistic manipulation (for example, the use of Greek recalls the *tele* in the hybrid "television"). In *Ulysses* the application of scientific discourses was riddled with errors of fact, whereas in the *Wake* matters of terminology predominate.

In the *Wake* scientific terms and concepts are used in multiple manners concurrently. For example, the sentence "Vetus may by occluded behind the mou in Veto but Nova will be nearing as their radient among the Nereids" (*FW* 267.22–4) might describe the occultation[59] of Venus by the moon and the simultaneous appearance of a nova shining in the constellation Eridanus (formerly known as Nereus), but it could also be a metaphorical expansion of the saying "out with the old (*vetus*), in with the new (*nova*)." There is also a sexual component to this passage enabled by the word "mou," which is French slang for the human body and also means a man of weak character as well as the contrary ironic sense of someone strong and vigorous. These senses allow for this passage also to be read as describing a (possibly old and impotent) man lying on top of, and thus occluding, an old woman, as during coitus, even as a new young buck makes merry with some charming nymphs (nereids, the daughters of Nereus). In this way, this simple passage is linguistically parallactic: multiple perspectives are allowed, which complement and subvert each other.

The primary way in which Joyce referred to the latest developments in physics in *Finnegans Wake* may have less to do with the specific content of these new theories and more to do with their estranging effects upon conventional wisdom. Put simply, relativity and quantum theory turned the world of physics upside down. While writing *Finnegans Wake*, Joyce was not so much a contemporary of the unveiling of a "new truth," but rather an observer of the overturning of the *ancien régime* of Newton et al. Thomas Kuhn describes this kind of epistemic discombobulation as revolutionary: "It is rather as if the professional community has been suddenly transported to another planet where familiar objects are seen in a different light and are joined by unfamiliar ones as well."[60] Such estranging occurs somewhat violently in the geometry lesson in II.2: "Thanks eversore much, Pointcarried! I can't say if it's the weight you strike me to the quick or the red mass I was looking at but at the present momentum, potential as I am, I'm seeing rayingbogeys rings round me" (*FW* 304.5–9). As Roland McHugh states, Henri Poincaré wrote an account of non-Euclidean geometries which wound up influencing Einstein and so here the point carried (Poincaré) is a "sock in the jaw for Newton."[61] However, this whack is described in terms entirely derived from Newtonian mechanics (mass, momentum, and potential energy). But, as Kuhn comments, during revolutionary episodes some terms and concepts from the paradigm that is being overthrown persist as scientists awkwardly adjust to a new *Gestalt*. The language of the new paradigm retains traces of the old. Therefore, during periods of revolution, a scientific discipline exhibits a fracturing of its language.[62] Here Poincaré's point carried is likewise fractured.

Another example of revolutionary science falls in III.3:

> Now, are you derevatov of yourself in any way? The true tree I mean? Let's hear what science has to say, pundit-the-next-best-king. Splanck!
> – Upfellbowm. (*FW* 505.26–9)

The true tree is apparently Newton's apple tree (*Apfelbaum*, German, "apple tree"), but through Joyce's pun, the apple falls up. Therefore Newton's world is upside-down. The reference to Planck, which makes for a nice onomatopoeic fall ("Splanck!"), introduces an inaccuracy: Einstein's theory of relativity was much more challenging to Newtonian concepts of gravity than Planck and quantum theory.[63] Like the "uncondensed milky way" in "Ithaca," the urge to pun trumps scientific accuracy. In any case, what we have is not the triumphant paradigm of modern physics, but rather the *multiplicity* of paradigms, a simultaneous multiplicity of enmeshed perspectives (where, for example, Einstein can cohabit with Theosophy). Joyce's "theory of everything" is not a syncretic one.

Joyce deploys the languages of science in the *Wake* not in any manner remotely resembling an attempt to represent or enframe the universe in a codifiable and verifiable manner (in other words not scientifically), but rather to draw a kind of mythopoesis out of the jargons of science as well as through other languages (such as myth, history, Checheno-Lesghien, and Dutch). In short, in *Finnegans Wake*, Joyce does to science what he does to other languages. He once remarked to the Danish writer Tom Kristensen: "I don't believe in any science ... , but my imagination grows when I read Vico as it doesn't when I read Freud or Jung" (*JJ II* 693). Simply put, Joyce uses the languages of science *imaginatively* in *Finnegans Wake*. His "theory of everything" is not just scientific, it is poetic and, ultimately, fluxile. Science becomes imaginative, and perhaps wondrous, despite or rather because of its epistemic frangibility. "Sifted science will do your arts good" (*FW* 440.19–20). Joyce's omni-science is fractured and fracturing. In this way, his use of the sciences is homologous to Feyerabend's pluralistic conclusion in *Against Method*, "No area is unified and perfect, few areas are repulsive and completely without merit."[64] The only principle that unifies in *Finnegans Wake* is Joyce's non-syncretic stylistic eclecticism. Joyce himself said in reference to his puns, "Yes. Some of the means I use are trivial – and some are quadrivial."[65] In other words, science is but one perspective (or rather one set of perspectives) among many. It is one "IMAGINABLE ITINERARY THROUGH THE PARTICULAR UNIVERSAL" (*FW* 260.R3–8) and not "Sare Isaac's universal of specious aristmystic" (*FW* 293.27–8).

notes

1. Paul Feyerabend very convincingly concludes *Against Method* with an analysis of the plurality of the sciences. "The word 'science' may be a single word – but there is no single entity that corresponds to that word. ... the assumption of a single coherent world-view that underlies all science is either a metaphysical hypothesis trying to anticipate a future unity, or a pedagogical fake." Paul Feyerabend, *Against Method*, third edition (London: Verso, 1993), pp. 238, 245.
2. Richard E. Madtes, *The Ithaca Chapter of Joyce's "Ulysses"* (Ann Arbor: UMI Research Press, 1983), p. 68.
3. Neil R. Davison, *James Joyce, "Ulysses," and the Construction of Jewish Identity* (Cambridge: Cambridge University Press, 1996), p. 197.

4. I am grateful to Will Lautzenheiser for pointing this out to me.

5. M.G.J. Minnaert, *Light and Color in the Outdoors* (New York: Springer-Verlag, 1993), pp. 1–2.

6. Ezra Pound, "James Joyce et Pécuchet," *Pound/Joyce*, ed. Forrest Read (New York: New Directions, 1970), pp. 200–11, 206.

7. J.A. Bennett, *Church, State and Astronomy in Ireland: Two Hundred Years of Armagh Observatory* (Belfast: Queens University, 1990), p. 215; quoted in Andrew Gibson, "'An Aberration of the Light of Reason': Science and Cultural Politics in 'Ithaca'," in *Joyce's "Ithaca,"* ed. Andrew Gibson (Amsterdam: Rodopi, 1996), pp. 133–74, 134. Gibson's essay provides an account of the cultural capital associated with the sciences in Ireland.

8. "During his leisure hours at Eltham Mr. Parnell took up the study of astronomy with that vigour that always characterized him when he was interested in a subject. He had picked out from my bookshelf a book of stars – one of Sir Robert Ball's I believe." Katherine O'Shea, *Charles Stewart Parnell – His Love Story and Political Life* (London: Cassell, 1914), p. 183; quoted in Daniel O'Connell, "Bloom and the Royal Astronomer," *James Joyce Quarterly* 5:4 (Summer 1968), pp. 299–302, 302.

9. The narrative voice in "Ithaca" redresses this confusion about the properties of heat in the account of the "phenomenon of ebullition" (*U* 17.257) occurring in Bloom's kettle as he boils some water.

10. Thomas H. Huxley, "The Progress of Science," *Collected Essays*, Vol. 1 (London: Macmillan, 1893), pp. 42–129, 60–1.

11. Ibid., pp. 63–6.

12. See Feyerabend, *Against Method*, p. 245.

13. Whilst Stephen represents the "artistic" temperament, he has had some formal training in the sciences with his Jesuit education and his aborted study of *"physiques, chimiques et naturelles"* (*U* 3.176–7) in Paris as part of the medical school curriculum.

14. Katie Wales, "'Stagnant Pools in the Waning Moon': The Poetry of the 'Ithaca' Episode of *Ulysses*," *A Collideorscape of Joyce*, eds. Ruth Frehner and Ursula Zeller (Dublin: Lilliput, 1998), pp. 156–70, 157.

15. For example, Joyce compiled thorough notes on palmistry for "Circe" (*U* 15.3677–716; see also Phillip F. Herring, *Joyce's "Ulysses" Notesheets in the British Museum* (Charlottesville: University Press of Virginia, 1972), pp. 43–7.

16. Jacques Derrida, "Limited Inc a b c … ," in *Limited Inc*, trans. Samuel Weber (Evanston: Northwestern University Press, 1988), pp. 29–110, 90.

17. John D. Barrow, *Theories of Everything* (Oxford: Clarendon Press, 1991), p. 210.

18. Henry Norris Russell, Raymond Smith Dugan, and John Quincy Stewart, *Astronomy II: Astrophysics and Stellar Astronomy* (Boston: Ginn and Company, 1927), pp. 601–11.

19. Ibid., p. 610. Joyce recorded the basic sequence "white yellow red" in one of the "Ithaca" notesheets (Herring, *Joyce's "Ulysses" Notebooks*, p. 428).

20. Dante Alighieri, *Inferno*, trans. Charles S. Singleton (Princeton: Princeton University Press, 1970), 34.137–9. See also Mary T. Reynolds, *Joyce and Dante* (Princeton: Princeton University Press, 1981), p. 125.

21. Reynolds, *Joyce and Dante*, p. 298.

22. Ball begins his book with the sentiment of providing a sense of the grandeur augured by astronomy: "We have indeed a wondrous story to narrate; and could we tell it adequately, it would prove of boundless interest and of exquisite beauty. It leads to the contemplation of grand phenomena in nature and great achievements of human genius". Robert Stawell Ball, *The Story of the Heavens* (London: Cassell, 1893), p. 1. See also Wales, "'Stagnant Pools in the Waning Moon'", pp. 165–6.

23. Russell et al., *Astronomy II*, pp. 804–5.

24. The proposition of a human lifetime being 70 years is not so much a scientifically established fact as it is a religious superstition, based on Psalms 90.10.

25. This scene is parodied in the *Wake*: "I publicked in my bestback garen for the laetification of siderodromites and to the irony of the stars" (*FW* 160.20–2). This line might also echo Wyndham Lewis's play *The Enemy of the Stars*, which he claimed had influenced *Ulysses*. Wyndham Lewis, *Time and Western Man*, ed. Paul Edwards (Santa Rosa: Black Sparrow Press, 1993), p. 107.

26. Ball, *The Story of the Heavens*, p. 429. Joyce recorded this basic information, as well as facts about other irregularities in the earth's motion, in a comparatively lengthy entry on a "Circe" notesheet: "Earth (moves) round Sun, oblique fall towards Hercules, diurnal rotation, oscillation of inclination, annual variation of elipse [*sic*], displacement of polar axis, (Vega was polar star 16000 y^{rs} & will be in 12000 years)" (Herring, *Joyce's "Ulysses" Notebooks*, p. 288).

27. W.M. Smart, *Text-Book on Spherical Astronomy* (Cambridge: Cambridge University Press, 1931), pp. 217–23, 260–2.

28. Ibid., p. 249.

29. See Michael Groden, *"Ulysses" in Progress* (Princeton: Princeton University Press, 1977), pp. 15–17.

30. Hugh Kenner, *"Ulysses,"* revised edition (Baltimore: Johns Hopkins University Press, 1987), p. 73 n.

31. Ibid, p. 75.

32. "He was very enthusiastic about this parallax work for some years before trouble with his eyesight obliged him to give it up ... he hurried up to Dublin and out to Dunsink whenever a very promising, clear evening occurred, in order not to spoil the parallax observations by leaving a gap of two months." Robert Stawell Ball, *Reminiscences and Letters of Sir Robert Ball* (Boston: Little, Brown and Company, 1915), p. 106.

33. Smart, *Text-Book on Spherical Astronomy*, pp. 37–9.

34. If the word "elliptic" were used in place of "ecliptic," the qualifying phrase would make some sense since, through the parallax effect, over the course of one year a star appears to trace out in the sky an ellipse whose diameter is inversely proportional to its distance (Ball uses the word "elliptic" in reference to stellar parallax [Ball, *The Story of the Heavens*, p. 412 *et passim*]). The word "subsolar" would still be a superfluous addition to the question, but the question would at least no longer be nonsensical.

35. Kelvin McKready, *A Beginner's Star-Book* (New York: G.P. Putnam, 1912), p. 139. Contemporary measurements place its parallax at 0.048 seconds of arc, meaning a distance of about 68 light years. Dorrit Hoffleit and Carlos Jaschek,

Bright Star Catalogue, fourth edition (New Haven: Yale University Observatory, 1982).

36. Russell et al. *Astronomy II*, p. 637.
37. *The Expanding Universe* is also the title of a book by Sir Arthur Eddington (Cambridge: Cambridge University Press, 1933).
38. In the *Wake*, this abnihilization is effected "*by the grisning of the grosning of the grinder of the grunder of the first lord of Hurtreford*" (FW 353.22–3), that is, Lord Rutherford (the "etyms" of his name rearranged to get the word "hurt"). Rutherford produced the first atomic transmutations, thereby effectively disintegrating or splitting the atom, in 1919 at Cambridge. Roger H. Stuewer, "Niels Bohr and Nuclear Physics," *Niels Bohr: A Centenary Volume*, eds. A.P. French and P.J. Kennedy (Cambridge: Harvard University Press, 1985), pp. 197–220, 197–201. Joyce must have been familiar enough with the implications of Rutherford's work because the "*abnihilisation of the etym ... explodotonates through Parsuralia with an ivanmorinthorrorumble fragoromboassity*" (FW 353.22–5). This is not a case of prescience since the OED records several citations of the destructive power of an atomic bomb from before 1932, the earliest being H.G. Wells's *The World Set Free* (New York: Dutton, 1914), p. 96.
39. On page 80 of Notebook VI.B.47 (November–December 1938), Joyce made a crude drawing of an atom; on the opposite page, across from the word "atom" Joyce wrote the word "word" in the same ink.
40. Donald F. Theall, *James Joyce's Techno-Poetics* (Toronto: University of Toronto Press, 1997), p. 158. Similar arguments are also advanced in S.B. Purdy, "Let's Hear What Science Has to Say: *Finnegans Wake* and the Gnosis of Science," *The Seventh of Joyce*, ed. Bernard Benstock (Bloomington: Indiana University Press, 1982), pp. 207–18. See also Clive Hart, *Structure and Motif in "Finnegans Wake"* (London: Faber and Faber, 1962), pp. 65–6.
41. According to Theall, Joyce's project "is the most radical crafting of a techno-poetics for rendering forth (i.e. making manifest or epiphanizing) the emerging techno-culture" (Theall, *James Joyce's Techno-Poetics*, p. xviii).
42. Such analogies to explicate and comprehend the *Wake* can be made with any number of *au courant* disciplines, such as Thomas Rice's attempt to describe the *Wake* in terms of chaos theory. Thomas Jackson Rice, *Joyce, Chaos, and Complexity* (Urbana: University of Illinois Press, 1997), pp. 112–40. Ultimately, while informative and perceptive, Rice's proposal is essentially Hart's theory of motif translated into a different register.
43. Heisenberg's principle states that, regardless of the accuracy of one's instrumentation, the position and velocity of an electron cannot be measured simultaneously with a degree of accuracy. Although it has been applied to other phenomena, "it is a total misrepresentation of Heisenberg's uncertainty principle to suppose that it applies to macroscopic observers making macroscopic measurements" (Douglas R. Hofstadter, "Heisenberg's Uncertainty Principle and the Many-Worlds Interpretation of Quantum Mechanics," *Metamagical Themas* (New York: Basic Books, 1985), pp. 455–77, 464.
44. A recent example of such an analogy came about during the "controversy" surrounding two brothers' – Grichka and Igor Bogdanov – successful attempt to publish articles of dubious merit and legitimacy in prestigious science

journals. Commenting on this affair and on the difficulty of evaluating highly-specialized work for publication, the physicist Lee Smolin remarked that the Bogdanovs' "paper is essentially impossible to read, like *Finnegans Wake.*" Dennis Overbye, "Are They a) Geniuses or b) Jokers?," *New York Times*, November 9, 2002.

45. Lewis, *Time and Western Man*, p. 87.

46. Ibid., pp. 137–9.

47. General relativity, unlike special relativity, does not require "a uniformly accelerated coordinate system" (Albert Einstein, "The Theory of Relativity," *Out of My Later Years* [New York: Philosophical Library, 1950], pp. 41–8, 45); therefore it does not posit a uniformly determinate space and time.

48. Jonathan Powers, *Philosophy and the New Physics* (London: Metheun, 1982), pp. 93–100.

49. I am grateful to Jed and Hsiu-Chuang Deppman for clarification on the Chinese. Joyce's use of Chinese here is part of the polemic he uses to respond to Lewis's criticisms. In June 1921, he wrote to Harriet Shaw Weaver: "Mr. Lewis was very agreeable, in spite of my deplorable ignorance of his art, even offering to instruct me in the art of the Chinese of which I know as much as the man in the moon" (*Letters I* 167).

50. Andrzej Duszenko, "The Relativity Theory in *Finnegans Wake*," *James Joyce Quarterly* 32:1 (Fall 1994), pp. 61–70; see also Andrzej Duszenko, "The Joyce of Science," unpublished Ph.D. dissertation, Southern Illinois University at Carbondale, 1989.

51. Adaline Glasheen, *Third Census of "Finnegans Wake"* (Berkeley: University of California Press, 1977), p. 83.

52. "Local colour" was the epithet Lewis used to chastise Joyce's bricolage. Lewis, *Time and Western Man*, p. 81.

53. These notebooks are currently being published with transcriptions and source identifications: *The "Finnegans Wake" Notebooks at Buffalo*, eds. Vincent Deane, Daniel Ferrer, and Geert Lernout (Turnhout: Brepols, 2001–).

54. These issues are discussed in detail in Jean-Michel Rabaté, "Back to Beria! Genetic Joyce and Eco's 'Ideal Readers,'" *Probes: Genetic Studies in Joyce*, eds. David Hayman and Sam Slote (Amsterdam: Rodopi, 1995), pp. 65–83.

55. Nigel Calder, *Einstein's Universe* (London: BBC, 1979), pp. 101–10.

56. See Geert Lernout, "Introduction," *The "Finnegans Wake" Notebooks at Buffalo, VI.B.1*, eds. Vincent Deane, Daniel Ferrer, Geert Lernout (Turnhout: Brepols, 2003). For an account of the development of the *via crucis*, see Wim Van Mierlo, "Shaun the Post: Chapters III.1–2," *A Genetic Guide to "Finnegans Wake"* (Madison: University of Wisconsin Press, forthcoming).

57. See Martin J. Klein, "Einstein and the Development of Quantum Physics," *Einstein: A Centenary Volume*, ed. A.P. French (London: Heinemann, 1979), pp. 133–51, 134–40.

58. Television is also described in the *Wake* at FW 150.32–5 and throughout II.3; see also Theall, *James Joyce's Techno-Poetics*, pp. 66–7.

59. Occultation is the technical term for when a brighter heavenly body, such as the moon, covers, whether wholly or partially, a dimmer body, such as a star or planet. The word eclipse is used when a dimmer body covers a brighter one, such as the moon covering the sun (*OED*).

60. Thomas S. Kuhn, *The Structure of Scientific Revolutions* (Chicago: University of Chicago Press, 1962), p. 111.

61. Roland McHugh, *The Sigla of "Finnegans Wake"* (Austin: University of Texas Press, 1976). Joyce took some notes on non-Euclidean geometry for *Ulysses* (Herring, *Joyce's "Ulysses" Notebooks*, p. 474).

62. Kuhn, *Structure of Scientific Revolutions*, pp. 129–30. The early development of quantum theory is a good illustration of this principle as scientists adapted, adjusted, and in some cases discarded principles from classical physics. See Edward MacKinnin, "Bohr on the Foundations of Quantum Theory," *Niels Bohr: A Centenary Volume*, eds. A.P. French and P.J. Kennedy (Cambridge: Harvard University Press, 1985), pp. 101–20, 106–10.

63. While relativity certainly displaced Newtonian mechanics, these were not completely invalidated or overthrown, at least not once the revolutionary furor had subsided. As Einstein said of the theory of gravitation postulated by relativity: "These equations yield Newton's equations of gravitational mechanics as an approximate law" (Einstein, "Theory of Relativity," p. 47).

64. Feyerabend, *Against Method*, p. 249.

65. Frank Budgen, "James Joyce," in *James Joyce and the Making of "Ulysses" and Other Writings* (Oxford: Oxford University Press, 1989), pp. 343–8, 347.

9
dialogical and intertextual joyce

r. brandon kershner

... he foreknew that as he passed the sloblands of Fairview he would think of the cloistral silverveined prose of Newman, that as he walked along the North Strand road, glancing idly at the windows of the provision shops, he would recall the dark humour of Guido Cavalcanti and smile, that as he went by Baird's stonecutting works in Talbot Place the spirit of Ibsen would blow through him like a keen wind, a spirit of wayward boyish beauty, and that passing a grimy marinedealer's shop beyond the Liffey he would repeat the song by Ben Jonson which begins:

> *I was not wearier where I lay.* (P 176)

It is arguable that, more than the work of any other major author, Joyce's writings are permeated by quotations, citations, literary allusions, and other traces of texts or voices. This becomes increasingly the case as he matures; while even the stories of *Dubliners* have significant traces of linguistic otherness, in *Ulysses* and *Finnegans Wake* there is less writing that we would confidently assign to Joyce and more that we identify as quoted, borrowed, cited, or somehow appropriated from "elsewhere." In *Finnegans Wake*, in fact, we are confronted by a language critics sometimes call "Wakese" that is wholly original, in that a passage of it sounds like nothing else in literature, while at the same time a great proportion of it is made up of warped quotation of literary passages, riddles, proverbs, clichés, and other sorts of "public language." Two of the most frequently cited works on Joyce are in fact Don Gifford's *Joyce Annotated: Notes for "Dubliners" and "A Portrait"* (1982), and his *"Ulysses" Annotated* (1988), and almost as often cited is Roland McHugh's *Annotations to "Finnegans Wake"* (1980), a fact which would tend to suggest that the man's work is a virtually continuous palimpsest of the writing of others; and yet Joyce is also widely regarded as an author of stunning, ground-breaking originality, and perhaps the most accomplished prose stylist of the century.

Clearly the problem of quotation, citation, and allusion in Joyce in particular highlights several paradoxes or aporias in our paradigms of writing. So it is that this discussion will necessarily proceed more by means of a series of questions and problems than by assertions. Joyce rather famously claimed to have invented nothing, and said he would be "quite content to go down to posterity as a scissors-and-paste man" (*Letters I* 297). Obviously he was exaggerating here for effect, and yet he was also emphasizing the degree to which his writings were a verbal collage of "given" or "found" elements – spoken and written quotations both from the immediate life-world of Dublin and from the broadest imaginable version of cultural history. As an apprentice writer, Joyce in his youth hung around stairways recording exactly the conversations he heard, and many of his "epiphanies" record banal, meaningless, or odd bits of conversation, complete with the frequent lacunae, ellipses, and pleonasms: the conversation between the young men and the girl running the stall at the end of "Araby" is such a passage. Indeed, Joyce has sometimes been attacked by the less literary sort of Dubliner, who feels that the frequency with which he simply recorded the pub talk of his time somehow demonstrates that he is a literary fraud.

In analyzing the role of quotation and allusion in Joyce we find ourselves struggling with the problem of what constitutes an allusion, at the furthest extreme. There is a spectrum running from direct, immediately recognizable verbal quotation – Stephen's use of the phrase "Agenbite of Inwit," for example, specifically and exclusively invoking Dan Michel of Northgate's 1340 translation of a French medieval manual of virtues – all the way to a possible broad thematic echo of a previous writer or thinker: the question whether Stephen's meditations on selfhood and reality on the beach in "Proteus" might echo similar meditations in, say, Descartes, even if there are no explicit verbal echoes of any of the relevant Cartesian texts. With an author such as Joyce who is generally inclined to the use of quotation and allusion, it soon becomes apparent that any given passage of his writing will resonate with a series of more or less explicit verbal and thematic echoes from previous writers and thinkers. The question, of course, is when these echoes are useful or important to identify and in what way they are significant.

To some extent, Joyce has guided his interpreters. It was he who signaled the importance of Giordano Bruno and Giambattista Vico to his thought in *Finnegans Wake* and ensured that Samuel Beckett brought that out in his contribution to *Our Exagmination* ... (Beckett et al. 1929). Indeed, this fact was responsible for a certain rebirth of interest in the iconoclastic philosophers (see, for example, Silverstein 1965, Church 1976, Verene 1987, Rabaté 1989). But Joyce delighted in directing interested parties to obscure or minor sources, such as when he suggested Edouard Dujardin as the originator of *monologue intérieur*, and this may have been in part an effort to discourage attention to sources whose influence he was less comfortable acknowledging, such as Yeats, or perhaps Wilde. No doubt he would have been ready to cite Bret Harte as a "source" for "The Dead" (Friedrich), given that neither he nor anyone else would doubt that "The Dead" is a far better story than anything Bret Harte ever produced. Joyce had no reluctance to acknowledge his classical models, though; in fact, it was oddly crucial for him to do so.

It could be said that the first serious extended critical work on Joyce, Stuart Gilbert's *James Joyce's "Ulysses"* (1930), is in great part an explanation of the ways in which the book alludes continuously to Homer's *Odyssey*. Simply because he discusses the book's episodes by their Homeric names as he runs through the novel, Gilbert implies that this allusion constitutes a fundamental level of meaning, and this assumption has been maintained in much later criticism. Of course Gilbert, who was something of a spiritualist, probably saw the motif of "metempsychosis" in more literal terms than Joyce may have intended, and this would lend the Homeric allusions an added significance. In addition, Joyce himself laid great stress on the Homeric allusions while working with Gilbert, who seldom questioned whether Joyce was always being either sincere or accurate. But Gilbert's stress on the Homeric parallels was also motivated by the broader literary-cultural situation. During the early years of Joyce criticism, from the 1930s up through the 1960s, at least part of the trajectory of literary criticism was determined by the New Critical campaign to lend legitimacy to high modernist works by exploring their references to (and thus, it is implied, continuity with) great literature of the past.

Eliot's well-known essay "*Ulysses*, Order, and Myth" made this argument explicit in his claim that Joyce's work, by invoking classical myth, provides a structuring principle for the chaos of modern life: "Instead of narrative method, we may now use the mythic method. It is, I seriously believe, a step toward making the modern world possible for art" (Eliot 1923: 681). A similar assumption lies behind Gilbert Highet's discussion of Joyce and Eliot in *The Classical Tradition* (1949). The "tradition" Highet invoked was essentially that of Eliot's essay "Tradition and the Individual Talent," (1920) an ideal array of the best work of the past which was always open to – and could be slightly modified by – the addition of modern works of sufficient genius. F.R. Leavis's *The Great Tradition* (1948) was a similar concept, although Leavis chose to put greater emphasis on moral seriousness (and chose Lawrence rather than Joyce as his modern exemplar). Such concepts, by restricting the canon to a limited number of aesthetically "serious" works and by implying that each member of the group is somehow in dialogue with all the rest, puts a formal premium on what would later come to be called "intertextuality."

Throughout the early "heroic period" of Joyce criticism, Joyce benefited from the New Critical revaluation of complexity, especially the sort of textual difficulty and density that the frequent use of allusion made possible. He also, perhaps wrongly, benefited from a basically conservative valuation of classical sources, so that the association of his writing with that of Homer was taken to suggest that the effect of Joyce's work should be similar to that of his classical model. But this of course is not necessarily the case. In a thoughtful essay on Joyce's relationship to Homer, Fritz Senn suggests that while

> ultramodernist Joyce always turned back to the classics, Aristotle, Homer, Ovid; to medieval figures like Augustine, Aquinas, Dante; and later to Giordano Bruno, Nicolas of Cusa, Pico della Mirandola, or Shakespeare … , history, *Vico*, and *Finnegans Wake* all say that each impulse of new life is a *re*vival. (Senn 1984: 71, original emphasis)

In other words, with each new invocation of a classical or medieval source everything starts afresh. As Keith Booker observes,

> For Senn, Joyce does not use *The Odyssey* as a structural model for *Ulysses*. Instead, Joyce sets up the relatively pure and homogeneous style and language of Homer's epic as a starting point against which he can define his radically heterogeneous text as the antithesis. (Booker 1995: 22)

There are several questions bearing on this issue, most fundamentally (a) how significant is Joyce's use of a series of allusions to Homer's *Odyssey* in *Ulysses*; and (b) if it is significant, in what way is it so? If we assume that the *Odyssey* bears importantly on *Ulysses*, it is possible, even likely, that it does so ironically. After all, Molly, Joyce's version of Penelope, is emphatically *not* faithful to her wandering husband; Bloom in confronting his "Cyclops" in a bar is more tongue-tied than verbally clever, and instead of slaying even one suitor he appears to be a relatively complaisant cuckold. Thus we would have a Joyce who, like the traditional Eliot, shows the destruction of traditional values in our debased modern world. If we invert this same reading, we might argue that Joyce's novel implicitly critiques the conservative, masculinist, militarist values of Homer, instead offering for our admiration Bloom's pacifism and androgyny. And of course most readings of Joyce find him located at neither extreme, but instead partially affirmative, partially oppositional in his relationship to his classical precursors. But an even more skeptical and pragmatic reading might emphasize that readers unaware of Joyce's sheets of correspondences and their elaboration by generations of critics might well miss virtually all the "parallels" cited there, just as the initial readers of *Ulysses* did. As A. Walton Litz has pointed out, a good number of the Homeric parallels Joyce listed were never actually used in his novel, while many others were added very late in composition, as finishing touches in the book's elaborate embroidery: certainly they were not "structural" in any meaningful way (Litz 1961: 21). And even if they are taken to be structural, that does not necessarily imply that they are important to the *reader's* experience. More than one critic has insisted that the Homeric references are precisely a scaffolding that allowed Joyce as author to create his masterpiece, lending it a form other than that dictated by simple narrative; but once the book was written, we readers could just as easily dispense with it.[1]

Still, during the early period of Joyce criticism critics were understandably eager to discover allusions and patterns of allusion, each of which promised to open onto a new vista of meaningfulness. Even Joyce's relatively naturalistic early work became grist for the mill of allusion-trackers. Once some of the allusions of *Ulysses* were laid bare, critics also began to find hidden allusions in *Dubliners* and *A Portrait of the Artist*. A representative work here is Richard Levin and Charles Shattuck's "First Flight to Ithaca: A Reading of Joyce's *Dubliners*" (1948), in which the authors argue with great ingenuity but somewhat dubious credibility that there are a rich series of parallels to the Homeric myth in Joyce's naturalistic stories. Similarly, once the importance of Giambattista Vico's work for *Finnegans Wake* was established – by Joyce himself among others – Margaret Church found a Viconian pattern operating on "religious, psychological, and mythical levels" in *A Portrait* (Church 1976: 77). Here, clearly, we are far beyond the level of explicit verbal echoes, but despite the indirectness and tenuousness of the evidence Church is patently convinced that she has identified a genuine set of allusions which Joyce preferred to deploy with considerable subtlety. And with Joyce, as Peter J. Rabinowitz (1994) has noted, readers grant critics a good deal more interpretive latitude than they do with other writers, if only because we can demonstrate that in some cases the historical Joyce indeed meant his readers to register some extremely subtle effects. Rabinowitz refers to this effect, or its abuse, as "interpretive vertigo."

Given the stress upon the classical roots of modernism during the heyday of the New Criticism, it is somewhat surprising that it is only recently that full-scale treatments of Joyce's debts to and uses of Latin and Greek writers have appeared. Joseph Schork's volumes *Latin and Roman Culture in Joyce* (1997) and *Greek and Hellenic Culture in Joyce* (1998) easily supersede the piecemeal work done earlier in the field. Schork's approach to Joyce's use of the classical languages is to stress that there is generally an element of mockery and designed difficulty in the writer's allusions:

> What was, in the classroom, touted as the linguistic instrument of logic has been transformed, in the artist's forge, into a medium of subterfuge, burlesque, and adroit vocabulary, or structural legerdemain ... . I do not mean to imply that Joyce always used Latin as an instrument of satire or to deny that some learned references concealed a serious point. Rather, the evidence I have found in his texts leads me to conclude that Joyce's skill in the classics ... was a major component of his sense of humor. (Schork 1997: 3)

Schork quotes a passage from Stuart Gilbert's notebooks that gives Joyce's apparent reaction to accusations that a reader would not detect his Odyssean references:

> Allusions to Homer
> You say these are farfetched.
> Exactly! (Schork 1997: 3)

Although it is not entirely clear what Joyce means by this affirmation, it brings to mind his famous reply to the accusation that some of the puns in the *Wake* are trivial: "Yes, and some are quadrivial" (Jolas 1948: 24).

After his textual relations to the classical authors – and in some ways even before them – the most obvious area to examine in Joyce is his participation in the language of Catholicism – the Bible in its several variations, the copious writings of the Church Fathers, and at the broadest approximation the full sweep of Joyce's involvement in Christian discourse. Joyce is supposed to have said to Francini Bruni, his colleague at the Berlitz School in Trieste, "I love Dante almost as much as the Bible" (cited in Moseley 1967: vii). In *Joyce and the Bible*, Virginia Moseley claims that she is concerned with "Joyce's use of the Bible as such, not with matters of theology, other analogies, or influences of other writers … ," but then she immediately admits that "in two instances I have employed a related analogy – that of Dante in 'The Dead' and of the *Daily Missal* of the Roman Catholic Church in *A Portrait*, where these threads are so tightly interwoven with the biblical that removal of one would seriously damage the other" (Moseley 1967: vi). Moseley distinguishes among Joyce's citations of the Latin Vulgate, the Douay Bible, and the King James version (which Joyce, despite his Catholic background, quotes surprisingly frequently). Naturally enough, Moseley finds that the narratives of the lives of Christ and of Satan are most frequently alluded to by Joyce and are most apt to echo behind the narratives in *Dubliners* and *A Portrait*, although she also finds a disguised structure for *A Portrait*:

No less than a master stroke, this hidden motif is the yearly liturgical cycles of the Roman Catholic Church displayed in the Daily Missal. What could be more ironic than the fact that the very thing from which Stephen Daedalus-Joyce seems to be escaping, the imitation of Christ … , affords the method of escape. (Moseley 1967: 32)

In *Ulysses*, on the other hand, Moseley stresses the structural use of the Martha/Mary opposition.

Moseley's book was preceded by a more sophisticated work that more generally addressed Joyce's use of Christian material, *The Sympathetic Alien: James Joyce and Catholicism*, by J. Mitchell Morse (1959). Morse strays over the whole of Joyce's corpus, dealing with allusions as they arise, but divides his book into chapters focusing on figures such as Augustine, Aquinas, and John Scotus Erigena, putting them and others into the context of major Catholic heretics, and also treating the influence of Ignatius Loyola and his *Spiritual Exercises*. Morse also deals with the narratives of Cain and Abel and that of Jacob and Esau, both of them prominent in *Finnegans Wake*. Morse is among the best of the early source critics at discussing the ways in which Joyce consciously attempted to adapt Catholic rites, terminology, and conceptual structures to the work of a fundamentally secular artist. Another excellent though somewhat quirky discussion of Joyce in the light of his religion is Robert Boyle's *James Joyce's Pauline Vision: A Catholic Exposition*. Boyle recognizes that he is hanging a complex reading of Joyce from debatable biblical citations, and faces the problem directly:

> My own conviction – that the Pauline text shines out from *FW* 482: 34–6 'What can't be coded can be decoded if an ear aye seize what no eye ere grieved for'[2] – may seem at first glance to require some relatively esoteric circumstances: ... a Catholic alertness to the religious profundities of the text; a philosopher's sensitivity to its metaphysical implications; a consideration of Joyce's constantly deeper use, and his decreasingly acrimonious toleration, of religious and specifically Catholic doctrines and attitudes to express his own literary theory and practice; and other elements. Maybe so. My own judgment is that what I see is actually present in Joyce's text, and not merely in my own reading of it. But even if it is not, ... I consider that the evidence I intend to bring to bear upon my perception of the text will, in illuminating Joyce's total product, justify my procedure. (Boyle 1978: x–xi)

Father Boyle's unusually open-minded self-questioning about his own assumptions here, centered on a single quotation, can be seen to reflect his personal situation as well, as a deeply committed Jesuit who at the same time deeply values Joyce's work and wishes to bring these two parts of his intellectual and spiritual life into some kind of harmony.

While allusions to particular Church Fathers or to the Bible itself may be relatively straightforward to identify, Catholicism as a whole constitutes a shared body of references and a vocabulary in which Joyce participates, and the mutuality of this moral and aesthetic universe makes it difficult to discuss in terms of specific citation or influence. To some extent, this is also true of Joyce's inheritance from the major European writers, many of whom were engaged like him in serious artistic iconoclasm. So many of the fiction writers or dramatists, for instance, displayed an innovative technique that it is impossible to say whether Joyce was indebted to a particular writer or to a group of them, or on the other hand was merely part of the artistic *Zeitgeist*, another innovator in a period of innovation. In an essay on "The European Background of Joyce's Writing" (1990), Klaus Reichert first names the great Realists Flaubert and Tolstoy; Tolstoy Joyce denigrated while he admired Flaubert, a relationship explored by Richard Cross in *Flaubert and Joyce: The Rite of Fiction* (1970). Reichert continues with the naturalist Zola and the late Romantic D'Annunzio, whom Joyce also praised, and the dramatist Arthur Schnitzler. Ibsen, of course, was a major influence, as for a time was Gerhart Hauptmann, whom Joyce translated. Reichert discusses Nietzsche at some length, arguing that the German philosopher was an early influence despite the scarcity of allusions to him in the early work. And Joyce of course shared Nietzsche's admiration for Wagner, a relationship Timothy Martin explores at length in *Joyce and Wagner* (1991), arguing as does Reichert that in his conception of *Ulysses* Joyce had in mind some sort of Wagnerian *Gesamtkunstwerk*. Valuable as many of his insights may be, there are still obvious problems of incommensurability in comparing the work of a musician with that of a novelist, among them the fact that many apparent parallels in the work of the two will necessarily be metaphorical.

But Joyce fits many more contexts than European modernism. Some of these contexts are formal: If *Portrait* is a *Bildungsroman* or a *Künstlerroman*, then that could make Joyce – consciously or not – heir to the tradition of these forms. Far more specifically, I have argued that around the turn of the century there was a spate of European Catholic novels portraying the spiritual crisis of adolescents, and that Joyce's shares a number of generic characteristics with them (Kershner 1989: 277–85). Similarly, the Joyce of *Dubliners* has been seen as one of a good number of Irish fiction writers giving shape to the modern short story around the turn of the century, a context within which the influence of George Moore may seem significant (Beckson 1972), despite the fact that Joyce is universally seen as the "stronger" writer of the two. In fact, Joyce's European roots have long obscured the fact that he may also be seen in the context of Irish literature – both Celtic and Anglo-Irish, since he had at least some knowledge of the native language and its literary tradition. Maria Tymoczko's *The Irish "Ulysses"* (1994) explores one dimension of this relationship thoroughly. Less historically, a number of critics have seen Joyce as in some way an essentially medieval mind, a metaphor whose implications are teased out by Umberto Eco in *The Aesthetics of Chaosmos* (1982) (see also Boldrini 2002).

The Catholic writer with whose work Joyce was most profoundly engaged was Dante, and we are fortunate that several highly accomplished works treat the relationship between the two writers. In the first of these, *Joyce and Dante: The Shaping Imagination*, Mary Reynolds observes that while some writers labor to disconnect themselves from their predecessors, others seek out a tradition to which they can comfortably conform. Joyce did neither. His estimate of his own genius would not have allowed subservience to a defined tradition, yet few writers have written with such an educated critical awareness. At an early stage he marked out a small number of his predecessors for lifetime engagement, attaching their work to his.

But this was a peculiarly loose attachment, which encroached while maintaining its distance. (Reynolds 1981: 3)

"Attaching their work to his" is an especially telling phrase, suggesting as it does that the meaning of Joyce's usage is by no means determined by the site of the quotation. If anything, it is implied that the significance of the passage quoted or alluded to might be altered by its attachment to Joyce's text – an effect that, from the point of view of reader psychology, is a perfectly reasonable outcome. Reynolds points out that while in *Ulysses* both Homer and Shakespeare are structural presences, Homer as a model and Shakespeare as an illustration, Dante is present "only by quotation" (1981: 3), which leaves open the question of whether there is a cumulative meaning to the citations. And Reynolds no less than Boyle is aware that Joyce's Dantean references may be extremely tenuous: "Joyce made use of Dante in a great variety of ways. The simplest are easily discernable as verbal clues, direct quotations, and allusions. The more subtle uses are much harder to detect" (1981: 4). One of the most useful aspects of Reynolds's book is that all the Dante allusions are printed together in an Appendix, so that the reader can decide for him- or herself how convincing each citation is.

Reynolds's book, like all the books we have discussed so far, could be termed "pre-theoretical" in the sense that it does not generally foreground the theoretical issues – in this context those raised by the structuralists, post-structuralists and their heirs – involved in the intersection between the works of two authors – a formulation of the problem which would be anathema to those, beginning with Barthes, who prefer to separate intertextual interactions from any putative "author-construct." Lucia Boldrini's *Joyce, Dante, and the Poetics of Literary Relations: Language and Meaning in "Finnegans Wake"* is in this regard a far more self-conscious work. Her main thesis is that

there is a poetics of *Finnegans Wake* (a conception of the relationship between language and literature, and between theme, structure, and style, as well as of the scope of a literary work, and of how a text signifies) which is comparable to the poetics of Dante's works ... and which I believe Joyce recognized and actively engaged with by reading and "raiding" Dante, "writing" Dante, exploiting both the words and the gaps left by his texts ... . (Boldrini 2001: 13)

According to Boldrini, "it is this radically eclectic and playful relationship to 'parent' texts that best distinguishes Joyce's literary practice from that of his fellow-modernists" (2001: 10), especially Pound and Eliot, whom she regards as being far more affirmative and even respectful in their use of allusions to past literary works.

Jennifer Fraser's *Rite of Passage in the Narratives of Dante and Joyce* (2002) is a substantially different book in form and intention from Boldrini's; she frames her work as a "diptych," equally a reading of Dante and of Joyce, rather than, as Boldrini's work might be described, a reading of late Joyce by way of Dante. In fact, these three books show some of the multitude of possibilities latent in comparisons of Joyce and a major source – questions of stress, significance, and the possible treatment of shared material, from the largest concepts – Fraser's concern with the larger cyclical pattern of life and narration in the two writers – to single verbal echoes. Like Reynolds, Fraser concentrates on Joyce's earlier production, but she is more likely to found her arguments in philology than is Reynolds, whose arguments are nearly always thematic. Fraser, for instance, argues that Dante's treatment of Ulysses has an effect on Joyce's portrait of Stephen Dedalus, in that Joyce "grafts these two cantos [*Inferno* 26 and *Purgatorio* 25] onto the initiatory experience that Stephen appears to have" (Fraser 2002: 97).

Interestingly, both Boldrini and Fraser question the dominant paradigm for interpreting the interaction between two writers, the Oedipal drama set out in Harold Bloom's *Anxiety of Influence* (1973) and *A Map of Misreading* (1975). Fraser points out that in Bloom's model "it is exactly the initiatory figure of the mother who is missing" (2002: 5), and she finds in both Joyce and Dante such a figure, even if in Dante's work this is sometimes a feminized version of Virgil. Boldrini, on the other hand, stresses the limitations of Bloom's version of "misreading":

If for Harold Bloom the only way forward for the later poet is to misread the precursor, and thus to be condemned to suffer from the anxiety of the latent "guilty" knowledge of this misreading even as the process allows the successor to achieve his own greatness, Joyce's fully conscious recycling of Dante ... shows, rather, how it is in fact the precursor that already contains, or even determines, the possibility, for the later poet, to distort his works; the operation should therefore be described not so much as "misreading" but as a reading between the lines which will expose *any* model's limitations. (Boldrini 2001: 7)

Clearly Boldrini's vision of textual interaction is more a product of post-structuralism than of the neo-Freudianism that underlies Bloom's paradigm, and to this extent she is probably representative of many contemporary Joyce critics.

Questions about the relative strengths of the writer cited versus the "belated" citer, of course, predate Bloom, as do critical issues regarding the use one particular text, rather than another, might make of an allusion. Bjørn Tysdahl points out that the basic principle of the *Wake* is inclusiveness, and that where allusions to Ibsen in Joyce's earlier work generally rework the dramatist to suit Joyce's purposes, "in one very special sense, *Finnegans Wake* makes indiscriminate use of Ibsen" (Tysdahl 1968: 219). This "indiscriminateness" or lack of significant transformation to a new context in fact may be one reason there are more books addressing the *Wake* that simply identify allusions, such as Roland McHugh's (1980) guide or Adaline Glasheen's three "censuses" of the *Wake* (1977), than there are interpretive studies of allusion and citation like Vincent Cheng's *Shakespeare and Joyce: A Study of "Finnegans Wake"* (1984). After all, we know that Joyce occasionally set friends of his to reading books he had not and invited them to identify for him passages or references they found interesting (*JJ II* 699n).[3] To put it another way, the *Wake* is so original a document that the mere presence of another author's words within it may mean relatively little to our interpretation of the book. James Atherton, in his ground-breaking work *The Books at the Wake: A Study of Literary Allusions* (1960), separates what he terms the "structural books" (by Giambattista Vico, Edgar Quinet, Nicholas of Cusa, Giordano Bruno, Freud and Jung, Morton Prince, James Hogg, Lévy-Bruhl, the Occultists, and Arthur Symons) from more casual references; and even here, it seems to me arguable that most of these influences aside from Vico and Bruno and perhaps the psychoanalysts, whether or not they fit the psychic and historical structure of Joyce's book, are decidedly minor embellishments rather than substantial contributions to Joyce's thought. A relatively long passage from Quinet, for instance, appears in several forms in the *Wake*, but seems to be an illustration of Joyce's penchant for finding obscure passages that pleased him by their wording rather than testifying to his embrace of another writer's vision.

In fact, faced with the *Wake*'s originality and Joyce's arrogant "strength" as a writer, we may feel that finding allusions in that book need count for little in our evaluation of it. Tysdahl continues:

> These considerations seem to leave little room for a study of literary influences; the better the work, the greater the inner necessity which governs the inclusion of material and the more completely changed the nature and purpose of elements from earlier works. This is, I think, a point of view which is ... sometimes disregarded with the disturbing result that authors are "hustled into mutuality" with insufficient regard for their uniqueness. (Tysdahl 1968: 219)

Here Tysdahl is implying that the integrity of the literary productions of a writer like Joyce is naturally resistant to significant influence by predecessors – or at least that such influences would necessarily be transformed into something Joycean. The problem is especially acute when we are dealing with precursors who may be less "strong" than Joyce. For instance, some reviewers have questioned whether Martha Black's monumental *Shaw and Joyce* in fact demonstrates that Shaw was Joyce's "spiritual father" and "private parent" while Joyce was the "ambivalent disciple" in his writing (Black 1995: 411). Yet clearly there are many significant parallels between the Irish literary rebels. The overriding problem may be that most contemporary readers simply regard Joyce as more important than Shaw in virtually every way. A more extreme example is offered by Grace Eckley's work on the crusading journalist W.T. Stead, as in *The Steadfast "Finnegans Wake": A Textbook* (1994). Eckley's scholarship is remarkable, and it is undeniable that Stead's concerns and Joyce's overlapped significantly; still, most Joyceans have been very reluctant to accept Stead as a significant "source" for Joyce, however we construe that position. And we should remember that whatever the merits of Eckley's arguments, the New Critical heritage weighs heavily against her in its emphasis on the organic unity and originality of the great writer and its assertion that the work of a journalist and that of an artist are simply of two different and unequal kinds.

Work on Joyce and his "influences" has proceeded from the 1920s until today, even as our paradigms of influence study have continued to evolve. It is something of an exaggeration but still fair to say that earlier studies tended to see the problem of influence on Joyce as a matter of Joyce's work being enriched by his receptiveness to classical and medieval sources – as is appropriate for a "classical Joyce" – while later studies sometimes cast the relationship in terms of a romantic agon of opposition between huge warring artist-heroes. After all, Joyce was notoriously reluctant to admit to having been influenced by many writers, especially by his contemporaries. He was happy enough to point to figures like Aquinas, possibly because it was so obvious that in making use of the Church Father for Stephen's aesthetic theory he had distorted the man's thought almost beyond recognition (see Noon 1957). Among his contemporaries, he was eager to speak of relatively minor figures such as Italo Svevo or Edouard Dujardin while disclaiming any knowledge of Proust or Woolf.

It is likely that Joyce was eager to acknowledge Ibsen as an early master partly because he was neither English nor Irish, but Dano-Norwegian. Walter Jackson Bate in *The Burden of the Past and the English Poet* (1970) begins by setting out the problem of belatedness, which he argues has existed since the beginning of writing. Bate finds that in each writer's search for innovation a revolt against the preceding generation of writers is commonplace, and sometimes accompanied by an embrace of an earlier or even a grandparental generation's work. Among the most famous examples of this is the modernist poets' rejection of the Victorian poets and their rediscovery of the metaphysicals. George Bornstein (1988) has pointed out that poets who wrote in a different language are not seen as the same sort of threat that the parental figures in the writer's own language represent. As Patrick Hogan (1995) points out, this might account for Joyce's relative silence about Yeats, whose figure obviously loomed large in his mind as a young man, and his praise for Ibsen.

Hogan is one of relatively few Joyceans who has attempted to discuss the theory of influence study. He begins by citing Bate's discussion, and then moves to an analysis of Bloom's paradigm, which he views rather critically: for example, he complains that there are no criteria given for identifying "strong" as opposed to "weak" poets in Bloom's terms. Further, Bloom offers no evidence – at least of a falsifiable sort – to support his claims. Bloom is often highly metaphoric in his descriptions of poetic activities: "It is very hard to say precisely what Bloom means when he speaks of 'the Primal Scene for a poet *as poet*' and explains that this is 'his Poetic Father's coitus with the Muse'" (Hogan 1995: 7). Hogan points out that a writer may have both conscious and unconscious "affective relations" with a poet who is a father figure, and that these may be quite different. He argues that authors have unconscious transferential relations with precursors as well as ones of identification, including "identificatory idealizations" (1995: 41). These relationships may apply to characters as well as authors, and their basic mechanisms, being matters of fantasy, may be construed in terms of plot as well as of character (1995: 45). Hogan then makes two unusual moves. In the first place, he posits a supplementary approach to influence in terms of cognitive science. Then Hogan "frames" his psychoanalytic discussion by observing that the value of innovation in the arts is in any case not a constant, and thus not an eternal source of anxiety for the belated poet. A historically oriented cultural studies perspective would dictate that "this entire psychological scenario is located within a historical economy of literary production" (1995: 46).

A unique aspect of the economy of literary production of high modernism was that, in drawing attention to the Homeric intertext by his encouragement of Gilbert's book and his direct contributions to it, Joyce – like Eliot providing footnotes for *The Waste Land* – was actually generating material whose literary status was uncertain: was it criticism or primary text? After-the-fact authorial commentary or an aspect of the creative endeavor? Where, exactly, were the borders of the "text itself" and where did commentary begin? Or, to put it another way, where did the author's responsibility for a given field of words stop, and where did they become the words of others, including readers? And, most crucially for literary-critical commentators, how should we discuss these textual and (perhaps) extra-textual interactions? Probably the most influential thinker to offer approaches, if not answers, to such questions was the Russian philosopher M.M. Bakhtin (1895–1975). Bakhtin's work was first brought to the attention of Western critics by Julia Kristeva in an essay entitled "Word, Dialogue, and Novel," published in a French journal in 1969 and reprinted in her *Desire in Language* (1980). Kristeva explains that for Bakhtin

> the three dimensions or coordinates of dialogue are writing subject, addressee, and exterior text. The word's status is thus defined *horizontally* (the word in the text belongs to both writing subject and addressee) as well as *vertically* (the word in the text is oriented toward an anterior or synchronic literary corpus). (1980: 66)

Kristeva, perhaps inevitably, at this stage saw Bakhtin in the light of the Russian formalists with whom he had serious differences, in the light of their inheritors the structuralists, and in the context of Derrida's early work as well, so that she is inclined to stress how in Bakhtin the "notion of *intertextuality* replaces that of intersubjectivity" (1980: 66). Kristeva's vocabulary of *text* and *textuality* to some extent distorts Bakhtin's stress on *voice* and what most translators render as *dialogism*, the interplay of textual "voices." Yet this is not as serious a distortion as it might seem, in that Bakhtin's concept of voice does not rely upon a singular, embodied subject; for him, each apparently unified voice is made up of numerous other voices, harmonizing, disputing, or simply jostling for position. Further, a voice for Bakhtin is always material, and grounded in a social and historical (and thus political) situation. In some ways, Bakhtin anticipated Barthes's and Derrida's vision of intersecting networks of textuality and their attack upon the unified subject as the "authenticator" of speech.

Bakhtin calls for a "trans-linguistics" because linguistics in its traditional form idealizes and de-materializes language; the "utterance" for Bakhtin is always unique, a materially grounded individual instance that determines meaning. The most important aspect of an utterance is its "addressivity," its quality of being in some respect spoken *toward* someone. Bakhtin uses the term *heteroglossia* to indicate the fact that speech, insofar as it is always embodied in a specific situation, is always multiple, always a mixture of "languages" which themselves could be further analyzed. The key to understanding language for Bakhtin is that

> our speech, that is, all our utterances (including creative works) is filled with others' words, varying degrees of otherness or varying degrees of "our own-ness," varying degrees of awareness or detachment. These words of others carry with them their own expression, their own evaluative tone, which we assimilate, re-work, and re-accentuate. (Bakhtin 1986: 89)

So language is inevitably "double-voiced," including both the language of the speaker (itself an amalgam of that speaker's significant interlocutors, such as parents, lovers, intellectual influences, etc.) and any present or anticipated addressee, toward whom the speaker may assume a great variety of postures.

Following on from my essay on dialogism in *Portrait* (Kershner 1986), my book *Joyce, Bakhtin, and Popular Literature* (Kershner 1989) was the first to explore Joyce's dialogism in his early works, including *Dubliners*, *Portrait*, and *Exiles*, and concentrated on identifying the "voices" of various examples of popular literature, such as Dumas's *Count of Monte Cristo* (to which Joyce makes explicit allusion) or *Tom Brown's School Days* (to which

I argue he implicitly alludes). To some extent, the Bakhtinian framework suggests that this undertaking is no longer a traditional "source study" in the sense of a *Quellenforschung*. Although the different "voices" involved are treated to some extent as though they represented different people, from the standpoint of theory that is a crude simplification. Bakhtinian voices are inevitably plural, internally riven and multitonal; they may as easily belong to a genre as to an individual, and their relationship can seldom be reduced to anything as simple as opposition or mutual support. From Bakhtin's standpoint, a novel's polyphony has the richness and complexity of a symphony, except that it would probably never be describable in terms of a succession of harmonies. For Bakhtin, all voices are also created equal, so that the strength of a voice is not necessarily related to its aesthetic or intellectual status. Keith Booker's *Joyce, Bakhtin, and the Literary Tradition* (1995) applies elements of Bakhtinian analysis to Joyce's dialogic interchange with Homer, Rabelais, Dante, Goethe, and Shakespeare, while Michael Patrick Gillespie in *Reading the Book of Himself* (1989) discusses the multiplicity of voices in Joyce's work, including the reader's participation, through the concepts of dialogism and polyvocality.

While Gillespie combines Bakhtinian criticism per se with elements of reader-response criticism, Booker attempts a bridge to Stephen Greenblatt's "cultural poetics," the term Greenblatt preferred to New Historicism. But in fact most contemporary critics who use Bakhtin's concepts respect the historical "embeddedness" of the voices whose interactions they analyze. Indeed, it is aguable that Bakhtinian readings – or at least those concentrating on dialogics rather than carnival – are an intermediate step between classical studies of literary sources, based as they are on the authorizing images of the great authors, and contemporary critical studies of discourses, based on Foucauldian analysis of social texts. Cheryl Herr's (1986) study certainly pointed in this direction, and recent work such as Tracey Teets Schwarze's *Joyce and the Victorians* (2002) is more inclined to examine the discourse of manliness in the late nineteenth century than the influence of, say, Matthew Arnold on Joyce. In general I think it is fair to say that literary source-study has been eclipsed in recent years by the broader conception of interacting discourses; both Jennifer Wicke (1988) and Garry Leonard (1998), for instance, have examined Joyce's relationship to the discourse of advertisement, and the implications of such a study are quite different from those of a book like William Schutte's *Joyce and Shakespeare* (1957). With the critical move away from psychologism and the figure of the author toward a broader social and historical focus has come an invigorated interest in intertextuality. Luckily for Joyce studies, both *Ulysses* and the *Wake* are networked by multiple and dense social discourses whose presence is easily as influential as that of the writers whose traces were the subject of so much early criticism. Our interest may have shifted from allusion to misreading to dialogics to intertextuality as we read Joyce, but as we move into the new millennium it shows no sign of abating.

notes

1. Raymond Queneau, a French admirer of Joyce, used his discovery of *Ulysses* with its Homeric structure to overcome a writer's block he had experienced after parting company with Breton's Surrealist group. His first important novel, *Le Chiendent*, uses a structure based on the seven letters of his first and last names, as well as a group of different "modes de récit" for the different chapters and sub-sections. See Kershner (1971).
2. "What no eye has seen, nor ear heard, nor the heart of man conceived, what God has prepared for those who love him" (I Cor. 2–9) in Father Boyle's citation (viii).
3. Ellmann reproduces a letter from Joyce to David Fleischman, then 18, asking him to summarize and annotate a copy of *Huckleberry Finn*, because Joyce has not read it and in the press of composition of the *Wake* has no time to do so. Such a letter certainly elicits questions for the critic regarding just what sort of depth of significance we may attribute to a literary allusion.

references

Atherton, James S. *The Books at the Wake: A Study of Literary Allusions in James Joyce's "Finnegans Wake."* New York: Viking Press, 1960.

Bakhtin, M.M. *Speech Genres and Other Late Essays.* Trans. Vern W. McGhee, ed. Caryl Emerson and Michael Holquist. Austin: University of Texas Press, 1986.

Bate, Walter Jackson. *The Burden of the Past and the English Poet.* Cambridge: Harvard University Press, 1970.

Beckett, Samuel, et al. *Our Exagmination Round his Factification for Incamination of Work in Progress.* Paris: Shakespeare and Co., 1929.

Beckson, Karl. "Moore's 'The Untilled Field' and Joyce's *Dubliners*: The Short Story's Intricate Maze." *ELT*, 15 (1972), pp. 291–304.

Black, Martha Fodaski. *Shaw and Joyce: "The Last Word in Stolentelling."* Gainesville: University of Florida Press, 1995.

Boldrini, Lucia. *Joyce, Dante, and the Poetics of Literary Relations: Language and Meaning in "Finnegans Wake."* Cambridge: Cambridge University Press, 2001.

Boldrini, Lucia. ed. *Middayeval Joyce: Essays on Joyce's Medieval Cultures.* Amsterdam: Rodopi, 2002.

Booker, M. Keith. *Joyce, Bakhtin, and the Literary Tradition: Toward a Comparative Cultural Poetics.* Ann Arbor: University of Michigan Press, 1995.

Bornstein, George. *Poetic Remaking: The Art of Browning, Yeats, and Pound*. University Park: Pennsylvania State University Press, 1988.

Boyle, Robert, S.J. *James Joyce's Pauline Vision: A Catholic Exposition*. Carbondale: Southern Illinois University Press, 1978.

Cheng, Vincent John. *Shakespeare and Joyce: A Study of "Finnegans Wake."* University Park: Pennsylvania State University Press, 1984.

Church, Margaret. "A Portrait and Giambattista Vico: A Source Study," in *Approaches to Joyce's "Portrait": Ten Essays*. Ed. Thomas F. Staley and Bernard Benstock. Pittsburgh: University of Pittsburgh Press, 1976, pp. 77–89.

Cross, Richard K. *Flaubert and Joyce: The Rite of Fiction*. Princeton, N.J.: Princeton University Press, 1970.

Eckley, Grace. *The Steadfast "Finnegans Wake": A Textbook*. New York: University Press of America, 1994.

Eco, Umberto. *The Aesthetics of Chaosmos: The Middle Ages of James Joyce*. Trans. Ellen Esrock. Tulsa, OK: University of Tulsa Press, 1982.

Eliot, T.S. "*Ulysses*, Order, and Myth," *The Dial* 75 (1923), pp. 480–3. Cited here as reprinted in *The Modern Tradition*. Ed. Richard Ellmann and Charles Feidelson, Jr. New York: Oxford University Press, 1965, pp. 679–81.

Eliot, T.S. "Tradition and the Individual Talent," in *The Sacred Wood* (1920). London: Methuen, 1972, pp. 47–59.

Fraser, Jennifer Margaret. *Rite of Passage in the Narratives of Dante and Joyce*. Gainesville: University of Florida Press, 2002.

Friedrich, Gerhard. "Bret Harte as a Source for James Joyce's 'The Dead,'" *Philological Quarterly* 33 (1954), pp. 442–4.

Gifford, Don. *Joyce Annotated: Notes for "Dubliners" and "A Portrait of the Artist as a Young Man."* Berkeley: University of California Press, 1982.

Gifford, Don, with Robert Seidman. *"Ulysses" Annotated*. 2nd edn. Berkeley: University of California Press, 1988.

Gilbert, Stuart. *James Joyce's "Ulysses". A Study* (1930). 2nd edn. Harmondsworth: Penguin, 1969.

Gillespie, Michael Patrick. *Reading the Book of Himself: Narrative Strategies in the Works of James Joyce*. Columbus: Ohio University Press, 1989.

Glasheen, Adaline. *Third Census of "Finnegans Wake": An Index of the Characters and Their Roles*. Berkeley: University of California Press, 1977.

Herr, Cheryl. *Joyce's Anatomy of Culture*. Chicago: University of Illinois Press, 1986.

Highet, Gilbert. *The Classical Tradition: Greek and Roman Influences on Western Literature*. New York: Oxford University Press, 1949.

Hogan, Patrick Colm. *Joyce, Milton, and the Theory of Influence*. Gainesville: University of Florida Press, 1995.

Jolas, Eugène, "My Friend James Joyce," in *James Joyce: Two Decades of Criticism*. Ed. Seon Givens. New York: Vanguard, 1948.

Kershner, Richard B., Jr. "Joyce and Queneau as Novelists: A Comparative Study." Dissertation, Stanford University, 1971.

Kershner, R.B. "The Artist as Text: Dialogism and Incremental repetition in Joyce's *Portrait*." *ELH* 53 (1986), pp. 881–94.

Kershner, R.B. *Joyce, Bakhtin, and Popular Literature: Chronicles of Disorder*. Chapel Hill: University of North Carolina Press, 1989.

Kristeva, Julia. *Desire in Language: A Semiotic Approach to Literature and Art.* Ed. Leon S. Roudiez. New York: Columbia University Press, 1980.

Leavis, F.R. *The Great Tradition.* New York: New York University Press, 1948.

Leonard, Garry. *Advertising and Commodity Culture in Joyce.* Gainesville: University of Florida Press, 1998.

Levin, Richard and Charles Shattuck. "First Flight to Ithaca: A Reading of Joyce's *Dubliners,*" in *James Joyce: Two Decades of Criticism.* Ed. Seon Givens. New York: Vanguard Press, 1948; reprinted 1963, pp. 47–94.

Litz, A. Walton. *The Art of James Joyce: Method and Design in "Ulysses" and "Finnegans Wake."* London: Oxford University Press, 1961.

Martin, Timothy. *Joyce and Wagner: A Study of Influence.* Cambridge: Cambridge University Press, 1991.

McHugh, Roland. *Annotations to "Finnegans Wake."* Baltimore: Johns Hopkins University Press, 1980.

Morse, J. Mitchell. *The Sympathetic Alien: James Joyce and Catholicism.* New York: New York University Press, 1959.

Moseley, Virginia. *Joyce and the Bible.* De Kalb: Northern Illinois University Press, 1967.

Noon, William T. *Joyce and Aquinas.* New Haven: Yale University Press, 1957.

Rabaté, Jean-Michel. "Bruno no, Bruno si: Note on a Contradiction in Joyce," *James Joyce Quarterly,* 27:1 (Fall 1989), pp. 31–9.

Rabinowitz, Peter J. "'A Symbol of Something': Interpretive Vertigo in 'The Dead,'" in *James Joyce's, "The Dead."* Ed. Daniel R. Schwartz. Boston: Bedford Books of St. Martin's Press, 1994, pp. 137–49.

Reichert, Klaus. "The European Background of Joyce's Writing," in *The Cambridge Companion to James Joyce.* Ed. Derek Attridge. Cambridge: Cambridge University Press, 1990.

Reynolds, Mary T. *Joyce and Dante: The Shaping Imagination.* Princeton, N.J.: Princeton University Press, 1981.

Schork, R.J. *Latin and Roman Culture in Joyce.* Gainesville: University of Florida Press, 1997.

Schork, R.J. *Greek and Hellenic Culture in Joyce.* Gainesville: University of Florida Press, 1998.

Schutte, William M. *Joyce and Shakespeare. A Study in the Meaning of "Ulysses."* New Haven: Yale University Press, 1957.

Schwarze, Tracy Teets. *Joyce and the Victorians.* Gainesville: University of Florida Press, 2002.

Senn, Fritz. "Remodeling Homer," in *Light Rays: James Joyce and Modernism.* Ed. Heyward Ehrlich. New York: New Horizon, 1984, pp. 70–92.

Silverstein, Norman. "Bruno's Particles of Reminiscence," *James Joyce Quarterly* 2 (1965), pp. 271–80.

Tymoczko, Maria. *The Irish "Ulysses."* Berkeley: University of California Press, 1994.

Tysdahl, Bjørn J. *Joyce and Ibsen: A Study in Literary Influence.* New York: Humanities Press, 1968.

Verene, Donald, ed. *Vico and Joyce.* New York: State University of New York Press, 1987.

Wicke, Jennifer. *Advertising Fictions: Literature, Advertisement, and Social Reading.* New York: Columbia University Press, 1988.

10

joyce, history, and the philosophy of history

margot norris

If Joyce's university friend Thomas Kettle could quip that "Irish history is the lie disagreed upon" (quoted in Spoo 1994: 4) there is today a more and more widespread agreement as to the centrality of the question of history in Joyce studies. One factor that has helped build this consensus is that the issue of history is not restricted to Irish history any more. Irish history is the nightmare from which Joyce scholars have awoken, but only to find themselves facing the even more loaded issue of Joyce's philosophy of history. Thus in October 1990, Yale University sponsored a conference on "Joyce and History," an event that resulted in a 1996 collection of essays entitled *Joyce and the Subject of History*, edited by Mark Wollaeger, Victor Luftig, and Robert Spoo. In their introduction, the editors point to the confluence of disciplines, theories, and movements that made historicity one of the major issues in Joyce criticism in the last two decades.

> Current attempts to establish a relation between "Joyce" and "history" face not only the expanding and continually reconceived archive but also the competing and rapidly changing claims of anthropology, psychoanalysis, Marxism, feminism, deconstruction, and postcolonial theory, to name only the most prominent. (Wollaeger et al. 1996: 2)

Harbingers of this attention to Joyce and history began appearing in the 1980s when Fredric Jameson, Terry Eagleton, and Seamus Deane began publishing essays on Ireland, colonialism, and Joyce. This same decade saw the first politically inflected culture criticism appear, led by Cheryl

Herr's (1986) *Joyce's Anatomy of Culture*, and R.B. Kershner's (1989) *Joyce, Bakhtin, and Popular Literature: Chronicles of Disorder*. These early studies were followed in the 1990s by a number of books specifically focused on the Joycean text in relation to Irish history. These works included James Fairhall's (1993) *James Joyce and the Question of History*, Robert Spoo's (1994) *James Joyce and the Language of History*, Enda Duffy's (1994) *The Subaltern "Ulysses,"* Vincent Cheng's (1995) *Joyce, Race, and Empire*, Thomas Hofheinz's (1995) *Joyce and the Invention of Irish History: "Finnegans Wake" in Context*, Emer Nolan's (1995) *James Joyce and Nationalism*, and Derek Attridge and Marjorie Howes' (2000) collection of essays entitled *Semicolonial Joyce*.

This rapid review of the critical history suggests a remarkable coherence, except for a striking disjunction between this panoply of work on the subject of Joyce and history, and the simultaneous – if less conspicuous – scholarly interest in Joyce and the philosophies of history that preoccupied him in his own day. Joyce's philosophical erudition may be assumed to have played a role in his own sense of historiography, and therefore influenced the narrativized history he may be presumed to have wished to produce in his fictions. In 1985 a conference was held in Venice, Italy, on the topic of Vico and Joyce, that also resulted in a volume of essays (*Vico and Joyce*) in 1987, edited by its convener and chair, Donald Verene. How do we connect the essays in Verene's volume, and others on Joyce and the Continental philosophies of history that he studied and explored throughout his writing career, to the contemporary Marxist, post-colonial, and cultural criticism that has been so dominant in the last two decades of Joyce studies? The problem is difficult and ultimately beyond the scope of this chapter. However, by taking a systematic look at Joyce's engagement with philosophies of history, and the range of scholarly commentary upon them over the last two decades, it may be possible to make some generalizations about the concepts and theoretical principles that may have informed Joyce's writings. These in turn may help to illuminate why Joyce's treatment of history has inspired such rich and gratifying interest from the range of politically engaged scholars who have studied Joyce and history during the last two decades.

Studies of history often begin with dictionary definitions of the term, and *Webster's Third International Dictionary* offers a set of entries useful for setting up the problem of history and the philosophy of history in Joyce's understanding and in his works. The entry begins with the intriguing etymology of the word "history": "L. *historia*, fr. Gk *historia* inquiry, information, narrative, history, fr. *historein* to inquire into, examine, relate" (p. 1073). As Fritz Senn notes, "The Greek *historia* is based on the idea of knowledge" (Senn 1996: 47). The *Webster* etymology suggests that *history* begins as a question or questioning, an examination that relates one thing to another, before the commencement of a telling. The *Webster* etymology is then followed by a first definition of "history" that points much more to the novel or the biography than to the state chronicle: "1: a narrative of events connected with a real or imaginary object, person, or career" (p. 1073). James Fairhall cites an *Oxford English Dictionary* definition that clarifies this seemingly paradoxical definition by explaining that early *histories* did indeed blur the line between fact and fiction, and that the expulsion of invention from the writing of history has been a relatively recent phenomenon. The *OED* speaks of *history* as "A relation of incidents (in early use, either true or imaginary; later only of those professedly true" (p. 1). And Fairhall goes on to remind us that history as we now commonly think of it, as a discipline of social science, came into existence only in the nineteenth century. This more modern sense of history is listed as *Webster's* second definition: "2: a systematic written account comprising a chronological record of events (as affecting a city, state, nation, institution, science or art) and usu. including a philosophical explanation of the cause and origin of such events" (p. 1074). In this sense of history, historical writing depends both on methodological rigor and, optionally, on philosophical theories of origin and causation. *Webster's* definition of *historiography* gives a fairly precise sense of the methodology, but omits, and therefore begs the question of, theories of origins and causations. It defines "historiography" as "1: the writing of history; esp: the writing of history based on the critical examination of sources, the selection of particulars from the authentic materials, and the synthesis of particulars into a narrative that will stand the test of critical methods" (p. 1073).

Against these definitions of history and historiography, Joyce emerges as a historian chiefly in the archaic sense, as one who narrates events or incidents that relate to real or imaginary objects, persons, and careers. *A Portrait of the Artist as a Young Man* could certainly exemplify a *history* of this kind, although the mediations and ironizations produced by its imitative form might undermine its reliability as history even in this *Bildungsroman* sense of the term. As a historian of the state, nation, or institutions, Joyce would also appear less as a revisionist than as a destabilizer or deconstructionist of disciplinary historiography. Thomas Hofheinz finds the status of "'history'" in Joyce's work to be always "dubious" because its form is a diffusion rather than a construction of civic or political narrative. "Joyce's historical moments are discrete, local, situational, their force distributed into the internal mysteries of the individual" (Hofheinz 1995: 40). Garry Leonard radicalizes this point further to make of Joyce's work a "history of now," and Joyce the historian of that which eludes historicization.

> Joyce is presenting the history of the everyday, the significance of ephemera, the memorable quality of forgotten experience, and the peculiar and particular haunting permanence of anything that has disappeared before being historicized. The nonhistoricized haunts us. (Leonard 1996: 19)

Another argument along these same general lines is Joseph Valente's notion that Joyce historically occupied a "border zone" between the imperial British culture and the irredentist Irish culture and that this position between the mainstream and the margin produced in him a "double vision" that Valente calls "cosmopolitan." He writes:

> I would call this vision cosmopolitan, not cosmopolitan in the pejorative Marxist sense of a view from nowhere, which registers only a gray neutrality or abstract universality, but cosmopolitan in the sense of a mobile decentered view, which registers more or less comprehensively the contradictions of a complex social situation and the endless unraveling those contradictions demand. (Valente 1996: 63)

These views of Joyce as a historian with a decidedly anti-positivistic and anti-scientific bent can be profitably related to his engagement with philosophers and philosophies of history, particularly those that were themselves oppositional and marginal to their own intellectual moments. The names of Giambattista Vico, Edgar Quinet, and Friedrich Nietzsche, come to mind in this respect. Joyce took an interest in other historical philosophies and theories as well, including G.W.F. Hegel, Jules Michelet, Benedetto Croce, and – if we stretch the sense of philosophy of history a bit – Henri Bergson and Sigmund Freud. Robert Spoo has shown that Joyce had read carefully the Anglo-Irish historian W.E.H. Lecky, whose *History of European Morals: From Augustus to Charlemagne* (1869) he owned, and who gave him the notion of a "moral history" of his times. He was also influenced, as his letters testify, by the Italian essayist Guglielmo Ferrero, whose *Grandezza e Decadenza di Roma* (1902–07) anticipates concerns and methods shared by *L'Ecole des Annales* and the New Historians (see Spoo

1994: 22–33). Such a list reflects Joyce's advanced education in modern European languages and interest in Continental intellectual history and philosophy, as well as his interest in the mythological as the "counter-historical," as Samuel Beckett termed it. Recent scholarship has uncovered additional intermediary sources in which Joyce encountered some of his historical philosophies, for example, Jacques Aubert's discovery of Bernard Bosanquet's *A History of Aesthetic* (1892) as a possible source of Joyce's Hegelianism. Another instance of such a mediated source is the famous sentence from Edgar Quinet that Joyce cites and parodies in *Finnegans Wake*. Inge Landuyt and Geert Lernout (1995) have traced this sentence to Leon Metchnikoff's *La civilisation et les grands fleuves historiques*. By first offering an overview of what we know of Joyce's engagement with philosophies of history, it may be easier to consider how he transformed these influences into essays and fictions in which history is given revisionary, dispersed, non-progressive, non-teleological, cyclical, and deconstructed forms.

Because the philosophies of history that engaged Joyce are themselves connected by influence and translation, clarity may be served by taking them up in roughly chronological order, beginning with Giordano Bruno. Although Lucia Boldrini makes Samuel Beckett's essay, "Dante … Bruno . Vico . . Joyce" the prelude for her study of Joyce and Dante, she approaches Beckett's mediating accounts of the Italian's influence on Joyce[1] with proper caution. Boldrini writes, "Beckett only mentions the coincidence of opposites (originally in fact not a Brunonian concept) after stating that at this point 'Vico applies Bruno – though he takes very good care not to say so' (DBVJ 5–6) – an assertion which is, at the very least, debatable" (Boldrini 2001: 17). Her point is that Beckett's explanations are themselves strategic and playful in glossing Bruno's and Vico's roles in Joyce's *Work in Progress*, and he may therefore distort and omit information and formulations when it serves his own creative purpose, and Joyce's.[2] This useful reminder positions us to consider, speculatively, whether the young Joyce found more in Bruno than just his dualism. We may wonder whether Bruno's theory on the art of memory, for example, may also have influenced Joyce, as Daniel Ferrer hints (Ferrer 1999: 357), and whether Joyce might have found in Bruno an early theory of natural recurrence and regeneration. Joyce probably discovered the works of Giordano Bruno on his own, in spite of – rather than through – the instruction of his Italian professor, Father Charles Ghezzi, during his studies in the Modern Languages curriculum at University College, Dublin. Father Ghezzi reminded Joyce that Bruno was a terrible heretic (*JJ II* 59). Joyce encountered in "the Nolan," as he called him in *The Day of the Rabblement*, a type of restless, questing, resistant intellectual exile[3] whose appeal to a Stephen Dedalus would be perfectly plausible. Bruno chiefly explored questions of epistemology and cosmology in his writings – expanding a post-Copernican position into a model of an infinite universe that contained an infinite number of potentially habitable worlds. At least one of his works, "On Cause, Principle, and Unity," gestures proto-historically toward later cyclical theories and theories of natural regeneration. In this work Bruno wrote, "This entire globe, this star, not being subject to death and dissolution and annihilation being impossible anywhere in Nature, from time to time renews itself by changing and altering all of its parts" (Kessler 2003).

In Giambattista Vico, Joyce encountered another philosopher of cyclical history whose work too "threatened both Christian orthodoxy and the body of mainstream rationalist Enlightenment thinking," according to John Bishop's illuminating discussion of Joyce and Vico in *Joyce's Book of the Dark* (Bishop 1986: 176). Richard Ellmann reports that Joyce, during his years in Trieste just before World War I, discussed ideas with a lively circle of friends and pupils that included beside the novelist Ettore Schmitz, the attorney Paolo Cuzzi, a man named Oscar Schwarz, and the Yugoslavian Boris Furlan with whom he discussed Benedetto Croce as well as Schopenhauer and Nietzsche. Paolo Cuzzi was particularly interested in Vico, and discovered to his delight that "Joyce was also passionately interested in this Neapolitan philosopher" (*JJ II* 340–2). This timing strengthens John Bishop's argument that Joyce read widely in *The New Science*, including the Third Book, "The Discovery of the True Homer," which "illustrates in detail the failures of nonevolutionary reconstructions of the past" (Bishop 1986: 178), and thereby richly illuminates Joyce's adaptation of Homer in *Ulysses*. Bishop also glosses the relationship between Vico and Hegel. He notes that, "Well before the appearance of Hegel's *Phenomenology of Mind*, *The New Science* necessarily implied that human consciousness was an evolutionary variable, changeable with history and society, and that it depended on the whole human past for its definition" (1986: 176). In his Preface to *Vico and Joyce*, Donald Verene credits Joyce with salvaging the eighteenth-century philosopher, who greatly influenced Michelet, Croce, and Marx, for a twentieth-century readership.[4]

Mary Reynolds cites Max Fisch's formulation of Vico's vision of history: "The ontogenetic pattern exhibited by each nation in its origin, development, maturity, decline, and fall" (Reynolds 1987: 111). Here is the description Attila Faj gives of the famous Viconian cycles:

> Vico claims that all pagan peoples must pass through a specific "course" consisting of four main stages preceded by a brutal primary barbarism. They are: the stage of gods, of heroes, of men, and, at last, a new kind of barbarism – the barbarism of reflection. Each stage has its political, social, and cultural characteristics. If a nation at the end of its cycle has not annihilated itself or is not compelled to follow the evolutive stages of another nation which conquered and subdued it definitively, this nation, after the stage of its own barbarism of reflection, will retrace the aforesaid course on a similar plane of existence. (Faj 1987: 21)

Joseph Mali then goes on to explain the methodological exigencies that led Vico to narrate these stages in the forms of myths, myths to which he gives status not as empirical fact but as psychological verities.

> The radical innovation in Vico's appraisal of myth of *vera narratio* was that mythology was thereafter perceived as neither ahistorical nor antihistorical but as counter-historical. Mythologies, according to Vico, often narrate those forbidden 'true stories' which have been systematically suppressed and omitted from the official, homogenous histories of nations, religions, social and political institutions, and so forth. (Mali 1987: 41)

This explanation also contributes to our understanding of how Vico may have influenced not only the structure of *Finnegans Wake*, as is widely held, but also the Homeric structure of *Ulysses*. Mali writes:

> Instead of dealing with heroic achievements of individuals and their world-views, the common stuff of the Renaissance tradition in cultural history, Vico concentrated on the attitudes of ordinary people toward everyday life. He was not interested so much in their conceptual ideas but in their sensual images of life, death, marriage, work, sex, family, and so on. All these were best expressed and preserved in their shared beliefs and myths. (Mali 1987: 37)[5]

Finally, Vico – writing against the rationalism of Descartes – is credited with introducing the irrational as a factor in the historical process (*Encyclopaedia Britannica* 19, 104). This may account for Joyce's own famous linkage of Vico with psychoanalytic theory, when he told the Danish writer Tom Kristensen that "I don't believe in any science ... but my imagination grows when I read Vico as it doesn't when I read Freud or Jung" (*JJ II* 693). This leads John O'Neill to begin his essay on Joyce, Freud, and Vico with a rhapsodic linkage of the three figures. He writes:

> Vico, Joyce, and Freud constitute a glad company of jubilant, somatologists (scientists of the intrarational senses) awakening the world's sleeping history to the body's dance down from the mountain tops, out of the primal forest into the familied self, all civil, murderous, and sinful. (O'Neill 1987: 160)

A number of critics, including Mary Reynolds, Bonnie Kime Scott, and Peter Hughes, argue, however, that Joyce would have learned his Vico through the translation by Jules Michelet, who launched his historical career with an 1827 translation of the *Scienza nuova*. Mary Reynolds writes that

> Joyce's first reading of Vico began in Trieste, probably in 1905 or 1906, perhaps stimulated by Croce's critical endorsements, and definitely connected with his first awareness of Freud. Indeed, Joyce had read Vico before he left Dublin, in Michelet's translation of *La Scienza nuova*. (Reynolds 1987: 119)

She postulates that this reading of Michelet could have occurred as early as 1901, when Joyce studied Romance Languages at the university. If Joyce did get his Vico through Michelet, then, Peter Hughes argues, he would have received Michelet's misreadings or creative interpretations of Vico, which include Michelet's effacement of the "aboriginal class struggle" in Vico (Hughes 1987: 85), his emphasis on renewal and rebirth and the role that writing and language play in that renewal, and his foregrounding of the historian as "omniscient author" (1987: 86–7). In fact, there has been relatively little serious exploration of Joyce's engagement with Michelet as a philosopher of history in his own right.[6] Lorraine Weir discusses Michelet's visitation of Vico in his *Introduction a l'Histoire Universelle* only to characterize it as a problematic appropriation:

> Thus Michelet's "strong reading" of the Vichian text effectively destroys the holistic, morphogenetic power of the system, putting in its place a patriarchal and paternalistic claim to ownership of the world and

its life forms. Adapting the metonymy of France in relation to the world, Michelet repeats the Vichian transformation of metonymic into metaphoric relation but this time the result is the proclamation of a French colonialist hegemony, a redemptive mission undertaken by France, "le pilote du vaisseau de l'humanité." (Weir 1989: 72)

Yet the descriptions of Michelet's ambition to have writing produce the resurrection of the past seem strongly resonant of Joyce's own ambitions in writing *Ulysses* and *Finnegans Wake*. Jacques Rancière's poetic description of Michelet's designation of the historian as archivist of the people's forgotten texts may express this most eloquently:

It is, on the contrary, the historian who is going to appear on stage, show himself to us, holding in his hand those narratives of federations that are much more than narratives, he tells us – they are love letters to the youthful native land: "I have found all that entire and glowing, as though made yesterday, when, sixty years afterwards, I lately opened those paper, which few persons had read." (Rancière 1994: 44)[7]

Peter Hughes finds this "concentration of history in the individual, that *biographing* of discourse" (Hughes 1987: 87) in both Edgar Quinet's and Michelet's reading of Vico.

Peter Hughes describes the link between Michelet and Quinet as "friends and colleagues who had been drawn to Vico and Herder as forerunners of the revolution in historical studies launched in France in the 1820s" (Hughes 1987: 87). And Lorraine Weir configures Quinet and Michelet as the dueling philosophers or enemy twins of French historiography. Analyzing some of the later chapters of *Finnegans Wake*, Weir finds that "the violent world [of Michelet] again intersects with the gentle, ecological view of Quinet with its heritage of medieval pastoral" (1989: 80). The role of Edgar Quinet in Joyce's thinking remains troubled by the paradox of its startling prominence in his writing, and the lack of context for Joyce's focus on the famous lyrical sentence promising that the wildflowers of nature will survive the wars of the world. In Ellmann's elegant translation: "the hyacinth disports in Wales, the periwinkle in Illyria, the daisy on the ruins of Numantia ... while around them the cities have changed masters and names, while some have ceased to exist, while the civilizations have collided with each other and smashed" (*JJ II* 664). The early studies of *Finnegans Wake* by James Atherton and Clive Hart gave considerable attention to Quinet's sentence, because it was the only quotation of any length included in the book, in the original French. Hart calls it "a single modulating sentence of quite remarkable architectural beauty which is fully stated on six occasions [in *FW*] and is always very clearly delineated" (1962: 182). Hart attributed the errors and corruptions in Joyce's French transcription to Joyce's "faulty memory" (1962: 183).

More recently, Inge Landuyt and Geert Lernout have attributed these anomalies to Joyce's recourse to an intermediary text, a geographical and anthropological study by Leon Metchnikoff in 1889 entitled *La civilisation et les grands fleuves historiques*. Basing their argument on notebook evidence, Landuyt and Lernout conclude that "Joyce chose the sentence for its beauty and for what the sentence itself says, not for Quinet's theories or for the function the sentence may have in *Introduction à la philosophie de l'histoire de l'humanité*, which he does not seem to have read" (Landuyt and Lernout 1995: 113). However, it may be premature to dismiss Quinet, who also published an epic prose poem called *Ahasverus*, as an influence on Joyce's notions of history. Ira Nadel writes of Quinet's importance to Joyce beyond the famous flower sentence, "Of equal if not greater importance to Joyce was Quinet's belief that an individual mind can be a complete history of an era, recording in its thoughts the ideas of its time" (Nadel 1989: 163). Clearly, the Quinet of this proposition would offer a significant structural concept to the author of *Ulysses*. And Nadel goes on to credit to Quinet two books on the Wandering Jew that address the Semitic Orient. The *Encyclopaedia Britannica* describes *Ahasverus* as a work "in which the legend of the Wandering Jew is used to symbolize the progress of humanity through the years" (8, 357). Ira Nadel notes that each of the four acts of *Ahasverus* correspond "to four days in the history of the world" (1989: 163). Joyce's library also included a copy of Eugene Sue's *Le Juif errant*, and Timothy Martin (1991) points out that there are many sources for the legend of the Wandering Jew. Martin himself singles out the pervasive influence of Richard Wagner's *The Flying Dutchman* on Joyce's work. While Martin explores the Wandering Jew chiefly as a Romantic type of the exiled artist, the legend's force as historical allegory, in Quinet's sense, may also have played a role in its literary deployment by Joyce.

Turning to the influence of nineteenth-century philosophers of history on Joyce, Derek Attridge reminds us that "[a]s early as 1923 Joyce had suggested to Harriet Weaver that the puzzle of his new project [*Finnegans Wake*] lay in the historical theories of Hegel and Vico, as well as the idea of metempsychosis [*Letters I* 205]" (Attridge 2000: 142). As Geert

Lernout (1990) has meticulously documented, it has been French critics – particularly those interested in deconstruction – who have explored the relationship between Joyce and G.W.F. Hegel. At the end of an early 1967 essay called "Violence and Metaphysics," later reprinted in *Writing and Difference*, Jacques Derrida ended his implicit dialogue with Emmanuel Levinas by asking a question that embedded a quotation from Joyce. "And what is the legitimacy, what is the meaning of the *cupola* in this proposition from perhaps the most Hegelian of modern novelists: 'Jewgreek is greekjew. Extremes meet'?" he writes (Derrida 1978: 152).[8] But in what sense has Joyce been "the most Hegelian of modern novelists"? Jacques Aubert and Jean-Michel Rabaté have explored this question most thoroughly, and it is to Jacques Aubert that we owe the discovery that Joyce's Hegelianism may have been deeply influenced by his reading of Bernard Bosanquet's 1892 study, *A History of Aesthetic*. In meditating on Joyce in relation to the status of the author and authority, Jean-Michel Rabaté invokes Derrida's formulation to point to the systematizing and totalizing impulse that Joyce ultimately deconstructs with excess (Rabaté 1988: 106).

> Hegel would stand as Joyce's direct ancestor, and Joyce would start precisely where Hegel had desisted, retracing the steps of a widening totality … . Joyce might well stand as our last author in the sense of *auctor*, the one who augments, adds to: he has clearly enlarged our notion of literary totality, a notion which, it might be recalled, is never too far from that of the monstrous. (Rabaté 1988: 105)

The influence of Hegel on Joyce's aesthetics[9] is clearer, however, than the impact of his philosophy of history on Joyce. The *Encyclopaedia Britannica* offers this summary of Hegel's philosophy of history:

> In his philosophy of history, Hegel presupposes that the whole of human history is a process through which mankind has been making spiritual and moral progress and advancing to self-knowledge. History has a plot, and the philosopher's task is to discern it. Some historians have found its key in the operation of natural laws of various kinds. Hegel's attitude, however, rested on the faith that history is the enactment of God's purpose and that man had now advanced far enough to descry what that purpose is: it is the gradual realization of human freedom. (*Encyclopaedia Britannica* 8, 731)

Joyce's yoking of Hegel and Vico may suggest that he saw in both models a dynamic sense of historical development in which human consciousness and human agency played active or reactive, but not passive or determined roles. The Hegelian model of history, with its emphasis on the spirit's drive for self-transcendence in the historical process, could be seen as one possible refutation for Haines's defensive comment in "Telemachus," that "It seems history is to blame" (*U* 1.649).

Given Joyce's early socialist and anarchist sympathies, the influence of Hegel's historical philosophy on Karl Marx may also have impressed him, his supposed disavowal notwithstanding. (This disavowal comes to us by way of Herbert Gorman's story that Joyce found the first chapter of *Das Kapital* so absurd that he instantly returned the book to the lender [*JJ II* 142].) Jacques Aubert believes that

> Joyce owed something to Marx, who is one of the "subversive writers" in whose company Stephen Dedalus is supposed to waste his youth [*P* 78] and who inspired the closing lines of "A Portrait of the Artist" (104): for he also spoke of the limits of human experience, of "the laws not only independent of human will, consciousness and intelligence, but rather, on the contrary, determining that will, consciousness, and intelligence." (Aubert 1992: 130)

The *Enclopaedia Britannica* articulates the connection between Hegel and Marx by noting:

> The notion that history conforms to a "dialectical" pattern, according to which contradictions generated at one level are overcome or transcended at the next, was incorporated, though in a radically new form – in the theory of social change propounded by Marx ... . Man, according to Marx, was a creative being, situated in a material world that stood before him as an objective reality and provided the field for his activities; this primitive truth, which had been obscured by Hegel's mystifying abstraction, afforded the key to a proper understanding of history as a process finally governed by the changing methods whereby men sought to derive from the natural environment the means of their subsistence, and the satisfaction of their evolving wants and needs. (*Enclopaedia Britannica* 8, 963)

Joyce may also have been aware that Marx was influenced not only by Hegel but also by Vico. Donald Verene points to an "important footnote to Vico in *Capital*" (Verene 1987: ix), and John Bishop considers "how Marx could find in Vico a prototype for his own more refined 'new science' of dialectical materialism" (Bishop 1986: 179). He writes, "*The New Science* gave Joyce a vision of a recurring patterning in social history that at once respected the unique problems and conditions of successive social eras, yet also isolated, as Marx did, social forces that manifested themselves in different cultures, in different material settings, and in different periods of history" (Bishop 1986: 180). R.B. Kershner and Donald Verene, in their thinking about Joyce and history, cite as relevant to Joyce, Marx's contention that "Men make their own history" (Kershner 1996: 42, Verene 1987: ix–x).

If Joyce's interest in, and use of, the historical philosophy of Marx is sketchy,[10] we receive clear references to Friedrich Nietzsche's *The Gay Science* in "A Painful Case," and to Nietzsche and Zarathustra in "Telemachus." These supplement Joyce's early play with Nietzschean tropes, when he called himself "James Overman" in a 1904 letter to George Roberts (*SL* 23). Jacques Aubert points out that at the beginning of the century "Public opinion, even in the most sophisticated circles was inclined to consider Nietzsche a profoundly immoral and perverse author, deserving contempt rather than consideration" (Aubert 1992: 25). This insight may explain Nietzsche's attraction to a young Joyce who favored heretics like Bruno for his philosophers. Both Jacques Aubert and Timothy Martin link Joyce's interest in Nietzsche to what Aubert calls "the Wagnerian craze" (1992: 24). We know that Joyce in Trieste owned a number of Nietzsche's works including *The Birth of Tragedy*, to which Aubert attributes the Dionysian argument of Joyce's early essay, "Royal Hibernian Academy 'Ecce Homo'" (Aubert 1992: 35). Spoo connects Nietzsche's meditation on "The Use and Abuse of History" (1874) with Joyce's repulsion for a Rome that he saw plagued by a burdensome sense of antiquity; the desire to forget history becomes the symptom that we are all affected by a modern "malady of history" (Spoo 1994: 18–19).

Joseph Valente goes further and argues that Nietzsche was not simply a youthful passion for Joyce, but that his appreciation of Nietzsche ripened and matured over time (Valente 1987). He believes that it exerted a powerful impact on *Ulysses* where Nietzsche's concept of *amor fati* and his perspectivism play major roles in the novel's deconstruction of the ego. Gregory Castle's essay on "Proteus" not only addresses the role of Nietzschean affirmation in Joyce's thinking but specifically relates it to Nietzsche's philosophy of history. "The Nietzschean theory of eternal recurrence is based on a world characterized as 'a play of forces' and waves of forces, at the same time one and many, increasing here and at the same time decreasing there," Castle writes (1992: 281). Nietzschean history is therefore non-teleological: "There is no great historical goal toward which the will to power tends, no manifestation of God, no absolute knowledge, no utopian paradise" (Castle 1992: 284). This is the philosophy of history Castle finds manifested in "Proteus." He writes:

> The alternative narrative limned in "Proteus," on the other hand, because it operates in accordance with principles of cyclical change, variable repetition and permutation, stands opposed to tradition and authority (at times a parodic, at times a critical stance), opposed to the teleological philosophy of history that "moves towards one great goal, the manifestation of God" [*U* 34]. (Castle 1992: 284)

Of twentieth-century philosophers of history, Joyce was clearly familiar with the work of Benedetto Croce, whose *Estetica* he owned, according to Richard Ellmann (*JJ II* 340). Ellmann also reports Joyce's friendship during his time in Trieste with Boris Furlan, who wrote essays on Croce, among others (*JJ II* 342). James Atherton lists one allusion to Croce in *Finnegans Wake*, and adds, parenthetically, "I do not understand the allusion but Joyce seems to have used many of Croce's works" (Atherton 1959: 243), without noting which ones. Joyce further complicated the question of his disposition toward Croce with a curious reference in a February 1, 1927 letter to Harriet Shaw Weaver, in which he reports to her about the international protest against the piracy of *Ulysses* by Samuel Roth. He writes, "The protest appears tomorrow. It has been cabled to 900 papers in U.S. I feel honoured by many of the signatures and humiliated by some, those of Gentile, Einstein, and Croce especially. It is curious about them too on account of Vico" (*SL* 319). Jean-Michel Rabaté refers to Croce as "the Italian philosopher who was most instrumental in restoring Giambattista Vico to his proper place on the map of modern culture." He further lists him among the thinkers whose debt Joyce never fully acknowledged – "using for instance Bernard Bosanquet's neo-Hegelian aesthetics to move from Aquinas to Hegel, then to Vico and Croce" (Rabaté 1996: 9). Croce's *Estetica* contained a chapter on Vico, and Ellmann quotes a section that he believes infuses Stephen's thoughts in *Ulysses*.

> Man creates the human world, creates it by transforming himself into the facts of society, by thinking it he re-creates his own creations,

traverses over again the paths he has already traversed, reconstructs the whole ideally, and thus knows it with full and true knowledge. (*JJ II* 340n)

This passage presents some of the salient features of Croce's theory that history is created by the human mind which encompasses its past and uses it to build its future – a creative sense of history particularly consonant with the interiorized Viconian historical consciousness of *Finnegans Wake*.

In addition to this considerable range of academic or professional philosophers of history who may have influenced Joyce or found resonance in his work, a number of other twentieth-century intellectuals whose theories have implications for the conception of history merit consideration. James Fairhall links Croce to William James and Henri Bergson as part of the "wave of new ideas in the hard and social sciences which swept across Paris and other centers of the leading industrial countries during the three decades prior to World War I" (Fairhall 1993: 200). Fairhall writes, "William James wrote about the rule of chance; Bergson about the importance of becoming rather than being; Croce about the plasticity of the historical past" (1993: 200). Joyce is known to have owned a copy of Henri Bergson's *The Meaning of the War: Life and Matter in Conflict* (1915) in his Zurich library, and, according to Michael Gillespie, to have consulted his *L'Evolution créatrice* (1914) while working on *Ulysses* (Gillespie 1983: 97). Bergson is considered a theorist of "process philosophy, one that stresses the open flow of time" (*Encyclopaedia Britannica* 2, 843). His theory of "creative evolution" proposes that "the whole evolutionary process should be seen as the endurance of an *élan vital* ("vital impulse") that is continually developing and generating new forms" (*Encyclopaedia Britannica* 2, 844). Although James Fairhall does not deal with Bergson's specific influence on Joyce, he nonetheless acknowledges that Joyce's interior monologue "evokes the flux of individual consciousness; it approximates what Bergson calls *la durée*, or time-as-experience, which he locates in our experience of our personalities of flowing through time" (Fairhall 1993: 213).

Sigmund Freud's psychoanalytical theories also construct a model of individual history that could be construed as a "process philosophy" or a dynamic model in which an unconscious historiography allows the past to influence the construction and experience of the present individual life. The question of Joyce's actual knowledge of Freud and respect for his theories was highly vexed until genetic criticism clarified some of the facts in the 1980s. Rosa Maria Bosinelli published an early essay that supplemented available evidence of Joyce's encounters with psychoanalytic theories in Trieste with interviews and judicious analysis (Bosinelli 1970). However, the first definite evidence of Joyce's serious attention to specific Freudian texts depended on Daniel Ferrer's examination of Notebook VI.B 19, which he published in the summer 1985 issue of the *James Joyce Quarterly*.

> We can now be absolutely certain that Joyce read attentively "Little Hans" and "The Wolf Man" ... that he took notes from them and that he used them in *Finnegans Wake*. There is also indirect but conclusive evidence that "Dora," "The Rat Man," and "President Schreber" ... passed through his hands, although we do not yet know whether he actually read them. (Ferrer 1985: 367)

Whether and how Joyce might have read Freud's *Totem and Taboo*, translated by A.A. Brill in 1918 or his 1930 *Civilization and its Discontents* is also not sufficiently clear to suggest what he might have taken from Freud's psycho-anthropological model of the process and development of civilization. Nonetheless, the Joycean texts themselves are so consonant with Freudian theory that critics find the connections difficult to resist. Brian Shaffer (1992), while acknowledging that Joyce could not have had Freud's *The Future of an Illusion* (1927) or the 1930 *Civilization and its Discontents* in mind while writing *Dubliners*, nonetheless produces provocative readings of the stories through them.

John Bishop makes the most interesting oblique case for Joyce's engagement with Freudian historical theory when he reads Viconian theory as producing a proto-Freudian psychology.

> In order to substantiate his dialectical account of history, essentially, Vico had to invent an elaborate depth psychology – a "metaphysics," in his own phrase – that would enable him to comprehend the unconsciousness out of which men made social choices "in the deplorable obscurity of the beginnings" of the human world. (Bishop 1986: 182)

Bishop goes on to delineate Vico's philology, with its focus on etymology, as a "protoform of psychoanalysis" (1986: 196). He writes:

> Vico's study of "the development of language" offered Joyce exactly this insight into "the language of dreams," his psychology of

unconsciousness in turn anticipating Freud's both because of its earlier emergence in history and because of its compass: not simply personality, but all of Vico's gentile humanity begins in an unconsciousness whose dynamic is revealed in the evolution of language and whose deep structure is yielded by etymology. (Bishop 1986: 196)

Having summarized the various philosophies of history Joyce attended during his writing, and interpretations of their influence by a range of Joycean critics, is it possible to generalize some principles of historical conceptualization that could be thought to characterize Joyce's view of history? Such an effort always risks some reductionism, but here are some of the features that may have appealed to Joyce in the various historical models he encountered over the course of his career. First, he seems to have been attracted to historical theorists who were themselves intellectual outliers or experimentalists, able to imagine worlds, as Bruno did, that are cosmically unimaginable. Other versions of such historical imaginations are those able to think of our planet's passage through time in ways that defamiliarize the familiar, as Vico did when he anthropologized the Book of Genesis or Homer. Joyce appears to have been drawn to speculative rather than positivistic methodologies in exploring possible origins or causations for events, and to postulations of unconscious and irrational motors behind temporal occurrences and cultural developments rather than the operations of immutable laws or a rational or purposive Providence. Philosophies of history that posit human agency in the production of history, and human possibilities for change and development aimed toward increased freedom appear to have interested Joyce. His lack of positivistic interest in questions of facticity or historical "truth" may also have inclined him toward historiographic theories and methodologies that recognized the role of perception, ideology, and interpretation in producing representations of history. Consequently anti-phenomenological theories of history that conflated history with consciousness, and historiography with narrative, seem to have engaged him. In addition, philosophers who recognized the potential of mythology for retrieving or representing that which remains unhistoricized (Vico, Quinet, Nietzsche, and Freud, among others) also had appeal for his poetic projects. Those philosophers able to encompass in their conceptualization the human activities whose cultural particularity traditional historiography ignores or elides – the everyday life of birth, death, childhood, marriage, earning a living, praying, eating, loving and playing – helped to legitimize Joyce's novelistic and experimental designs.

And finally, philosophies that collapse past, present and future – either by positing recurring cycles or by assuming the saturation of the present with the past and the present pregnant with the future,[11] also point toward the historical spirit of the range of Joycean texts.

These projects cannot be aligned perfectly with any or all of the specific philosophers of history Joyce encountered and attended but they point to possible connections between historical models and processes Joyce might have considered as relevant to his project and deployed in his fiction. These are currently reflected in contemporary historical criticism of the Joycean texts. Significantly, some of the contemporary critical theories of history turned to Joyce offer surprisingly provocative insights into his complexity of styles and the difficulties it produces. Enda Duffy looks to such contemporary theorists as Fredric Jameson rather than to Joyce's philosophical influences when he argues that *Ulysses* was written "with the forces of anticolonial revolution in view" and that it "profoundly embodies the subaltern concerns of a postcolonial text" (Duffy 1994: 7). He then goes on to argue for a possible anti-colonialist impetus behind the very features traditionally thought to be manifestations of high modernism.

> The fractured viewpoints, impetus toward allegory, rhetorics of obscurity, and comic defamiliarizations that enliven the [subaltern] writing make for strategies close to the literary defamiliarizations of metropolitan modernism, that are set off in the anticolonial moment by a mechanics developed out of fear. (Duffy 1994: 8)

It is interesting to consider the extent to which a Bruno or a Vico, writing in the shadow of a censorious Church, or a Michelet or Quinet, writing in shifting and dangerous intellectual climates in revolutionary France, would confront similar problems and even conditions that might translate themselves into certain features of their historical philosophies that in turn would catch Joyce's attention. Thomas Hofheinz offers a variant historical explanation for Joyce's difficult writing. He proposes

> that the *Wake*'s semantic opacity is a performance of crucial problems in historical understanding, enabling the book's readers to "resolve" its meaning in the optical sense, to focus on historical information which seems opaque because it is so intensely compounded in the human present. (Hofheinz 1995: 4)

James Fairhall intriguingly appeals to contemporary theorists – Fredric Jameson and Jacques Derrida in particular – when he looks at the relationship between history and language, or more specifically, Jameson's "prison-house of language" in relation to Joyce. He refers here to both the way history "is itself contained within language" or rhetoricity (Fairhall 1993: 9), and the deconstructive consignment of historical discourse to linguistic uncertainty. The solution to this impasse for Fairhall is Joyce's "infinite semiotic openness."

> It is this idea of freedom or liberation which links Joyce's attitudes toward history and language, and provides a common ground for both Jamesonian and Derridean perspectives on his work. Joyce struggled throughout his adult life to wrest a realm of freedom from history; though this was above all a struggle to save himself, we do find, in his fiction from *Dubliners* to *Finnegans Wake*, a liberating impulse directed toward the consciousness of his readers. (Fairhall 1993: 9)

History, and the philosophy of history, vastly exceed the matter of the merely thematic in the Joycean text, as we have seen. Historical excavations of the philosophies of history Joyce may himself have encountered, understood, and transmuted in some form in his writing are themselves doomed to speculative modes and methods with compromised rigor. We can only gesture toward what sort of historical principles might have guided Joyce in transforming the paralysis of Irish politics in the wake of the death of Parnell into varieties of desultory political conversations, heated family arguments, bad poems, allegories, or sentimentalia in *Dubliners*, *Portrait*, *Ulysses,* and *Finnegans Wake*. The myriad genres the Parnell story and its effects assume in Joyce's writing fracture and fragment what Fairhall calls "the Parnellite martyrology" (1993: 42) without entirely betraying it. The fight at the Dedalus Christmas dinner table, for example, evokes some of the subtexts of the Parnell scandal, like the one Joseph Valente calls "the gambit of sparing Parnell direct criticism by focusing the umbrage and vitriol of Irish popular opinion upon his paramour, Katherine O'Shea" (1995: 60). In "Eumaeus," the problematic intersection of public and private at the heart of the Parnell scandal receives further generic translations, as Enda Duffy points out. "What is done to [Parnell's] reputation here is that it is removed from the public, political sphere and, processed in Bloom's mind, is transformed into a cliched love story from the genre of realist romance" (Duffy 1994: 179).

Any single conventional history of the fall of Parnell has been fractured in the Joycean text and reproduced in proliferating versions with its marginal and occluded subtexts and popular translations that give the Irish patriot a strangely skewed and demythified historical afterlife. Fairhall writes, "We see in Joyce's writings a hostility to official history similar to and, at least in *Ulysses* and *Finnegans Wake*, influenced by Vico's own rejection of such history" (1993: 62). The Parnell of *Finnegans Wake* is effaced even further by a literal text and a textual error, the misspelling of the word "hesitency" in the letter by which Pigott sought to implicate the politician in the Phoenix Park murders. The *Wake* foregrounds the power of the single alphabetical letter to change the course of history at the same time that it throws documentary evidence into question. Patrick Parrinder writes of *Finnegans Wake*:

> This fictional combination of fable and deconstruction implies, not only that Joyce's weird jumble of stories could be made to yield a new sort of historical consciousness, but that both the new historical consciousness and the "scientific" history it offers to complement are nothing other than forms of mythology. To this extent, Isaiah Berlin is perhaps correct to regard Joyce as a "modern irrationalist" follower of Vico, whose work "would destroy, at least in theory, all distinctions between history as a rational discipline and mythical thinking." (Parrinder 1984: 211)

notes

1. Northrop Frye points out that "Since the fourteenth century, there has never been a time when English literature has not been influenced, often to the point of domination, by either French or Italian literary traditions, usually both at once" (1987: 3). He finds it curious that except for Joyce, "no previous writer in English except Coleridge seems to have been much interested [in Giordano Bruno of Nola], although he lived in England for a time and dedicated two best-known books to Sir Philip Sidney" (1987: 4).
2. Peter Hughes makes a similar point about Beckett's treatment of Vico in the essay, claiming that Beckett "read Vico through Joyce, laying Joyce's echoes and puns on top of Vico's axioms and etymologies, as in a palimpsest" (1987: 91).
3. Giordano Bruno was born in 1548 and became a Dominican priest after schooling in the monastery in which Thomas Aquinas had himself been a Dominican priest. In 1581 he went to Paris to lecture on philosophy, and began publishing his works on "The Shadows of Ideas," "Art of Memory," architecture, Lully, and "The Incantation of Circe," on the

Homeric sorceress. In 1582 he published a play called "The Chandler," then moved on to Oxford in England, where he wrote his Copernican treatise, "The Ash Wednesday Supper," and met Queen Elizabeth I. From England he went on to Germany and over a number of years published, among other works, his "On Cause, Principle, and Unity," "The Universe and its Worlds," "The Transport of Intrepid Souls," "The Expulsion of 'The Triumphant Beast'," and "Principle of Many Practical Arts," and "On Images, Signs, and Ideas." He eventually returned to Venice, where charges of heresy brought him before the Inquisition, which eventually transferred him to a Papal prison in Rome, where he languished between 1593 and 1600. During his imprisonment he recanted and reneged on his recantations – leading him to be condemned to burn at the stake. His books were placed on the Index expurgatorius and were not resurrected and circulated again until the late nineteenth century.

4. Verene writes, "There is an important footnote to Vico in *Capital*, and Marx's notion that 'men make their own history' is very close to Vico's conception of making. Michelet and Croce were both strongly influenced by Vico's conceptions of history and knowledge, and made them the bases of their own original thought. Michelet translated Vico into French, and Croce, with Nicolini, produced the standard edition of Vico's works. Michelet, Vico, and Marx all come together in Edmund Wilson's study of history, *To the Finland Station* ... But Joyce, more than any other figure, has circulated [or recirculated: 'a commodius vicus of recirculation'] the name of Vico to a wide audience" (1987: ix–x).

5. Hugh Kenner attributes a similar novelistic view of myth as the history of everyday life to Samuel Butler's archeologically inspired *The Authoress of the Odyssey*, which he considers a significant influence on the writing of *Ulysses*. See Kenner (1969: 285–98).

6. Bonnie Kime Scott's essay on "Joyce and Michelet" (1992) explores chiefly Michelet's writings on women, *La Femme* and his defense of witches in *La Sorcière*.

7. My thanks to Vivian Folkenflik for her helpful consultation on the subject of Michelet.

8. Geert Lernout uses this quotation to illustrate the methodological differences between "conventional" and "deconstructionist" critics exploring Hegel's influence on Joyce: "A conventional Joyce critic who wants to show the importance of Hegel in Joyce's work must establish the connection by proving that Joyce read Hegel, that his thought was influenced by the German philosopher, or that it is structured similarly. A deconstructionist critic will simply refer to Jacques Aubert's book (1973), or better still, to Derrida's description of Joyce as 'the most Hegelian of novelists' (1964b, 473) without having to add Derrida's qualifying 'peut-être' or the source of the comment which is Jean Paris's *James Joyce par lui-même* (1957), not mentioned by Derrida" (Lernout 1990: 198).

9. Robert Scholes and Marlena Corcoran's essay, "The Aesthetic Theory and the Critical Writings" in the 1984 Bowen and Carens' *Companion to Joyce Studies* discusses Hegel's history of aesthetic development in relation to Joyce (Scholes and Corcoran 1984: 690–705). See also F.C. McGrath's

essay, "Laughing in His Sleeve: The Sources of Stephen's Aesthetics," for a discussion of Hegel's possible influence on Stephen's theory of aesthetics (McGrath 1986: 259–75).

10. Thomas Hofheinz's book offers one of the fuller discussions of Marxist concepts of history, but he discusses the topic chiefly through Fredric Jameson's interpretations of Joyce's works (Hofheinz 1995: 7–12).

11. Cheryl Herr reads "*Finnegans Wake* as in part a response to the historical dynamic that has placed provisionality at the heart of Irish politics." She thus transforms the *Wake* into "a history of the future, designed to evolve with its culture and actually to authorize the size and shape of that future's construction of histories for the various contending groups in Irish politics" (Herr 1996: 197).

references

Atherton, James. *The Books at the Wake: A Study of Literary Allusions in James Joyce's "Finnegans Wake."* Carbondale: Southern Illinois University Press, 1959.

Attridge, Derek. *Joyce Effects: On Language, Theory, and History.* Cambridge: Cambridge University Press, 2000.

Attridge, Derek, and Marjorie Howes, eds. *Semicolonial Joyce.* Cambridge: Cambridge University Press, 2000.

Aubert, Jacques. *The Aesthetics of James Joyce.* Baltimore: Johns Hopkins University Press, 1992.

Beckett, Samuel, et al. *Our Exagmination Round his Factification for Incamination of Work in Progress.* London: Faber and Faber, 1929.

Bishop, John. *Joyce's Book of the Dark: Finnegans Wake.* Madison: University of Wisconsin Press, 1986.

Boldrini, Lucia. *Joyce, Dante, and the Poetics of Literary Relations.* Cambridge: Cambridge University Press, 2001.

Bosinelli Bollettieri, Rosa Maria. "The Importance of Trieste in Joyce's Work, with Reference to his Knowledge of Psycho-analysis," *James Joyce Quarterly* 7:3 (Spring 1970), pp. 177–85.

Castle, Gregory. "'I am Almosting It': History, Nature, and the Will to Power in 'Proteus'," *James Joyce Quarterly* 29:2 (Winter 1992), pp. 281–96.

Cheng, Vincent J. *Joyce, Race, and Empire.* Cambridge: Cambridge University Press, 1995.

Cheng, Vincent J., and Timothy Martin, eds. *Joyce in Context.* Cambridge: Cambridge University Press, 1992.

Derrida, Jacques. "Violence and Metaphysics," in *Writing and Difference.* Trans. Alan Bass. Chicago: University of Chicago Press, 1978, pp. 79–153.

Duffy, Enda. *The Subaltern "Ulysses."* Minneapolis: University of Minnesota Press, 1994.

Ellmann, Richard. *James Joyce.* New and revised edition. New York: Oxford University Press, 1982.

Fairhall, James. *James Joyce and the Question of History.* Cambridge: Cambridge University Press, 1993.

Faj, Attila. "Vico's Basic Law of History in *Finnegans Wake*," in *Vico and Joyce*. Ed. Donald Verene. Albany: State University of New York Press, 1987, pp. 20–31.

Ferrer, Daniel. "The Freudful Couchmare of Λd: Joyce's Notes on Freud and the Composition of Chapter XVI of *Finnegans Wake*," *James Joyce Quarterly* 22:4 (Summer 1985), pp. 367–82.

Ferrer, Daniel. "Loci Memoriae: Joyce and the Art of Memory," *Classic Joyce. Joyce Studies in Italy 6*. Ed. Franca Ruggieri. Roma: Bulzone Editore, 1999, pp. 355–60.

Frye, Northrop. "Cycle and Apocalypse in *Finnegans Wake*," in *Vico and Joyce*. Ed. Donald Verene. Albany: State University of New York Press, 1987, pp. 3–19.

Gillespie, Michael Patrick. *Inverted Volumes Improperly Arranged: James Joyce and His Trieste Library*. Ann Arbor: UMI Research Press, 1983.

Hart, Clive. *Structure and Motif in Finnegans Wake*. London: Faber, 1962.

Herr, Cheryl. *Joyce's Anatomy of Culture*. Urbana: University of Illinois Press, 1986.

Herr, Cheryl. "Ireland from the Outside," in *Joyce and the Subject of History*. Eds. Mark A. Wollaeger, Victor Luftig, and Robert Spoo. Ann Arbor: University of Michigan Press, 1996, pp. 195–210.

Hofheinz, Thomas. *Joyce and the Invention of Irish History: "Finnegans Wake" in Context*. Cambridge: Cambridge University Press, 1995.

Hughes, Peter. "From Allusion to Implosion. Vico, Michelet, Joyce, Beckett," in *Vico and Joyce*. Ed. Donald Verene. Albany: State University of New York Press, 1987, pp. 83–99.

Kenner, Hugh. "Homer's Sticks and Stones," *James Joyce Quarterly* 6:4 (Summer 1969), pp. 285–98.

Kershner, R.B. *Joyce, Bakhtin, and Popular Literature: Chronicles of Disorder*. Chapel Hill: University of North Carolina, 1989.

Kershner, R.B. "History as Nightmare: Joyce's Portrait to Christy Brown," in *Joyce and the Subject of History*. Eds. Mark A. Wollaeger, Victor Luftig, and Robert Spoo. Ann Arbor: University of Michigan Press, 1996.

Kessler, John. *Giordano Bruno: the Forgotten Philosopher*. Accessed at: <www.infidels. org/library/historical/john_kessler/giordano_bruno.html> (2003).

Landuyt, Inge, and Geert Lernout. "Joyce's Sources: *Les grands fleuves historiques*," *Joyce Studies Annual 1995*. Ed. Thomas F. Staley. Austin: University of Texas Press, 1995, pp. 99–138.

Leonard, Garry. "The History of Now: Commodity Culture and Everyday Life in Joyce," in *Joyce and the Subject of History*. Eds. Mark A. Wollaeger, Victor Luftig, and Robert Spoo. Ann Arbor: University of Michigan Press, 1996, pp. 13–26.

Lernout, Geert. *The French Joyce*. Ann Arbor: University of Michigan Press, 1990.

McGrath, F.C. "Laughing in his Sleeves: The Sources of Stephen's Aesthetics," *James Joyce Quarterly* 23:3 (Spring 1986), pp. 259–75.

Mali, Joseph. "Mythology and Counter-History: The New Critical Art of Vico and Joyce," in *Vico and Joyce*. Ed. Donald Verene. Albany: State University of New York Press, 1987, pp. 32–47.

Martin, Timothy. *Joyce and Wagner: A Study of Influence*. Cambridge: Cambridge University Press, 1991.

Nadel, Ira B. *Joyce and the Jews: Culture and Texts*. Iowa City: University of Iowa Press, 1989.

The New Encyclopaedia Britannica. 15th edition. Chicago: Encyclopaedia Britannica, Inc., 1984.

Nolan, Emer. *James Joyce and Nationalism*. New York: Routledge, 1995.

O'Neill, John. "Vico Mit Freude Rejoyced," in *Vico and Joyce*. Ed. Donald Verene. Albany: State University of New York Press, 1987, pp. 160–74.

Parrinder, Patrick. *James Joyce*. Cambridge University Press, 1984.

Rabaté, Jean-Michel. "A Portrait of the Artist as a Bogeyman," in *James Joyce: The Augmented Ninth*. Ed. Bernard Benstock. Syracuse: Syracuse University Press, 1988, pp. 103–34.

Rabaté, Jean-Michel. *The Ghosts of Modernity*. Gainesville: University of Florida Press, 1996.

Rancière, Jacques. *The Names of History*. Trans. Hassan Melehy. Minneapolis: University of Minnesota Press, 1994.

Reynolds, Mary. "The City in Vico, Dante, and Joyce," in *Vico and Joyce*. Ed. Donald Verene. Albany: State University of New York Press, 1987, pp. 100–22.

Scholes, Robert, and Marlena G. Corcoran. "The Aesthetic Theory and the Critical Writings," in *A Companion to Joyce Studies*. Eds. Zack Bowen and James F. Carens. Westport, Conn.: Greenwood Press, 1984, pp. 689–705.

Scott, Bonnie Kime. "Joyce and Michelet," in *Joyce in Context*. Eds. Vincent Cheng and Timothy Martin. Cambridge: Cambridge University Press 1992, pp. 123–37.

Senn, Fritz. "History as Text in Reverse," in *Joyce and the Subject of History*. Eds. Mark A. Wollaeger, Victor Luftig, and Robert Spoo. Ann Arbor: University of Michigan Press, 1996, pp. 47–58.

Shaffer, Brian W. "Joyce and Freud: Discontent and its Civilizations," in *Joyce in Context*. Eds. Vincent Cheng and Timothy Martin. Cambridge: Cambridge University Press, 1992, pp. 73–88.

Spoo, Robert, *James Joyce and the Language of History*. Oxford: Oxford University Press, 1994.

Valente, Joseph. "Beyond Truth and Freedom: The New Faith of Joyce and Nietzsche," *James Joyce Quarterly* 25:1 (Fall 1987), pp. 87–103.

Valente, Joseph. *James Joyce and the Problem of Justice*. Cambridge: Cambridge University Press, 1995.

Valente, Joseph. "James Joyce and the Cosmopolitan Sublime," in *Joyce and the Subject of History*. Eds. Mark A. Wollaeger, Victor Luftig, and Robert Spoo. Ann Arbor: University of Michigan Press, 1996, pp. 59–80.

Verene, Donald Phillip, ed. *Vico and Joyce*. Albany: State University of New York Press, 1987.

Webster's Third New International Dictionary of the English Language Unabridged. Chicago: Encyclopaedia Britannica, Inc., 1981.

Weir, Lorraine. *Writing Joyce: A Semiotics of the Joyce System*. Bloomington: Indiana University Press, 1989.

Wollaeger, Mark A., Victor Luftig, and Robert Spoo, eds. *Joyce and the Subject of History*. Ann Arbor: University of Michigan Press, 1996.

11
genetic joyce:
textual studies and the reader

__michael groden__

As the "Aeolus" episode of *Ulysses* nears its conclusion, Stephen Dedalus comes to the end of his short vignette about two old ladies who have climbed to the top of Nelson's Pillar. Feeling dizzy from the height, the women "pull up their skirts" and "settle down on their striped petticoats, peering up at the statue of the onehandled adulterer." The text continues:

DAMES DONATE DUBLIN'S CITS
SPEEDPILLS VELOCITOUS AEROLITHS, BELIEF

– It gives them a crick in their necks, Stephen said, and they are too tired to look up or down or to speak. They put the bag of plums between them and eat the plums out of it, one after another, wiping off with their handkerchiefs the plumjuice that dribbles out of their mouths and spitting the plumstones slowly out between the railings.

A few lines later, the focus shifts briefly from Stephen's story to Dublin's tram system:

HELLO THERE, CENTRAL!

At various points along the eight lines tramcars with motionless trolleys stood in their tracks, bound for or from Rathmines, Rathfarnham, Blackrock, Kingstown and Dalkey, Sandymount Green, Ringsend and Sandymount Tower, Donnybrook, Palmerston Park and Upper

Rathmines, all still, becalmed in short circuit. Hackney cars, cabs, delivery waggons, mailvans, private broughams, aerated mineral water floats with rattling crates of bottles, rattled, rolled, horsedrawn, rapidly.

Finally, "Aeolus" ends after Stephen names his tale "*A Pisgah Sight of Palestine* or *The Parable of The Plums.*" One of his listeners, Professor MacHugh, reacts ("We gave him that idea") and then, like the trams, stops his motion:

He halted on sir John Gray's pavement island and peered aloft at Nelson through the meshes of his wry smile.

DIMINISHED DIGITS PROVE TOO TITILLATING
FOR FRISKY FRUMPS. ANNE WIMBLES, FLO
WANGLES – YET CAN YOU BLAME THEM?

– Onehandled adulterer, he said smiling grimly. That tickles me, I must say.
– Tickled the old ones too, Myles Crawford said, if the God Almighty's truth was known. (*U* 7.1013–75)

Critics have analyzed this short scene in many different ways. First, it parallels one in the *Odyssey*: Odysseus and his men are stuck on Aeolia after Aeolus's winds blew them almost home to Ithaca but then back to the island, and in *Ulysses* the women are motionless and silent, the men have stopped walking, and the trams are short-circuited. At the end of an episode full of noise and movement, almost everything is quiet and motionless.

Second, Stephen's parable calls out for interpretation. His short tale is full of realistic detail and strong language, and, unlike his anemic vampire poem from a few pages earlier (or the villanelle in *A Portrait of the Artist as a Young Man*), it obeys Myles Crawford's request that he produce "something with a bite in it. Put us all into it" (*U* 7.621). Stephen weaves several details from *Ulysses* into his narrative: the two midwives with their umbrellas whom he saw on Sandymount Strand (*U* 3.29ff.); Fumbally's lane, where, he recalled on the strand, he once met a prostitute (*U* 3.379) and where his two women live; Garrett Deasy's "little savingsbox," which finds an echo in the women's "red tin letterbox moneybox" (*U* 2.218, 7.932); Nelson's Pillar, towards which Stephen and Professor MacHugh walk after they leave the newspaper office; Buck Mulligan's song about

Mary Ann "hising up her petticoats" (*U* 1.384, 3.462), clothing which becomes part of Stephen's story; and Seymour Bushe's speech about Michelangelo's statue of Moses (*U* 7.768–71) and John F. Taylor's about "the youthful Moses" (*U* 7.833), which provokes J.J. O'Molloy's remark that Moses "died without having entered the land of promise" (*U* 7.873; see C.H. Peake's *James Joyce: The Citizen and the Artist* [1977: 196–7] for these and other echoes). Stephen's story has been discussed as a study in frustration and disappointment (Blamires 1996: 58–9); as a metaphoric presentation of a sterile Ireland in which two old women "spit potential seeds upon concrete where they cannot grow" (Schwarz 1987: 122) or in which the women are "representative of sterile Ireland and his own self-censure" (Schwaber 1999: 154); and as a story linking politics and sex, since the Irish women are transfixed and paralyzed by the English conqueror Nelson, a man who, even without an arm, can still tickle them (and MacHugh, too, who admits that "the onehandled adulterer," as Stephen refers to Nelson, "tickles me") and whose reputation remained unharmed even though, as an adulterer, he committed the act that later ruined the Irish Parnell (Peake 1977: 197). The story's plumstones evoke the name Plumtree, the company whose ad for potted meat remains in Leopold Bloom's mind all day (*U* 5.144–7), and like the potted meat they serve as a marker of sexual frustration and satisfaction. Finally, as Stanley Sultan notes, Stephen's story ironically inverts and refutes Taylor's Romantic identification of the "youthful Moses" and the "youth of Ireland" (*U* 7.833, 829; Sultan 1964: 115–16) and can inspire such post-colonial readings as those by Enda Duffy, who points out that, in various ways including Stephen's parable, "a gendered division of labor in the colony is implicitly posited early in the novel" (1994: 170), and by Patrick McGee, who notes that Stephen, in identifying with "the woman who labors ... has aligned himself with the figure of the subaltern, the bondwoman" (1999: 87).

Third, the bold interpolations in the passage – critics usually describe them as newspaper headlines, subheads, captions, or simply heads – break up any traditional narrative momentum. These interruptions include a sensationalistic restatement of the women's actions ("DAMES DONATE DUBLIN'S CITS"), a colloquial phone call seeking help for the tram system ("HELLO THERE, CENTRAL!"), and alliterative descriptions of Nelson ("DIMINISHED DIGITS") and the old women ("FRISKY FRUMPS").

Readers might understandably think that responding to the words in the printed *Ulysses* is a sufficiently large task. They might be forgiven for not knowing that when Joyce first considered "Aeolus" finished and sent it to his typist and then to the printer of *The Little Review* (the New York magazine that was serializing *Ulysses*), no newspaper heads or trams were in the episode, Stephen's name for his narrative was simply *"A Pisgah Sight of Palestine,"* and the last words were slightly fewer.[1] They might also be unaware that "Sandymount Tower" was "Sandymount tower" in the printed editions until 1932 and that in all the printed editions from 1922 through 1968, Professor MacHugh said "Onehandled adulterer" only "grimly." Not until the Gabler edition in 1984 did he speak "smiling grimly."[2]

Ulysses alone does not account for readers' indifference to Joyce's revisions or to variations among the printed versions. Textual critics, who study such matters (textual criticism investigates how texts are produced and transmitted and applies that investigation to scholarly editing), have long bemoaned the tendency of other critics to ignore textual matters completely. But faced with remarks like Fredson Bowers's from 1959 – "Every practising critic, for the humility of his [*sic*] soul, ought to study the transmission of some appropriate text" (Bowers 1959: 4) – who wouldn't stay away?[3] Furthermore, the dominant critical attitudes during most of the twentieth century restricted attention to the final printed text. In their influential *Theory of Literature* from 1948, René Wellek and Austin Warren argued for an "intrinsic study of literature," an approach in which textual study and establishing accurate editions are "preliminary to the ultimate task of scholarship," and drafts and other evidence of a work's development are "not, finally, necessary to an understanding of the finished work or to a judgement upon it. Their interest is that of any alternative, i.e. they may set into relief the qualities of the final text" (Wellek and Warren 1949: 137, 57, 91). Critical assumptions based upon statements like these were ubiquitous, even in specific considerations of drafts. In a 1948 essay called "Genesis, or The Poet as Maker," for example, Donald A. Stauffer asked, "What light ... does the composition of a poem throw upon its meaning and its beauty? What difficulties in a finished poem may be explained, what pointless ambiguities dispelled, what purposeful ambiguities sharpened, by references found in its earlier states?" (Stauffer 1948: 43–4). The situation did not change as New Criticism (of which Wellek and Warren are prime theorists) faded and was supplanted by deconstruction and post-structuralism, whose practitioners emphasized the indeterminacies and instabilities of texts but only in relation to meaning and interpretation and not to the state of the texts themselves.[4]

And yet, 50 years after Bowers, Wellek and Warren, and Stauffer, in a complete turnaround Jean-Michel Rabaté called for an "ideal genetic reader" of Joyce (Rabaté 2001: 203). How did such a reversal come about?

*

Despite claims like Wellek and Warren's, interest in how Joyce wrote *Ulysses* is as old as the work itself. Even before *Ulysses* was published in 1922, Valery Larbaud described "abbreviated phrases underlined in various-coloured pencil" (1922: 102) on Joyce's working papers. Most prominently, Frank Budgen in 1934 described Joyce pulling out "little writing blocks especially made for the waistcoat pocket" and jotting down "a word or two ... at lightning speed as ear or memory served his turn." Budgen noted that this "method of making a multitude of criss-cross notes in pencil was a strange one for a man whose sight was never good. A necessary adjunct to the method was a huge oblong magnifying glass" (1934: 172). Joyce acknowledged this interest in *Finnegans Wake*: the manuscript of Anna Livia Plurabelle's "untitled mamafesta" is described there as "writing thithaways end to end and turning, turning and end to end hithaways writing and with lines of litters slittering up and louds of latters slettering down" (*FW* 114.16–18), as "not a miseffectual whyacinthinous riot of blots and blurs and bars and balls and hoops and wriggles and juxtaposed jottings linked by spurts of speed: it only looks as like it as damn it" (*FW* 118.28–31), and as "engraved and retouched and edgewiped and puddenpadded ... all those red raddled obeli cayennepeppercast over the text, calling unnecessary attention to errors, omissions, repetitions and misalignments" (*FW* 120.10–16). The *Wake* narrator recommends that the manuscript's students "see all there may remain to be seen" (*FW* 113.32–3).

Scholars predictably tried to "see all," looking more systematically at the documents that Larbaud and Budgen described anecdotally. Making such investigations possible was the establishment of major Joyce collections at the British Library, the University at Buffalo, State University of New York, Cornell University, the National Library of Ireland, the University of Texas at Austin, the University of Tulsa, and Yale University; with important documents also at Harvard, Princeton, and Southern Illinois Universities and at the University of Wisconsin at Milwaukee.[5] In 1975 the Rosenbach Museum published a beautiful facsimile of its *Ulysses* manuscript, and in 1977–79 all other extant and available prepublication materials for Joyce's works were published in the 63-volume *James Joyce*

Archive. The manuscript collections remained relatively static from the 1970s until 2000, when two early drafts of *Ulysses* episodes came to light and were sold at auction for huge sums. First the National Library of Ireland bought a "Circe" draft for $1.5 million, and then an unidentified private collector purchased a "Eumaeus" draft for $1.2 million. Even more astonishing, in May 2002 the National Library of Ireland acquired about 25 previously unknown Joyce manuscripts, mostly notes and early drafts of *Ulysses* episodes, for $11.7 million.[6] In contrast, in the late 1940s the University of Buffalo bought its huge collection of Joyce manuscripts for $10,000, a sum considered exorbitant at the time.

Early scholarly work on the *Ulysses* manuscripts focused on Joyce's writing of specific episodes or on particular stages in the book's development, such as the proofs. A pioneering study was A. Walton Litz's *The Art of James Joyce* (1961), which studied the *Ulysses* notesheets and proofs and demonstrated how Joyce's notesheets led to his revisions to *Ulysses*. Litz also sketched out the process by which Joyce moved from a concept of revision as compression to revision as expansion. My book, *"Ulysses" in Progress*, built on previous work and established two important aspects of Joyce's writing. First, it worked out a stemma, or family tree, of the *Ulysses* manuscripts, placing the documents in relation to each other. Second, it showed that Joyce's conception of *Ulysses* evolved as he moved from an "early stage" (the first nine episodes) to a "middle stage" ("Wandering Rocks" through "Oxen of the Sun") and then to a "last stage" ("Circe" to the end), with each stage featuring writing styles and techniques that seemed to come into being only as he worked. Joyce left traces of his early ideas and plans as he moved beyond them rather than eradicating them. "Aeolus" was my main example: the newspaper heads were grafted onto an existing text, but that existing text was basically like the episodes that precede it. In presenting *Ulysses* as a "palimpsest involving all three stages" (Groden 1977: 4), Joyce made it possible to read any passage in his book vertically – as the result of an elaborate composition process and a series of choices – as well as horizontally – as part of an unfolding text in the published book.

These early manuscript studies shared certain features. For one thing, they took for granted that the study of manuscripts and the writing process made sense only in relation to the published work. As I wrote in *"Ulysses" in Progress*, "Once [Joyce] finished the book ... the tasks of interpreting and assessing the complete work necessarily take precedence over any questions about the methods of composition" (Groden 1977: 200–1). Second, these studies looked at the manuscripts in order to interpret the works rather than to establish accurate texts of them. Third, the manuscript studies operated pragmatically and untheoretically: the scholar saw a specific problem and looked to the documents for possible answers. Critics once hoped that the manuscripts "would ultimately provide ... a thread for the labyrinth," but, as Litz notes, "somehow the controlling design that I sought eluded me, and I have long since relinquished the comforting belief that access to an author's workshop provides insights of greater authority than those provided by other kinds of criticism" (1961: v; elsewhere, Litz suggests that every scholar approaching Joyce's manuscripts should be forced to read "The Figure in the Carpet," Henry James's marvelous short story about an obsessive and ultimately doomed quest for an authorially sanctioned key to a writer's works [1966: 103]). Manuscript scholars now are more likely to share the assumption of Luca Crispi and Sam Slote, who, in the introduction to their forthcoming collection of genetic essays on *Finnegans Wake*, remark that genetic criticism cannot provide an answer or a key to the works but "should help make the questions more interesting."

I am focusing mostly on *Ulysses* here, but I want to briefly consider *Finnegans Wake*. Litz studied the manuscripts for the *Wake* as well as for *Ulysses* in *The Art of James Joyce*, and at about the same time, other scholars produced editions of the manuscripts for individual *Wake* chapters and notebooks. David Hayman devoted a full-length article to the 13 composition stages of one *Wake* sentence, and in 1963 he published *A First-Draft Version of "Finnegans Wake,"* an edition containing the earliest available state of each passage in the *Wake*. The *Finnegans Wake* materials occupy 36 of the 63 volumes in the *James Joyce Archive*, and the *Archive* has inspired a great deal of scholarship primarily focused, it has turned out, much more on the notebooks than on the drafts. This work has culminated in the *"Finnegans Wake" Notebooks at Buffalo* project, an enormously ambitious edition of the 49 notebooks, including photo-reproductions and transcriptions of each notebook page along with an identification of every note's source that the editors were able to identify and indications of Joyce's use of each note that found its way into a draft or into the published text of the *Wake*.

Even though manuscripts were used by critics more than by textual editors, scholarly editions were produced. William York Tindall edited the poems in *Chamber Music* in 1954, and in the 1960s Robert Scholes edited *Dubliners* and Chester Anderson *A Portrait of the Artist as a Young Man*. When Hans Walter Gabler published his *Critical and Synoptic Edition* of *Ulysses* in three volumes in 1984 (a one-volume reading text appeared in 1986), *Ulysses* became the first, and so far only, Joyce work to appear in a "critical edition" – one prepared by comparing extant manuscript and printed versions of the work and including an apparatus that explains the editorial principles and lays out the evidence on which the editor based the decisions. (In the 1990s, Gabler also produced editions of *Dubliners* and *Portrait*.) Joyce's other works remain unedited, although in 1979 John MacNicholas produced a "textual companion" to *Exiles* which shows how to mark up an existing text to produce a more accurate one.

If the story had ended here, this essay would not be part of this book. Two important developments occurred in the 1970s and 1980s, however. First, the attention Gabler's edition of *Ulysses* received on its release and the "Joyce Wars" it provoked a few years later made all Joyce's readers, critics, and scholars and even the general reading public aware of textual matters. Second, the age of theory curtailed most interest in manuscript study and other kinds of archival work for about twenty years, but in France, where much of the theory imported into English-speaking countries originated, scholars thoroughly conversant with the theoretical texts, in several cases students of the major theorists themselves, formalized manuscript study and even institutionalized it as *critique génétique*, or genetic criticism. We continue to work in exciting ways with the consequences of these two events.

*

Writing in the famous eleventh edition of the *Encyclopaedia Britannica*, J.P. Postgate concludes his entry on textual criticism with incredibly naive optimism: "As time goes on, textual criticism will have less and less to do ... . In the newer texts ... , it will have from the outset but a very contracted field" (Postgate 1911: 715). Almost as if in response, Sylvia Beach included a startlingly direct note in the first edition of *Ulysses* that said, "The publisher asks the reader's indulgence for typographical errors unavoidable in the exceptional circumstances," and in his letters Joyce noted the errors and hoped that they would be corrected (*Letters I* 180, *Letters III* 86). For many years, however, *Ulysses* was considered uneditable: the existing texts seemed too corrupt, and the manuscript record too uncertain, to make an edition possible. But after the manuscripts became available in libraries and in the *James Joyce Archive*, and the patterns of Joyce's writing were adequately established, Hans Walter Gabler saw a theoretical way out of the dilemma by combining English and North American editing practices with quite different German procedures. In

Anglo-American practice, the editor creates a new version of a work by choosing one extant text as "copytext" and emending the copytext with readings from other surviving documents, thus producing an "eclectic text" (it combines readings from more than one extant text) in order to reflect what Fredson Bowers called the "final authorial intention." German genetic editing, in contrast, has been more concerned with documenting the stages through which the work passed during its composition.[7]

The main impediment to editing *Ulysses* involved the existing states of the text: none seemed adequate as a copytext.[8] The Rosenbach Manuscript offers a handwritten beginning-to-end version of the text, but because Joyce revised the text so heavily on the typescript and proofs, it sometimes represents only about two-thirds of an episode's text. The first edition contains the full text but its many errors seemed to rule it out as a copytext. Gabler reasoned, however, that in theory the Rosenbach Manuscript plus all Joyce's additions on the many sets of typescripts and proofs should add up to the full *Ulysses* and that he could reject all the existing versions of *Ulysses* as copytext in favor of a "continuous manuscript text." (In reality, sometimes we cannot know what Joyce wrote because documents are missing, sometimes the printers set a different word from the one Joyce wrote and he changed it to something else. The most complicated uncertainty involves the Rosenbach Manuscript, because only about half of it was the document that the typist used to create the typescript from which the proofs and so the first edition were set, and in several places it contains words, phrases, and even sentences that were never typed or printed.) To construct the "continuous manuscript text," Gabler used German genetic practices to assemble a "virtual" text (it never existed as a single text before) that could serve as a copytext in Anglo-American practice. Once this copytext was assembled, he then compared it to the extant states of the text, and he emended it whenever that seemed appropriate. His goal, as he explained it, was to produce "*Ulysses* as Joyce wrote it,"[9] which signaled a substantial break with the Anglo-American goal of reproducing the "final authorial intention." The edition is authorial – it privileges Joyce's writing over the contributions of everyone else connected with the publication – but it reflects what Joyce did (activities for which we have evidence) rather than what he might have intended.

For the *Critical and Synoptic Edition*, which Garland Publishing released in three volumes in 1984, the left-hand pages provide a coded, synoptic version of the text that indicates the composition stage at which Joyce entered each word or phrase as well as Joyce's revisions and deletions, and the right-hand pages offer a clear reading text, which is the left-hand page without the codes and the words that Joyce either changed or deleted. The synoptic text is not a complete genetic edition – rather, it is a visualization of how the continuous manuscript text came into being. (This is different from a visualization of how *Ulysses* itself came into being.) In 1986, Random House in the United States and Bodley Head and Penguin in England released a one-volume version of the reading text alone, at first called *Ulysses: The Corrected Text* and later, in a slightly revised version in 1993, *Ulysses: The Gabler Edition.*

In his foreword to the three-volume edition, Gabler states that the "main editorial achievement, centered on the establishment of the text and the analysis of its evolution in the synoptic display of the edition's left-hand pages, is submitted to the scrutiny of every critical reader and adventurous explorer of the novel" (*U* viii), and in a review Jerome McGann noted that the *Critical and Synoptic Edition* should "be a required object of study for every scholar working in English literature" because it "raises all the central questions that have brought such a fruitful crisis to literary work in the postmodern period" (McGann 1985: 174). Things progressed differently, however, and Gabler's *Ulysses* is now known for the controversy it provoked almost as much as an edition.

In June 1988, the *New York Review of Books* published John Kidd's article "The Scandal of *Ulysses*," which contained a variety of charges: Gabler misread the manuscripts, relied too heavily on facsimiles, spelled the names of historical figures incorrectly, departed too often from the book as it was originally published. Here and in "An Inquiry into *Ulysses: The Corrected Text,*" his 170-page expanded version of his charges, Kidd provided specific examples of Gabler's supposed errors, and in focusing on precise details in the reading text, he deflected attention from the three-volume *Critical and Synoptic Edition*, with its synoptic presentation and apparatus that scholars assumed would be the focus of attention, to the one-volume *Corrected Text*, where the reading text stands isolated from the editorial principles and procedures that produced it. He argued that Random House should stop distributing the Gabler edition and that a new edition of *Ulysses* was needed.

In a response to Kidd's "Inquiry," I wrote that two narratives regarding the achievement and reception of the Gabler edition had already been constructed – the initial flurry of glowing newspaper reports and supporting scholarly articles and then the attacks – and I hoped that a third narrative, one in which the edition would be studied and assessed in a scholarly manner, would begin (Groden 1990: 81, 108). The dispute eventually subsided – Random House decided to keep the edition in print, although it reissued its 1961 version and started selling it along with the Gabler edition; Gabler provided his own response to Kidd's "Inquiry"; and the publisher W.W. Norton offered Kidd a contract to edit *Ulysses*, an edition he failed to produce.[10] The debate, however, precluded almost all discussion about the conceptual, theoretical, and practical significance of this particular edition of this work and about what the edition might say about works in general.

Such discussions were and remain few, but they do exist. In "Intentional Error," written in the midst of the debate, Vicki Mahaffey highlights the paradox between textual editing, which strives to "eliminate error," and the much more tolerant attitude towards error that *Ulysses* exhibits. Bloom, for example, notices and then toys with Martha Clifford's two typos in her letter to him – "I called you naughty boy because I do not like that other world" and "So now you know what I will do to you, you naughty boy, if you do not wrote" (*U* 5.244–5, 252–3) – and even though he is "nettled not a little" by seeing his name misprinted in a newspaper account of Paddy Dignam's funeral as "L. Boom," he is also "tickled to death" at seeing the names of two absentees in the list of mourners (*U* 16.1260–3). For Mahaffey, "the difference between the tolerant, even opportunistic attitude the book encourages its readers to take toward the vagaries of print and the precise, scholarly attitude an editor must take to allow the narrative to convey the message is something that should be explicitly stated: the book's theory is necessarily and meaningfully at odds with editorial *and* critical practice" (Mahaffey 1991: 183, Mahaffey's emphasis). She links this dichotomy to a more basic distinction between writing as process (which Gabler's theory and synoptic text largely promote) and as product (as in the reading text [1991: 172]).

McGann claimed that Gabler's edition "should remove forever that illusion of fixity and permanence we normally take from literary works because they so often come to us wearing their masks of permanence" (1985: 182). Some recent considerations of the edition have followed up on this suggestion. Writing ten years after the controversy began, and noting that the debate "has been characterized by missed opportunities and missed understandings throughout" (Spoo 1997: 108), Robert Spoo argues that "for all our celebration of textual indeterminacy, ... we Joyce critics have placed great importance on stable, reliable texts of our author's works" and as a result resist looking at the principles and theory that lie behind the "Gablerian indeterminacy" of the left-hand synoptic pages in favor of the "particularized instances (however numerous) of alleged textual misconduct" that Kidd deduced from the right-hand reading text and the paperback editions (Spoo 1997: 110–11). J.C.C. Mays, observing how few editors, much less general readers, have considered the implications of the left-hand synoptic text, remarks that "I find it eerie that the instability of texts is widely discussed and increasingly acknowledged, as is the fact that texts exist in multiple versions, and that at the same time texts continue to be presented as if they constituted univocal expression" (Mays 1997: 10), especially since a choice regarding editions "situates a chooser in a different – I think looser – relation to any one of them. Absolute authority becomes relativised by the consideration of use: the version you call up is determined by why and how you want to read it" (1997: 12). Most recently, in *Material Modernism*, George Bornstein argues that Gabler's diacritical symbols in the synoptic presentation "signal that there is no 'the' text, but only a series of texts built up like a layered palimpsest over a variety of compositional stages; further, they signal that any text is always already a constructed object, and that other constructions would have been (and are) possible" (Bornstein 2001: 138). As an indication of how far away Gabler's edition – both as a concept and as a presentation of a text – takes us from New Critical assumptions, Bornstein concludes that "the synoptic pages signal that far from being a well-wrought urn, the text itself contains gaps and fissures, opportunities for revealing differences as well as concealing it" (2001: 138–9).

In the United States, readers selecting a copy of *Ulysses* need to make a choice between the Gabler edition and the 1961 text, and thus in at least a rudimentary sense they must make a textual decision.[11] Individuals buy a particular version of a book for various reasons: price, binding (hardcover or paperback), cover design, name recognition of the introduction's author. Teachers choosing an edition for their classes might consider whether the text is edited or not, and they are almost certain to consider price in relation to the amount of time they will spend on the work and any accompanying materials in the edition (introduction, notes, critical essays). Sometimes, readers unexpectedly discover that all texts are not equal. For example, if they inadvertently compare a reprint of the first edition of *Dubliners* (such reprints are readily available) with a later edition, they immediately confront, and are usually disoriented by, what McGann has called the "bibliographical codes," that is, aspects of the presentation of the text other than the words, or the "linguistic codes" (McGann 1991: 13). In this case, the first edition prints all Joyce's dialogue using traditional quotation marks (single inverted commas in the English format), a manner of visual presentation which Joyce disliked. Later editions feature his preferred method for indicating spoken dialogue: a dash at the start of the line. These two presentations of *Dubliners* offer strikingly different reading experiences simply because of their manner of indicating dialogue.

*

If the Gabler edition of *Ulysses* represents one major recent development in scholarship and criticism involving Joyce's manuscripts, then French genetic criticism is the other. As I mentioned earlier, early American and English manuscript studies shared certain features: they were more concerned with studying the manuscripts as evidence of writing processes than with establishing accurate texts; they were pragmatic, looking at the documents to see what they could find without any overriding plan or theoretical perspective; and they saw manuscript study as valuable only if it shed light on the final, published works. The models for looking at manuscripts in this way were powerful ones. If you consider the finished work to be an organism or an icon or a monument, then anything that did not end up in the work will be secondary, a discard, reject, or (in film terminology) outtake. In Wellek and Warren's conception, it will be "extrinsic" to the "actual work" (Wellek and Warren 1949: 73, 91). The metaphors that Henry James used in his 1907–09 prefaces to the New York edition of his novels all assume the works to be organic wholes: he "remount[ed] the stream of composition"; he sought the "germ" of a story, the "virus of suggestion," the "prick of inoculation" that instigated a work; he considered "the growth of the 'great oak' from the little acorn" (James 1934: 27, 119, 119, 121, 140).

At the same time as the age of theory ended the dominance of New Criticism and its view of a literary work as an organism or icon, a new kind of criticism and scholarship centered around manuscripts began to develop in France. Earlier French manuscript scholars shared many of the assumptions of their English-language counterparts, but in the late 1960s and early 1970s this criticism – eventually called *critique génétique* or genetic criticism (and this is how I will use this term from here on)[12] – began to look at manuscripts in relation to the final work in two different ways: the traditional teleological view, in which the drafts and other documents are seen as leading to the final work, and an opposite view in which every moment in the writing process that can be documented in surviving manuscripts reveals a series of possibilities, dilemmas, and choices, and these options – seen more as a series of variant possibilities than as rejected options – are fascinating in their own right. Almuth Grésillon speaks of metaphors of "the road … : travelling, course, path, way, match, route, tracks, trails, progression, movement," as well as "forks, junctions, losing one's way, clearing the way, diversion, detours, short cuts, retracing one's steps, dead ends, accidents, false starts, taking a wrong turn" (Grésillon 1992: 110), and she suggests balancing metaphors "borrowed from organicism" with "those borrowed from constructivism." She cites the conclusion of Baudelaire's introduction to his translation of Edgar Allan Poe's 1846 essay "The Philosophy of Composition" (a seminal text for genetic critics, which Baudelaire translated under the title "Genesis of a Poem"): "We shall now see *behind the scenes*, the *workshop*, the *laboratory*, the *inner workings*" (Grésillon 1992: 108, Grésillon's emphasis). (Conveniently and probably not coincidentally, these two views of literary creation – James's stream and Grésillon's road – parallel the dualism often evoked in the digital age of the line and the network.)

To genetic critics, the final work appears not so much as the result of pruning the great oak to let the inferior chaff fall away and the beautiful fruit remain as one possibility chosen and singled out among many others. Pierre Marc de Biasi claims that the drafts reveal "a mobile image, far more hypothetical and often richer then the one the published text will eventually give us to be read as its *truth* after many reworkings" (de Biasi 1997: 125) – the work, once seen as a monument, has evolved into a mobile. As the editors of *Drafts*, a special issue of *Yale French Studies* put it,

> Whatever autonomy and internal logic formal analysis may reveal in a work of art, the actual work is only one among its multiple possibilities … . The work now stands out against a background, and a series, of potentialities. Genetic criticism … attempts to reinscribe the work in the series of its variations, in the space of its possibilities. (Contat et al. 1996: 2)

Louis Hay provocatively argues that "perhaps we should consider the text as a *necessary possibility*, as one manifestation of a process which is always virtually present in the background, a kind of third dimension of the written work" (Hay 1985: 75). Readers of *Ulysses* will probably find the thrust of these arguments familiar because Stephen Dedalus considered them in a very different context in the "Nestor" episode:

Had Pyrrhus not fallen by a beldam's hand in Argos or Julius Caesar
not been knifed to death. They are not to be thought away. Time has
branded them and fettered they are lodged in the room of the infinite
possibilities they have ousted. But can those have been possible seeing
that they never were? Or was that only possible which came to pass?
… It must be a movement then, an actuality of the possible as possible.
(*U* 2.48–52, 67)

Genetic critics tend to see the two poles inherent in all manuscript
studies – the process by which the work came into being and the product
that resulted – in oscillation with, not opposition to, each other. The
term "avant-texte," the central concept of French genetic criticism (there
is no adequate English equivalent), stresses a continuity between the
manuscripts and the final text. The term designates all the documents
that come before a work when it is considered as a text and when those
documents and the text are considered as part of a system. Built into
the conception of the avant-texte is the assumption that the material of
textual genetics is not a given but rather a critical construction – not all
documents that survive are part of the avant-texte for a work – elaborated
in relation to a postulated terminal state of the work.

As a result, whereas time for traditional manuscript critics involves
looking back to see how the present work came into being, time becomes
a fascinating multifaceted factor for genetic critics. According to Jean
Bellemin-Noël, "We must never forget this paradox: what was written
before and had, at first, no *after,* we meet only *after,* and this tempts us to
supply a *before* in the sense of a priority, cause, or origin" (Bellemin-Noël
1982: 31). For Daniel Ferrer, genetic critics cannot renounce teleology,
no matter how much they might want to, but teleology is ultimately
double-edged: "Once the text is declared as such … nothing prevents
it from retrospectively engendering its avant-texte" (Ferrer 1994: 230).
We can read the manuscripts as evidence of works in progress, even if
we remain aware of the end result (like reading a novel for a second
time), or from the perspective of the final text. In either case, the genetic
materials reveal a richer, fuller set of possibilities than the final text alone
can provide; as Ferrer puts it, "If the study of manuscripts is necessary, it
is indeed because the final text *does not contain* the whole of its genesis"
(Ferrer 1994: 234; Ferrer's emphasis).

If earlier manuscript studies follow the implications of Archibald
MacLeish's poem "Ars Poetica" – "A poem should not mean / But be"
(MacLeish 1926: 1284) – genetic critics endorse Frank Paul Bowman's

description of the text as "becoming, not being" (Bowman 1990: 644). The writer stopped writing for all kinds of reasons (he or she considered the work to be finished, got tired of working on it, died; an arbitrary deadline arrived; the publisher snatched the work away), but, set among the rich array of its possibilities, the work no longer appears as a complete, self-contained, finished entity. This concept, too, is built into *Ulysses*. When Bloom recalls lying with Molly on Howth Hill 18 years previously and then thinks, "Me. And me now" (*U* 8.917), and when Stephen summarizes the changes in his body over time with the phrase "I. I and I. I," (*U* 9.212), they are imaging something like a text as genetic critics see it.

When studied genetically, even the most monumental works start to move. In "**Still** *Lost Time*: **Already** the Text of the *Recherche*," for example, Almuth Grésillon (1983) studies a draft of what became the opening of *À la recherche du temps perdu* and concentrates on Proust's use of the terms *encore* and *déjà* ("still" and "already"). Declaring that she "knew nothing of [the draft's] date or its eventual fate," she sees Proust's struggles with temporal markers as an instance of a writer coming to grips linguistically with a crucial problem in an evolving text. Focusing on a conclusion rather than a beginning, Raymonde Debray-Genette in "Flaubert's 'A Simple Heart,' or How to Make an Ending" (1984) looks at Flaubert's tortuous path towards the last words of his story. "He goes from expansion to blockages and from blockages to displacements," she concludes, revealing a writer struggling to delay the ending as much as to complete it. Finally, and more directly relevant to this essay, in "Paragraphs in Expansion (James Joyce)" (1989) Daniel Ferrer and Jean-Michel Rabaté study Joyce's uses of paragraphs in his writing. "Do paragraphs belong to the text or to its layout?" they ask, formulating a version of the distinction that McGann calls the linguistic and bibliographic codes. For Joyce, paragraphs are internal borders. Rather than dividing the inside of the text from the outside, they separate units of prose from each other, and once Joyce created paragraph divisions, he tended to retain them no matter how much a paragraph grew. Joyce's addition of the heads in his late work on "Aeolus" does not disrupt the paragraph divisions, because, with only one exception, he inserted the heads into already established paragraph breaks. And so his startling overhaul of the appearance of "Aeolus" maintains the paragraph structure intact. Ferrer and Rabaté (1989) conclude that paragraphs "play the role of mediation between the book, understood as a formal organization, and the proliferating letter of which they are ... the very vessels of expansion."[13]

More recently, Rabaté has argued that Joyce's works – he speaks directly of *Finnegans Wake* but his claim applies in many ways to *Ulysses* as well – call for an "ideal genetic reader," "genetic reader," or "genreader" (he uses all three terms): "a reader who has to approach the difficult and opaque language less with glosses and annotations than through the material evidence of the notebooks, drafts, corrected proofs reproduced by the *James Joyce Archive*" (Rabaté 2001: 196). This genetic reader "confronts a new type of materiality and temporality" – a text, like Bloom, is "Me. And me now." Joyce's avant-textes reveal a series of possibilities, many of which Joyce never implemented, as well as his tendency to work with and build on whatever happened, correctly or erroneously, as he wrote, and just as Bloom connects time's passage with his human limitations and fallibility, so the archive teaches a reader to live amidst error. The genetic reader "will have the choice between varieties of error" (2001: 202), because, confronting *Ulysses* and the *Wake*, "we keep misreading, missing meanings, producing forced interpretations, seeing things which are not there" (2001: 207). What Ferrer revealed as the avant-texte's fullness ("the final text *does not contain* the whole of its genesis") is for Rabaté an excess that will always overwhelm any single interpretation: "Facing an expanding archive, the 'genreader' progresses through an excess of intentions and meanings that never adequately match each other" (2001: 207).

*

And what about Stephen Dedalus, the men who listen to his parable, his two old ladies at the top of Nelson's Pillar, and the stalled tramcars? We left them many pages ago in a tableau that contrasted with the bustle and noise of the preceding pages of "Aeolus." Like the figures on Keats's Grecian urn, the trams will not move again, and the women will remain atop the pillar – they are suspended in time. When we look at the passage from the perspective of Joyce's writing of it, however, all is mobile.

The ending of Joyce's first, provisionally finished version of "Aeolus" contained Stephen, his parable, and his listeners, but when Joyce inserted the trams at the beginning and end, he turned the mechanized Dublin – already important because of the machines in the newspaper office – into a frame for "Aeolus." With the trams cut off from their origins and destinations, the new words at the end emphasize the breakdown of the mechanized city. When the trams were absent from the episode, they presumably went on their journeys without any interruptions, but after

Joyce added them, naming their origins and destinations but declaring them "becalmed in short circuit," they become simultaneously present and paralyzed. In the trams' oscillation between absence and presence, their stillness and stasis reveal a text perpetually in motion.

The newspaper heads – those artificial, stunning, and visually loud intrusions, usually considered as breaking the narrative's flow or interrupting the text's movement – are aswirl in motion, and Joyce's revisions after he first inserted them increase the movement. The first head in our excerpt originally described only the two ladies' "donation" of the plumstones before Joyce added a line emphasizing the falling objects' speed ("SPEEDPILLS VELOCITOUS AEROLITHS, BELIEF"). The second head – "HELLO THERE, CENTRAL!" – suggests a frantic emergency phone call. The final one is full of motion, with its "TITILLATING" missing fingers and its "FRISKY" women who "WIMBLE" and "WANGLE" (whatever "WIMBLES" might mean, it certainly suggests more motion, although less sadness, than "SIGHS," the word it replaced). Even the often absent word "smiling" in the last section – MacHugh speaks "grimly" or "smiling grimly" depending on the version of *Ulysses* – appears and disappears like Lewis Carroll's Cheshire Cat's grin.

In adding the trams and heads (as well as many allusions to wind elsewhere in the episode), Joyce revised "Aeolus" to conform with the kind of writing he was doing on "Eumaeus," "Ithaca," and "Penelope." He was not writing stream-of-consciousness interior monologues any longer but constructing more abstract structures for each episode, and his interpolation of newspaper heads into an episode located in a newspaper office is consistent with this late practice. As critics from as far back as Stuart Gilbert in 1930 have pointed out (Gilbert 1930: 179), the heads themselves progress historically; formal and static at the start, they become loud and colloquial at the end. These intrusions make their presence known visually, but they also move in time.

Crucially, *Ulysses* itself is reinscribed back into time. A genetic view reveals that *Ulysses* as a text has its own history, one that became obscured by the book's publication but is far removed from Stephen's "nightmare from which I am trying to awake" (*U* 2.377). This history is also far from Joseph Frank's influential early approach to *Ulysses* as "spatial form": literary works are "apprehend[ed] ... spatially, in a moment of time, rather than as a sequence," with their elements "juxtaposed in space rather than unrolling in time" (Frank 1945: 10, 12). "Past and present," Frank argues, are "locked in a timeless unity" (1945: 63). A critic writing in 1945 might understandably want to make the Dedalian move of eradicating time and awakening from the nightmare of history, but time has been restored to *Ulysses* in many different ways since Frank wrote, most prominently in the view that *Ulysses* has changed over the years as readers have approached it in their various ways. In that view, *Ulysses* has changed continuously starting from the moment of its publication, but reinserting *Ulysses* into the history of its writing gives it a changing past as well. The published text becomes a still point at the fulcrum of the teeming histories of its production and reception. Everything suspended at Nelson's Pillar begins to move again as the monument becomes a mobile.

notes

1. Joyce added the heads to the first set of *placards*, although the first one in our passage contained only its first line, and in the last one "ANNE WIMBLES" was "ANNE SIGHS" (*JJA* 18, 67–8, 87; *placards* are the first stage of proofs, the French equivalent of galley proofs). On the same proof page on which he wrote "HELLO THERE, CENTRAL!," he also added the paragraph about the short-circuited tramcars, but the destinations were slightly shorter and in a different order. In the list of moving non-electric vehicles he first wrote "delivery cars" before changing "cars" to "waggons." Another addition makes Myles Crawford refer not simply to "the truth" but to "the God Almighty's truth" (all *JJA* 18, 87). On the second set of *placards* Joyce corrected several printing mistakes, especially but not only in the names of the tramcar destinations, expanded "Sandymount" to "Sandymount green and Sandymount tower" and then made an addition to an addition when he inserted "Ringsend" after "green." He also added Stephen's narrative's second title, *"The Parable of The Plums,"* and in the final head changed "ANNE SIGHS" to "ANNE WIMBLES" – recasting an archaic word for a tool used to bore holes into a verb (*JJA* 18, 95). On the first set of page proofs he added the first head's second line, "SPEEDPILLS VELOCITOUS AEROLITHS, BELIEF," capitalized the "g" in "green," and reinserted a question mark after "THEM" at the end of the final head that the printer neglected to include (*JJA* 23, 69–71). All his other activities on the three sets of page proofs for this passage involved correcting printer's errors (*JJA* 23, 69–71, 85–7, 101–3).
2. Joyce wrote "tower" on the second *placards* and never changed it, but the word appeared as "Tower" in the 1932 Odyssey Press edition, the version corrected by Stuart Gilbert by comparing the proofs with the earlier printed texts and by occasionally consulting with Joyce. Joyce wrote "smiling gently" on the Rosenbach manuscript ("Aeolus" p. 32), but the typist – who probably worked from another, now lost, handwritten manuscript from which both the typescript and the extant Rosenbach Manuscript derived – did not include "smiling" on the typescript (*JJA* 12, 302), and the word never appeared on any proofs or in print until Gabler included it in his edition.
3. Bowers also noted that "many a literary critic has investigated the past ownership and mechanical condition of his [*sic*] second-hand automobile, or

the pedigree and training of his dog, more thoroughly than he has looked into the qualifications of the text on which his critical theories rest" (1959: 5).

4. See Thomas Tanselle's "Textual Criticism and Deconstruction" (1990) for an analysis of the uses of the word "text" in the essays by Harold Bloom, Paul de Man, Jacques Derrida, Geoffrey Hartman, and J. Hillis Miller in *Deconstruction and Criticism*. See also Jerome McGann's discussion of how, in seeking to demonstrate that "textual indeterminacy is a function of the 'reader' rather than of the 'text,'" Stanley Fish in his reader-response criticism "wants to take the text as physical object at face value" (McGann 1985: 185).

5. For an account of these collections, see my "Library Collections of Joyce Manuscripts," (1984) and for checklists of them, see my *James Joyce's Manuscripts: An Index* (1980).

6. See the auction catalogs of the "Circe" and "Eumaeus" manuscripts (Christie's 2000, Selley 2001), Sam Slote's "Preliminary Comments on Two Newly-Discovered *Ulysses* Manuscripts" (2001) and my "The National Library of Ireland's New Joyce Manuscripts: A Statement and Document Descriptions" (2001).

7. A succinct account of copytext editing is in Williams and Abbott's *Introduction to Bibliographical and Textual Studies* (1999), pp. 82–3, 87–102. The most complete discussion and justification of the issue of "final authorial intention" is Tanselle's "Editorial Problem of Final Authorial Intention." For German editing, see Gabler et al.'s *Contemporary German Editorial Theory* (1995), especially Gabler's introduction (pp. 1–16).

8. This account of Gabler's edition is a condensed version of what I wrote in the afterword to the 1993 *Ulysses: The Gabler Edition* and in "Perplex in the Pen," pp. 231–9 (pp. 38–46 as reprinted in *Joyce and the Joyceans*).

9. The phrase "the work as he wrote it" is in Gabler's afterword to *Ulysses: A Critical and Synoptic Edition*, 3:1891, and "*Ulysses* as Joyce wrote it" is in his afterword to the 1986 *Ulysses: The Corrected Text*, p. 649, and in his foreword to the 1993 *Ulysses: The Gabler Edition*, p. xvii.

10. A new edition of *Ulysses* did appear in 1997. Danis Rose's *Ulysses: A Reader's Edition* treats *Ulysses* as a text in need of copy-editing and alters the text in many places in a dubious attempt to produce a more reader-friendly *Ulysses* than the editor considers Joyce to have written.

11. Not only American readers of *Ulysses* need to make a choice. In the U.K. and Canada, the primary *Ulysses* options are an Oxford Worlds Classics reprint of the 1922 first edition and a Penguin reprint of the 1960 Bodley Head edition, both of which, unlike the two U.S. editions, contain introductions and extensive notes, and readers in the UK also have the choice of the Gabler edition published by Bodley Head. Because both *Dubliners* and *Portrait* are out of copyright in the U.S. and Canada, reprints of earlier editions are widely available along with the Scholes, Anderson, and Gabler editions. *Finnegans Wake* has never been edited, but various printings since the first edition in 1939 have attempted to correct the text, with several basing their corrections on errata lists which Joyce prepared. In a bizarre complication, the newest Penguin printing in the U.S. – the Twentieth-Century Classics version from 1999 – reproduces the uncorrected first edition of 1939.

12. The term "genetic criticism" is not new, however. Donald Stauffer used it, for example, in his 1948 essay in *Poets at Work* (Stauffer 1948: 41), a set of four essays based on and introducing the new collection of manuscripts (called "worksheets") in the University of Buffalo's Poetry Collection.

13. English versions of Grésillon's, Debray-Genette's, and Ferrer and Rabaté's essays are in *Genetic Criticism: Texts and Avant-textes*, edited by Deppman, Ferrer, and Groden. Parts of the preceding account of genetic criticism are based on the editors' introduction to that volume. Other English-language collections of French genetic studies include *Drafts*, edited by Contat, Hollier, and Neefs (a special issue of *Yale French Studies*, 1996) and *Genetic Criticism*, edited by Claire Bustarret (a special issue of *Word and Image*, 1997).

references

Bellemin-Noël, Jean. "Psychoanalysis and the Avant-texte" (1982) in Jed Deppman, Daniel Ferrer, and Michael Groden, eds. *Genetic Criticism: Texts and Avant-textes*. Philadelphia: University of Pennsylvania Press, 2004, pp. 28–35.

Blamires, Harry. *The New Bloomsday Book: A Guide Through "Ulysses."* 1966. 3rd edn. London: Routledge, 1996.

Bloom, Harold, et al. *Deconstruction and Criticism*. New York: Continuum, 1979.

Bornstein, George. *Material Modernism: The Politics of the Page*. Cambridge: Cambridge University Press, 2001.

Bowers, Fredson. *Textual and Literary Criticism*. Cambridge: Cambridge University Press, 1959.

Bowman, Frank Paul. "Genetic Criticism." *Poetics Today* 11 (1990), pp. 627–46.

Budgen, Frank. *James Joyce and the Making of "Ulysses"* (1934). Reprinted Bloomington: Indiana University Press, 1960.

Bustarret, Claire, ed. *Genetic Criticism*. Special issue of *Word and Image* 13:2 (April–June 1997).

Christie's. *James Joyce's "Ulysses": The John Quinn Draft Manuscript of the "Circe" Episode*. New York: Christie's, December 14, 2000.

Contat, Michel, Denis Hollier, and Jacques Neefs, eds. *Drafts*. Special issue of *Yale French Studies* 89 (1996).

Crispi, Luca, and Sam Slote, eds. *A Genetic Guide to "Finnegans Wake."* Madison: University of Wisconsin Press, forthcoming.

de Biasi, Pierre-Marc. "Horizons for Genetic Studies," trans. Jennifer A. Jones, in Claire Bustarret, ed. *Genetic Criticism*. Special issue of *Word and Image* 13:2 (April–June 1997), pp. 124–34.

Debray-Genette, Raymonde. "Flaubert's 'A Simple Heart,' or How to Make an Ending: A Study of the Manuscripts" (1984), in Jed Deppman, Daniel Ferrer, and Michael Groden, eds. *Genetic Criticism: Texts and Avant-textes*. Philadelphia: University of Pennsylvania Press, 2004, pp. 69–95.

Deppman, Jed, Daniel Ferrer, and Michael Groden, eds. *Genetic Criticism: Texts and Avant-textes*. Philadelphia: University of Pennsylvania Press, 2004.

Duffy, Enda. *The Subaltern "Ulysses."* Minneapolis: University of Minnesota Press, 1994.

Ferrer, Daniel. "Clementis's Cap: Retroaction and Persistence in the Genetic Process" (1994), trans. Marlena G. Corcoran, in Michel Contat, Denis Hollier, and Jacques Neefs, eds. *Drafts*. Special issue of *Yale French Studies* 89 (1996), pp. 223–36.

Ferrer, Daniel, and Jean-Michel Rabaté. "Paragraphs in Expansion (James Joyce)" (1989), in Jed Deppman, Daniel Ferrer, and Michael Groden, eds. *Genetic Criticism: Texts and Avant-textes*. Philadelphia: University of Pennsylvania Press, 2004, pp. 132–51.

Frank, Joseph. "Spatial Form in Modern Literature" (1945), in *The Idea of Spatial Form*. New Brunswick, N.J.: Rutgers University Press, 1991, pp. 3–66.

Gabler, Hans Walter. "What *Ulysses* Requires." *Papers of the Bibliographical Society of America* 87 (1993), pp. 187–248.

Gabler, Hans Walter, George Bornstein, and Gillian Borland Pierce, eds. *Contemporary German Editorial Theory*. Ann Arbor: University of Michigan Press, 1995.

Gilbert, Stuart. *James Joyce's "Ulysses": A Study* (1930). Reprinted New York: Vintage, 1952.

Grésillon, Almuth. "**Still** *Lost Time*: **Already** the Text of the *Recherche*" (1983, 1990), in Jed Deppman, Daniel Ferrer, and Michael Groden, eds. *Genetic Criticism: Texts and Avant-textes*. Philadelphia: University of Pennsylvania Press, 2004, pp. 152–70.

Grésillon, Almuth. "Slow: Work in Progress" (1992), trans. Stephen A. Noble and Vincent Vichit-Vadakan, in Claire Bustarret, ed. *Genetic Criticism*. Special issue of *Word and Image* (April–June 1997), pp. 106–23.

Groden, Michael. *"Ulysses" in Progress*. Princeton, N.J.: Princeton University Press, 1977.

Groden, Michael. *James Joyce's Manuscripts: An Index*. New York: Garland, 1980.

Groden, Michael. "Library Collections of Joyce Manuscripts," in Zack Bowen and James F. Carens, eds. *A Companion to Joyce Studies*. Westport, CT: Greenwood Press, 1984, pp. 783–5.

Groden, Michael. "Perplex in the Pen – and in the Pixels: Reflections on *The James Joyce Archive*, Hans Walter Gabler's *Ulysses*, and 'James Joyce's *Ulysses* in Hypermedia.'" *Journal of Modern Literature* 22 (1989–99), pp. 225–44. Reprinted in *Joyce and the Joyceans*. Ed. Morton P. Levitt. Syracuse, N.Y.: Syracuse University Press, 2002, pp. 32–50.

Groden, Michael. "A Response to John Kidd's 'An Inquiry into *Ulysses: The Corrected Text*.'" *James Joyce Quarterly* 28 (1990), pp. 81–110.

Groden, Michael. "Afterword," in James Joyce. *Ulysses: The Gabler Edition*. New York: Vintage, 1993, pp. 647–57.

Groden, Michael. "The National Library of Ireland's New Joyce Manuscripts: A Statement and Document Descriptions," *James Joyce Quarterly* 39 (2001), pp. 29–51.

Hay, Louis. "Does 'Text' Exist?" (1985), trans. Matthew Jocelyn and Hans Walter Gabler, *Studies in Bibliography* 41 (1988), pp. 64–76.

Hayman, David. "From *Finnegans Wake*: A Sentence in Progress," *PMLA* 73 (1958), pp. 136–54.

James, Henry. *The Art of the Novel: Critical Prefaces*. New York: Scribner's, 1934.

Joyce, James. *Chamber Music*. Ed. William York Tindall. New York: Columbia University Press, 1954.

Joyce, James. *A First-Draft Version of "Finnegans Wake."* Ed. David Hayman. Austin: University of Texas Press, 1963.

Joyce, James. *Ulysses: A Facsimile of the Manuscript.* Ed. Clive Driver. Three vols. New York: Octagon, and Philadelphia: Philip H. and A.S.W. Rosenbach Foundation, 1975.

Joyce, James. *Ulysses: Annotated Students' Edition.* Ed. Declan Kiberd. London: Penguin, 1992.

Joyce, James. *A Portrait of the Artist as a Young Man.* Ed. Hans Walter Gabler with Walter Hettche. New York: Garland, 1993a; New York: Vintage, 1993a.

Joyce, James. *Dubliners.* Ed. Hans Walter Gabler with Walter Hettche. New York: Garland, 1993; New York: Vintage, 1993b.

Joyce, James. *Ulysses: The 1922 Text.* Ed. Jeri Johnson. London: Oxford University Press, 1993.

Joyce, James. *Ulysses: A Reader's Edition.* Ed. Danis Rose. London: Picador, 1997.

Joyce, James. *The "Finnegans Wake" Notebooks at Buffalo.* Ed. Vincent Deane, Daniel Ferrer, and Geert Lernout. Six vols. to date. Turnhout, Belgium: Brepols, 2001 – .

Kidd, John. "An Inquiry into *Ulysses: The Corrected Text.*" *Papers of the Bibliographical Society of America* 82 (1988a), pp. 411–584.

Kidd, John. "The Scandal of *Ulysses.*" *New York Review of Books* (30 June 1988b), pp. 32–9.

Larbaud, Valery. "James Joyce." *La Nouvelle Revue Française* 18 (1922), pp. 385–407. Partly translated anonymously as "The *Ulysses* of James Joyce," *Criterion* 1 (1922), pp. 94–103.

Litz, A. Walton. *The Art of James Joyce: Method and Design in "Ulysses" and "Finnegans Wake."* New York: Oxford University Press, 1961.

Litz, A. Walton. "Uses of the *Finnegans Wake* Manuscripts," in Jack P. Dalton and Clive Hart, eds. *Twelve and a Tilly: Essays on the Occasion of the 25th Anniversary of "Finnegans Wake."* Evanston, IL: Northwestern University Press, 1966, pp. 99–106.

McGann, Jerome J. "*Ulysses* as a Postmodern Work" (1985) Reprinted in *Social Values and Poetic Acts: The Historical Judgment of Literary Work.* Cambridge, MA: Harvard University Press, 1988, pp. 173–94.

McGann, Jerome J. *The Textual Condition.* Princeton, N.J.: Princeton University Press, 1991.

McGee, Patrick. "Machines, Empire, and the Wise Virgins: Cultural Revolution in 'Aeolus,'" in Kimberly J. Devlin and Marilyn Reizbaum, eds. *Ulysses: En-Gendered Perspectives.* Columbia: University of South Carolina Press, 1999, pp. 86–99.

MacLeish, Archibald. "Ars Poetica" (1926), in Ronald Gottesman et al., eds. *The Norton Anthology of American Literature.* Vol. 2. New York: Norton, 1979, p. 1284.

MacNicholas, John. *James Joyce's "Exiles": A Textual Companion.* New York: Garland, 1979.

Mahaffey, Vicki. "Intentional Error: The Paradox of Editing Joyce's *Ulysses,*" in George Bornstein, ed. *Representing Modernist Texts: Editing as Interpretation.* Ann Arbor: University of Michigan Press, 1991, pp. 171–91.

Mays, J.C.C. "Gabler's *Ulysses* as a Field of Force," *Text* 10 (1997), pp. 1–13.

Peake, C.H. *James Joyce: The Citizen and the Artist*. Stanford: Stanford University Press, 1977.

Poe, Edgar Allan. "The Philosophy of Composition" (1846), in Vincent B. Leitch et al., eds. *The Norton Anthology of Theory and Criticism*. New York: Norton, 2001, pp. 739–50.

Postgate, J.P. "Textual Criticism," *Encyclopaedia Britannica*, 11th edn., Vol. 26. New York: Encyclopaedia Britannica Co., 1911, pp. 708–15.

Rabaté, Jean-Michel. *James Joyce and the Politics of Egoism*. Cambridge: Cambridge University Press, 2001.

Schwaber, Paul. *The Cast of Characters: A Reading of "Ulysses."* New Haven: Yale University Press, 1999.

Schwarz, Daniel R. *Reading Joyce's "Ulysses."* New York: St. Martin's, 1987.

Selley, Peter. *The Lost "Eumaeus" Notebook: James Joyce, Autograph Manuscript of the "Eumaeus" Episode of Ulysses*. London: Sotheby's, July 10, 2001.

Slote, Sam. "Preliminary Comments on Two Newly-Discovered *Ulysses* Manuscripts," *James Joyce Quarterly* 39 (2001), pp. 17–28.

Spoo, Robert. "*Ulysses* and the Ten Years War: A Survey of Missed Opportunities," *Text* 10 (1997), pp. 107–18.

Stauffer, Donald A. "Genesis, or The Poet as Maker," in Rudolf Arnheim et al., eds. *Poets at Work: Essays Based on the Modern Poetry Collection at the Lockwood Memorial Library, University of Buffalo*. New York: Harcourt, Brace, 1948, pp. 37–82.

Sultan, Stanley. *The Argument of "Ulysses"* (1964). Reprinted Middletown, CT: Wesleyan University Press, 1987.

Tanselle, G. Thomas. "The Editorial Problem of Final Authorial Intention," *Studies in Bibliography* 29 (1976), pp. 167–211.

Tanselle, G. Thomas. "Textual Criticism and Deconstruction," *Studies in Bibliography* 43 (1990), pp. 1–33.

Wellek, René, and Austin Warren. *Theory of Literature* (1949). 3rd edn. New York: Harcourt, Brace, and World, 1962.

Williams, William Proctor, and Craig S. Abbott. *An Introduction to Bibliographical and Textual Studies*. 3rd edn. New York: Modern Language Association, 1999.

12
classics of joyce criticism

jean-michel rabaté

Early in the spring of 1931, Joyce faced a new worry in addition to the deteriorating mental health of his daughter: an Italian painter named Gianni Corte, who had lived for a while in Paris before returning to Capodistria, not far from Trieste, was under the delusion that Joyce had cast a spell on him and his family: according to him, the Corte family had been forced to live inside *Ulysses*; they had all been trapped in this novel as in a prison. Corte's letters had grown violent, and he threatened to kill the author if he did not lift the spell immediately. Thereupon Joyce enlisted friends like Louis Gillet to help him get rid of this "lunatic." Gillet and others prevailed, and soon the Corte incident was forgotten. I want to take this psychotic acting out as an extreme case of reader participation, a participation that seems to have been willed or engineered by Joyce himself. Indeed, readers of *Finnegans Wake* often feel that a spell has been put on them as soon as they get engrossed in the book; they testify to their experiencing the reading as a curious initiation until they see themselves caught up in a web, imprisoned in a non-Euclidian textual space from which escape seems dependent upon finding clues planted by the author, like references to one's name hidden in the midst of the pages, deciphering cryptic allusions to certain books, historical events or characters. Derrida has summed up this peculiar impression very aptly in a dialogue with Joyce specialist Derek Attridge:

Ulysses arrives like one novel among others that you place on your bookshelf and inscribe in a genealogy. It has its ancestry and its descendants. But Joyce dreamt of a special institution for his oeuvre, inaugurated by it like a new order. And hasn't he achieved this, to some extent? When I spoke of this as I did in "Ulysses Gramophone," I did indeed have to understand and share his dream too: not only share it in making it mine, in recognizing mine in it, but that I share it in *belonging to the dream* of Joyce, in *taking a part* in it, in walking around in *his* space. Aren't we, today, people or characters in part constituted (as readers, writers, critics, teachers) *in* and *through* Joyce's dream? Aren't we Joyce's dream, his dream readers, the ones he dreamed of and whom we dream of being in our turn?[1]

What is true of *Ulysses* appears even more relevant when considering *Finnegans Wake*, a book that Joyce claimed had been written not by him but by all the people around him, and that could be studied or just read forever. One difficulty created by the mass of commentaries on Joyce (almost as huge as the critical literature on Shakespeare and Dante) is that many critics sense that anything that they can write about the works has been anticipated by Joyce. This has again been called up with almost apocalyptic fervor by Derrida, who starts from the premise that Joyce's later works force us to remain "in memory of him" which is tantamount to inhabiting his memory, a hypertrophied memory that summons the most varied religions, languages and mythologies on top of universal history and literature: "Can one pardon this hypermnesia which *a priori* indebts you, and in advance inscribes you in the book you are reading?"[2] Joyce's position would be not far from that of a "sadistic demiurge" who has set up

a hypermnesiac machine, there in advance, decades in advance, to compute you, control you, forbid you the slightest inaugural syllable because you can say nothing that has not been programmed on this 1,000th generation computer – *Ulysses, Finnegans Wake* – beside which the current technology of our computers and our micro-computerized archives and our translating machines remains a *bricolage* of a prehistoric child's toy.[3]

Indeed *bricolage* describes quite adequately what we do when we struggle to read an author who was a self-professed "engineer" or *bricoleur* of texts; let us then explore the remaining possibilities left for us, Joycean tinkers that we are.

Current interest in Joycean hypertexts (particularly the *Ulysses* hypertext soon to be completed by a team supervised by Michael Groden) and in new editions of the James Joyce "Archive" with new annotations of the *Finnegans Wake* notebooks seems to confirm Derrida's speculation.

Indeed, if Joyce's extreme interest in his own critical reception has often been documented, I want to argue that this very interest has made the issue of interpreting the works much more complex right from the start. To show this, I will start with a typical passage from Ellmann's canonical biography. Ellmann covers the years immediately following the publication of *Ulysses* and evokes Joyce's reaction to criticism:

> Like other modern writers, such as Yeats and Eliot, Joyce made a point of not challenging any interpretation; the more controversy the book aroused, the better pleased he was, though he noted wistfully that no critic pursued Larbaud's insistence upon the relation of *Ulysses* to the Odyssey, and through Miss Weaver urged Eliot to take it up. Even Pound, in the several excellent notices he wrote of the book, minimized the Odyssean parallels, but Eliot perceived and wrote in the *Dial*, that "manipulating a continuous parallel between contemporaneity and antiquity" had "the importance of a scientific discovery." Joyce was gratified and his note of thanks urged Eliot to coin some short phrase such as one Eliot had devised in conversation, "two-plane." Larbaud's phrase, "interior monologue," was worn out after six months, Joyce said (underestimating critical habit), and the reading public had need of a new one. (*JJ II* 527)

Here we catch Joyce at his most scheming: while on the one hand he pretends to leave interpretations open, he carefully selects a few friends or confidants who will act as go-betweens (here Valery Larbaud and Miss Weaver) and who will discreetly prod and urge other critics to work in a certain way. As Nora Joyce confided to their friend Jacques Mercanton in 1938: "He is full of tricks."[4] But an aside from Joyce himself throws another light on this systematic pre-emption of critical discourse by the work itself; Joyce was talking to Mercanton about the almost completed *Finnegans Wake* and sounded for once skeptical about the result. He added: "The book has to do with the ideal suffering caused by an ideal insomnia. A sentence in the text describes it in those terms. When you say it in advance yourself, you silence the critics."[5] Did Joyce really want to silence the critics, or on the contrary keep them not only busy for three centuries but also, using that extra time afforded by their "ideal insomnia" (*FW* 120.14), actively reading and re-reading and writing on the text forever?

If the "ideality" of the reading is the offshoot of a strategy defined quite early by "silence, exile and cunning," we need to take seriously the means by which Joyce creates his own reader. Making a principle of indirection and discreetly oblique strategies, Joyce refused to enter into the arena of drumming self-promotion. Thus he never used the political tactics of a Pound, who had adopted an avant-garde practice of promotion via scandal, cliques, organized debates, and concerted assaults by a vociferous group of friends. Rather, Joyce relied on a more subtle use of critical discourse, as he knew that criticism could pave the way to new conditions of promotion, while at the same time conditioning the subsequent interpretation of the works. Besides, as Ellmann notes in this passage, Joyce's pedagogical efforts were not always successful: for decades one could still hear critics state that the whole of *Ulysses* was written in the style of interior monologue. And then it was the term of "epiphanies" that became fashionable, before being replaced by other terms like "parody," "gnomon," "parallax," "dialogism," or "subaltern." A history of these critical metaphors, which were often borrowed from the texts themselves, is indispensable, and tends to converge with the history of the Joyce industry I will be sketching here.

Ellmann sounds embarrassed in this passage, as his wish to be objective forces him to adopt a spurious equanimity, which generates something like a contradiction: here Joyce is both a model modern author who lets his readers free, never claiming ownership over the meaning contained in his books (an attitude one sees with writers like Gide or Valéry) and a cunning arranger, jealous of his own posterity, a writer who knows the ropes, remains aware of the ups and downs of critical fads, working underhand in the launching of critical concepts that will deal adequately with his literary strategies. This dual attitude has generated more than hesitations, it has created endless debates: for instance, critics still argue today about the respective merits of Eliot's assessment (that the novelty of *Ulysses* lies in continuous "correspondences" with a mythical layer of reference that provides deeper meaning to a contemporary world otherwise deprived of intrinsic significance) or Pound's curt dismissal according to which the Odyssean pattern is a mere scaffolding – more decorative than substantial – since it functions like the constraints systematized by the Oulipo (Queneau, Perec, Calvino, Harry Matthews are good representatives of the school of *Ouvroir de Littérature Potentielle*), "constraints" that would have given Joyce the impetus to write an epic of the modern world and explore language as an independent medium. I want to insist upon the alternative as these views of authorship, the "arranger" who controls everything from a distance and the skeptical combiner of mythical patters chosen almost at random to deal with contemporary issues have been both ascribed to the aesthetic ideology of high modernism. This is the unfinished task that has attracted many commentators, and I shall have to return to their worthwhile attempts. But I would like first to suggest that Joyce, having despaired of providing a theoretical treatise on literature that would not be, in some way, included in his works, decided at least to leave a complete, cleaned-up, as it were, image of his life.

This is what happened when, by a planned "coincidence," Joyce succeeded in getting his biography published in 1939, the year *Finnegans Wake* was made available to readers as a single volume. Gorman's *James Joyce*[6] is fascinating because so much in it has been either written directly or censored by Joyce (nothing is said about Lucia's psychological problems for instance, and she has completely disappeared from the postcard family picture depicted at the end). Moreover, Gorman's work is curiously replete with factual mistakes. We know that in 1933, annoyed at the slowness of his biographer's progress, Joyce withdrew his authorization for the book (*JJ II* 666) whereas in 1938 he begged Gorman to delay publication of the then almost completed book so that it would not be out before the *Wake* (*JJ II* 705), which annoyed Gorman considerably. Joyce's masterminding of the coincidence by having a 17-year creative process reach completion at the same time as a biography that had been nine years in the making was not a mean feat. Beyond the obvious devotion to issues of his own reception, one can see here an instance of Joyce's tendency to think in pairs: the work, at last made available to the public, had to be accompanied by a guide to the man behind it.

Despite its by now well-known unreliability, there is still something to learn from Gorman's biography. First, the portrait of the young Joyce that emerges is largely antipodal to the "Joyce as Stephen" conception that has beset so many naive readers. Gorman stresses James Joyce's youthful energy, social popularity, contagious sense of fun and even athletic prowess: when in Dublin, he is seen "swimming strongly in the salt water of Clontarf" (G, *JJ* 64) – not exactly what you would expect from an introverted hydrophobic like Stephen. Accordingly, Gorman concludes an evocation of the Dublin scene in 1899–1901 that owes a lot to Joyce's own reminiscences by stating: "This was a very human Joyce with a sense of the ridiculous that was often extravagant and a vitality that was inexhaustible" (G, *JJ* 64). Joyce's character appears thus true to his name, as we learn early: "The name is obviously of French extraction – Joyeux" (G, *JJ* 8). Even if, as Ellmann noted, Joyce forced his biographer to tone down a number of passages (*JJ II* 725–6), the self-deprecating jibe in the *Wake* referring to "*the martyrology of Gorman*" (*FW* 349, 24) is partly misleading. True, Gorman often sounds like Joyce himself, especially in his repeated diatribes against bigoted Catholicism or Irish nationalism:

> For the patriotic importance of Irish, he did not care a fig. ... And he feared, too, that a national immersion in Gaelic would cut Ireland still further off than she was from the great central current of European culture, a culture that recognized no fixed country boundaries but was universal to all. (G, *JJ* 60)

The theme is sounded at the beginning and reiterated at the end: "Like Flaubert and Dostoevsky and Proust, he belonged to the international world of letters where national boundaries mean nothing at all" (G, *JJ* 337). Such a view cannot be credited to Gorman only – in fact, as John Whittier-Ferguson has deduced from a careful examination of Joyce's corrections and deletions in the Gorman manuscript, many such grandiose pronouncements were in Joyce's hand. When Gorman described Joyce's stay in neutral Zurich during World War I as potentially rife for conflict with the British Consulate after his clash with one of its officials, he was aware of the comic overtones of the fight between the exiled Irish writer and the British official. Tom Stoppard's amusing 1975 play *Travesties* was based upon Ellmann's canonical biography, but he would have found exactly the same material in Gorman. It is in this context, however, that Gorman had originally alluded to Joyce's distant sympathy with the Easter Rebellion in 1916, writing that Joyce "was delighted when determined opposition in Ireland prevented the English from enforcing conscription there."[7] Joyce, no doubt afraid of passing for a traitor (he had kept a British passport), decided to delete it all, explaining in a note that the situation was much more complicated. The final version stresses again an apolitical stance:

> Joyce did not meddle in politics in any way. He was above the conflict as were all the wise impassioned minds of the time and his entire devotion and travail were concentrated on the development and perfection of his art. (G, *JJ* 257)

The reiteration of the Flaubertian principle of the divine indifference of the artist spinning his web while history passes by does not preclude a few barbs. Two vignettes added by Joyce illustrate this. In the first, he tells a British official in 1915 that the British Consul was not "the representative of the King of England" but "an official paid by my father for the protection of my person"; in the second, when asked whether he would welcome the emergence of an independent Ireland, he retorts: "So that I might declare myself its first enemy?" (G, *JJ* 234). What is suggested here is a more paranoid Joyce, closer to Wyndham Lewis's embattled profession of universal enmity. Besides, he is not indifferent to issues of racism; when he states how he feels that he cannot take sides in the world war, the indictment is sweeping:

> There was not even a cause to be admired. There was nothing but rapaciousness and the complicated duels of commercial supremacies. If the conflict had arisen because of a persecuted people he might have sympathized, but who could say that Great Britain, France, Germany, Austria, Russia and the United States were persecuted peoples? For God's sake, let things be finished and let men think of the arts again. (G, *JJ* 241)

I have quoted the first biography at some length to indicate how the issue of framing the text in a given hermeneutic system can become complex. Clearly, this purification in the name of art is merely the other side of the chaos of history made up of persecutions and exclusions that *Finnegans Wake* recreates so hauntingly.

If we can see in Gorman's biography a Shaunian approach applied to a self-designed Shem,[8] the same principle of a duality of incompatible or slightly divergent approaches holds true for the framing of *Ulysses*. Stuart Gilbert had been drawn into the Joyce circle in 1927 when he was asked to help with the French translation of *Ulysses*. Already the maneuvers that led him to revise an almost finished French version by Morel would not have worked without Joyce's usual diplomatic skills (Gilbert explains that Joyce saw himself as "a diplomat negotiating among major powers" [*JJ II*, 601]). Having been in contact with Joyce almost daily over the minute problems of the novel, it was logical that Gilbert thought of writing a study of it. Joyce helped in two ways, first by asking pointedly whether Gilbert had read such and such a book, then by directly giving new details once a draft had been made. For instance, when he heard that Gilbert was brushing up his Greek and reading the *Odyssey* in the original, Joyce suggested he read Victor Bérard's *Les Phéniciens et l'Odyssée*.[9] This reading then influenced Gilbert's presentation to the point that his analysis of most episodes begins with allusions not only to Homer's epic but to Bérard's linguistic and topographical speculations that are based upon the idea of a Semitic origin for a poem that was evolved by making sense of Phoenician maps and nautical charts then translated into Greek: for Bérard, each location of Odysseus's wanderings through the Mediterranean world provided a real-life basis for Homer's imaginative reconstruction.

As Gilbert acknowledges, Joyce read the text as it was being prepared, and in a sense this is an "authorized" commentary. Thus it comes as no surprise to see Joyce presented as less Irish than European:

> There has been a tendency to overemphasize the Irish element in Joyce's works, because, for obvious reasons, he invariably chose Dublin as the setting of his narratives. But, in reality, he always aimed at being a European writer and, in his major works, linked up the local theme with wider references in Space and Time. (*JJU* 90)

The capitalized words alert to one of Gilbert's defects: he is pedantic and likes showing off his erudition. This is why he is so precious for first-time readers, as well as slightly unpalatable. He often quotes directly in Greek, Latin, French or German without translating, and makes most of the system of correspondences elaborated by Joyce. In fact, Gilbert takes up where Larbaud had stopped (originally it was Larbaud who had been asked to write this guide). Joyce had given, along with a developed "scheme" of Homeric correspondences, the reference to Edouard Dujardin's *Les Lauriers sont coupés* (later translated into English by Stuart Gilbert) in conversations with Larbaud when he acknowledged a debt to Dujardin as to the invention of "interior monologue." Larbaud was extremely well-read but his poetic sensibility made him eschew the dry pedantic prose favored by Gilbert. By the time Gilbert wrote his guide, Joyce's concern with revolutionary literary innovation became more a heuristic "technique" than an instrument of psychological discovery:

> ... from the point of view of the author of *Ulysses* (*ipse dixit*!) it hardly matters whether the technique in question is "veracious" or not; it has served him as a bridge over which to march his eighteen episodes, and, once he has got his troops across, the opposing forces can, for all he cares, blow the bridge sky-high. (*JJU* 16)

Unhappily, the same can be said about historical accuracy: the facts of Joyce's biography could be manipulated at will, provided they let him reach the position of eminence as "literary genius" that he was looking for.

The version of *Ulysses* that is presented by Gilbert is clearly high modernist: Joyce's novel is a serious novel that deals with "eternal" themes such as creation as paternity, the atonement of the son with the father, the dialectical relationship between the artist and the citizen, and the intractability of feminine otherness, in a *periplum* of exile and return to a City that becomes all cities. As a stylistic tour de force, it rivals the literary masterpieces of the past starting with Homer and Shakespeare. *Ulysses* is a purified "aesthetic image of the world; a sublimation of the *cri de coeur* in which the art of creation begins" (*JJU* 21). As a consequence, there is nothing indecent about it (*JJU* 20): we only hear the voice of nature as Molly Bloom unfolds her deepest thoughts in her monologue. It is a static masterpiece that slowly reworks age-old truths infused with a revitalized language; it becomes experimental once in a while, and its verbal pyrotechnics take their cue from suggestions contained in the *Odyssey*, a continuous subtext translated and modernized in an hyper-realistic recreation of the Dublin of 1904; by these will the author's mastery be measured. It is surely with Gilbert's study in mind that Joyce told Beckett: "I may have oversystematized *Ulysses*."[10]

Joyce attempted to correct this first critical approach to his own novel when his old Zurich friend, Frank Budgen, told him that he felt up to the task of writing about the war years spent together discussing the genesis of *Ulysses*. In *James Joyce and the Making of Ulysses*,[11] published in 1934, Budgen sounds quite a different note. When they met for the second time, Joyce tried his method of indirect allusion, and told Budgen that he was writing a book in which the *Odyssey* would serve as a ground plan. Budgen remained silent for a while, imagining a few terrible academic illustrations. Immediately, Joyce shifted the discussion to different types of consideration when he asked whether Budgen could name one "all-round character" in European culture (*JJMU* 15). The answer was of course neither Jesus nor Hamlet but Ulysses. This is not to say that concerns for style and technique are absent from this wonderful guide, but they are never divorced from the physicality of the body and a concern for the humanity of the characters. Thus the slightly arcane reference to Bérard's thesis on the *Odyssey* is reduced to its simplest expression – one day, remarking that a group of Greek friends looked very Jewish, Budgen elicited the following comment from Joyce: " ... there's a lot be said for the theory that the *Odyssey* is a Semitic poem" (*JJMU* 170)

Moreover, unlike Gilbert who discreetly skirts the issue, Budgen acknowledges that there is obscenity in *Ulysses*; true, it is of a sane and Rabelaisian type and not at all "pervert" but it is undeniably there: "There is much in *Ulysses* that, in the normal acceptation of the word, is obscene, but very little that is perverse" (*JJMU* 69). In his rapid overview of the "Penelope" episode (not more than four pages altogether), he quotes Joyce's letter to him mentioning that the four cardinal points in the chapter were the breasts, arse, womb and sex of Molly (*JJMU* 263). Finally, Budgen anticipates the debate about sex and gender that marked the feminist reception of *Ulysses* in the 1970s and 1980s; for him, there is no doubt that Molly is a male projection:

> Her obscenities of thought lack no verisimilitude. They are of woman: but no obscenity is womanly. The province of social woman is the erotic: the obscene is to her a kind of brawling in church. Molly Bloom is the creation of a man; and Joyce is, perhaps, as one-sidedly masculine as D.H. Lawrence was one-sidedly feminine. (*JJMU* 263)

This does not preclude an appreciation of Joyce's affirmative spirit (*JJMU* 71), yet Budgen does not see this as a sign of feminine empathy or complicity. What he defines as Joyce's province is the exact point where mind and body meet and interact, that is, through words. "Not all thoughts are in words, but all other material is specialists' material. Words are the substance of everybody's thoughts" (*JJMU* 91). When this is coupled with remarks on the fascination of Joyce for certain words, we are not far from an assessment of Joyce as an abstract painter who uses words as colored squares on a canvas. In fact, if Gilbert's approach was high modernist, Budgen's is more precisely early modernist. This is why, as a painter he compares Joyce pell-mell with Rembrandt, Rodin, Matisse, the Cubists and the Impressionists. All these references aim at capturing Joyce's fearless realism when it comes to new ways of perceiving the world (a fact that determined the Impressionists' quest for complementary colors and mosaic-like compositions: their experimental method wanted to be true to a nature observed through fresh eyes) combined with a sense for symbols, linking minute details to an overall scheme or general design. Joyce is a Zola doubled with a Verlaine, or a Matisse who would have created the intricately self-contained mythology of a Blake. But unlike Blake, Joyce does not want to connive us or convert us, he asks us to contemplate the world in all its humorous comedy. This is why Joyce told Budgen that his countrymen would never appreciate *Ulysses*:

it was the work of a skeptic lacking passionate convictions about the world and politics; however, he added that he would not want it appear as the work of a cynic (*JJMU* 152).

Ironically, and thanks to the alphabetical order, Budgen and Gilbert follow one another in *Our Exagmination Round His Factification for Incamination of Work in Progress*, the notorious collection of essays mostly published in *transition* and written by the twelve "apostles" chosen by Joyce to "explicate" *Finnegans Wake* – just ten years *before* its publication! The way they begin their pieces is diametrically opposite; Budgen stresses the organic logic of the work ("Joyce is not to be described by an etiquette or located within the four walls of any aesthetic creed. His logic is that of life and his inventions are organic necessities")[12] while Gilbert opens with his usual display of erudite quotes and polyglot puns to address the central issue of the work's intractable difficulty. Now, in Gilbert's account, Vico has replaced Homer as a key, while for Budgen Joyce's new language attacks "intelligence" in the name of "poetic freedom." Typically, Gilbert concludes with a detailed reading of a passage, with all the glosses provided, while Budgen praises Joyce for having explored the dark recesses of the human mind.

Both are true to the spirit of *transition* that found its bearings in the philosophy of language developed by Ogden and Richards in *The Meaning of Meaning*, a treatise in which the authors explored among other things how the mind invents "hybrid formless onomatopoeic" so as to express certain rare feelings.[13] The belief in a "Revolution of the Word" spearheaded by Joyce promotes the secondary, non-utilitarian functions of language. Joyce is truly revolutionary because he dared invent a new syntax with which he was at leisure to explore the "dream world" and create a new "mythos" (a term that recurs in Gorman's biography), that is, a new universe in which language and unconscious symbols of the most universal kind keep interpenetrating one another. Because this and other references now appear dated, most Joyce scholars dismiss *Our Exagmination* as an oddity, a series of essays that can be kept in the museum of early and misguided efforts.[14] Indeed, Joyce himself mocks his "disciples" when he introduces them into his book as the "twelve deaferend dumbbawls of the whowl abovebeugled to be the contonuation through regeneration of the ururteration of the word in pregross" (*FW* 284.19–23). There is good reason, however, to treat this collection seriously: it remains an exciting and user-friendly introduction to the *Wake* because it does not attempt to impose a dominant interpretive grid and is always attentive to the way its strange language unfolds. All the pieces analyze subtly the poetical and musical aspects of the text. Above all, these essays convey the pleasure of discovery and enjoyment of a multilayered writing defined as "polyphony" (*OE* 136).

Our Exagmination gives us a sense of how Joyce's friends were interested in redefining the conditions of possibility of literature by inventing a new language that required a new reader as well. John Rodker even describes *Work in Progress* as bringing about a "complete symbiosis of reader and writer" (*OE* 143). The final version of the *Wake* echoes this: "His producers are they not his consumers? Your exagmination round his factification for incamination of a warping process" (*FW* 497.1–3). The "warping process" is the constant misprision of deluded even if well-meaning critics, but it is also the only way to "work" and "play" at the same time with the text. What is revealing in all this is the way Joyce not only anticipates or deflates criticism but plays with it, inserts it into the work, making of the twelve commentators characters of the *Wake* – the twelve customers of Earwicker's pub. Besides, he could not consider the task completed, which is why already in May 1929, he was planning a collection of four longer essays on the night, mechanics and chemistry, humor, and one unhappily unidentified topic: typically, Joyce knew that he wanted *four essays* even when he hadn't decided upon the last theme, so as to make the new collection fit the pattern of the Four Old Irish masters who dominate Book III of the *Wake* (*JJ II* 613–14).

Joyce's strategy was dependent on criticism while "warping" it in advance, which forced Joyce scholars to imitate only one model at a time. It is quite tempting to see in the long feud that opposed Richard Ellmann and Hugh Kenner something larger than personal dislikes. It is safe to assume that Gilbert's successor was Ellmann, who even published a book on Joyce's schemes and correspondences (*Ulysses of the Liffey*); Hugh Kenner, closer to Ezra Pound in spirit, tended to denigrate the value of Homeric parallels and to stress the quirky realism and the satirical dimension of the text. It was no accident that Kenner wrote the preface for the re-edition of Budgen's book on *Ulysses* and that he was always the most vocal critic of Ellmann's biography. In a review of the revised 1982 edition of Ellmann's *James Joyce*, Kenner made fun of the "Irish facts" that would crop up unreliably in the book.[15] He was not the only one who denounced a biographical approach to Joyce: as it appears in an often quoted chapter from Ellmann's book, "The Backgrounds of 'The Dead'" (*JJ II* 243–53), the thesis that the text duplicates the artist's life generates readings of the life as already transformed by the works. It becomes very hard to know whether the life is a key to the works or the works a key to the life. This tendency exerted dangerous effects, as one sees in the French translation of *Finnegans Wake*, a "novel" explicitly presented as an autobiographical narrative. The biographical fallacy can be summed up in trite teacher's advice to students: when you have nothing to say about a text, you can always read it as a biographical document.

In his 1955 book on Joyce, Kenner attempts to get a different sense of textuality that will not bracket off the real world of Dublin, Joyce's life and Joyce's borrowings.[16] In his acknowledgments, Kenner pays homage to Frank Budgen, and then to Wyndham Lewis and to Ezra Pound – as he admits, his thesis develops the main insight of Pound's famous "James Joyce and Pécuchet," an early review published in French in 1922[17] that compares *Ulysses* with Flaubert's *Bouvard et Pécuchet*. Thus Kenner's analysis of *Exiles* goes as far as presenting a "Flaubertian Ibsen." Kenner's groundbreaking and incisive book has many merits, but it has struck contemporaries by its offhand treatment of Stephen; it is true that Kenner judges Stephen rather harshly, as he states in remarks about the ending of *A Portrait of the Artist as a Young Man*:

> we are not to accept the mode of Stephen's "freedom" as the "message" of the book. The "priest of the eternal imagination" turns out to be indigestibly Byronic. Nothing is more obvious than his total lack of humour. ... [O]ur impulse on being confronted with the final edition of Stephen Dedalus is to laugh ... .[18]

As Joyce said to Budgen, he needed Bloom since Stephen's shape was too limited, could "not change" and its immaturity needed the relay of a mature "all-round man"; however, he added that the reader should not identify with Buck Mulligan, whose continuous jesting should begin to be felt as boring and sterile half-way through the book,[19] a sensible tip not always heeded to by Kenner. Joyce was clearly warning against the tendency to treat everything as parody in the novel, a tendency already present in the readings of Pound and Lewis.

Nevertheless, by the late 1950s, the camp of the Stephen-haters had swollen its numbers, until Wayne Booth pointed to troubling inconsistencies and unresolved dilemmas. Booth concluded a review of both positions – the cynical ironists versus the Romantics – in this way: "The truth seems to be that Joyce was always a bit uncertain about his attitude toward Stephen."[20] This will not surprise readers of Flaubert who cannot miss Flaubert's ambivalence facing characters who look very much like him, like Frédéric Moreau in the *Sentimental Education* or unlike him, like Emma Bovary.[21] What is specific to Joyce is that his own uncertainties or ambivalences were always reinscribed in the works themselves first, so as to make them part of the plot and structure, and then in the critical legacy they spawned. The same debate came up later in issues of textual scholarship when Hans Walter Gabler published his "corrected edition" in 1984 only to be attacked by a younger scholar, John Kidd, who ended up winning the day in spite of more uncertain credentials. At least John Kidd knew how to exploit latent rifts in the works and to play the part of the young "cad" who challenges authority.

The textual battle over *Ulysses* took place between 1984 and 1993. By that time, the institutions of the "Joyce industry" already existed and were running at full speed, producing more articles and books than any person could hope to read in one lifetime. I can only refer to Joseph Kelly's wonderful survey of the growth of the "Joyce Industry" in the United States (a term that became current as early as 1956, first used in a non-critical way by Magalaner and Kain in their important book *Joyce: The Man, the Work, the Reputation*).[22] Kelly retraces the steps that have been necessary to reach such streamlined production of critical texts, in North America especially, albeit allied with an openness, a non-hierarchical mode of functioning and a sense of hospitality rare in academia, this being due, as Fritz Senn has noted, to the fact that the first generation of Joyceans was made up for a great part not of academics but of gifted "amateurs".[23] What is sure is that the critical mass is steadily augmenting. In order to find our bearings, we now dispose of at least five regular publications in English that are entirely devoted to Joyce scholarship, the *James Joyce Quarterly*, the *James Joyce Annual*, the *James Joyce Broadsheet*, the *James Joyce Literary Supplement*, and *James Joyce European Studies*, without counting similar publications in France, Spain and Italy. Joyce has indeed become an "icon" as Kelly has it, and he insists quite appositely on Joyce's decision not to reproduce the famous schema of correspondences in the first American edition of *Ulysses*: in his creator's mind, the text has to stand on its own, and this "celibate" status will continue generating more and more criticism.

For, in spite of all the articles and books published, many gaps remain. For one thing, the fact is that, unlike Yeats, Eliot, Woolf or Pound, Joyce did not leave us a full-fledged critical theory that would help unpack his texts. If Joyce is often taken as an example of the intricate links between modernism and contemporary literary theory, no one has yet brought a satisfactory solution to the following puzzle: why is it that Joyce wrote enough critical essays to make up a volume of *Critical Writing* and then decided to abandon the project he had caressed in his youth of writing a self-contained aesthetic treatise? One may argue that for pragmatic reasons of writerly concentration, he refused to spend too much time or energy in the kind of critical writing that gives the works of modernist contemporaries like Woolf, Pound, Lewis or Eliot that useful horizon of secondary references and self-commentaries. Yet one needs to account for the discrepancy that arises between earlier texts like *Stephen Hero* in which the main protagonist repeatedly flaunts an aesthetic theory in front of friends and adversaries and texts like *Ulysses* from which similar theories are either taken as signs of immaturity or fade in front of more important issues.

In his Dublin years, however, Joyce would assert that his mind worked better than contemporaries like Yeats or Synge because he had crafted a rigorous theory of art and literature that could provide a secure foundation while they were still trying to outgrow Romanticism or Symbolism. In a letter sent in March 1903 to his mother from Paris, Joyce outlines a schedule covering the next decades: "My book of songs will be published in the Spring of 1907. My first comedy about five years later. My 'Esthetic' about five years later again. (This *must* interest you!)" (*SL* 19). Surprisingly, Joyce's anticipation turned out being almost right: *Chamber Music* was published in 1907, and the action of *Exiles* takes place in the summer of 1912, while Joyce's first notes for the play date from 1913. However, no "Esthetic" was written by Joyce. If one puts together the reviews, articles and essays from the *Critical Writings*, adding excerpts from Stephen's ruminations on art, paternity, creation, and rhythm in *Ulysses*, one can try to reconstitute the coherence of an aesthetic system. This unfinished task has attracted many commentators, who first equated theory in the Joycean mode with "Esthetic theory."

Among the first serious attempts dating from the 1950s and 1960s, one can mention invaluable books by William T. Noon, *Joyce and Aquinas* (1957), W.Y. Tindall, *A Reader's Guide to James Joyce* (1959), S.L. Goldberg, *The Classical Temper* (1961), Arnold Goldman, *The Joyce Paradox* (1966). Noon was the first to point out inconsistencies in Joyce's bowdlerized adaptation of Aquinas, and his groundbreaking study was followed by important contributions by Umberto Eco with his *Opera Aperta* (1965) and *Problema estetica in Tommaso d'Aquino* (1970) and also by Jacques Aubert's *Introduction à l'esthétique de James Joyce* (1973) (English [revised] edition, *The Aesthetics of James Joyce*, published 1992). Scholes and Kain had already published in 1965 all the documents used by Joyce to cobble together an aesthetic theory in *The Workshop of Dedalus*. In 1974, Wolfgang

Iser published the first rigorous phenomenological approach to *Ulysses* in terms of its "loopholes" and its concept of style in *The Implied Reader*. A little earlier, Robert Greer Cohn had pointed to a common Hegelian basis in Mallarmé and Joyce (*Toward the Poems of Mallarmé* [1965] and the earlier but influential *L'oeuvre de Mallarmé: Un coup de dés*[24] [1951]), an insight taken up by Derrida in a systematic parallel between Joyce who was seen as a Hegelian historicist and Husserl in his 1962 *Introduction to Husserl's "Origin of Geometry."*

Thus, if Joyce's place in modernism appeared fundamental in the second half of the twentieth century, it is not only because his works have played a role of keystone in all definitions of the field (to the point that for Kenner, Woolf and Stevens had to be excluded from the modernist canon on logical grounds[25]), but also because he has acted as a logical attractor for all the various discourses deployed in literary theory. His marvelous adaptability has excited envy from scholars who have worked on less favored authors: after deconstructive, Lacanian, post-colonial, feminist, and new historicist waves, Irish nationalists, late Marxist or post-nationalists have followed suit. None of the recognized critical schools ever forgot Joyce who often stood as a privileged testing ground for the validity of their methods. The pre-eminence of Joyce came to the fore when Jacques Lacan experienced a late conversion to Joyce (or an identification with Joyce?) in 1975 and gave the opening address to the Paris James Joyce Symposium in 1975. After Lacan took Joyce's works as privileged corpus for his later seminar in 1976–77, psychoanalysts throughout the world were given the arduous task of mastering Joyce's work as a prerequisite should they want to understand Lacan's last word on the symptom, sublimation, gender, psychosis and the "fourth knot" of Joyce's writerly ego.[26]

In another key, Trevor Williams identified the 1975 Paris International James Joyce Symposium as a watershed in the internationalization of the institutions of Joyce criticism, the moment when the "apolitical" view of Joyce was shattered, and I cannot agree more.[27] Most of the presentations have been preserved in a fascinating two-volume publication. It has been said too often that the division in two volumes, one in French and one in English, reflected a deep Franco-American divide. In fact, one can take an exemplary panel gathering Bernard Benstock, Seamus Deane, Paul Delany, Leslie Fiedler, Suzette Henke, Maria Jolas and Philippe Sollers to confirm that there was indeed a dialogue going on about the "political perspectives on Joyce's work." Besides Sollers' mild provocations – he asserted that English had turned into a "dead language" after the publication of *Finnegans Wake* and dramatically showed the book (pointing to the adequately red hardback cover of the jacketless Faber edition of *Finnegans Wake*) with the declaration: "I show you one revolution"[28] – the audience sensed that a real discussion was taking place. After all, Joyce's works had been banned just as Freud's books had been burned by the Nazis. Even if the time and place did not coincide, such homology was striking. Fiedler expressed an awareness of experimental language that tallied with Sollers', while Deane stressed the Irish point of view on Joyce as a colonial writer, caught up in a defeatist time warp; Henke reflected upon the then emergent feminist discourse on Joyce and Maria Jolas intervened to assert that Joyce had been political all along while an auditor quoted Franz Fanon and concluded that Joyce was essential to debunk colonialist prejudice.

Besides, serious work on the generative linguistics of the *Wake* was being presented by Change, a dissident group battling with *Tel Quel*. One perceptive person in the audience wondered aloud why 96 percent of the time, the French were referring to *Finnegans Wake* and not *Ulysses*[29] – less than betraying ignorance, this pointed to the possibility of bridging the gap between Joyce's works as taught more and more widely in academic contexts, with a corpus limited to selections like Harry Levin's *Portable Joyce* or *Essential Joyce*, in which earlier texts were well represented, *Ulysses* excerpted and *Finnegans Wake* reduced to a minimum and the cultic aspects of the later Joyce, cornered by a coterie of *Wake* aficionados who subscribed to the *Wake Newlitter* and exchanged precious information about arcane sources. Finally what was rendered manifest was how the discourse of Jolas and his friends on the "Revolution of the Word" had met half-way the language of high theory revised by the Parisian avant-garde; the experimentalism of the 1930s had returned with a vengeance to haunt the avant-gardism of the 1970s, then under the domination of the *Tel Quel* group for whom Lacan, Althusser, Foucault and Derrida conveyed household truths. Some of these pronouncements antagonized a more academic group influenced by New Criticism, since even when semiotics was introduced, the dominant reading practice relied on close readings, source hunting and communal discussions of textual riddles and conundrums. A critical language inspired by Marxism, psychoanalysis, feminism, linguistics, post-structuralism and deconstruction was brought to bear on Joyce for the first time. Yet how could one stress the political element in Joyce given biographical evidence testifying to his aloof position in Irish matters, his projection into a youthful fictional double, a pure aesthete who leaves behind him Ireland's burden of tangled responsibilities, and his refusal of involvement in nationalist or internationalist causes after *Ulysses*?

Clearly, the answer was the issue of a "revolutionary language," which for the *Tel Quelians* automatically placed Joyce in the avant-garde, on a pedestal including Lenin, Mao and Artaud, whereas more conservative American Joyce specialists would stick to aesthetics or to a biographical basis. Sollers adapted Mallarmé's famous statement that "the Book was the bomb!" while other Joyceans only saw in the "artist's" politics non-involvement, detachment and indifference. It took another decade to allow the Joyce industry to digest the impact of 1975 – this is nowhere more visible than in the enormous compendium called *A Companion to Joyce Studies* edited in 1984 by Zack Bowen and James F. Carens.[30] In more than 800 pages, the main aspects of Joyce scholarship are surveyed, with detailed analyses of all the individual works and important synthetic chapters like Scholes and Corcoran's on the "Aesthetic Theory and the Critical Writings." Yet Colin MacCabe's groundbreaking 1978 *James Joyce and the Revolution of the Word* (in which a neo-Marxist approach is coupled with Lacanian theory) is not even mentioned, nor are the names of Eco, Lacan or Derrida quoted. Nothing is said of gender issues or of textual problems like the genetic versions provided by various manuscripts and editions. It is revealing to compare this thick book with the slim "Introduction" by Alan Roughley, *James Joyce and Critical Theory*,[31] published seven years later. There, chapter headings bear on Joyce as approached by various schools ranging from structuralism, post-structuralism, semiotics, feminism, and psychoanalytic theory to Marxism, and most of the names do not figure in the *Companion*.

As Seamus Deane wrote in 1985, the prevalent critical assumption up to then had been that Joyce was apolitical and limited his genius to formal and stylistic innovation:

> Repudiating British and Roman imperialism and rejecting Irish nationalism and Irish literature which seemed to be in the service of that cause, he turned away from his early commitment to socialism and devoted himself instead to a highly apolitical and wonderfully arcane practice of writing. Such, in brief, is the received wisdom about Joyce and his relationship to the major political issues of his times.[32]

Deane estimated that the critical tide had turned around 1985, when systematic revision of this opinion started. One can push back the watershed in time, send readers back to Dominic Manganiello's nuanced appraisal in *Joyce and Politics* (1980) or to Colin MacCabe's already mentioned *James Joyce and the Revolution of the World*. What has changed since 1985 cannot be attributed only to a gradual acceptance by American academics of "French" or "continental" approaches to literary theory. The spate of books written on Joyce in the perspective of post-colonial theory like Enda Duffy's *The Subaltern Ulysses* (1994), Vincent Cheng's *Joyce, Race and Empire* (1995), or Declan Kiberd's influential *Inventing Ireland* (1996) seem to show that there is by now almost a consensus. Even more seminal perhaps has been Cheryl Herr's *Joyce's Anatomy of Culture* (1986), a Marxist analysis of Joyce's use of the popular culture of this time. The rich lore provided by advertisements and newspaper cuttings along with lower forms of entertainment or social containment like cheap pantomimes, religious tracts, absurd sermons, and early jazz music proved to be an inexhaustible source of inspiration for subsequent investigations.

   If it looks as if approaches inspired by cultural studies or neo-Marxism have won the day, it is also because they address a different critical predicament, like Joyce's position facing Irish nationalism. While Vincent Cheng remained prudent, Irish scholars like Emer Nolan[33] have reassessed positively the nationalist discourses in *Ulysses*, seeing in a character like the Citizen a counterpart to Bloom's idealism, thus criticizing a liberal complacency in other critics' internationalist positions. Seamus Deane, Terry Eagleton and David Lloyd belong to a camp more prone to striking a balance between Bloom's measured tolerance and the political struggle that was going on in Ireland at the time. But for Emer Nolan, Colin MacCabe's Marxism is deemed too Lacanian, and he is accused of betraying the cause of "subaltern" resistance in being blind to the way "minor" literature is a vehicle for revolutionary aspirations.

   Symptomatically, it was also in 1984 that, in a major address given at the Frankfurt Joyce Symposium, Derrida went further and took to task the very concept of a James Joyce International Foundation. His deconstructive gesture was based upon previous readings of Joyce. We have seen that Derrida defines *Ulysses* and *Finnegans Wake* as totalizing masterpieces whose programs modify our reading habits. Reading them, being read by them, we have to accept to recognize ourselves as read in advance by the author, traversed by Joyce's reading. In this phrase, a double genitive is at play, both objective and subjective: we read Joyce, and Joyce reads us, in a strategy of Wakean "hesitency" inevitably produced by the writing in us of an unconscious inscription. Stephen Dedalus spoke of Shakespeare as the father of his grandfather and his own grandson, presenting him as the paradigm of the self-generating artist who thereby constitutes a world we happen to be inhabiting too. Aware of this circularity, and in awe of it, Derrida sees in Joyce's hypermnesic machine a program from which our interpretations cannot disentangle themselves either from the materiality of an archive or from the ghostly inheritance of actual families. We are aware of the fascination of Joyce scholars for manuscripts, drafts, first editions, autographs, holographs, letters, notebooks, all culled in the more than 60 volumes of the *James Joyce Archive* – with the constant addition of recently discovered proofs and unpublished manuscripts sold for a fortune at auctions. Now that the *Finnegans Wake* notebooks have been annotated, thoroughly edited and published one by one, the Joycean "archive fever"[34] will perhaps abate but will never be extinguished.

This is a scene that has involved Joyce's own grandson: Stephen Joyce, heir and addressee of certain texts, occupies today the position of moral and rightful owner even after manuscripts have been acquired by national libraries and academic institutions in what remains the "object" of Joyce scholarship, namely the texts. Stephen Joyce has been known to intervene in the choice of translators, editors, and texts that can or cannot be anthologized. Thus Derrida dedicated the first version of *Ulysses Gramophone* to Stephen Joyce, proving that in this spectral genealogy, we were all "Joyce's grandsons," all responding to the apparatus imagined by Bloom in *Ulysses* when he imagined that one would be able to play recordings of the dead or to Stephen's fantasy of being telephonically connected to "Edenville" via the cables of our umbilical cords. Derrida leads us to question the basis of Joycean competence as ratified by academic discourse, with the usual rivalries between American and European scholars, and the crucial exception of Irish specialists. As we have seen, the Joycean problems of transmission started with scholars like Gorman, who, before writing the first biography, first published a pioneering book on Joyce's work, *James Joyce: His First Forty Years* (1926), an introduction to *Ulysses* whose bibliography is refreshingly limited to two pages as it lists pieces written in 1922 and 1923 only.[35] Gorman was relayed by other critics until something like an institution was formed in the 1940s and 1950s when Joyce's name became an unavoidable reference in discussions of modernism. When Ellmann and Kenner came upon the scene, both tried to get in touch with people who had known Joyce himself. Kenner has documented how he first visited Ezra Pound with Marshall McLuhan in 1948, then managed to talk with T.S. Eliot and Wyndham Lewis during an English tour in 1956.[36] Meanwhile, during those same years, Richard Ellmann was busy interviewing all the survivors who had been in contact with Joyce, such as Maria Jolas; he then relied heavily on Stanislaus Joyce (whose posthumous memoirs, *My Brother's Keeper*, he helped publish) to the point that he has been accused of being uncritically influenced by the point of view of Joyce's embittered brother.[37]

Joyce, who had dramatized the brothers' struggle to control truth in the *Wake*, was keenly aware of the importance of the active role he played in the dissemination of a tradition; he had made the decision as early as the redaction of the "Scylla and Charybdis" episode to dramatize literary theory, and, following the model of Plato's *Symposium*, to let characters act it out without providing an authorized synthesis or a dogmatic closure. He knew all along that he was "forging" theories like Shem the Penman while also needing the intermediary of Shaun the Postman, that is, relays like Valery Larbaud, Stuart Gilbert, Frank Budgen, Louis Gillet, Carlo Linati, Eugène and Maria Jolas, Jacques Mercanton, Ernst Robert Curtius, Nino Franck and a few others who were instrumental to ensure his own immortality, an immortality measured by the number of books and theses devoted to him. In that sense, as Nora Joyce herself said more naively, there was only one other chap her husband had to get the better of, William Shakespeare. Judging from the number of publications, it seems that Shakespeare keeps his lead. There is hope for Joyce, nevertheless, since the corpus with its attendant academic scholarship is caught up in a double affiliation, hesitating between a *perpetuum mobile* sustained by the myth of an infinitely self-generating text and an historical responsibility, both ethical and cultural, that addresses a European tradition forced to open its ear to the Other, as European becomes "earopen" (*FW* 419.14) in the *Wake*.

Facing such a formidably programmed critical "double bind," Derrida wielded a deconstructive scalpel in 1984 when he confronted the "Joyce scholars" perceived as an intimidating body but also an institution in need of a more secure foundation. As he expresses it in *Ulysses Gramophone*, the International James Joyce Foundation is a concrete example of a tradition that had invested cultural capital aiming at universality in a writer's name. But then it needs someone else, coming from the outside like Plato's Stranger in the *Sophist*, to authorize the foundation from a position of marginal difference. Even if Joyce scholars have at their disposal the "totality of competence in the encyclopedic field of the *universitas*" (*AL* 281), they crave for the non-expertise of a foreigner who will both question the "foundation" and then reassure them. Such a foreigner will end up confessing:

As a matter of fact, you do not exist, you are not founded to exist as a foundation, which is what Joyce's signature gives you to read. And you can call on strangers to come and tell you, as I am doing in replying to your invitation: you exist, you intimidate me, I recognize you, I recognize your paternal and grandpaternal authority, recognize me and give me a diploma in Joycean studies. (*AL* 284)

Derrida's barbed irony should not hide a real Husserlian question: under what conditions can something like "James Joyce studies" become a rigorous discipline? Is there a type of Joycean competence that can be measured and posited as a prerequisite? Is it enough to have read all the works and most of the critics (not all of them, that would be impossible), or should one commit oneself more actively and join a Joycean reading group or website? Such remarks not only query a type of knowledge but also its transmission and the rites that accompany it (such as the James Joyce symposia, the Bloomsday celebrations, the regular meetings of *Finnegans Wake* or *Ulysses* reading groups throughout the world). All the witnesses and friends of Joyce during the Paris years have underlined that Joyce relished birthdays, celebrations, anniversaries, forcing them upon his friends as a way of entreating them (and us by implication) to join the extended family of his readers. If this collection of essays helps Joyce readers to answer this question (everyone has to answer privately), it will have succeeded insofar as it will make us take a legitimate place, albeit reserved in advance, among the numerous grandchildren of the auspiciously named Telemachus.[38]

notes

1. "An Interview with Jacques Derrida," in Jacques Derrida, *Acts of Literature*, ed. Derek Attridge (New York: Routledge, 1992), p. 74. Henceforth referred to as "*AL*."
2. Jacques Derrida, "Two words for Joyce," in *Post-Structuralist Joyce*, ed. Derek Attridge and Daniel Ferrer (Cambridge: Cambridge University Press, 1984), p. 147.
3. Ibid.
4. Jacques Mercanton, *Ecrits sur James Joyce* (Vevey: L'aire Bleue, 2002), p. 44; in English in the text.
5. Jacques Mercanton, "The Hours of James Joyce," in *Portraits of the Artist in Exile: Recollections of James Joyce by Europeans*, ed. Willard Potts (Seattle: Wolfhound, 1979), p. 221. Joyce's original expression is more condensed: "Ce livre est la souffrance idéale de l'idéale insomnie." Mercanton, *Ecrits sur James Joyce*, p. 47.

6. Herbert Gorman, *James Joyce* (Farrar and Rhinehart, 1939). Henceforth referred to as 'G, *JJ*'.

7. Quoted by John Whittier-Ferguson in "Embattled Indifference: Politics on the Galleys of Herbert Gorman's *James Joyce*," in *Joycean Cultures/Culturing Joyces*, eds. Vincent Cheng, Kimberley J. Devlin and Margot Norris (Newark: University of Delaware Press, 1998), p. 137.

8. I am alluding here to the rival brothers of *Finnegans Wake*, Shaun the Post and Shem the Penman, the latter having inherited many features of Joyce's personality and biography.

9. Stuart Gilbert, *James Joyce's Ulysses. A Study* (1930) (New York: Random House, 1955), p. vii. Henceforth referred to as "*JJU*".

10. See *JJ II*, p. 702. Unless otherwise specified, all the subsequent references are to this edition.

11. Frank Budgen, *James Joyce and the Making of Ulysses* (Bloomington: Indiana University Press, 1960), p. 15. Unless otherwise specified, all the subsequent references are to this edition and are referred to as "*JJMU*."

12. Frank Budgen, "James Joyce's *Work in Progress* and Old Norse Poetry," in Samuel Beckett et al., *Our Exagmination Round His Factification for Incamination of Work in Progress* (London: Faber, 1972), p. 38. Henceforth referred to as "*OE*."

13. C.K. Ogden and I.A. Richards, *The Meaning of Meaning* (1923) (London: Harcourt and Brace, 1968), pp. 142–3.

14. Suzette Henke, "Exagmining Beckett & Company," in *Re-Viewing Classics of Joyce Criticism*, ed. Janet Egleson Dunleavy (Urbana and Chicago: University of Chicago Press, 1991), pp. 60–81.

15. Hugh Kenner, "The Impertinence of Being Definitive," *Times Literary Supplement*, December 17, 1982, p. 1384, reprinted in *Mazes* (San Francisco: North Point, 1989), pp. 101–12.

16. Hugh Kenner, *Dublin's Joyce* (New York: Columbia University Press, 1955; 2nd edn. 1987).

17. See *Pound/Joyce: The Letters of Ezra Pound to James Joyce with Pound's Essays on Joyce*, ed. Forrest Read (London: Faber, 1975), pp. 200–11.

18. Kenner, *Dublin's Joyce*, p. 132.

19. "'(Buck Mulligan) should begin to pall on the reader as the day goes on,' Joyce said. ... 'And to the extent that Buck Mulligan's wit wears threadbare,' Joyce continued, 'Bloom's justness and reasonableness should grow in interest.'" Budgen, *James Joyce and the Making of Ulysses*, p. 116.

20. Wayne Booth, "The Problem of Distance in *A Portrait of the Artist*," in *The Rhetoric of Fiction* (Chicago: University of Chicago Press, 1961), p. 330.

21. I am here alluding too rapidly to a fascinating dispute, which has triggered an abundant critical literature; a very good account is provided by Michael Groden in "Perplex in the Pen – And In the Pixels," in *Joyce and the Joyceans*, ed. Morton P. Levitt (New York: Syracuse University Press, 2002), pp. 32–50.

22. See Joseph Kelly, *Our Joyce: From Outcast to Icon* (Austin: University of Texas Press, 1998), pp. 203–4.

23. See the whole of Fritz Senn's remarkable "The Joyce Industrial Evolution According to One European Amateur," in Levitt, *Joyce and the Joyceans*, pp. 1–7.

24. Paris: Minard, 1951.
25. Hugh Kenner, "The Making of the Modernist Canon" in *Mazes*, p. 40.
26. I have analyzed this crucial seminar in *Jacques Lacan: Psychoanalysis and the Subject of Literature* (Houndmills and New York: Palgrave Macmillan, 2001), pp. 154–82. See also my *James Joyce and the Politics of Egoism* (Cambridge: Cambridge University Press, 2001) and Roberto Harrari, *How James Joyce Made His Name* (New York: The Other Press, 2002).
27. "Appropriately, it was in Paris at the 1975 Joyce Symposium that these various strands of the political Joyce were first drawn together." Trevor L. Williams, *Reading Joyce Politically* (Gainesville: University of Florida Press, 1997), p. 28.
28. In *Joyce & Paris, 1902 ... 1920–1940 ... 1975*, Vol. 2, ed. J. Aubert and Maria Jolas (Lille and Paris: Publications de Lille-III and CNRS, 1979), p. 107.
29. Aubert and Jolas, *Joyce & Paris, 1902 ...*, Vol. 1, p. 87.
30. Zack Bowen and James F. Carens, eds, *A Companion to Joyce Studies* (Westport: Greenwood Press, 1984).
31. Alan Roughley, *James Joyce and Critical Theory: An Introduction* (Ann Arbor: University of Michigan Press, 1992).
32. Seamus Deane, *Celtic Revivals: Essays in Modern Irish literature, 1885–1980* (London: Faber, 1985), p. 92.
33. Emer Nolan, *James Joyce and Nationalism* (New York: Routledge, 1995).
34. See Jacques Derrida, *Archive Fever: A Freudian Impression*, trans. Eric Prenowitz (Chicago: University of Chicago Press, 1996) and the series of *The Finnegans Wake Notebooks at Buffalo*, eds. Vincent Deane, Daniel Ferrer and Geert Lernout (Turnhout, Belgium: Brepols, 2002). So far six notebooks have been transcribed, edited and published.
35. Herbert Gorman, *James Joyce: His First Forty Years* (London: G. Bles, 1926). It is interesting to notice that this "authorized" work (it had been revised by Joyce) denies any strict use of Homeric parallels: " ... the parallelisms with the Odyssey do not follow the absolute scheme of Homer's work except in a general fashion. Rather are these parallelisms subdued to the exigencies of this momentous day traversed by Stephen Dedalus and Leopold Bloom" (p. 218). It is true that Gorman repeats that his point of view may be limited and at any rate very "American": one may wonder – would Joyce have decided to leave the anti-Homeric position to his American critics and asked the British guides to stress them? See Hugh Witemeyer, "'He Gave the Name': Herbert Gorman's Rectifications of *James Joyce: His First Forty Years*," *James Joyce Quarterly* 32:3–4 (Spring/Summer 1995), pp. 523–32.
36. Hugh Kenner, *The Elsewhere Community* (Oxford: Oxford University Press, 2000), pp. 33–88.
37. This is a point that has been made very forcibly by Joseph Kelly in *Our Joyce*, pp. 142–79.
38. Stuart Gilbert explains that the etymology of "Telemachus" refers to someone who "fights from afar" and thus remains "out of the fray" (*JJU* 104). One might be tempted to see in "Telemachus" someone who, like Joyce, knew how to wage war from afar by exploiting the "telephony" of a well-chosen transmission.

selected bibliography

joyce bibliographies

Cohn, Alan M., followed by Brockman, William S., "Current James Joyce Checklist," regularly published in the *James Joyce Quarterly*.

Deming, Robert H. *James Joyce: The Critical Heritage*. Routledge, London, 1970.

Deming, Robert H. *A Bibliography of James Joyce Studies*. G. K. Hall, Boston, 1977.

Rice, Thomas Jackson. *James Joyce: A Guide to Research*. Garland, New York, 1982.

Slocum, John J. and Herbert Cahoon. *A Bibliography of James Joyce 1992–1941*. Greenwood, Newport, 1971.

Staley, Thomas F. *An Annotated Critical Bibliography of James Joyce*. Harvester, Brighton, 1989.

biographies

Beja, Morris. *James Joyce. A Literary Life*. Ohio State University Press, Columbus, 1992.

Costello, Peter. *James Joyce: The Years of Growth 1882–1915*. Kyle Cathie, London, 1992.

Costello, Peter, and John Wyse Jackson. *James Stanislaus Joyce. The Voluminous life and genius of James Joyce's father*. St. Martin's Press, New York, 1998.

Curran, C. P. *James Joyce Remembered*. Oxford University Press, London, 1968.

Ellmann, Richard. *James Joyce* (1959, revised and augmented 1982). Oxford University Press, Oxford and New York, 1982.

Fargnoli, Nicholas, ed. *James Joyce: A Documentary Volume*. Gale Group, Detroit, 2001.

Fitch, Noel Riley. *Sylvia Beach and the Lost Generation*. Norton, New York, 1983.

Gilbert, Stuart. *Reflections on James Joyce: Stuart Gilbert's Paris Journal*. Ed. Thomas E. Staley and Randolph Lewis. University of Texas Press, Austin, 1993.

Gorman, Herbert. *James Joyce*. Farrar and Rhinehart, 1939.

Joyce, Stanislaus. *My Brother's Keeper*. Ed. Richard Ellmann. Faber, London, 1958.

Joyce, Stanislaus. *The Complete Dublin Diary*. Ed. George Healey. Cornell University Press, Ithaca, 1971.

McCourt, John. *The Years of Bloom: James Joyce in Trieste*. Lilliput Press, Dublin, 2000.

Maddox, Brenda. *Nora: A Biography of Nora Joyce*. Hamish Hamilton, London, 1988.

Potts, Willard, ed. *Portraits of the Artist in Exile: Recollections of James Joyce by Europeans*. Columbia University Press, New York, 1974.

Power, Arthur. *Conversations with James Joyce*. Ed. Clive Hart. Millington, London, 1974.

general approaches

Attridge, Derek, ed. *The Cambridge Companion to James Joyce*. Cambridge University Press, Cambridge, 1990.

Attridge, Derek. *Joyce Effects*. Cambridge University Press, Cambridge, 2000.

Attridge, Derek, and Daniel Ferrer, eds. *Post-Structuralist Joyce: Essays from the French*. Cambridge University Press, Cambridge, 1984.

Attridge, Derek, and Marjorie Howes, eds. *Semicolonial Joyce*. Cambridge University Press, Cambridge, 2000.

Aubert, Jacques, and Maria Jola, eds. *Joyce and Paris – Joyce et Paris*. Editions du CNRS, Lille and Paris, 1979.

Aubert, Jacques, ed. *Joyce avec Lacan*. Navarin, Paris, 1987.

Aubert, Jacques. *The Aesthetics of James Joyce*. Johns Hopkins University Press, Baltimore, 1992.

Begnal, Michael, ed. *Joyce and the City*. Syracuse University Press, Syracuse, 2002.

Beja, Morris, ed. *James Joyce: The Centennial Symposium*. University of Illinois Press, Urbana, 1986.

Benstock, Bernard. *James Joyce: The Undiscover'd Country*. Barnes and Noble, New York, 1977.

Benstock, Bernard, ed. *Critical Essays on James Joyce*. Hall, Boston, 1985a.

Benstock, Bernard. *James Joyce*. Lorrimer, London, 1985b.

Benstock, Bernard, ed. *James Joyce: The Augmented Ninth*. Syracuse University Press, Syracuse, 1988.

Benstock, Bernard and Shari Benstock. *Who's He When's He's At Home*. University of Illinois Press, Urbana, 1980.

Bloom, Harold, ed. *James Joyce: Modern Critical Views*. Chelsea House, New York, 1986.

Boheemen-Saaf, Christine van. *Joyce, Derrida, Lacan and the Trauma of History*. Cambridge University Press, Cambridge, 1999.

Bonheim, Helmut. *Joyce's Benefictions*. University of California Press, Berkeley, 1964.

Bowen, Zack. *Musical Allusions in the Works of James Joyce*. Gill and Macmillan, Dublin, 1975.

Bowen, Zack and James F. Carens, eds. *A Companion to James Joyce Studies*. Greenwood, Newport, 1984.

Boyle, Robert. *James Joyce's Pauline Vision: A Catholic Exposition*. Southern Illinois University Press, Carbondale, 1978.

Brannigan, John, Geoff Ward, and Julian Wolfreys, eds. *Re: Joyce. Text. Culture. Politics*. Macmillan, London, 1988.

Brivic, Sheldon. *The Veil of Signs: Joyce, Lacan and Perception*. University of Illinois Press, Urbana, 1991.

Brown, Carole, and Leo Knuth. *The Tenor and the Vehicle: A Study of the John McCormack Connection*. Wake Newslitter Press, Colchester, 1982.

Brown, Richard. *James Joyce and Sexuality*. Cambridge University Press, Cambridge, 1985.

Burgess, Anthony. *Joysprick: An Introduction to the Language of James Joyce*. Andre Deutsch, London, 1973.

Burns, Christy L. *Gestural Politics. Stereotype and Parody in Joyce*. State University of New York Press, Albany, 2000.

Burkdall, Thomas. *Joycean Frames: Film and the Fiction of James Joyce*. Routledge, New York, 2001.

Chace, William M. *Joyce: A Collection of Critical Essays*. Prentice-Hall, Englewood Cliffs, 1974.

Cheng, Vincent. *Joyce, Race and Empire*. Cambridge University Press, Cambridge, 1995.

Cheng, Vincent, Kimberley Devlin, and Margot Norris, eds. *Joycean Cultures/ Culturing Joyces*. Associated University Presses, Cranbury, 1998.

Cixous, Hélène. *The Exile of James Joyce*. Trans. Sally Purcell. Calder, London, 1976.

Conley, Tim. *Joyces Mistakes*. University of Toronto Press, Toronto, 2003.

Cotter, David. *James Joyce and the Perverse Ideal*. Routledge, New York, 2003.

Dettmar, Kevin J. H. *The Illicit Joyce of Postmodernism. Reading Against the Grain*. University of Wisconsin Press, Madison, 1996.

Devlin, Kimberley. *James Joyce's "Fraudstuff."* University of Florida Press, Gainesville, 2002.

Dunleavy, Janet Egleson, ed. *Re-viewing Classics of Joyce Criticism*. University of Illinois Press, Urbana, 1992.

Eco, Umberto. *The Aesthetics of Chaosmos: The Middle Ages of James Joyce*. Trans. Ellen Rock. University of Tulsa Press, Tulsa, 1989.

Eide, Marian. *Ethical Joyce*. Cambridge University Press, Cambridge, 2002.

Ellmann, Richard. *The Consciousness of James Joyce*. Faber, London, 1977.

Fairhall, James. *James Joyce and the Question of History*. Cambridge University Press, Cambridge, 1993.

Ferrer, Daniel, and Claude Jacquet, eds. *Writing Its Own Wrunes For Ever. Essays in Joycean Genetics*. Du Lérot, Tusson, 1998.

Fraser, Jennifer Margaret. *Rite of Passage in the Narratives of Dante and Joyce*. University of Florida Press, Gainesville, 2002.

Frehner, Ruth, and Ursula Zeller, eds. *A Collideorscape of Joyce. Festschrift for Fritz Senn*. Lilliput Press, Dublin, 1998.

Friedman, Susan Stanford, ed. *Joyce/The Return of the Repressed*. Cornell University Press, Ithaca, 1993.

Froula, Christine. *Modernism's Body. Sex, Culture and Joyce*. Columbia University Press, New York, 1996.

Garvin, John. *James Joyce's Disunited Kingdom and the Irish Dimensions*. Gill and Macmillan, Dublin, 1976.

Gillespie, Michael Patrick. *Reading the Book of Himself: Narrative Strategies in the Works of James Joyce*. Ohio State University Press, Columbus, 1989.

Gordon, John. *James Joyce's Metamorphoses*. Gill and Macmillan, Dublin, 1981.

Harrari, Roberto. *How James Joyce Made His Name. A Reading of the Final Lacan.* Trans. Luke Thurston. The Other Press, New York, 2002.

Hayman, David. *Joyce et Mallarmé*. Minard, Paris, 1956.

Heller, Vivian. *Joyce, Decadence and Emancipation*. University of Illinois Press, Urbana, 1995.

Henke, Suzette. *James Joyce and the Politics of Desire*. Routledge, New York, 1990.

Henke, Suzette and Elaine Unkeless, eds. *Women in Joyce*. University of Illinois Press, Urbana, 1982.

Herr, Cheryl. *Joyce's Anatomy of Culture*. University of Illinois Press, Urbana, 1986.

Herring, Phillip F. *Joyce's Uncertainty Principle*. Princeton University Press, Princeton, 1987.

Hogan, Patrick Colm. *Joyce, Milton and the Theory of Influence*. University of Florida Press, Gainesville, 1995.

Jaurretche, Colleen. *The Sensual Philosophy. Joyce and the Aesthetics of Mysticism.* University of Wisconsin Press, Madison, 1997.

Kenner, Hugh. *Dublin's Joyce*. Columbia University Press, New York, 1955, 2nd edn. 1987.

Kenner, Hugh. *Joyce's Voices*. University of California Press, Berkeley, 1978.

Kershner, R. B. *Joyce, Bakhtin and Popular Literature: Chronicles of Disorder.* University of North Carolina, Chapel Hill, 1989.

Kershner, R. B., ed. *Joyce and Popular Culture*. University of Florida Press, Gainesville, 1996.

Kimball, Jean. *Joyce and the Early Freudians*. University of Florida Press, Gainesville, 2003.

Lawrence, Karen, ed. *Transcultural Joyce*. Cambridge University Press, Cambridge, 1998.

Lernout, Geert. *The French Joyce*. University of Michigan Press, Ann Arbor, 1990.

Levin, Harry. *James Joyce: A Critical Introduction* (1941), revised edn. Faber, London, 1960.

Levitt, Morton. *James Joyce and Modernism: Beyond Dublin*. Edwin Mellen Press, Lewiston, 2000.

Levitt, Morton P., ed. *Joyce and the Joyceans*. Syracuse University Press, Syracuse, 2002.

Litz, A. Walton. *The Art of James Joyce*. Oxford University Press, Oxford, 1964.

Lyons, J. B. *Thrust Syphilis Down to Hell and other Rejoyceana*. Glendale Press, Dublin, 1988.

MacCabe, Colin. *James Joyce and the Revolution of the Word*. Macmillan, London, 1979, revised edn 2003.

MacCabe, Colin, ed. *James Joyce: New Perspectives*. Harvester, Brighton, 1982.

McGee, Patrick. *Joyce Beyond Marx*. University of Florida Press, Gainesville, 2001.

Mahaffey, Vicki. *Reauthorizing Joyce*. Cambridge University Press, Cambridge, 1988.

Manganiello, Dominic. *Joyce's Politics*. Routledge, London, 1980.

Martin, Augustine, ed. *James Joyce: The Artist and the Labyrinth*. Ryan, London, 1990.

Milesi, Laurent, ed. *James Joyce and the Difference of Language.* Cambridge University Press, Cambridge, 2003.

Miller, Nicholas A. *Modernism, Ireland and the Erotics of Memory.* Cambridge University Press, Cambridge, 2002.

Morse, J. Mitchell. *The Sympathetic Alien: James Joyce and Catholicism.* New York University Press, New York, 1959.

Moseley, Virginia. *Joyce and the Bible.* Northern Illinois University Press, De Kalb, 1967.

Mullin, Katherine. *James Joyce, Sexuality and Social Purity.* Cambridge University Press, Cambridge, 2003.

Nadel, Ira. *Joyce and the Jews.* University of Florida Press, Gainesville, 1996.

Nash, John, ed. *Joyce's Audiences.* Rodopi, Amsterdam, 2002.

Nolan, Emer. *James Joyce and Nationalism.* Routledge, New York, 1995.

Noon, William T. *Joyce and Aquinas.* Yale University Press, New Haven, 1957.

Norris, Margot. *Joyce's Web. The Social Unraveling of Modernism.* University of Texas Press, Austin, 1992.

O'Sullivan, J. Colm. *Joyce's Use of Colors. Finnegans Wake and the Earlier Works.* UMI Research Press, Ann Arbor, 1987.

Parrinder, Patrick. *James Joyce.* Cambridge University Press, Cambridge, 1984.

Peake, C. H. *James Joyce: The Citizen and the Artist.* Stanford University Press, Stanford, 1977.

Rabaté, Jean-Michel. *James Joyce, Authorized Reader.* Johns Hopkins University Press, Baltimore, 1991a.

Rabaté, Jean-Michel. *Joyce Upon the Void: The Genesis of Doubt.* Macmillan, London, 1991b.

Rabaté, Jean-Michel. *James Joyce and the Politics of Egoism.* Cambridge University Press, Cambridge, 2001.

Read, Forrest, ed. *Pound/Joyce.* New Directions, New York, 1967.

Reizbaum, Marilyn. *James Joyce's Judaic Other.* Stanford University Press, Stanford, 1999.

Restuccia, Frances. *Joyce and the Law of the Father.* Yale University Press, New Haven, 1989.

Reynolds, Mary T. *Joyce and Dante: The Shaping Imagination.* Princeton University Press, Princeton, 1981.

Reynolds, Mary T., ed. *James Joyce: A Collection of Critical Essays.* Prentice Hall, Englewood Cliffs, 1993.

Rice, Thomas Jackson. *Joyce, Chaos and Complexity.* University of Illinois Press, Urbana, 1997.

Riquelme, John Paul. *Teller and Tale in Joyce's Fictions.* Johns Hopkins University Press, Baltimore, 1983.

Roughley, Alan. *James Joyce and Critical Theory.* Harvester, Hemel Hempstead, 1991.

Schlossman, Beryl. *Joyce's Catholic Comedy of Language.* University of Wisconsin Press, Madison, 1985.

Scholes, Robert. *In Search of James Joyce.* University of Illinois Press, Urbana, 1992.

Schork, R. J. *Latin and Roman Culture in Joyce.* University of Florida Press, Gainesville, 1997.

Schork, R. J. *Greek and Hellenic Culture in Joyce*. University of Florida Press, Gainesville, 1998.

Schwarze, Tracey Teets. *Joyce and the Victorians*. University of Florida Press, Gainesville, 2002.

Scott, Bonnie Kime. *Joyce and Feminism*. Harvester, Brighton, 1984.

Scott, Bonnie Kime. *James Joyce*. Harvester, Brighton, 1987.

Seidel, Michael. *James Joyce. A Short Introduction*. Blackwell, Oxford, 2002.

Senn, Fritz. *Joyce's Dislocations*. Ed. John Paul Riquelme. Johns Hopkins University Press, Baltimore, 1984.

Senn, Fritz. *Inductive Scrutinies: Focus on Joyce*. Ed. Christine O'Neill. Lilliput Press, Dublin, 1995.

Spoo, Robert. *James Joyce and the Language of History: Dedalus's Nightmare*. Oxford University Press, New York, 1994.

Spurr, David. *Joyce and the Scene of Modernity*. University of Florida Press, Gainesville, 2002.

Sultan, Stanley. *Joyce's Metamorphosis*. University of Florida Press, Gainesville, 2001.

Tindall, William York. *A Reader's Guide to James Joyce*. Thames and Hudson, London, 1959.

Tysdahl, Bjorn J. *Joyce and Ibsen*. Norwegian University Press, Oslo, 1969.

Valente, Joseph. *James Joyce and the Problem of Justice*. Cambridge University Press, Cambridge, 1995.

Valente, Joseph, ed. *Quare Joyce*. University of Michigan Press, Ann Arbor, 1998.

Verene, Donald, ed. *Vico and Joyce*. State University of New York Press, Albany, 1987.

Verstraete, Ginette. *Fragments of the Feminine Sublime in Friedrich Schlegel and James Joyce*. State University Press of New York, Albany, 1999.

Wall, Richard. *An Anglo-Irish Dialect Glossary for Joyce's Works*. Syracuse University Press, Syracuse, 1987.

Wawrzycka, Jolanta, and Marlena Corcoran, eds. *Gender in Joyce*. University of Florida Press, Gainesville, 1997.

Weir, Lorraine. *Writing Joyce: A Semiotics of the Joyce System*. Indiana University Press, Bloomington, 1989.

White, David. *The Grand Continuum. Reflections on Joyce and Metaphysics*. University of Pittsburgh Press, 1983.

Williams, Trevor. *Reading Joyce Politically*. University of Florida Press, Gainesville, 1997.

Wollaeger, Mark A., Victor Luftig and Robert Spoo, eds. *Joyce and the Subject of History*. University of Michigan Press, Ann Arbor, 1996.

the first works

Beck, Warren. *Joyce's Dubliners: Substance, Vision and Art*. Duke University Press, Durham, 1969.

Beja, Morris, ed. *Dubliners and A Portrait of the Artist as a Young Man. A Casebook*. Macmillan, London, 1973.

Benstock, Bernard. *Narrative Con/Texts in Dubliners*. University of Illinois Press, Urbana, 1994.

Bidwell, Bruce, and Linda Heffer. *The Joycean Way: A Topographic Guide to Dubliners and A Portrait of the Artist as a Young Man*. Wolfhound Press, Dublin, 1982.

Bosinelli, Rosa Maria, and Harold F. Mosher, eds. *Rejoycing: New Readings of Dubliners*. University of Kentucky Press, Lexington, 1998.

Brandabur, Edward. *A Scrupulous Meanness. A Study of Joyce's Early Works*. University of Illinois Press, Urbana, 1971.

Epstein, Edmund L. *The Ordeal of Stephen Dedalus*. Southern Illinois University Press, Carbondale, 1971.

Fuger, Wilhelm. *A Concordance to James Joyce's Dubliners*. Georg Olms, Hildesheim, 1980.

Garrett, Peter K., ed. *Twentieth Century Interpretations of Dubliners*. Prentice-Hall, Englewood Cliffs, 1968.

Gifford, Don. *Joyce Annotated. Notes for Dubliners and A Portrait of the Artist as a Young Man*. University of California Press, Berkeley, 1982.

Harkness, Marguerite. *A Portrait of the Artist as a Young Man, Voices of the Text*. Twayne, Boston, 1990.

Hart, Clive, ed. *James Joyce's Dubliners: Critical Essays*. Faber, London, 1969.

Ingersoll, Earl. *Engendered Trope in Joyce's Dubliners*. Southern Illinois University Press, Carbondale, 1996.

Leonard, Garry. *Reading Dubliners Again: A Lacanian Perspective*. Syracuse University Press, Syracuse, 1993.

MacNicholas, John. *James Joyce's Exiles: A Textual Companion*. Garland, New York, 1979.

Magalaner, Marvin. *Time of Apprenticeship: The Fiction of Young James Joyce*. Abelard-Schuman, New York, 1959.

Norris, Margot. *Suspicious Readings of Joyce's Dubliners*. University of Pennsylvania Press, Philadelphia, 2003.

Power, Mary, and Ulrich Schneider, eds. *New Perspectives on Dubliners*. European Joyce Studies, Rodopi, Amsterdam and Atlanta, 1997.

Scholes, Robert, and Richard M. Kain. *The Workshop of Dedalus*. Northwestern University Press, Evanston, 1965.

Scholes, Robert, and Walton A. Litz, eds. *Dubliners: Text, Criticism and Notes*. Viking, New York, 1969.

Schwarz, Daniel R., ed. *James Joyce's "The Dead": Case Studies in Contemporary Criticism*. Bedford Books, Boston, 1994.

Staley, Thomas, and Bernard Benstock, eds. *Approaches to Joyce's Portrait: Ten Essays*. University of Pittsburgh Press, Pittsburgh, 1976.

Thornton, Weldon. *The Antimodernism of Joyce's Portrait of the Artist as a Young Man*. Syracuse University Press, Syracuse, 1994.

Werner, Craig H. *Dubliners: A Pluralistic World*. Twayne, Boston, 1988.

ulysses

Adams, Robert M. *Surface and Symbol. The Consistency of Joyce's Ulysses*. Oxford University Press, Oxford, 1962.

Arnold, Bruce. *The Scandal of Ulysses*. St. Martin's Press, New York, 1992.

Bell, Robert H. *Jocoserious Joyce. The Fate of Folly in Ulysses*. Cornell University Press, Ithaca, 1991.

Blamires, Harry. *The Bloomsday Book. A Guide through Joyce's Ulysses*. Methuen, London, 1966.

Bowen, Zack. *Ulysses as a Comic Novel*. Syracuse University Press, Syracuse, 1989.

Brannon, Julie Sloan. *Who Reads Ulysses? The Rhetoric of the Joyce Wars and the Common Reader*. Routledge, New York, 2003.

Budgen, Frank. *James Joyce and the Making of Ulysses, and Other Writings*. Oxford University Press, Oxford and London, 1972.

Card, James Van Dyck. *An Anatomy of "Penelope."* Associated University Presses, London and Toronto, 1963.

Davidson, Neil R. *James Joyce, Ulysses, and the Construction of Jewish Identity*. Cambridge University Press, Cambridge, 1996, revised edn. 1998.

Devlin, Kimberley, and Marilyn Reizbaum, eds. *Ulysses En-gendered Perspectives: Eighteen Essays on the Episodes*. University of South Carolina Press, Columbia, 1999.

Duffy, Enda. *The Subaltern Ulysses*. University of Minnesota Press, Minneapolis, 1994.

Ellmann, Richard. *Ulysses on the Liffey*. Faber, London, 1974.

French, Marilyn. *The Book as World. James Joyce's Ulysses*. Harvard University Press, Cambridge, 1976.

Gibson, Andrew. *Joyce's Revenge: History, Politics and Aesthetics in Ulysses*. Oxford University Press, New York, 2002.

Gifford, Don and Seidman, Robert J. *Notes for Joyce. An Annotation of James Joyce's Ulysses*. Dutton, New York, 1989.

Gilbert, Stuart. *James Joyce's Ulysses. A Study* (1930). Penguin, Harmondsworth, 1969.

Goldberg. S. L. *The Classical Temper: A Study of James Joyce's Ulysses*. Chatto and Windus, London, 1961.

Gottfried, Roy K. *The Art of Syntax in Ulysses*. University of Georgia Press, Athens, 1980.

Gottfried, Roy K. *Joyce's Iritis and the Irritated Text: The Dis-lexic Ulysses*. University of Florida Press, Gainesville, 1995.

Groden, Michael. *Ulysses in Progress*. Princeton University Press, Princeton, 1977.

Hart, Clive. *James Joyce's Ulysses*. Sydney University Press, Sydney, 1968.

Hart, Clive, and David Hayman, eds. *James Joyce's Ulysses. Critical Essays*. University of California Press, Berkeley, 1974.

Hart, Clive, and Leo Knuth. *A Topographical Guide to James Joyce's Ulysses*. Wake Newslitter Press, Colchester, 1975.

Hayman, David. *Ulysses. The Mechanics of Meaning*. University of Wisconsin Press, Madison, 1970, revised edn. 1982.

Heffernan, Laura. *Ulysses*. Spark Notes, New York, 2002.

Kenner, Hugh. *Ulysses*. Allen and Unwin, London, 1980.

Knowles, Sebastian D. G. *The Dublin Helix: The Life of Language in Joyce's Ulysses*. University of Florida Press, Gainesville, 2001.

Lawrence, Karen. *The Odyssey of Style in Ulysses*. Princeton University Press, Princeton, 1981.

McBride, Margaret. *Ulysses and the Metamorphosis of Stephen Dedalus*. Bucknell University Press, Lewisburg, 2001.

McCormick, Kathleen, and Edwin R. Steinberg, eds. *Approaches to Teaching Joyce's Ulysses*. Modern Language Association of America, New York, 1993.

McKenna, Bernard. *James Joyce's Ulysses. A Reference Guide*. Greenwood Press, Westport, 2002.

McMichael, James. *Ulysses and Justice*. Princeton University Press, Princeton, 1991.

Melchiori, Giorgio, ed. *Joyce in Rome. The Genesis of Ulysses*. Bulzoni, Rome, 1984.

Mitchell, Breon. *James Joyce and the German Novel 1922–1933*. Ohio University Press, Athens, 1976.

Norris, Margot. *A Companion to James Joyce's Ulysses*. Bedford, Boston, 1998.

Osteen, Mark. *The Economy of Ulysses*. Syracuse University Press, Syracuse, 1995.

Pearce, Richard, ed. *Molly Blooms. A Polylogue on "Penelope" and Cultural Studies*. University of Wisconsin Press, Madison, 1994.

Rickard, John S. *Joyce's Book of Memory. The Mnemotechnics of Ulysses*. Duke University Press, Durham, 1999.

Rose, Danis and O'Hanlon, John, eds, *James Joyce: The Lost Notebook*. Split Pea Press, Edinburgh, 1989.

Schutte, William M. *Joyce and Shakespeare. A Study in the Meaning of Ulysses*. Yale University Press, New Haven, 1957.

Schutte, William M. *Index of Recurrent Elements in James Joyce's Ulysses*. Southern Illinois University Press, Carbondale, 1982.

Segal, Jeffrey. *Joyce in America. Cultural Politics and the Trials of Ulysses*. University of California Press, Berkeley, 1993.

Seidel, Michael. *Epic Geography*. Princeton University Press, Princeton, 1976.

Shechner, Mark. *Joyce in Nighttown. A Psychoanalytic Inquiry into Ulysses*. University of California Press, Berkeley, 1974.

Sherry, Vincent. *James Joyce. Ulysses*. Cambridge University Press, Cambridge, 1994.

Sicari, Stephen. *Joyce's Modernist Allegory: Ulysses and the History of the Novel*. University of South Carolina Press, Columbia, 2001.

Staley, Thomas F., ed. *Ulysses: Fifty Years*. Indiana University Press, Bloomington, 1974.

Staley, Thomas F., and Bernard Benstock, eds. *Approaches to Ulysses. Ten Essays*. University of Pittsburgh Press, Pittsburgh, 1970.

Sultan, Stanley. *The Argument of Ulysses*. Ohio State University Press, Columbus, 1964.

Theoharis, Theoharis Constantine. *Joyce's Ulysses*. University of North Carolina Press, Chapel Hill, 1988.

Thomas, Brook. *James Joyce's Ulysses. A Book of Many Happy Returns*. Louisiana University Press, Baton Rouge, 1982.

Thornton, Weldon. *Allusions in Ulysses*. University of North Carolina Press, Chapel Hill, 1985.

Ungar, Andras. *Joyce's Ulysses as National Epic: Epic Mimesis and the Nation State.* University of Florida Press, Gainesville, 2002.

Voyitzaki, Evi. *The Body in the Text. James Joyce's Ulysses and the Modern Greek Novel.* Lexington Books, Lanham, 2002.

Wicht, Wolfgang. *Utopianism in James Joyce's Ulysses.* Winter Verlag, Heidelberg, 2000.

finnegans wake

Atherton, James S. *The Books at the Wake.* Faber, London, 1959.

Balsamo, Gian. *Scriptural Poetics in Joyce's Finnegans Wake.* Edwin Mellen Press, Lewiston, 2002.

Beckett, Samuel, et al. *Our Exagmination Round His Factification for Incamination of Work in Progress* (1929), Faber, London, 1972.

Begnal, Michael H., and Fritz Senn, eds. *A Conceptual Guide to Finnegans Wake.* Pennsylvania University Press, University Park, 1974.

Benstock, Bernard. *Joyce's Again's Wake.* University of Washington Press, Seattle, 1965.

Bishop, John. *Joyce's Book of the Dark.* University of Wisconsin Press, Madison, 1986.

Boldrini, Lucia. *Joyce, Dante and the Poetics of Literary Relations. Language and Meaning in Finnegans Wake.* Cambridge University Press, Cambridge, 2001.

Brivic, Sheldon. *Joyce's Waking Women. An Introduction to Finnegans Wake.* University of Wisconsin Press, Madison, 1995.

Burell, Harry. *Narrative Design in Finnegans Wake: The Wake Lock Picked.* University of Florida Press, Gainesville, 1996.

Campbell, Joseph, and H. M. Robinson. *A Skeleton Key to Finnegans Wake.* Harcourt, New York, 1944.

Christiania, Dounia Bunis. *Scandinavian Elements of Finnegans Wake.* Northwestern University Press, Evanston, 1965.

Connolly, Thomas E. ed., *Scribbledehobble. The Ur-Workbook for Finnegans Wake.* Northwestern University Press, 1961.

Dalton, Jack P., and Clive Hart, eds. *Twelve and a Tilly.* Northwestern University Press, Evanston, 1965.

Deane, Vincent, Daniel Ferrer, and Geert Lernout, eds. *The Finnegans Wake Notebooks at Buffalo.* Brepols, Turnhout, 2001–05.

Devlin, Kimberley. *Wandering and Return in Finnegans Wake.* Princeton University Press, Princeton, 1991.

Glasheen, Adaline. *Third Census of Finnegans Wake.* University of California Press, Berkeley, 1977.

Hart, Clive. *Structure and Motif in Finnegans Wake.* Faber, London, 1962.

Hart, Clive. *A Concordance to Finnegans Wake.* Paul P. Appel, Mamaronek, 1973.

Hart, Clive, and Fritz Senn, eds. *A Wake Digest.* Sydney University Press, Sydney, 1968.

Hayman, David. *A First-Draft Version of Finnegans Wake.* University of Texas Press, Austin, 1963.

Hayman, David. *The Wake in Transit.* Cornell University Press, Ithaca, 1990.

Higginson, Fred, H. *Anna Livia Plurabelle. The Making of a Chapter*. University of Minnesota Press, Minneapolis, 1960.

McCarthy, Patrick. *The Riddles of Finnegans Wake*. Fairleigh Dickinson University Press, Rutherford, 1980.

McHugh, Roland. *The Sigla of Finnegans Wake*. Edward Arnold, London, 1976.

McHugh, Roland. *Annotations to Finnegans Wake*. Johns Hopkins University Press, Baltimore, 1980, revised edn. 1991.

McHugh, Roland. *The Finnegans Wake Experience*. Irish Academic Press, Dublin, 1981.

Mink, Louis O. *A Finnegans Wake Gazeteer*. Indiana University Press, Bloomington, 1978.

Norris, Margot. *The Decentered Universe of Finnegans Wake*. Johns Hopkins University Press, Baltimore, 1976.

O'Hehir, Brendan. *A Gaelic Lexicon for Finnegans Wake*. University of California Press, Berkeley, 1967.

Rose, Danis, ed. *James Joyce's Index Manuscript. Finnegans Wake Holograph Workbook VI. B. 46*. Wake Newslitter Press, Colchester, 1978.

Rose, Danis. *The Textual Diaries of James Joyce*. Lilliput Press, Dublin, 1995.

Rose, Danis, and John O'Hanlon. *Understanding Finnegans Wake*. Garland, New York, 1982.

Skrabanek, Peter. *Nightjoyce of a Thousand Tiers. Studies in Finnegans Wake*. Ed. Louis Armand and Ondrej Pilny. Literaria Praguensia, Prague, 2002.

Solomon, Margaret C. *Eternal Geomater. The Sexual Universe of Finnegans Wake*. Southern Illinois University Press, Carbondale, 1969.

Tindall, William York. *A Reader's Guide to Finnegans Wake*. Thames and Hudson, London, 1969.

Troy, Mark. *Mummeries of Resurrection*. Almqvist and Wiksell, Stockholm, 1976.

current joycean periodicals in english

European Joyce Studies. Rodopi, Amsterdam.

James Joyce Broadsheet. Leeds University, UK.

James Joyce Literary Supplement. Coral Gables, Florida.

James Joyce Quarterly. Tulsa, Oklahoma.

Joyce Studies Annual. University of Texas, Austin.

Joyce Studies in Italy. Bulzoni, Rome.

index